continued. . .

DEMON ANGEL

Titles by Meljean Brook

DEMON ANGEL
DEMON MOON
DEMON NIGHT
DEMON BOUND

Anthologies

HOT SPELL
(with Emma Holly, Lora Leigh, and Shiloh Walker)

WILD THING
(with Maggie Shayne, Marjorie M. Liu, and Alyssa Day)

FIRST BLOOD
(with Susan Sizemore, Erin McCarthy, and Chris Marie Green)

DEMON BOUND

meljean brook

BERKLEY SENSATION, NEW YORK

THE BERKLEY PUBLISHING GROUP
Published by the Penguin Group
Penguin Group (USA) Inc.
375 Hudson Street, New York, New York 10014, USA
Penguin Group (Canada), 90 Eglinton Avenue East, Suite 700, Toronto, Ontario M4P 2Y3, Canada
(a division of Pearson Penguin Canada Inc.)
Penguin Books Ltd., 80 Strand, London WC2R 0RL, England
Penguin Group Ireland, 25 St. Stephen's Green, Dublin 2, Ireland (a division of Penguin Books Ltd.)
Penguin Group (Australia), 250 Camberwell Road, Camberwell, Victoria 3124, Australia
(a division of Pearson Australia Group Pty. Ltd.)
Penguin Books India Pvt. Ltd., 11 Community Centre, Panchsheel Park, New Delhi—110 017, India
Penguin Group (NZ), 67 Apollo Drive, Rosedale, North Shore 0632, New Zealand
(a division of Pearson New Zealand Ltd.)
Penguin Books (South Africa) (Pty.) Ltd., 24 Sturdee Avenue, Rosebank, Johannesburg 2196,
South Africa

Penguin Books Ltd., Registered Offices: 80 Strand, London WC2R 0RL, England

DEMON BOUND

A Berkley Sensation Book / published by arrangement with the author

PRINTING HISTORY
Berkley Sensation mass-market edition / November 2008

Copyright © 2008 by Melissa Kahn.
Cover art by Phil Heffernan.
Cover design by George Long.
Interior text design by Laura K. Corless.

ISBN: 978-0-425-22453-3

BERKLEY® SENSATION
Berkley Sensation Books are published by The Berkley Publishing Group,
a division of Penguin Group (USA) Inc.,
375 Hudson Street, New York, New York 10014.
BERKLEY SENSATION and the "B" design are trademarks of Penguin Group (USA) Inc.

PRINTED IN THE UNITED STATES OF AMERICA

10 9 8 7 6 5 4 3 2 1

To Brad.
Whether here or Over There—may you always
make it home safe, little brother.

THE ORIGIN OF
THE GUARDIANS

In the First Battle, Lucifer the Morningstar led his rebel angels against Heaven. After their defeat, the rebels received their punishment: they were transformed into demons and tossed into Hell. Although they were free to travel to Earth through the Gates, the demons were bound by the Rules:

They cannot take human life. They cannot prevent a human from acting of his free will.

Those angels who refused to take sides in the First Battle were transformed into nosferatu, cursed with bloodlust and vulnerability to daylight, and sent to Earth. Unlike demons, nosferatu are not bound by the Rules.

For a time, seraphim—warrior angels loyal to Heaven—resided in the realm of Caelum and watched over humans, protecting them from the demons' temptations and the nosferatu's violence. The seraphim could never completely pass for human, however, and so the people on Earth began worshipping them as gods. When Lucifer realized this, his jealousy led him to wage another war against the angels.

The Second Battle took place on Earth, and Lucifer brought with him a dragon from the Chaos realm. The angels began to falter before the dragon—but mankind, witnessing the battle taking place, joined the angels in their fight against the demons. One man, Michael, destroyed the dragon by cutting through its heart with his sword. With the dragon slain, the angels regrouped and were victorious.

After the Second Battle, the seraphim retreated from Caelum and from Earth. They bestowed upon Michael the power to protect humans, and to transform into Guardians any men or women who had sacrificed their lives to save another from otherworldly threats. In addition to immortality, wings, strength, and the ability to alter their appearance, these Guardians were given individual Gifts to assist in their fight against the demons and nosferatu.

Because they had once been human, Guardians can easily walk among those they protect. But despite their great powers, Guardians are also limited by the Rules.

Human life must always be protected, and free will must always be honored.

—As recorded in the Scrolls by the Doyen, Michael, with ink made of his blood (date unknown). Translated from the Latin by Alice Grey, 1892.

CHAPTER I

How easy killing a Guardian would be. Even Michael, the most powerful of all the Guardians, would fall if a sword cleaved through his heart or his neck.

But although the methods by which Guardians could be killed were simple, accomplishing it was another matter entirely. The Guardians' strength, speed, and training enabled them to fight the demons and bloodthirsty nosferatu who preyed on humans; their Gifts could be employed as weapons or defense.

And slaying Michael would be more difficult than slaying any other Guardian. His Gift of teleportation allowed him to disappear before a blade could touch him. In his thousands of years, Michael had developed unmatched skill with his weapons, lightning reflexes, and great physical power. His heightened senses warned him of an enemy's approach.

He might not be so wary of an ally's approach, however. It was no surprise, then, that a demon had arranged for a Guardian to kill him.

But a Guardian worthy of her wings did not slay other Guardians.

Even if she was bound by a demon's bargain to do that very

thing, a Guardian should not kill a fellow warrior. Even if it would save her soul from eternal, frozen torment, a Guardian should not cut the heart from the Doyen's chest and deliver it to his enemies.

And a Guardian should not imagine killing Michael whenever she was faced with him, whether in person . . . or while studying his carved granite features in the upper chambers of an abandoned desert temple.

Yet as Alice Grey traced her fingers over Michael's sculpted likeness, she could almost feel his heart, warm and bleeding in her hand. In the one hundred and twenty years since she'd been transformed into a Guardian, the image had become frighteningly easy to conjure.

Perhaps she'd never been worthy of her wings.

Alice dropped her hand away from Michael's stone chest and tried to ignore the tightening around her own heart. What a fool she was, to imagine freeing herself from the bargain she'd made. Even if she paid the price that Teqon had demanded, she would be neither safe nor saved. She would be a murderer.

And either way, she was damned.

But not yet. Not until she was dead—or Teqon was. Until then, there was hope.

It would not do, however, to think of how very little hope there was.

Seeking a distraction, Alice stepped back from the granite frieze, gaining a wider view of the sculpted panels so that she would not see *Michael*, but the story illustrated by the stone, in which he merely played a part.

When she'd found this temple, she'd been gripped by the same anticipation and excitement that had accompanied each of her discoveries. But aside from one—very large—difference, this temple did not tell her anything new.

Her battery-powered lantern illuminated the dozens of friezes that covered the walls of this enormous stone chamber, but every Guardian was familiar with the tale they told. At the far end was a panel representing the First Battle, with Lucifer leading his rebels against the angels loyal to Heaven.

Other scenes filled out the history—the transformation of rebel angels into demons and the descent into Hell. Here, and in every other temple Alice had found, scenes from the Second Battle were shown more often than any other. The frieze directly in front of her celebrated the moment Michael had slain the dragon. The artist had styled the Doyen's hair in classical Greek curls rather than shorn close to his scalp, but his hard features were unmistakable. Other panels depicted Michael and several companions, who must have been the first Guardians he'd transformed.

The sculpted pieces were a mystery, but only as to their creation. Though almost two decades had passed since she'd found the first temple, she still did not know who had built them.

And she could not account for the missing pieces of the timeline.

Alice glanced toward the early panels. One of those rebelling angels in the First Battle had become the demon known as Belial. Once Lucifer's lieutenant, he'd turned against the other demon, and had begun a campaign to take Lucifer's throne.

That much had been recorded in the Scrolls—but Alice did not know *when* Belial had turned against Lucifer. How she would have loved to put it all in order.

And there were other pieces that had not been mentioned in the Scrolls, pieces that she and other Guardians had not learned until the past year—such as the nephilim. There was no indication when Lucifer had created the strong race of demons whose purpose had been to assist him in enforcing the Rules. At some point, the nephilim had tried to overthrow Lucifer's throne. With the help of Belial and his armies, Lucifer had defeated the nephilim and imprisoned them in Hell—but Alice had no idea whether their insurgency had been before or after the Second Battle.

Some time after the nephilim's imprisonment, a prophecy had been delivered to Belial and his followers, assuring him that he would prevail over Lucifer after the nephilim were destroyed. Nothing in these friezes or the Scrolls said anything of that prophecy—not who had foreseen it, or any details regarding how Belial would triumph. Alice only knew of the prophecy because Belial's demons had revealed its existence to a fellow Guardian—but since she'd learned of it, she'd thought of little else.

Not now, though. Alice closed her eyes. Not now.

That hope was so very small, a thin thread in a fragile cloth. Tugging too often might unravel it all.

She took a long, steadying breath, and looked again at the sculpted wall. What else was missing?

Ah, yes. None of the friezes showed when—or how—Michael had lost the sword he'd used to slay the dragon.

The recovery of the powerful weapon from an English manor in the early nineteenth century was also missing from the history, but that omission was easier to explain: this temple had been abandoned more than two thousand years before the sword was found.

The hem of Alice's heavy woolen robes brushed the gleaming stone floor as she walked along the panels, studying the final scenes. Most depicted battles between Guardians and demons or Guardians and nosferatu. A few included Michael, but there were also other, unknown Guardians. The last was of a gathering in Caelum—hundreds of Guardians stood before Michael's temple. Behind them, the city rose in spires and domes; even in black granite, Caelum's beauty was breathtaking.

She'd sketched the panel, but her precise drawings could not convey the skill of these artists. How, she wondered, would they have sculpted the more recent events in Guardian history? Could they have expressed the emptiness of Caelum after the Ascension, when thousands of Guardians had moved on to their afterlife, leaving only a few dozen warriors and novices in the Guardian corps?

And was it possible to show Michael's victory two years before, when he'd won a wager with Lucifer—closing every Gate between Hell and Earth for five centuries, and locking all but a few hundred demons in that dark realm? A wager could not be sculpted; an invisible Gate couldn't, either.

Perhaps they would have only shown Michael being forced to give up his sword to Belial, who would use it in his war against Lucifer. That scene would appear to be a defeat—but Alice thought the loss was not so terrible, particularly if the demons in Hell completely slaughtered one another by the time the Gates were opened again.

Easier to sculpt would be the nephilim, who had been released from their prison. Unable to remain in corporeal form outside of Hell, the nephilim had possessed the bodies of humans who'd died, and whose souls had been bound for Hell. Now, the nephilim policed the demons remaining on Earth, enforcing the Rules—but they'd also begun slaughtering vampires in various cities around the world.

Those massacres would be all too easy to depict, Alice thought grimly. As was the Guardians' frustration that, so far, they'd only been able to prevent the slaughter in one city.

Demons, nosferatu, and now nephilim. The Guardians remaining after the Ascension had enough to fight.

They should not have to fear one of their own.

She was, Alice realized, looking at Michael again. She tore her gaze from his likeness—and felt the touch of a Gift, muffled by distance and stone.

A Guardian was outside the temple. Frowning, Alice reached out in an ever-widening circle with quick, light flicks of her own Gift.

She didn't get as far as the Guardian. Startled, she extinguished her lantern and listened. She could not hear anyone, but her Gift did not lie.

A Guardian was near . . . but he was not the only one.

❧

Moments after terrifying himself with memories of bloodsplattered foliage and a splintered bamboo cage, Jake Hawkins opened his eyes and realized he had no idea where the hell he'd teleported.

At least it wasn't *Hell*. Though chances were, he'd end up in that realm sooner or later. Until he got his Gift under control, only dumb luck prevented him from taking a swim in the Lake of Fire. Or worse, landing on a warmongering demon horde.

Backstroking through burning lava was a damn good alternative to being skewered by a thousand swords—or kept alive so the demons could play a gleeful game of Torture the Guardian.

Fun for everyone but him.

But his dumb luck had held for one more jump, and instead of screaming Below, Jake stood at the edge of a sheer cliff on the side of an arid, rock-studded mountain. A waxing crescent moon was setting behind the sand dunes on the horizon; early evening stars shot holes through the sky.

Not Hell, but he wasn't in Caelum, either—although the Guardian realm with its white marble and never-setting sun was almost as empty of people. No fires flickered in the foothills; no human odors floated in the air.

And there was no one to see Jake form his wings and step over the cliff.

Wind sifted through his white feathers, and Jake resisted the urge to look at his satellite positioning device. He'd been taking these unexpected jaunts since discovering his Gift; unfamiliar geography had become a challenge. If he used his GPS receiver to figure out his location, he'd failed.

But this place almost had him beat. The low-growing prickly scrub and the distant stretch of desert could be anywhere in North Africa or the Middle East. The recent sunset and mountain range narrowed it to Tunisia, Morocco, or Algeria; but as one of three Guardians who could teleport, Jake needed to learn how to identify a specific region within seconds.

He needed to be able to go where he intended, too.

A Gift ain't nothing but knowledge and willpower. Drifter, his mentor, had tossed out that not-so-helpful advice ten minutes before when Jake had been trying to teleport from Drifter's home in Seattle to the Archives building in Caelum.

Jake shook his head, circled back toward the cliff. Ignorance wasn't his problem. He wasn't spineless, either. He'd known where Caelum was, and he'd wanted to visit the Archives—but he'd still had to scare himself shitless in order to make the jump.

He'd also been praying he wouldn't run into the Black Widow. An image of the archivist's cold, disapproving stare had filled his mind just before he'd teleported.

So he hadn't focused hard enough; his Gift had picked up on his reluctance and landed him here. Wherever here—

Hot diggety damn.

With a snap of his wings, he drew up vertical and stared at the wall of stone.

A temple had been carved into the face of the cliff.

And he was catching flies. Jake closed his mouth, vanished his wings. The drop and knee-jarring thud against the ground shook away the last of his surprise.

No way could something like this have remained undiscovered, not for the length of time the architecture suggested. The portico of columns was unmistakably Greek. The pediment and entablature recalled the Parthenon's—only lacking the ornamental sculptures.

The interior extended farther back into the mountain than even his Guardian sight could determine.

He'd seen rock-cut buildings before. Petra, in Jordan—though those were of sandstone. The Hindu caves at Ellora were granite, like this was; but they were far more ornate, and completely excavated from the surrounding mountainside.

With a quick mental touch, Jake pulled the GPS receiver from his hammerspace. Screw failure—and, for now, the Archives.

He was in Kebili, a sparsely populated governorate in southwestern Tunisia. After marking the coordinates, Jake vanished the device back into his mental storage. He couldn't contain his awe and excitement as easily.

But only a fool rushed into something like this. He opened his psychic senses. Nothing. No unusual sounds, either. Insects, the small squeaking of a shrew or rodent, his own heartbeat.

A light wind lifted and skimmed over his head, carrying grains of sand that settled on his scalp, rasped against his jeans, gathered at the neckline of his T-shirt. Each particle irritated his heightened nerves, distracting him. He scrubbed his hand over his buzz cut, brushing out the worst of the grit.

The forward chamber was a tall stone box, and hadn't escaped the desert wind. Sand lay thick on the floor, shifting beneath his feet.

And his weren't the only feet to have crossed it, Jake realized. Several sets of human footprints led to—or from—the inner chambers. The impressions had sunk deep in the soft sand, leaving the edges indistinct and making it impossible to determine size and direction.

No human scent lingered in the air. Either the footprints were well over a week old . . . or a human hadn't made them.

Jake performed another mental sweep, but knew it wouldn't be reliable. Any demon or Guardian knew how to conceal his presence, and dense stone could dull psychic probes.

The footprints were probably nothing—but he wouldn't go in unprepared.

He stored several pistols and swords in his hammerspace, but called in a crossbow. The grip was comfortable when the weapon appeared in his hand; he practiced with it often.

The prints vanished past the second chamber, where the corridor angled to the right and led to a narrow stairwell. It was too far inside for the wind to blow, and only a trace amount of sand lay scattered on the bare floor.

He jogged up the stairs—three hundred and fifty—and into another corridor, his weapon ready at his shoulder. There were dozens more chambers on this level, and each he passed was stripped to its square bones. A few had stone benches carved around the perimeter of the room; more had recesses cut into the walls like shelves. The ceilings were high and flat.

At the top of another long stairwell, the darkness, which had threatened with shadows in the corners of each chamber, became absolute.

Surprised, Jake stopped. Even on moonless, overcast nights and in closed rooms, objects were clear to his Guardian eyesight. He only needed the faintest illumination to see: star shine, refracted light, the tiny glow of an LED indicator.

But this was like closing his eyes and wrapping his head in a heavy black sack—and it was the first time he'd seen true darkness since he'd done exactly that as a kid. He'd walked out to the middle of a Kansas cornfield, put on the hood, and stumbled around with his arms out—

His short laugh echoed in the stone chamber, revealing its enormous size and pressing away the suffocating darkness. Fifty years had passed, and he'd thought of that cornfield often, but had forgotten how that particular adventure had ended: his granddad had snuck up behind and scared the piss out of him.

He'd screamed and taken off running.

Jake shook his head, grinning. No wonder he'd tried to forget that part. His ten-year-old pride had been shredded.

His sixty-year-old pride withstood being scared all the time—but stumbling around here wouldn't get him very far.

He searched through his hammerspace, his mind skipping over each item. There'd be something he could use. He'd never bothered to store a flashlight; he'd never needed one.

Still didn't. The dim backlight from his cell phone lit the chamber like a carbide lamp.

It took a moment to register what he was seeing. The enormous chamber was terraced. A deep, rectangular pit had been carved into the floor of each level, with steps leading to the bottom. A colonnade surrounded the room; behind the rows of columns, giant arched entryways led east, west, north.

A bath, he realized. A Roman bath. Sculpted out of solid granite. *Inside* a mountain.

Two or three thousand years ago, someone in Tunisia had been flippin' insane.

Jake lowered the crossbow to his side, tossed a coin out of his hammerspace. Heads, so he went east.

An antechamber lay past the bath. Jake stopped, blinking up at the arch leading out—a line of symbols had been carved above it. Aside from the columns and the design of the temple, it was the first indication of a specific culture he'd seen.

But the symbols weren't Latin or Greek. He'd have recognized those. No, this reminded him of a script he'd only seen engraved in living flesh and used to cast spells.

A shiver ran up his spine. He turned and backed beneath the arch into the next chamber.

It didn't have to be the demonic script. There were many ancient languages he didn't know. He'd take a picture on his way out—another Guardian would recognize it, or he'd find a reference in the Archives.

Where he'd probably have to ask the Black Widow.

The shiver worked its way back down. The woman was straight-up creepy: always draped in black, playing with her spiders, and moving like a mechanical bird that'd been wound too tight. Talking to her made him feel eight again, his buddies daring him to trick-or-treat at Old Man Marley's house.

Finding the courage had been easy enough, but he'd still walked away with runny Jell-O for knees.

They almost gave out again when he turned and his phone illuminated the chamber. *Whoa, boy.*

The bath had been enormous; this was a cavern. His light didn't penetrate to the ceiling. The black granite floor had been polished to a mirror sheen—and at the opposite side of the chamber, a winged statue overlooked the room.

Her braids were a crown, her wings folded behind her, her arms bare. Despite the sword she brandished in her left hand, her expression was serene.

Jake estimated that, even at an inch over six feet, he stood no taller than her ankle.

There'd been crazy bastards living here, for sure. But they were talented crazies. The statue all but breathed with life.

But damn if he would be intimidated by it.

Awe was acceptable, though, he decided, forming his wings and crossing the chamber by air. He did awe very well: wide eyes, slack jaw. Hell, the first couple of decades in Caelum, surrounded by amazing architecture and beautiful, often-naked women, he'd done nothing *but* awe.

He missed those years.

Unfortunately, the statue wasn't naked. Even in granite, her draped gown appeared fluid, as if caught by a wind.

Jake landed, casting measuring glances to the sides of the chamber. His gaze narrowed on the walls behind the colonnade. There were the friezes he'd expected throughout the temple, ringing the room with their life-sized scenes. From this distance, shadows obscured their details.

And, he realized, the primary statue was just off-center. Judging by the large rough patch on the floor, there'd once been another figure in front and to the left of her.

Kneeling, he thought. Her face was downturned, and her right hand extended before her thigh, like a benevolent queen bestowing grace upon her subject.

Had it been a willing supplicant, he wondered . . . or a conquered one?

The tips of her fingers were broken off. She'd probably been touching the other figure, had been sculpted from the same stone. So removing it had destroyed part of her, as well.

Jake eyed the fingertips. They were too lifelike, and he was too accustomed to scaring himself—he expected blood to drip from them at any moment.

Time to move on, then. Fighting his girly shudder, he crossed to the south side of the room.

As soon as his light revealed the first sculpted panel, Jake froze.

He'd seen *this* before.

There was the dragon that Lucifer had called forth from Chaos during the Second Battle, and the human Michael thrusting his sword into its heart.

And it was a near replica of a frieze carved into the doors of Michael's temple in Caelum.

Why was it *here*? Jake's heart kicked into overdrive.

And he heard a footstep from behind him.

A gloved palm slapped over his mouth before he could react. A slim hand rose in front of his face, fingers flashing a warning in the Guardians' sign language.

Do not move, novice. Do not even breathe if you wish to live.

He nodded, but didn't relax. Demons also knew how to sign. And like a demon, she had no odor.

Quickly, he tucked his phone into his jeans pocket, leaving the backlit screen exposed, and raised his own hand. *How do I know what you are?*

As if not being dead wasn't a gigantic hint.

The gloves vanished; the fingers pressing over his lips were strong, slender—and warm. A demon's would have been hot.

All right, he signed, and she released him after another warning to be silent.

The moment he faced her, she asked, *Can you teleport away?*

Probably not. Right now, he was more curious than afraid. Since she'd known about his Gift, she obviously recognized him—but he didn't recognize her. A hijab covered her hair and forehead; layers of loose robes concealed her tall form. Her dark eyes studied him from beneath black brows.

When he shook his head in response, the dusky skin over her jaw whitened and she looked toward the chamber entrance.

Jake knew almost every Guardian by sight, and most by mannerism. She'd probably shape-shifted into this form to blend with the regional population, but he didn't have a clue who she was.

And he wasn't going to get the opportunity to ask. Her weapon appeared in her hand: a tall staff topped by a long, curving blade.

Which Guardian wielded a naginata? Jake wondered as he replaced his crossbow with his sword. Even Mariko, the Guardian who'd introduced Jake to the weapon, didn't use it except for practice the wooden staff splintered too easily.

But this one had obviously been modified to withstand a Guardian's strength and frequent use: the staff was fashioned of steel. To counter its weight, the blade extended half again a naginata's typical length.

With a wince, Jake glanced down at his own sword. He didn't quite measure up.

The Guardian's gaze followed his, and when she met his eyes again, he thought humor quirked her lips.

Use the crossbow, she signed. *They'll flare their eyes to see.*

Demons. Jake's grip tightened on the sword before he exchanged it with the crossbow again. Their eyes shone crimson; in the dark, they'd serve as a bright red target.

But rarely an easy one.

The Guardian was watching the entry again, and the low psychic thrum of her Gift pushed through his body. Her fingers moved at her side. *They've entered the bathing chamber. Three of them.*

No telling what her Gift was, except that it had helped her locate the demons. Jake couldn't hear or sense them—but because she'd used her Gift, they'd have sensed her.

She turned back to him. *Do the bolts in your crossbow have venom?*

Yes. The shafts and arrowheads had been coated with hellhound venom—not enough to paralyze a demon, but it'd slow one down.

Don't miss, she signed, and with an elegant sweep, she caught the edge of his cell phone on the point of her blade and flicked it out of his pocket.

Taking the hint, he vanished it into his hammerspace. Darkness surrounded them. Her hand clasped his, and he felt the brush of her wings before she tugged him into the air.

Okay. Apparently, her Gift was the ability to see in the dark. Jake dangled beneath her, aware that they were flying upward, expecting to smash into the ceiling at any second.

But she slowed, hovered, and maneuvered forward until stone was at his back, his side, and formed a shelf behind his knees. She lowered him onto the ledge, pressed her hand against his chest in an unmistakable *Stay put.*

He heard the air rip through her wings as she dove away. A moment later, light flashed from the antechamber. A grating screech accompanied it, like iron fingernails scraping a rough chalkboard.

What the flippin' hell was she doing? Jake tried to stand, whacked his head on the ceiling, and bit back his curse. But he didn't need to be silent to hear her. She wasn't flying anymore, but running. Her footsteps would make it stupidly easy for the demons to pinpoint her movements. Crazy.

And she'd stuck him up here in the corner, useless and—

On the opposite side of the cavern, a shower of sparks fell. For an instant Jake saw her, the blade of her naginata slashing across the granite wall.

Not so crazy, after all. Jake settled back down. The demons might not know there were two Guardians. Even if they did, she was forcing them to focus in her direction and making enough noise to cover Jake's heartbeat. He'd be able to get at least two shots before they located him.

In the antechamber, a female demon spoke. Another female answered her, then a male. Scarlet light gleamed across the floor before it was extinguished.

The female demon sang out a melodic stream of words.

Arabic. Jake didn't know the language, but the insult was plain enough. He firmed his jaw, waited.

From the direction of the statue came the Guardian's derisive snort. Then she was across the cavernous chamber, her steps echoing against the far wall.

The demon spoke again, in a lower tone. Her voice caught the Guardian mid-swing. The sparks illuminated her shocked expression; her head whipped around as she stared toward the antechamber. Dismay stabbed from her psyche before she blocked it.

The chamber went dark. Her whispered denial filled the silence. "No."

A crimson glow moved through the antechamber, and the first demon stepped through. Wearing robes and—except for her eyes and the batlike wings folded at her back—in her human form.

Come on, Jake urged the others. There was movement behind her, but he didn't have a shot yet.

In the wash of red light, he saw the Guardian standing in the center of the chamber, her arms slack at her sides, the tip of the naginata on the floor.

The demon smiled. Glowing eyes, leathery wings, *and* fangs. "And we've been charged to take something back to him as proof that you received his message. What shall it be—your hands? Your tongue?"

Just great. The demon had switched to English in response to the Guardian's "no," but Jake still had no idea what had stunned her. It wasn't the threat; between demons and Guardians, bloodshed was pretty much a given.

But whatever it'd been, she was coming out of it. A slow smile crept up the sides of her mouth. She no longer held her weapon in a slack grip, but with the loose confidence of a seasoned warrior.

Who the hell was she?

"Come, then," she challenged the demons. "Take them."

The male emerged, his unclothed body covered in crimson scales, a sword in each taloned hand.

Jake fired.

The bolt flew faster than sound, embedding in the demon's side before he could react to the snap of the bowstring. He fell to his knees, clawing at the shaft.

Jake reloaded as the second female burst from the antechamber. The first female dove forward; Jake's next shot pierced her wing.

That was all he'd get. Her movements as fluid as a dancer's, the Guardian slipped around the male. The blade of her naginata flashed. She leapt into the air in pursuit of the second female before his horned head hit the floor.

The first demon had vanished her injured wings, and a semi-automatic pistol appeared in her grip. She aimed it at the flying Guardian.

Not in this lifetime. Jake plummeted toward the demon, calling in his sword. She heard him coming, shifted her stance. He looked down the barrel of the gun, saw her finger tighten on the trigger.

And felt his Gift activate as terror ripped through him. A memory of pain and failure.

No, goddammit. Can't leave her alone—

He jumped, opened his eyes to a giant statue bathed in scarlet light. Gunshots cracked.

Holy shit. A miracle.

Jake pivoted, scything his blade through the demon's neck before she realized that he'd teleported behind her.

He glanced up, then threw himself to the side as a mass of scales and taloned wings hurtled toward him. The last demon smashed to the floor at his feet, the naginata buried in her heart.

The crimson glow in the cavern faded. In the darkness, Jake heard the Guardian land, and the wet sound of tearing flesh as she removed her weapon from the demon's chest—then the thunk as the blade sliced through the neck.

His cell phone lit the scene. Blood pooled beneath the mound of demon bodies. The Guardian began cleaning off her blade with the hem of her robe.

Jake carelessly wiped his sword on his jeans and made himself look at the demon he'd slain.

To his surprise, his knees didn't wobble, his stomach didn't churn.

Hot *damn.* His first kill since becoming a Guardian, but he wasn't staggering off to the side and blowing chunks. The miracles just kept on coming.

Grinning, he vanished his sword and shoved his hands into his pockets, told his feet to stay still. Slaying his first demon deserved a victory dance, but judging by the sharp glance she gave him, the Guardian probably wouldn't appreciate his version of the twist.

Then her naginata disappeared, and he thought, *What the hell.*

He caught her beneath her arms, swept her around in a circle. She didn't try to stop him, though her lips clamped together. Probably to stifle a shriek of delight or laughter, he guessed, because it was flippin' impossible not to be thrilled at this moment. The demons were dead, he didn't have a bullet in his head, and this chamber was the most incredible thing he'd ever seen—on Earth, anyway.

Her mouth didn't relax when he put her down, and Jake suddenly found the tight line irresistible.

He closed his eyes and swooped in.

Her fists balled at his shoulders, but she didn't push him away. Nor did her lips soften.

Her clothes did. The robes disappeared beneath his hands, and his palms slid from her underarms to a slim, silk-covered waist.

God, what made women feel so good?

Even the unreceptive ones. Damn, damn, damn. He broke the kiss, fighting his disappointment. The nice thing about female Guardians, though—and he knew from experience—was that they generally wouldn't kill a man just for making a move.

Jake lifted his head, and his blood froze.

Her eyes were blue now, and icy with disapproval. A heavy brown braid snaked over her shoulder. Her dress wreathed her in black from her neck to her pointy witch-boots.

The Black Widow smiled, and Jake's stomach lurched. Something moved inside her mouth. A hairy, segmented leg thrust between her parted lips—

Oh, Jesus—

A tarantula crawled out.

—Jesus, Jesus—

Jake stumbled back, tripped. Wood thudded beneath his ass. Sunlight speared his eyes.

"Jesus Christ in Heaven!" he shouted, then scrubbed at his lips, his tongue. He could almost *feel* that thing in his mouth. He'd kissed a flippin' nut job.

A shadow fell across his face, and Jake looked up. A long way up. His mentor wasn't a short man, by any measure.

"I reckon you yelling that name means you didn't make it to the Archives," Drifter said, his gaze running over the bloodstains on Jake's jeans. "Though I'm doubting it was him who scared you back here."

Seattle. Jake flopped back on the deck outside Drifter's house, breathed in the clean scent of Lake Washington. "I ran into the Black Widow."

"Alice?"

That was her name? If he'd ever learned it in his forty years as a Guardian, Jake had forgotten it.

"The Black Widow fits better," he said. Alice was a soft, sweet name. It belonged on girls in pretty dresses chasing after white rabbits and attending tea parties.

The Guardian was more like the frightening side of Wonderland. The Jabberwock, or the queen who ordered beheadings.

Scowling, Drifter shoved a flat-brimmed hat over his brown hair. "She ain't as bad as you novices make out. You all oughta—"

"I kissed her."

"Well, hell." Drifter whistled low, shaking his head. "I never figured you as suicidal. Why do a fool thing like that?"

Ah, that sweet elation was washing over him again. Jake grinned, laced his fingers behind his head. "I killed a demon."

"I suppose that's as good a reason as any." With a short nod, Drifter turned for the house. The wind from the lake kicked up the tails of his duster. "She do that spider-out-of-her-mouth trick?"

Jake jackknifed up to sitting. "That was a *trick*?"

❦

Oh, dear God.

The light had vanished along with the novice. Surrounded by darkness, Alice stood absolutely still, holding in the scream that swelled in her throat.

Teqon had sent the demons to tell her that his patience was at an end.

But she would not think of it yet—not until she mended the cracks in her composure and in her psychic shields. For a short time, she would allow herself to push thoughts of her bargain aside.

With shaking hands, Alice called her lantern and looked away from the spot where the novice had been standing. She'd heard he couldn't yet control his Gift—that his fear took him over.

But he didn't lack bravery, she thought as her gaze slipped over the demons' bodies, lingering on the head of the one he'd slain. And his vivid imagination would serve him well. A creative mind was an asset to a warrior—but it was a hindrance so long as he let it run wild. If the novice had taken even a moment to rein it in, he'd have perceived the illusion she'd created.

Alice touched her lips. Yes. Much too impulsive, but also skilled for his age. Ethan had taught him well—and, even now, was likely teaching him how she'd accomplished the illusion.

It was one of her best tricks. That did not mean very much, however, when she had so few.

And to be truthful, there wasn't much to it. Guardians couldn't hear thoughts or read minds; their psychic abilities were primarily empathic. But they could receive images if their psychic shields were penetrable and if someone focused hard enough.

The novice's shields hadn't been until Alice shifted into her natural form. His shock had given her an opening, like a small rip in a seam. The suggestion of a spider leg had been the tug to tear it wide, and his overwhelming revulsion concealed Alice's psychic scent as she shoved the larger, more horrific image past his defenses.

Simple, yet the illusion wouldn't have succeeded if the novice hadn't believed that Alice might ferry spiders about in such a way.

She wouldn't, of course. There were few spiders on Earth with which she had more than a passing acquaintance, and no self-respecting woman let a strange spider crawl through her mouth.

And if Alice couldn't remember the last time she'd respected herself . . . well, that was hardly the point.

A novice would expect it of her. She hadn't listened to the stories they told about her, but she was aware of them.

Enough to know they'd gotten most of it wrong.

Her sigh echoed through the chamber, and when it returned it sounded like a breath from the statue. As always, the warrior woman wore her serenity like a mask, but her sculptors revealed a wealth of power and emotion in the tangle of her braids, the riot of her gown, the lift of her sword.

Alice had seen her before. But this statue, dating from the seventh century BC, was the most recent of the woman's likenesses. It was also the only one with wings, and by far the largest.

It was, finally, something new: not the woman herself, but the wings and the kneeling figure. Alice didn't know what the difference meant, however—if it meant anything at all.

And she didn't know why the male companion who'd appeared with the woman in so many of the friezes no longer stood beside her. Had the missing statue been of the same man? Or had another knelt before her?

In the two weeks since Alice had discovered the temple and this room, she hadn't found the answers. She'd photographed, measured, and sketched. There was no more to record now; there was only much to wonder about.

But she did not have time left for that. Her chest was heavy as she turned back to the demons. Two were nude, and there was nothing unique about the third's robes to indicate her origin. They'd said the demon Teqon had sent them, but Alice had no idea where he'd sent them *from*. She'd preferred not knowing how to find him.

How had they located her? Not by following the novice. No demon could teleport.

Perhaps Teqon had been tracking her movements. She'd been using the Gate near Marrakech to travel between Caelum and Earth, then flying from Morocco to Tunisia. If she'd been identified and the location of the Gate revealed, she needed to warn the other Guardians; otherwise, anyone passing through the portal might be ambushed by demons.

And Teqon *would* send more if Alice didn't inform him that she'd received his message.

Her gaze drifted to the male's chest, and a knife appeared in her hand. It would not be the heart Teqon wanted.

But it would serve as an effective message in return.

CHAPTER 2

The Pontic Steppe was even less welcoming than the Sahara. Once, it had been home to the Scythians and the Sarmatians, the Goths and the Huns. In her mind, Alice could see the paths those ancient peoples had taken on foot and by horse, their trading routes, and maps blazed with violence and bloodshed.

These days, the people rode harvesting combines instead of horses, and the only paths they cut were through fields of wheat.

But they did not harvest now—and blood would be spilled again, very soon.

From the air, Alice searched the flat, snowy landscape. Though the cold did not affect her any more than the heat of the desert had, she shivered.

She rarely felt alone; here, she did. The early winter had killed off the spiders or driven them to shelter in homes and outbuildings. In the endless frozen stretch below, there were no minds to connect to, no whispers for her Gift to collect.

If she had been thinking clearly when she left, Alice would have brought a few of the cave weavers that had served her so well in the temple. Their ability to detect the slightest vibration—a footstep, the disturbance of air from a passing body or the flap of a wing—had allowed Alice to track the demons' progress through the temple better than her hearing could have, and to navigate through the dark.

Without a spider's senses enhancing her own, she was bereft.

She glanced down. A hare raced across the field below, then disappeared in a burrow beneath the snow. Its heartbeat fluttered in her ears.

Alice smiled into the night sky. What a wretched creature she was. A Guardian possessed of extraordinary powers, yet blind and deaf without eight-legged companions.

How very pitiable. Hardly fit to crawl through the sewers of Cairo, let alone the marble courtyards of Caelum. She ought to be eating rats . . . No, she ought to be feeding them her own contemptible entrails. That was, if they would not turn up their twitching noses at such an offering—

If she went any further, she would burst into laughter.

Satisfied that she'd trampled her melancholy mood, she reached out. Finally, a tendril from a familiar psychic scent flicked against her mind. Alice grabbed hold and followed it east.

§

She found Irena hunting roe deer sheltered within a copse of stunted trees.

There would be little contest. As fleet as the deer were, a Guardian could easily outrace them. Irena's bow made it more sporting, perhaps—but she would be upon her target so quickly, ending its suffering immediately after the arrow struck, that Alice wondered why Irena didn't just run the animal down with her kukri knives.

Irena crawled forward through the snow. A white mantle concealed her shoulders and auburn hair, chopped short by her own sword, its reds as varied as the hide of the deer she stalked. The wind carried the scent of dried blood and soot that stained her leather leggings, yet they were barely discernible beneath the musk of the herd.

Better to have come from upwind, Alice thought. Irena's victory over her prey was certain, so she should have given them an opportunity to flee. Not picked them off while they slept.

Alice's boots crunched the snow as she landed. Irena froze, and cast a killing look over her shoulder.

With a wave of her hand, Alice called, "A very good evening to you!"

Though Alice didn't know the word Irena spat, it was blunt and unmistakably Slavic.

Alice didn't *have* to yell over the thundering hooves for Irena to hear her, but once a task was begun, it was best to do it well. And besides, she needed to practice her Russian. "It is a cold night for hunting, yes?"

Irena was already streaking through the trees. Alice followed at a leisurely pace. When she emerged from the opposite side of the copse, Irena was working over a steaming body.

The deer snorted and circled, watching them warily. Blood darkened Irena's forearms, obscuring to her elbows the blue tattoos that decorated the length of her arms. She'd vanished her white mantle. Her smithy's apron protected her chest, leaving her arms and back bare.

Alice ran her hands down her sleeves. She could never be comfortable with so much exposed.

"And now you are quiet." Irena did not look up as she disemboweled the deer. The grisly task was not so different from the one Alice had performed on the demon, only hours before. "You creep up on me like Zorya Polunochnaya, swathed in darkness. You only lack the white hair and hunched back."

Like the midnight aurora? Alice frowned, until she realized that she'd translated *zorya polunochnaya* to English instead of hearing it as a name. Oh, dear. When had she last read about the Zorya? To the best of her recollection, they were three mythical goddesses watching over a sky hound chained to a constellation. The hound would destroy the universe if he broke his bonds.

Alice considered that as Irena rolled the deer's body onto its back. The heat of its blood and innards had melted the snow to pink slush.

Irena might have been the morning Zorya, Alice decided. The fierce young warrior. Neither of them would be the mother.

And Alice would rather the world not rely on her as their defense against annihilation by a godhound. Demons were quite enough. "If I must be a crone," she said, "I would prefer to be Baba Yaga."

"Would you aid the lost, or abduct children and eat them?"

"Both. It would lend more variety to my day. I should also like to have invisible servants."

Irena snorted. "And a home built on dancing chicken legs? With no windows, no doors—"

"And you will not build a chimney through which I could leave."

The angled knife in Irena's hand hesitated. Then she finished the cut, jaggedly slicing through the breastbone.

Alice's voice did not tremble. She could take pride in that, she supposed. At this point, it was the small things that counted. "A room of metal I cannot escape. Twenty years ago, Irena, you promised me this. If you hadn't, I never would have returned to Earth after I completed my training."

"We also promised never to speak of it again until necessary. Is it?"

"Teqon contacted me. I'm to fulfill my bargain, or be killed."

Irena's knife regained its former precision. "You are still trying to find an alternative?"

Trying, but not succeeding very well. "Yes. There must be something he wants more than Michael's heart. Something that would release me."

"Something tied to this prophecy Drifter told us about?"

Alice laced her fingers together, as if protecting the spark of hope that had burned in the months since she'd heard of the prophecy. "Perhaps."

Irena sat back on her heels, brushed her hair from her forehead with a bloody hand. "Teqon follows Belial in his war against Lucifer."

"Yes." Belial claimed that he fought for redemption, to return to the glory of Heaven. Alice didn't believe him—didn't think any Guardian believed him.

"And according to the prophecy, Belial will be victorious."

"Perhaps," Alice said again. What Ethan had told them was vague, at best. Belial's demons would defeat Lucifer, but first they had to win other battles.

What those battles were and how they would be won was still unknown, to Guardians and demons both.

Irena reached into the chest cavity, tore out the heart. Alice waited quietly as the other woman said a few reverent words over it. When Irena tore off a chunk with her teeth, Alice said, "It is Michael's opinion that the prophecy has no validity—that nothing can be foretold. He dismisses it entirely."

Irena swallowed, then vanished the remaining heart and the body of the deer into her cache. "I am of the same mind as the Doyen. And Michael is rarely incorrect about such things." She cocked a brow and stood. "But it does not matter as long as Teqon believes it, yes?"

"That is what I hope."

"Have you found evidence of the prophecy? Any mention that did not originate from a demon?"

"Not yet." Nothing in the temples, nothing in the Scrolls.

"Keep trying," Irena said, as if Alice might have considered anything else. "The options you've chosen—there is no victory, Alice. Eternal torment or eternal prison. If you become mad enough, they will be the same."

Yet it would be fitting. She'd been thought insane when she'd made the bargain. How elegant that she would be reduced to insanity by it. "I shall spend eternity creeping around the room."

Smiling, Irena knelt and began washing the blood from her arms with the snow. "You are an odd woman, Alice."

"Given enough time, I will be odder still. But even if my mind is gone, my soul would be safe."

Irena's mouth reshaped into a hard line. "Our souls are never safe. Not so long as there are demons who know the prices for which we will sell them." She scooped up more snow, roughly scrubbed her face and hair. Her ivory skin glowed when she finished. "I will help you as much as I can, Alice. But if you cannot face imprisonment, and choose to fulfill your bargain, I will kill you myself."

Irena had said the same twenty years ago, and so Alice was prepared for the sadness and dread the words stirred inside her.

She concealed it remarkably well, she thought. "You may not have the opportunity. Very likely, a queue of Guardians will be waiting to take my head."

"Then I will push to the front." Irena stood and looked to the east. Her wings sprouted from her naked back, the feathers a deeper, purer white than the snow around them. "I must deliver the meat to the village before dawn. Will you come to Seattle tonight? Charlie completed her training in Ashland, and Drifter wants to make an evening of it. I was to invite you if we met."

"I'll come," Alice said without hesitation, amazing herself. How simple that decision had been. Several months ago, only Irena's nagging and her own curiosity had propelled her to meet the woman Ethan had chosen for a partner. But to Alice's surprise, she'd been comfortable in Charlie's company. The woman had a gift of putting anyone she spoke with at ease—a gift that Ethan shared.

A gift Alice had never possessed.

In any case, she needed to talk with Ethan. Not only would he know how to find Teqon, Ethan was also the Guardian most familiar with the prophecy—and he would ask few questions in return.

Not that there were answers she could give. Or that she *would* give. Only Irena and Michael knew of her bargain. Her debt to Teqon made her a traitor at worst and a coward at best—and she'd never had the spine to tell Ethan or any of the other Guardians with whom she'd become close.

Irena turned, her wings arching, and for a moment Alice was reminded of the statue in the temple. Then the Guardian lifted into the sky, signing a farewell.

No, Alice thought. She had no answers. But if she were lucky, perhaps the photographs in her cache would finally offer a clue.

§

Blast!

Alice firmed her lips before the curse escaped. It was shameful to lose her temper—even more so to lose it over a piece of godforsaken technology.

She'd known trying to maintain a computer in Caelum would be more of a hassle than it was worth, but she'd been seduced by the cleverness of the machine.

The photographs of the temple interior had transferred from camera to hard drive with amazing speed. No film to develop, no negatives to store. And the resolution on her screen was incredible. Much more detailed than her best drawings could be, and it was easier to enlarge sections of each picture for printing.

But she'd almost drained her tenth—her *last*—battery. Caelum lacked electricity; she'd have no opportunity to recharge them until she visited Earth.

The warning light blinked again.

Worthless, wretched machine. But there was no reasoning with it. She selected photos to print and wrote them to a flash drive. For now, she would have to rely on her memory and her sketches.

Her senses hummed, and she glanced up, reaching out with her Gift. Beyond the entrance to her apartment, Remus and Romulus buzzed with excitement over some disturbance.

Alice heard laughter a moment later. Her mouth slackened in what must have been an idiotic expression of incomprehension. *Silly, softheaded cow.* What was there not to comprehend? With a few exceptions, only Guardians had stepped foot in Caelum since the angels had transferred the realm over to Michael.

Therefore, Guardians must be in her courtyard.

Straightening, she moved to the marble doors that led from her quarters. On her portico, a web stretching between two columns trembled as Remus scurried upward to hide in the scrollwork. Romulus remained behind, repairing a limp thread like a nervous old woman tidying a room for unexpected guests.

Alice resisted the urge to smooth her hand over her hair. An ache took up residence in her chest, but she repressed that as well.

Though many Guardians had once lived in this part of Caelum, it had been empty since the Ascension. Since, more than a decade earlier, silence had abruptly fallen over the city as thousands of heartbeats and voices were extinguished. Alice hadn't comprehended then, either—until she'd walked into the courtyard, and none of her students had been there to greet her.

They'd spoken of Ascending before. Unconvinced that Guardians were needed in a modern world, they'd all chosen to move on to their afterlife.

So had thousands of other Guardians; less than forty remained after the Ascension. Since then, only a few bored novices had wandered in this direction.

And two years ago, when the novices had begun training in San Francisco instead of Caelum, "few" had dwindled to "none."

Now there was laughter in the courtyard again. The ivory buildings surrounding the tiled square were not as tall as they were in other parts of the city, or as graceful. There were more straight edges here, fewer domes and spires. But the marble ivy climbing their walls seemed to seek the touch of the sun, and was found nowhere else in Caelum. In the center of the courtyard, a sculpted ash tree spread its translucent stone leaves over an unmoving shadow. The pavers at the base of the trunk buckled, as if a root system fought for space below the ground.

She could have sketched every detail in the courtyard with her eyes closed, yet with that sound warming the air, the familiar scene suddenly looked foreign to her.

Oh, dear. Alice pressed her lips together. Foreign was a bit of an overstatement, wasn't it? Next she would be decrying that the appearance of true life had stripped the courtyard of its illusions, leaving only coldness and death, woe and fie!

If she let herself, the depths of histrionics she might plumb were dizzying.

This was not something foreign, but something forgotten. And the courtyard was just as lovely and unique as it had ever been.

Folding her arms over her chest, Alice watched the novice from the temple—Jake, she reminded herself—perform an odd, hip-and knee-twisting dance beneath the tree. Drusilla had doubled over, holding her sides and begging him to stop. Next to her, Pim had bent as well; but instead of laughing, the novice had her hands braced on her knees. Her sleek bowl of black hair slanted forward across her cheeks, and her psychic scent billowed with nausea.

Nausea? Guardians didn't need to eat and were never sickened by it. So Jake's queer dance probably celebrated a successful teleportation, Alice decided. Drusilla, older and more accustomed to the disorientation that accompanied the jump, wasn't as affected as the novice she mentored.

Only Michael, Selah, and Jake could teleport, so Alice rarely used that method to travel between realms. But although the Gates were not as convenient—they were spaced great distances apart on Earth—she enjoyed flying. It was far better, she mused, than wobbling.

Pim lifted her head, met Alice's eyes, and the sallow color that had been ebbing from the novice's face oozed back in.

How easily unsettled these novices were. A cackle would have been just the thing—but now that Drusilla's laughter had faded into a smile of greeting, much too heavy-handed.

Drusilla vanished her physician's coat, called in a sword, and used it to wave. "Good afternoon, Alice darling!"

Alice's lips curved. The salutation was as light and bubbly as soda water—and so was Drusilla.

She stepped from beneath the portico roof, brushing her hand across the web and scooping up Romulus. "You must be coming from San Francisco if it was afternoon."

Several Guardians and all of the novices were connected to a law enforcement facility headquartered in that city, where they received their assignments and training. Alice hadn't bothered to see it yet. Aside from the occasional task that Michael gave her when he was in Caelum, Alice was still largely self-directed.

"Pim and I decided to practice in Caelum; the gym at the warehouse was packed. And that tree is marvelous!" Drusilla's smile widened, and she bobbed back and forth on cherry red athletic shoes. "I'd totally forgotten it was here. But if the noise will disturb you, we can head down to Zephyrus Quarter in a jiffy."

"Of course not," Alice murmured. Movement near the tree caught Romulus's attention, and she glanced past Drusilla to see Jake collecting a small carton from the ground. Through the holes in the lid came a chorus of squeaks.

An early delivery, but perhaps Selah had been unable to bring them to her. Or Jake intended to mollify her for the kiss.

If so, Alice wouldn't tell him she'd only thought of that kiss two or three times since—and never with anger.

But she might tell him that she hadn't thought of it with pleasure, either.

"Great!" Drusilla gave another little bob, then turned to Pim.

Alice wasn't certain how Drusilla remained so effervescent when, as a Healer, she saw more carnage than most Guardians. Perhaps it was because Drusilla rarely failed the tasks given her; her Gift could instantly heal everything but decapitation or a severed heart.

Alice frowned, her eyes narrowing. "Drusilla—do you suppose a Guardian might survive having his heart removed in a surgical manner, so long as it was not cut in two?"

She heard Jake's step falter slightly, and Pim's indrawn breath. If the answer hadn't been so important, Alice would have cackled merrily.

Drusilla bounced back around. "I don't know. I've never encountered an injury like that. When a demon or a nosferatu gets to a heart, that's usually all she wrote." A crease formed between her brows as she considered it. "Removed whole, and then healed?"

"Yes."

"I doubt it," Drusilla said. "But I'm not sure."

"I am." Jake stopped a few feet in front of Alice, his wary gaze on her mouth. He seemed relieved not to see any spiders there until Romulus crawled up to her shoulder for a better look, raising his two front legs.

To his credit, Jake did not blink or vanish. Nor did he do anything else, until Drusilla prompted, "Jake?"

"Yeah. All right." He grinned and shook his head, as if silently laughing at an inner joke. His fingers tapped against the white box, and he was answered by curious squeak. He grimaced and stilled his hands. "I've been specializing with Alejandro—for my blade work—most nights when Drifter's with Charlie. So two months ago, Alejandro and I went back to Philadelphia, because we'd heard one of Lucifer's demons moved in after the nephil was gone."

Alice nodded. Earlier in the year, the nephilim had massacred the vampire communities in Rome, Berlin, and Washington, D.C. Alejandro and Jake had slain one in Philadelphia, but not before hundreds of vampires had died.

Though the nephilim usually lived in the bodies of the humans they possessed, not much stronger than vampires, they were almost unstoppable in their own form. And although they both originated from Hell, the nephilim wouldn't hesitate to kill a demon. Any intelligent demon would flee a city a nephil inhabited.

"I caught it with a bullet," Jake said, rapping his knuckle against his temple to show where he'd shot the demon, "and Alejandro got him through the chest."

Jake jabbed the air in front of him, miming a sword and drawing a protest from the mice as they were jostled. "But he missed the heart."

"Alejandro had a *sword* and he missed?" Alice said, and held out her hand for the box. When Jake ignored her outstretched palm, she lowered it again.

"Unheard of, right? I was like this." Jake's eyes widened, and Alice had to firm her lips against a laugh. He'd had the same expression after kissing her. "But the assho— Er, the demon dodged at the last second. So Alejandro got him right here instead." He tapped his sternum. "And the demon had ahold of him, so Alejandro couldn't back up for another strike. So he just . . ."

Jake twisted his wrist, as if carving a tight circle with his blade, then yanked his arm back. "And the heart popped right out. Along with some ribs and lungs and sh— *stuff*."

"And Alejandro calls Irena barbaric," Alice murmured. An upward slice would have sufficed.

"Does he?" Jake shrugged, and his arm dropped to his side. "So the heart was whole, but the demon was dead. Instantly."

A Guardian and a demon had similar powers—and similar

weaknesses. What had killed a demon would likely kill a Guardian, too.

Disappointment swept through her, stronger than she'd expected. She hadn't truly believed removing the heart whole might be a solution, but however tiny the spark of hope had been, it was still a hope extinguished.

And she needed to go, or soon there would be some histrionic scene, after all. Alice signed a thank-you to Drusilla and set off for her apartment at a brisk walk.

"Hey!" Jake jogged up beside her, kept pace. Blades rang behind them as Drusilla and Pim began their fencing practice. "Hey. Uh, Alice—"

Blast and bother! She'd forgotten the box. "You're terrifying the mice," she observed tightly.

"And being eaten by a giant spider won't?" But he steadied the carton. "Does he use your shoulder as a table?"

"Romulus is an adult, and doesn't feed," she said, and paused to return him to his web. "Nefertari eats the mice."

"Nef—" He gave his head a shake. "And the vampire blood?"

"Is for the young and the females." She faced the novice. "Did Selah ask you to bring that as well?"

"No, I'd just heard that you used it." He glanced over her shoulder, into her quarters. Searching for Nefertari? He was looking too high. "But if you want it, I carry some in case I need to heal or transform a human. Or if I run into the nephilim."

Vampire blood weakened the nephilim, and might save a human. Her spiders did not have priority over that. "Keep it."

Alice began to turn away, but stopped when he said, "Well, it's Mackenzie's, so I can get more tomorrow night when I'm in San Francisco. I have two units, anyway."

A plastic bag appeared in his hand. Alice took it, and regretfully vanished the liquid. Blood would spoil if not stored in her cache, but it left a distinctly unpleasant taste in her mind and on her tongue.

"Thank you, Jake." She saw his surprise and sighed. She was not incapable of niceties, and she performed one more—though only because she was certain he'd refuse. "Would you like to come in?"

His grin surprised her, and his "Hell, yes" left her on the verge of incomprehension again. He winced and ran his hand over the dark stubble of his hair. "Sh— I mean, 'Heck, yes.'"

Alice stared at him. At least, she mused, her histrionics no longer threatened. "Come, then. Mind your step."

She walked past the threshold, but didn't hear him follow. She turned and found him with an odd expression shading his eyes. Realization or amusement—she couldn't tell.

"What is it?"

"The way you move. I couldn't work it out before. But it's—" He strode forward, his joints working as if he were fashioned of pistons and pulleys. "You don't slow down or speed up by making your muscles move slower or faster. No, your muscles are moving fast all of the time—so your speed depends on how long you wait between movements. Like a pendulum that hangs in the air before swinging back down. When you go slow, the wait is long, even though the actual movement is fast." He stopped in the center of the room and nodded, looking pleased with himself. "And that was why when you moved quickly, fighting the demon, it was smoother. Not so jerky."

Alice squelched her sudden self-consciousness. What did she care of his opinion? "It's efficient."

"Maybe, but it's also creepy as— Never mind." He set the box of mice next to her laptop. "Drifter won about fifty dollars from me last month because I keep saying stuff like this. I don't know what happens when women are around. There's a filter between my head and my mouth—but it only lets the stupid shit out." His mouth twisted, then he smiled with wry humor. "Obviously."

So they were both uncomfortable. That suited her. He would probably leave soon. And until he did, she'd take pleasure in his discomfort as retribution for causing hers.

His gaze began to sweep the large room, curiosity leaking from his psychic scent. Alice crossed her arms, wishing that she'd vanished the contents of her quarters into her cache. The sketches and photographs filling the white marble walls, the painted vases, the bronze and stone figures were not just artifacts—they recorded the past twenty years of her research. The past twenty years of her life. They were not meant to be put on display in this intimate context.

Jake moved closer to a Minoan vase, crouching to examine it.

Alice's fingers twitched. Where was Nefertari? Likely sleeping upstairs. Oh, if only the novice could not detect the use of her Gift, she would rouse the spider.

She'd use other means, then. Utterly conscious of the motion of her body now, resenting it, Alice crossed to the arch leading from the main room. "Come. Learning how I use the vampire blood will be more stimulating than that vase."

He glanced at her in a distracted manner. "Actually, I'd rather—"

"Come," Alice repeated, and walked into the next chamber. Square and high-ceilinged, the room was empty but for the tall wooden frames she'd constructed, and the giant orb webs filling them like silk screens.

Jake's reluctance didn't turn into fear when he saw the webs and the large spiders weaving them, but more of that maddening curiosity.

Alice found it difficult to wish him gone when he took such genuine interest.

"Holy mama," he said softly, tilting his head to study the spotted brown spider.

"These are the *Nephila*," Alice said, plucking the gossamer threads. Nero raced along the strands toward her fingers. "And though their names are similar, they have no relation to the nephilim."

Jake glanced at her sharply, as if trying to determine whether she was joking or lecturing. "And does she have a name?"

"He. It is Nero," Alice said, and with a small push of her Gift, she urged him onto her palm. It would confuse and disturb him to remain in his web while she gave her demonstration.

"A male? Aren't they usually—" He lifted his hand, thumb and forefinger a short distance apart.

"Smaller than females? Yes. Shall I introduce you to his mother?" When he gave her another of those sharp glances, she relented. "It is the vampire blood."

"You've made vampire spiders?"

Now it was her turn to wonder if he was serious. He should know that wasn't a possibility. "They don't transform, just as animals and insects don't if they drink vampire blood."

"Can you imagine vampire mosquitoes? Or immortal, blood-sucking ants who make you feel all sexy when they bite?"

"No. I can't."

He was undeterred. "Picnics would never be the same."

"But rather popular, one would think."

Self-reproach instantly followed the thoughtless response. Her dismay was compounded when Jake's blank expression of surprise broke into a grin.

That would simply not do.

And if humor put him at ease, then she would be ponderous. "The blood offers these spiders strength and longevity. Furthermore, the male and female offspring are of equal size—though both male and female are larger than natural spiders. And there is also this."

She hooked her forefinger around a thread near the center of the orb and pulled. The web bowed slightly—then it held. She applied more pressure, and the silk threatened to bite into her finger.

It sprang back into place when she let go.

"You're kidding." Jake looked from the web to Nero combing his tufted legs on her right hand. "Can I?"

"You may," she said, then caught his wrist when he reached for a radial thread. "Not there. See how it's flat? They're like razors. Try the spirals. They're thicker—and round."

"Here?" At her nod, he slipped two fingers around a strand. The muscles in his forearms flexed as he pulled. His teeth set, and his brows lowered in concentration. The frame creaked and listed toward them.

Men were such strange creatures. "You *are* strong enough to break it," Alice said when she smelled blood. "But lacking protection, not without damage to yourself. A blade will cut through, however."

Jake released the thread, and righted the frame with a push of his hand.

"Okay," he admitted as Alice returned Nero to his web. "That *was* worth coming in to see."

"Very good then." Alice injected as much dismissal into her tone as she could, satisfied that it hid the delight his acknowledgment had wrought. "It was kind of you to—"

"But," he interrupted with a smile and enough charm to set her teeth on edge, "I'm here about the temple in Tunisia."

Of course. "An apology isn't necessary."

"Well, no. I'm—"

"Then we agree." She strode toward the main chamber.

"Agree about what?" Jake came after her. "Oh, I get you. Sure, I'm sorry for kissing *you*, but I'm not sorry for . . . And there's no flippin' chance this will come out right."

She frowned and faced him again.

Though his laughter never escaped, his amusement rolled through his psychic scent with the subtlety of a boulder. He flattened his lips and leaned his shoulder against the archway. He glanced up at the ceiling, then back at the webs. A wooden toothpick appeared in his hand, and he twirled it between his fingers.

Finally, he looked at her. "So, spiders are safe to discuss, right? And everything else is off-limits."

Alice lifted her brows.

"All right. I can do that." Jake looked toward the spiders again, then his gaze shifted to the room beyond. "So, do you have any . . . Okay, I probably shouldn't ask if you have—"

"Black widows?"

He slipped the toothpick into the corner of his mouth and dug his hands into his pockets. "Yeah."

"Thirty in the upper levels of this building." She paused. "You must have a dog."

His forehead creased in puzzlement. "No."

"But I have heard that in San Francisco, the woman who doles out your assignments calls you Ethan's puppy."

His short laugh was not the abashed response she'd anticipated. Her frown deepened.

"That's true," he said. "But coming from Lilith, 'puppy' is practically a declaration of love."

"How so?"

"Well, there are two things in the world she loves more than any other: her hellhound, and Hugh Castleford. Hugh mentored you, didn't he?" At her nod, he said, "Me, too. Until Drifter took over."

"Ethan is a brave man. And patient."

Jake's eyes narrowed, and he regarded her steadily before shrugging. "Yeah, he's a hero. Anyway, Lilith named both Hugh and her hellhound 'Sir Pup'—and she also calls her hellhound 'puppy.' So I see it as a compliment."

"How very optimistic you are."

With an easy grin, he strolled into the room. "I am. And *you* called Lilith 'woman' instead of 'Lucifer's hellspawn.' So you don't have a problem with her heading Special Investigations? Some other Guardians do."

"In truth, I hardly know of her." Except that, through trickery and lies, Lilith had convinced Lucifer to release her—Lilith—from a bargain. Alice had taken particular notice of that. "Michael approves. As does Hugh, who knows her best. I will defer to their judgment."

"And she's human now, so you couldn't kill her without breaking the Rules, anyway."

Alice smiled thinly. "That is also true."

Jake stopped in front of her, and Alice decided she did not like that he stood over her by several inches. Why had she never shapeshifted into an immense height? But doing so now would be too obvious.

"You shouldn't have shown me your spiders," he said. "Now that I've seen you with them, you don't freak me out anymore. If you'd bitten their heads off, maybe. But being so careful with them? Nope."

What a terrible miscalculation. "That is unfortunate," she said. "What if you need to teleport?"

"I'll manage. If it helps, you're still creepy. Thirty black widows—and you're feeding them vampire blood? Weirdsville."

She would *not* be amused. "I also have a tarantula."

"I think I've seen it." His gaze dropped to her mouth. "All right, aside from Daddy Longlegs, that taps out my knowledge of different spider species. How about we move on to the temple in Tunisia?"

"Literally?"

"Well, I would, but here's the thing: I already went back earlier today.—and it's gone." He spread his hands, shook his head in disbelief, and repeated, "Just, gone. There's a cliff, but no temple."

Alice looked away from him, fought the ache again. Her gaze slipped over the sketches on the walls, the photographs.

"It is such a bother when that happens," she said quietly.

CHAPTER 3

Alice hadn't expected her answers, such as they were, to satisfy the novice. After all, they'd never satisfied her.

But that was where the similarity between them ended. She hadn't stalked around her quarters, muttering to herself in the way Jake was now, his hands linked behind his head like a prisoner on the march. He didn't lower them, even when he stopped in front of a photo and studied a male figure painted in profile.

She'd memorized the figure's sword, his simple tunic and sandals, years before. Though there weren't any hieroglyphs to identify him, Alice was certain it was Michael.

"And this one?"

"From a temple about fifty miles west of where Abu Simbel stands now. That is a site in—"

"Southern Egypt. Constructed during the reign of Rameses the Great, and relocated in the seventies when they built the Aswan Dam. Yes, I know."

His interruption was the first sign of irritation at her lecturing tone. He'd listened patiently through a monotonous history lesson about Mesopotamia and India, though he'd seemed to be biting his tongue. She'd pushed on, certain she'd been boring him.

But he'd just been polite, letting the eccentric natter on; he'd already known all she'd told him.

"It seems you do." She'd tired of it as well. His reaction reminded her too much of her human years, when she'd smile and nod as people lectured to her on subjects that she already knew as well—or even better—than they, and then go on about her business. "I have no idea how long this temple stood before I discovered it, and it disappeared four days later." Her gaze skimmed the wall below the photograph. A deep gouge scarred the smooth marble surface.

No, she hadn't paced the room in her frustration—she'd taken her weapon to it. She'd gained nothing, and left a blemish on her home.

Oh, why didn't he leave?

A soft noise from the mice reminded her how he'd tricked her into inviting him in. He hadn't brought them in apology, but as a bribe. She would attempt her own if it meant he would go.

"I have photographs from Tunisia on my computer," she said, lifting the carton of mice. Their cage hung from the ceiling, a heavy contraption with steel mesh and bars as thick as her finger. "You're welcome to take them."

Jake joined her, tapped the laptop's touchpad. "Your battery's dead."

"How observant you are."

She ignored his quick grin, but appreciated his doubtful glance at the cage when she opened its door. "Don't tell me," he said. "You feed them vampire blood, and they can gnaw through metal."

"No." She slid the brown mice into their nest. After vanishing the empty carton to her cache, she pulled a mangled pet-store cage out of it. "This is what Nefertari did to the previous one, so Irena made another."

Jake looked at the gaping hole in the side, the twisted wires. Something flickered through his psychic scent—remembered terror, remembered pain. She vanished the cage again.

She'd intended him to speculate about Nefertari, not reopen a wound. She had too many scars of her own to take pleasure in that.

Reaching over her desk, Alice tugged the flash drive from the port. "I've already copied the pictures. If you would only return the—"

Jake held up a large rectangular battery, and she thought there was a slight smirk on his mouth when he looked from it to the small memory stick she offered. "Or, I can just get your computer rocking again and save them to my own."

"Oh, but surely that can't be for the same model—"

"It is." Without waiting for her consent, he flipped her computer over. "I requisitioned laptops, weapons, and a bunch of other shi—*stuff*—for the Guardians working at Special Investigations," he said. "I ordered fifteen extra batteries for Drifter. But I kept five, because he never remembers to charge anything. His cell phone is a joke." He clicked the new battery into place, set the machine down, and powered it up. "I haven't seen him use his computer since I gave it to him—which wasn't a surprise, considering he can't touch one without it locking up. But apparently there was another reason."

Only her failure to hide how much she'd coveted the machine when Ethan had shown it to her. "Apparently," Alice said.

Jake hefted the depleted battery in his hand. "Do you want the other four?"

She hesitated only a moment before nodding. Acceptance did not make her indebted to him. This was nothing but a service he provided many Guardians.

They appeared on her desk in a neat stack. Jake was already bending over the computer, his gaze fixed on the screen, when she said her thank-you. His response was a careless lift of his shoulders.

Uncertain whether she was perturbed or amused by his dismissal, Alice watched him scroll through the pictures. He could have easily copied the files and looked them over later, but here he was, oblivious to her presence in his eagerness to study them *now*.

She could see why he'd been called a puppy. There was no awkwardness in his tall, wiry form, nothing that suggested a lack of control. His every step revealed his confidence; indeed, his movements were almost cockily self-assured. But even when he was still, he seemed to contain a boundless energy resembling the exuberance of youth.

Yet he couldn't be so very young. They'd had the same mentor for their basic training, but she'd already moved on to her specializations by the time Jake had come to Caelum—so that must have been forty or fifty years ago. She could recall him among

Hugh's students, so he hadn't significantly altered his appearance since becoming a Guardian. Perhaps his blue jeans hung a little lower, his T-shirt fit a little tighter against his leanly muscled torso—but that reflected contemporary human fashions more than a change in his body type.

Her gaze skimmed his back pockets, noting the slim outline of a wallet. Strange that he hadn't vanished it into his cache; it was more convenient. He'd likely carried it in his pocket as a human, then. Even centuries after transformation, there were actions many Guardians automatically performed: breathing, blinking, and individual habits engrained while they'd lived on Earth.

Habits, such as appreciating a superior example of male anatomy.

Alice hadn't been human for almost a hundred and twenty years, but she still hadn't broken that particular habit—and she saw no reason to do so now. Jake's fingers on the keyboard were long and nimble, his forearms strong and deeply tanned. The long plane of his back melded into a taut backside that was neither too spare nor too full.

Her gaze settled on his pockets again, and recognition slipped through her, curving her lips.

She'd sketched him once. He'd been nude, lazing about in a courtyard after participating in one of the orgies that had once been so commonplace. A Vietnamese phrase had been tattooed over that firm swell of muscle.

What had the phrase been? Alice couldn't recall, and the sketch was probably lost amid her jumble of personal papers upstairs. But she remembered that he'd seemed to possess boundless energy then, too.

And—according to the gossip she'd overheard from his fellow students—not much finesse.

"I see you've got more folders here, more pictures," Jake said, then turned from the screen. After a glance at her face, he darted a wary look over his shoulder, then at her feet. "Do you mind if I copy those, too?"

"Of course not," Alice said.

Eyes narrowed, Jake straightened. "What's with the smile?"

"Something amused me. Why else would I smile?"

"Maybe you've got something waiting to take a bite of me." He studied her mouth. "Your teeth are longer now."

So they were. Not by very much—but enough to be good practice, should she ever have to imitate a vampire. Such a need had not yet arisen, but one never knew.

"How suspicious you are, novice."

"How creepy you are, Alice." But Jake's own smile lifted the corners of his mouth as he focused on the computer again.

Perhaps she ought to tell him how nicely put together he was. Men so often mistook simple admiration for physical attraction. Surely, coming from her, a suggestion of interest would discomfit him so badly that he would finally go.

He'd responded contrary to her expectations on each of her previous attempts, however. Rather than retreat, he might make an advance—then she would be forced to reject him.

What an awkward scene that would be.

With a resigned sigh, Alice left him poring over a photograph she'd taken in India. The temple had punched through the surrounding jungle like a bare stone fist but had vanished before the wilderness could cast a single vine over its knuckles.

A print from its interior hung near the entrance to her quarters. Alice stopped to examine the temple's statues, then moved along the wall—searching, she imagined, for the same thing Jake was: a clue as to who had sculpted them, a hint of why and how and who.

"Mycenaean, right?" Jake suddenly spoke beside her, and her heart jumped.

Alice barely kept the rest of her body from following it. She held herself still, and wondered if she was surprised more by his sudden appearance or his correct identification.

She stole a glance at his profile, saw his concentration on the painting in front of them. "Yes. From a small island near Crete."

"The hair's distinctive. The braids, the beads. The little beehive thing—" He made a gesture over his head, indicating the high-set roll of hair. "She's sharper, though, than in any other Mycenaean art I've seen. More angular. Egyptian influence?"

He'd recognized that, too? Excitement sparked in her chest. Passion, almost as old as she was, and rarely shared.

Tread lightly, Alice.

She laced her fingers together. "Perhaps," Alice said. "But I wouldn't rule out Akkadian, or Sumerian."

Jake scanned the walls and the pottery again, his expression hopeful. "Have any ziggurats appeared?"

"Unfortunately, no." Exploring one of the Sumerian stepped

pyramids might have sent her into ecstasies. "This fresco is from the oldest temple I've yet found. Radiocarbon dating placed it—"

"*You* used carbon dating?" His quick survey of her form suggested that he thought her dress—or Alice herself—also should have been put under a spectrometer.

"What do you use, novice? Tree rings?"

His unapologetic gaze was steady on hers. "I know a few Guardians who would."

That was true, she reflected. And other Guardians who didn't use computers, guns, or even ballpoint pens.

Very well. She'd made her own assumptions about him and been surprised; she would allow him this surprise in return. This *one*. If he did not learn from it, then she would allow herself to be irritated.

She drew in a short breath. "As I was saying—"

"I'm a dick."

And an observant one at that. But Jake had that internally amused look again, and Alice couldn't decide whether he hoped she would return his smile or if he was laughing at her, so she only continued, "I sent the samples to a lab. This fresco is from 1250 BC."

His expression changed to confusion. "And that's the oldest?"

"Yes."

"But, that panel of Michael and the others . . ." Jake moved to the Egyptian piece from outside Abu Simbel. "Yeah. Check out the others—are they Guardians?"

"I believe so," Alice said quietly.

"Hot damn." He shook his head, then continued, "But the others, they're lounging—the woman and those two men. Their arrangement, their poses all look more natural. All they need are some potbellies and skinny arms." Jake turned and frowned at her. "Are the dates in my head screwy? I'm thinking: eighteenth dynasty, the Amarna period—and a hundred years earlier than your Mycenaean fresco."

She would lure him away from Ethan, Alice decided. Take over his mentoring, and have him teleport her to archeological sites around the world. She would not even care if each jump made her wobble.

Oh, my. How very scandalous her fantasies had become in her old age!

Jake's eyes narrowed, and Alice realized she was smiling again.

"You head isn't screwy," she said, joining him at the panel. "But when I tell you the date, you might begin to think mine is."

"I already—"

"Your filter is leaking again, novice."

His self-disparaging grin was too appealing, she thought. Half-amiable, half-wiseacre. And, when he held out an American five-dollar bill, all cheek.

"Give it to Drifter," Jake explained. "He'll know you've kept me in line."

"Then I shall keep it." Alice took the money. "I've earned it— and he'll only gamble it away."

And Ethan had fleeced her so many times when they'd been training together, she felt no compunction against getting the jump on his winnings now.

Jake sighed when Alice vanished the bill into her cache. "I hoped he would. That's how I planned to get it back."

"So when you say these things, your loss is only temporary?" Alice asked, frowning slightly. "Little wonder your behavior hasn't changed. There are no consequences when you are disciplined."

Except that Jake had begun to recognize his more thoughtless responses—perhaps that was all Ethan intended.

She met his eyes again, and saw that the good humor had deserted his smile. "Golly gee, Alice. I never thought of it that way. Maybe Drifter should make me shape-shift into a girl and crawl around on my hands and knees." His brows lifted, and the texture of his psychic scent was tipped with sardonic barbs. "But what if I liked it too much?"

Alice held his gaze, her own expression cool. No, Jake didn't appreciate a lecture any more than she did. But she had no intention of letting him see that he'd managed to make her feel like a pedantic prig.

And there was obviously only one topic they could discuss that wouldn't result in a mutually annoying exchange.

She turned back to the panel. "Ninth century BC," she said, and as he mulled over the date, she waited, wondering if he'd reach the same conclusion she had.

The distinctive naturalistic style had only flourished for a short period—beginning after Akhenaton had converted to monotheism, and ending when an heir restored the polytheistic religion of the earlier kingdoms. The formal art of the earlier kingdoms had been restored, as well—and rigidly enforced.

And although it was possible that a secret sect of monotheists had carried on the Amarna tradition for five hundred years, another group was far more likely to have created these—particularly considering the subject of the frescoed panels.

"So either you've got a bunch of rebels hiding out for centuries—and building big temples isn't such a smart way to hide," Jake said. "Or you've got someone—or *someones*—who saw this style in person. And liked it enough to use it five hundred years later."

She could forgive his thoughtlessness, Alice decided. "An immortal," she agreed.

"But obviously not a demon." He gestured to another fresco from the Abu Simbel temple, that one depicting a scene from the Second Battle. A figure's status could be determined by his size—and the demons were half as tall as the seraphim.

And Lucifer, at the head of the dragon, was the smallest of all the demons.

This time, Jake didn't go on alert when she smiled. "Obviously not. And you'll note the Guardians are equal to one another—even Michael. Only the angels are given divine rank."

"But no wings. Here, or on any of the other pieces." Jake scanned the room again as if making certain, then glanced over at her. "In Tunisia, I assumed the female was a goddess figure. Nike or Nemesis, maybe. Until I saw the friezes."

Alice nodded. "I believe it's the same woman who is one of Michael's companions in the early transformation scenes—but if so, it is also the first time I have seen her winged."

Jake returned to the Mycenaean figure. "Yeah. Her sword, her posture, her position. The hair and clothes change a little, but . . ." He trailed off, leaning in before slanting an assessing look at Alice. "Actually, she's kind of like you."

"Pardon me?"

He nodded to himself. "Yeah. All angular. Her—I know it's the style. But you, you're just kind of sharp and bony. And she's softened by her clothing instead of being all buttoned up and choked by her—" Jake clasped his neck in both hands. He glanced at her, froze. His arms fell back to his sides, and he cleared his throat. "But, uh, you're American, right? Not Greek."

"My father was American." Alice held out her hand. Her self-control was truly remarkable, she thought. When the five-dollar bill appeared in her palm, she vanished the money without tearing it to pieces. "My mother was Egyptian. *Like that panel.*"

Not so remarkable then; her irritation had slipped through. But he looked almost grateful for her pointed change of subject.

"What about Michael?"

She might have looked stiff to Jake before, but she *felt* stiff now—her braid pulling too hard on her scalp, her arms crossed too tight. "What of him?"

"What does he say that all of this is?"

"He says it is 'something best left buried by history, and forgotten.' But he also tells me that I am, of course, free to excavate it."

Jake frowned, clearly disappointed. "But—"

"Michael also cannot see it. Any of it, except for my sketches. He teleported to Abu Simbel with me, and couldn't see or enter the temple—even when I took his hand and tried to lead him over the threshold."

That left Jake speechless. He ran his hand over his head and looked at Alice, then the artifacts, several times.

Finally he asked, "What about the symbols over the antechamber entrance? Have they shown up before?"

"No, this is the first time." Something else that was new. But although she was eager to discover the symbols' meaning, she did not look forward to taking the steps to learn it. "I will have to ask Michael for the translation—"

" 'We go north,' " Jake interrupted. He met her surprise with a quick grin. "I asked Lilith. So, they left directions in this one, but not the others."

"Apparently."

"Then how'd you find them?"

"My Gift." She saw that response wouldn't satisfy him, and added, "When these temples appear, it *disturbs* the spiders in the area." There was no other word for it. "The disturbance spreads quickly, but the farther away it is, the weaker it feels. So I follow it to the strongest point."

He studied her for a long time, she thought. Turning it all over in his mind, looking for answers. "And you've been finding these since— When did you finish your training?"

"Nineteen hundred and eighty-eight."

"Over twenty years ago? Then why doesn't anyone know about this?"

"Anyone? Or you?" Alice watched acknowledgment touch his expression, and continued, "There are some who know. Anyone who has cared to ask me, or who has come across the photographs in the Archives—"

"These are in the library?" he said mournfully, as if already grieving over the two decades he'd not known of their existence.

"Perhaps if you'd ventured into the corner I usually inhabit, you'd have come across them."

Unexpectedly, he grinned. "Well, now that you don't freak me out, maybe I will. You've been working on them alone all this time?"

She shook her head. "Only since the Ascension. Before that, I had a team of novices to assist me."

"Oh," he said, and winced. "Yeah. Sorry."

If her spine had been rigid before, now it became a steel bar. She'd forgotten about the stories the novices told. One was that she'd helped a few of her students to "Ascend" with her blade, but vanished the bodies.

What the novices said didn't matter—much of it had probably arisen out of their boredom in the years after the Ascension and before they'd moved to San Francisco. It was the truth the stories were rooted in that had her turning away from him.

Of all the mentors who remained in Caelum after the Ascension, only Alice had lost every student. She was the only one who hadn't inspired a single novice to stay, to fight—to live.

And she didn't want to see his sympathy, or his pity.

"Hey," he called.

Short of breaking into a run, Alice couldn't prevent him from moving in front of her. She stopped, her lips set in a firm line.

He shoved his hands into his pants pockets, but instead of appearing cowed when his shoulders hunched, he only seemed taller. "Look, I know you want me gone."

Her response was a lift of her brows.

That must have amused him. His appealing smile returned. "I've just been waiting for you to sic Nefertari on me."

She should have. "Is that how you intended to leave? You wanted her to frighten you?"

"Nope. Just to see if you'd do it. I hoped you would."

"I'm sorry I disappointed you, then."

"I'll bet." He laughed to himself again, closing his eyes as if to contain it. After a moment, he opened them. "I'll be looking through the stuff you have in the library."

"I assumed as much, yes. You don't need my permission—"

"I'm going to bother you." His gaze didn't leave hers. "You've got twenty years on it already, and I'll have questions."

He also had both knowledge and curiosity. If that continued, there might be someone to carry on the research when—*if*—she no longer could.

Her fingers were clenched painfully tight, but she managed to perform a cool nod. "Very well. If, of course, it doesn't interfere with your training."

"I'll convince Drifter that it'll be a good experience for me."

Considering that Jake was the youngest Guardian in the field—and that he'd been made active long before the typical century of training had been completed—Ethan was likely more concerned that Jake mastered his weapons and Gift.

"I doubt that he'll be so easy to convince."

"No, he will be." Jake shrugged and looked over her head, his gaze moving keenly along her walls—already anticipating the opportunity to dig deeper into their mysteries, she supposed. "You're pretty much the only female who doesn't make me think about sex when I'm near you. So I'll point out that you'll be good practice for when I'm around real women."

Real women? Stunned, Alice could only stare at him. Her mouth was agape, she realized dumbly—and shut it at the same moment Jake's mortified gaze snapped to hers.

"Oh, shit—"

Alice pushed past him, threw open her front doors. If he ignored the blatant message, she would toss him out.

But she would not look at him yet; her control was too tenuous. She stared out into the empty courtyard and measured each icy word. "You may come to me, novice, if it teaches you how to behave around real women. But I suggest you return to Ethan's training, where you might learn to behave like a real man."

His footsteps approached. She heard his deep breath as he halted next to her.

"I'm sorry, Alice."

She closed her eyes. The sound of his heart beat against her ears. His remorse lay heavy over his psychic scent.

And with three words, Jake had proved himself more of a man than some she'd known.

"Thank you," she said. "But please leave."

He did. Not by teleporting or flying, as she'd expected—but walking across her courtyard with a slow, even gait.

CHAPTER 4

A fifteen-minute hike took Jake to the city's rounded edge. From high above, Caelum looked like a giant white plate in a waveless blue sea; the surrounding water sat level with the marble pavers, forming a smooth, unbroken plane.

As a human, Jake hadn't seen the ocean until he'd been on a foreign shore, preparing to go into combat—and wearing the brave face and swagger that they'd all learned to put on. Everyone had been afraid then, but the fear hadn't taken form yet.

And piss-scared hadn't come until later.

But despite the memories the sight of the ocean could wash up, he preferred it to this eerie, endless stillness. There wasn't anything out there. Not long after the Ascension, he and a few other novices had flown out over the sea, just to see if it ended. They'd given up after two weeks—at the same speed, they'd have circled the Earth eight times.

It was just as empty below the surface. Jake didn't know how far he'd followed the gigantic, submerged column that was Caelum's base, but he hadn't hit bottom. And though he must have swum dozens of miles underwater, Caelum's sun had penetrated even to those depths, lighting his way.

There were stories about Guardians who were still diving, still flying—spending their immortality looking for the end.

If the stories were true, they must be flippin' nutcases by now.

Jake grimaced and looked over his shoulder at the city. He couldn't see Alice's home behind the taller buildings nearer the water, but he almost expected to find spiders creeping up, preparing to make him pay for the insult to their mommy.

Yeah, he'd fucked that up but good.

But damn if he knew why. Halfway across her courtyard, Jake had realized it hadn't just been a stupid thing to say aloud—it'd been wrong to boot.

He'd always assumed his hormones were partially to blame for the crap that came out of his mouth. But in the forty-five minutes he'd spent with her, his only sexual thought had been a passing curiosity about spider reproduction—and yet he'd still managed to set a new record in dickery.

Unfortunately for them both, he couldn't stop thinking about that temple, and everything in that badass museum she called her quarters. They'd just have to get used to each other.

Something tickled the nape of his neck. Jake spun around, slapping at his shoulders, his hair. His fingers brushed a strand of . . . web? A spider leg?

With a shudder, he yanked it away from his skin—and ripped a hole in the neck of his shirt.

A cotton thread was pinched between his fingers. Jake stared at it, disbelieving. Jesus Christ in Heaven. He'd crawled through jungles without giving spiders a second thought. He'd taken bullets to his head. He'd tracked nosferatu, nephilim, and demons—and killed one.

Why was he going girly over a string?

Hell. Maybe spending more time with the Black Widow *would* be good for him.

♪

Alice fed the spiders, bathed, and settled her nerves before she heard the novice's return. Two hours. She moved to her front doors, musing that Jake must have been surrounded by passive and forgiving people during his formative years if he thought that was enough time for tempers to cool.

Or he was just clever. He waited on the opposite side of Remus and Romulus's web, and when Alice emerged from her quarters, he said, "There's no hourglass. Just these red dots."

So these will be our safe zones, Alice thought. Arachnids and artifacts.

"Only the females have the hourglass mark," she said.

Jake leaned his shoulder against the column. A casual pose, but his alert gaze didn't leave her face. "So they're just two guys sharing a web. Alone."

"It's for their safety." At his questioning look, she explained, "Only the females live upstairs. Remus and Romulus will sire the next generation, but unless I rescue them after each mating . . ." Alice shrugged lightly. "Well."

"A good way to go, though."

"Better than some, I suppose."

"You *suppose*? Then you obviously haven't had—" He stopped. Started again with "Did you take a bath?"

A laugh startled from her. "How on Earth did you decide that question was preferable to your original statement?"

"It's why I'm here." He shook his head. "Not to bathe you, but— Where'd you get the hot water?"

He'd already leapt out of their safe zone, but Alice followed him, curious now to where this led. "Irena's smithy."

"So you brought it from Earth in your hammerspace? That's a good idea."

"Indeed. But—"

"I thought you might be going to Seattle. For Charlie's thing at Cole's."

Another leap. But was this a new direction? "I am."

"I came here to see, but I couldn't tell if you were going, because you're still wearing that black thing. But the air's humid, so you must have taken a bath."

Guardians could remove dirt from their bodies and clothing by vanishing it into their cache—so Jake apparently thought that the only reason a Guardian woman might bathe was to prepare for a party.

Amused now, Alice said, "I did."

He sighed. "Look, I just didn't want to insult you. I was trying to decide if you knew about it. I've known people who become all offended if they don't get a formal invitation, even when it's just a thrown-together thing like this is."

How surprisingly thoughtful. "I've known several people like that, too." Her eyes narrowed. "You're here to offer me transport?"

"Yeah. But it might be a little bumpy."

That was of no consequence. Teleporting would save her an hour's flight—and if Ethan knew Teqon's location, it would allow her another advantage, as well. She couldn't carry living things in her cache or through the Gates, but they could be teleported.

"May I bring a passenger?"

Jake appeared confused for all of a second. Then he grinned. "A spider?"

"Yes."

"Go for it."

Alice focused her Gift upstairs. Most of the widows were sleeping, full and lazy after their feeding. But although her body was heavier than the others', Lucy was awake and moving restlessly beneath her web.

Alice caught hold of Lucy's mind and pushed.

"So that's how you knew where you were going in the temple," Jake said. "You had spiders in there."

"Yes. I brought in cave weavers."

Lucy reached the window. Alice stepped out into the courtyard, watching her descend on a gossamer dragline.

"What happened to them when the temple vanished?"

Nothing *should* have happened. Alice usually took the spiders with her when she left—but, preoccupied by thoughts of Teqon, she'd forgotten.

"I don't know," she finally said. With her Gift open like this, she couldn't hide the sorrow in her psychic scent.

Sorrow, for weavers she hadn't even bred and raised.

Her crimson markings gleaming against her ebony exoskeleton, Lucy dropped into Alice's outstretched palm. She lowered her Gift to a soothing hum, hoping to quiet the widow's anxiety—and her own.

Jake looked at her curiously, but he only said, "Grab on to me, then. And she'll have to be touching me, too."

He only tensed a little when Lucy crept onto his forearm and secured herself with silken thread. Alice took his hand.

And waited.

His brow had creased with concentration. A powerful wave swept over her psychic senses—his Gift. His mind was strong, his effort undeniable. Yet they hadn't teleported.

"Would you like help?" She adjusted the focus of her own Gift until she heard the rapid click of Nefertari's claws from inside her quarters.

"I don't think it'd work this time." He expelled a long breath. "Not when I know it's an illusion."

The skittering paused just long enough for Nefertari to push open the front door.

He glanced over Alice's shoulder—and laughed. "Come on. You can't expect me to believe that."

"Jake." She tightened her grip on his hand. "Am I projecting anything?"

His eyes widened.

"You wanted to meet her," she reminded him, just as Nefertari jumped.

❦

He lay on short, dried grass that pricked and itched, even through his shirt. He opened his eyes. Stars shone above, too bright to be near a city.

At least he hadn't screamed, Jake thought. He'd just landed on his back in the middle of God-knew-where. A little awkward, but not emasculating.

Warm fingers brushed his arm, and Jake lifted his head. Alice knelt beside his hip, murmuring to the spider she'd scooped into her palm.

"That wasn't a tarantula," Jake said. "That was a bear."

"Oh, come now. She isn't that large."

"A dog, then. A wolf."

"She's more like a cat. She even purrs."

"I'll bet." Probably while eating kittens. "A mountain lion."

"*Perhaps* an ocelot."

"Too small."

Alice met his gaze, and instead of freezing him, the ice in her eyes sparkled with humor. "But she so loves to jump."

Hot damn. So the Black Widow didn't always bristle with disapproval. And with her mouth set in that prim, trying-not-to-laugh line, Jake remembered why kissing her in the temple had seemed like such a good idea.

He must've hit his head. "How's your friend?"

The spider wasn't in her palm now, and he was pretty sure the itch on his left arm wasn't just the grass.

"She's fine. The disorientation only lasted a moment." She got to her feet in that disjointed, creepy way. "Shall we go?"

"Just a second. Let me figure out where we are."

He rolled onto his knees. They were in a farmhouse's backyard—the kind that was just a scraggly patch of dead grass cut out of a larger field. Judging by the smell, chickens scratched out here during the days.

There was something familiar about the lay of the fields, the neighboring houses, but he supposed there were thousands just like it in the Midwest.

"Oh, dear," the Black Widow said.

He followed the direction of her gaze to a window on the second floor of the farmhouse. A dark-haired girl stood in her ruffled nightgown, her eyes wide, her breath fogging a circle in the glass.

Her arms tightened, bending in half the pink rag doll she clutched. "Princess Mandy, look," she whispered. Her psychic scent boiled with more excitement than fear. "It's the Wicked Witch."

Jake fell forward onto his hands, laughing so hard he thought his gut would burst.

Small, running footsteps sounded from upstairs, and the girl yelled for her grandma.

"Shall we go?"

They'd be lucky if anything could get him to teleport now, but Jake nodded through his laughter and stood. The spider clung to his left arm, so he wiped away his tears with his right before taking Alice's hand. She frowned, gestured for him to quiet.

He tried. Damn, but he tried.

Alice's bristle was back. She signed, *Shall we fly? Do you know where we are—or how far it is to Seattle?*

He shook his head, turning in a circle as he attempted to narrow their location, pulling her with him.

Halfway around, he stopped. At the opposite edge of the yard, an old red tractor and a Mustang with pancake tires rusted next to a weathered shed. Recognition stabbed through his chest, killing his amusement.

"Jake?"

From inside the house, a woman's voice joined the little girl's.

"We're in Kansas," he said, wishing they were anywhere else.

Instantly, they were.

❧

He was the damn cowardly lion.

Jake slumped in his chair and watched the foam on his beer dissolve. Now and then, he felt the concern of the others around the table, but their chatter went over him.

He'd leapt to Seattle—but he couldn't get his flippin' head out of Kansas.

Of all places, the Hopewell farm. The silo and barn that had been behind the house were gone now, but he couldn't mistake that tractor. He and Billy Hopewell had tinkered with that thing and ridden it around the Hopewell fields—down the roads, through town—too many times.

But the car had been Jake's. Cherry, back in the day, and he'd lost count of how many bales he'd tossed, how much slop he'd waded through to buy it.

A piece of shit now.

And the woman he'd heard inside that house . . .

Goddamn. Nineteen years he'd tried to get out of that town. It just wasn't fucking right for his Gift to send him back now, when there was nothing he could do for anyone he'd left behind.

"Jake." Charlie scooted her chair closer to his and leaned in. When she spoke in a whisper, the rasp in her voice all but disappeared. "You okay?"

"Yeah." He sat up straight, scrubbed his hand over his face. He was such a dick. "Just one too many jumps today."

She smiled and squeezed his hand before turning back to the table.

Jake picked up his beer. Drifter was a lucky, lucky man. Charlie was the kind of girl you took home to Mom—if Mom was the kind to appreciate a girl with fangs, cold skin, and a right jab that could knock a Guardian's tooth loose.

Strange, then, that it'd been a while since Jake had wondered what she looked like naked.

Was it just that she'd been away from Seattle these past two months? Just for the hell of it he imagined undressing her, and mentally covered her up again an instant later.

Jesus. If he'd had a sister, Jake thought that was pretty much what taking a peek at her would have felt like.

And Selah, sitting on the other side of Charlie, was out, too. God knew she had a body worth stripping—but with her light blond hair and flawless face, she actually *looked* like an angel.

She'd also assisted Hugh in mentoring Jake when he'd first

come to Caelum—and as the only other Guardian besides Michael who teleported, Selah constantly gave him pointers, helping him get a handle on his jumps. It'd be like turning his Sunday school teacher upside down to see if her skirt went up.

Then there was her partner, Lucas Marsden. The vampire was all right, but Jake could happily live the rest of his life without imagining any guy naked.

Selah suddenly laughed at the vampire, who was shaking his head in embarrassment. Jake finally tuned in, and realized that Charlie was halfway through a story. In Charlie's hands, what had probably been a mildly amusing exchange became an epic encounter, with Marsden heroically resisting a geriatric vamp's increasingly desperate attempts to sex him up beneath a spotlight.

The last two months, Charlie had been learning the ropes at Marsden's theater in preparation for opening a similar theater for the Seattle vampire community. Chances were, she had many years' worth of these stories now.

And he'd probably feel more like laughing at them later. Jake finished his beer just as she wound up her tale, and used his empty glass as a non-dick reason to get up and head to the bar.

Old Matthew Cole didn't need to ask his preference. A new beer was in front of Jake almost before he slid onto the bar stool.

Jake took a deep swallow. It didn't do anything for him—and he'd have sworn beer tasted better when he'd been human.

But even though they didn't need to eat or drink, Cole's bar had become the unofficial gathering place for Guardians and vampires in Seattle. Ordering helped them fit in with the humans, and made sure that Old Matthew wasn't stiffed for his hospitality—not to mention his silence about their true nature.

But then, Old Matthew probably enjoyed flipping the bird to whatever authority he thought might take exception to their existence.

Jake watched the old man make change at the register, then glanced in the mirror behind the shelves of bottles. Shit. The "old man" was his age. And it was possible the only reason Old Matthew wasn't sitting in Jake's place was that instead of being drafted, he'd been in prison—making time for murders he hadn't committed.

From the direction of the table, Jake heard a chair scrape, and he tracked Charlie's approach in the mirror. She was already smiling at Old Matthew, and his dark face wrinkled when he grinned in response.

"You come on back here, Charlie girl."

"I thought I quit," she said, but she rounded the bar, and wrapped her arms around his waist. "You're going to make me work?"

"Well, now that you mention it, I could use five. Robbie called in sick."

"I can give you more than five if you need it."

"Not at your own to-do. And not when your man isn't here. You got trouble tonight, Charlie?"

"I hope not." She tied on the apron Old Matthew gave her. "Cora and Angie called when we were on our way over here. They found a vampire ashed up in the University District, and the partner was missing. The partners hated each other, so it might have just been a fight and she took off, but . . ." Her shrug hid the worry from Old Matthew, but Jake could feel it in her psychic scent. "They've got to check."

One nephil had moved into Seattle last spring and picked off the leaders of the vampire community. Drifter had managed to slay the nephil, preventing the full-scale vampire massacre that had followed similar assassinations in other cities—but there was no way of knowing if the nephilim intended to move against Seattle again.

Cora and Angie were the Seattle community's new heads, and the probable targets if the nephilim's MO held—but Drifter made a point to investigate any unusual vampire death, and rule out nephilim involvement.

"Golly gee," Jake said. "I bet Drifter's having a great time."

Charlie rolled her eyes, but her worry faded. "And I bet you're glad you got in too late to go with him."

"You'd win that bet." Cora and Angie required more patience than Jake had in supply.

"I thought you came in with Alice, Jake." Old Matthew looked over at the table. "Did you lose her?"

Charlie answered for him. "When Irena showed, they went over to the theater. They haven't seen it since we've started remodeling."

"I'll tell you, Charlie girl—I sure am looking forward to you opening up. We didn't get many coming over from the theater before, but it's been feeling quieter in here since they closed."

Jake grimaced, and slid a stack of fives across the bar. Old Matthew began to frown at him, but nodded when Jake said, "The money talk reminded me. It's to cover Alice's bill. Whatever she drinks or eats."

Charlie clubbed her hay-colored hair into a long ponytail. "What did you say to her?"

"Something stupid."

Old Matthew fanned the money. "Son, that's a lot of stupid."

"Yeah. Well, part of it is an advance payment."

The bartender laughed and turned toward the employees' door. Charlie stepped out of his way, then grinned at Jake, the tips of her fangs barely visible.

Jake had been responsible for those fangs. Charlie hadn't wanted them—but he'd failed to protect her. And because she hadn't been willing, the transformation had almost killed her.

Her smile faded. "You sure you're okay?"

"Yeah." He set his beer down, faced her squarely. "I told you I was sorry, right? For letting Sammael get to you."

"Only about twenty or thirty times." She leaned in and her tone softened. "Jake, he unloaded six bullets into your head. But you still managed to teleport, and send Ethan after me."

His first jump, and how he'd discovered his Gift. With his brain shot to pieces, it'd been pure fear and instinct. Not exactly the stuff of heroes.

"As far as I'm concerned, you don't have much to be sorry about." She arched her brows. "But if you're feeling guilty, there is one thing you can do to make it up to me."

Jake eyed her warily, not trusting the laughter in her voice. "What?"

"Just hold still."

He did, then had to chuckle when she began rubbing her hands all over his head.

"God. I've wanted to do that since I met you," she said when she finished. "And Jake—you know more than anyone that everything's good with me. Better than ever. So if you're going to beat yourself up over something, don't pick that."

"All right. I've got more to pick from anyway." But he grinned. "I *know* I haven't told you that you're just all-around swell, Charlie."

She snorted out a laugh. "Don't," she said. "That 'swell' shit and 'golly gee' crap just isn't playing fair. And . . . and . . ."

Her gaze shifted beyond him, and Jake didn't need to see Drifter in the mirror to know the Guardian had entered the restaurant.

Charlie sighed. "I can't even remember what I was saying."

Neither could Jake. Drifter must have stopped by the theater first, because Alice and Irena came in with him. And Jake couldn't miss the pair of human women who sniggered into their hands as Alice passed them.

"Jake." Charlie gripped his arm before he could stand.

He glanced at her, his jaw tight.

I'd be over there, too, if she cared what anyone thought of her, Charlie gestured slowly. He and Drifter had been teaching her the sign language since she'd been transformed, but two months focusing on the theater had put her out of practice. *But Alice doesn't care. At all.*

"How do you know?"

She told me. It happened before—a vampire who didn't realize she wasn't human and could hear. I almost went over the bar for it, but Alice stopped me. Charlie paused. *Of course, if I could shape-shift, I'd be turning into Mr. Sexy, strutting past them, and laying one on her.*

That sounds great, Charlie—except for the "laying one on her" part.

She covered her mouth again, laughing. "Ethan told me that you, uh—"

"Yeah."

In the mirror, Drifter was pulling out Alice's chair. Already seated, Irena turned and gave the still-sniggering ladies a look. They fell silent.

"Or a Death Stare works, too," Charlie said.

He watched the reflection a second longer. Alice didn't appear bothered. How much of that was real?

Maybe you should give her advice, Charlie. On what to wear, at least. Something modern.

She gave him a funny look. *You're kidding, right? Yes, they're old-fashioned—but gorgeous. The cut, the detailing. I'd kill for any one of them.*

Jake frowned. There was more than one dress? They all looked the same to him.

"Men," Charlie muttered.

Considering she then smiled up at another man, Jake assumed she actually just meant *him*. But at least he wasn't paying out money this time.

"Miss Charlie, your city is safe for one more day." Drifter settled onto the stool next to Jake.

So Jake hadn't missed anything by showing up late. If it had been the nephilim, he and Drifter—along with the other Guardians here—would have already been headed back out to search for them.

Jake nodded his response, but missed Charlie's reply; he was distracted by Alice's voice behind him—telling the others at the table that she'd been mistaken for the Wicked Witch.

He looked into the mirror, surprised. She wasn't laughing with Marsden and Selah, but her psychic scent rippled with it, warm and dark as velvet.

"Alice mentioned that you took a trip to Oz," Drifter said quietly. "Is it going to hang on you?"

Drifter knew that Jake had grown up in Kansas, and it probably wasn't a stretch to guess he'd landed somewhere familiar. But as long as Jake wouldn't let it affect him out in the field, he knew Drifter wouldn't pry any deeper.

"Nope."

"All right, then." Drifter stood as Old Matthew returned, and Charlie began to clean up.

Jake headed back to the table, took the seat facing Alice. His eyes narrowed.

The dresses *were* different. Earlier, she'd been wearing a long black thing with tiny buttons up the front. On her current long black thing, the buttons went from her right shoulder up the side of her neck. The sleeves hugged her arms to just below her knuckles, and more buttons ran from her wrists to her pointy elbows. The top might have fit like a second skin, but all of those vertical seams made it look as rigid as body armor.

So it was still like something from a Victorian funeral parlor. And Jake was sure that her spider was hiding somewhere in those loose skirts.

Charlie leaned over the table in front of him. "Irena—your water. Food is coming up, Alice." Charlie set a glass of wine in front of her. "This is on Jake."

"On Jake—?" A startled look passed over her features before she met his gaze. "Oh. Thank you."

He shrugged.

Irena pointed at him. "I need someone to please explain this wicked witch. They will not."

A man didn't argue with a woman who smelled like blood. Or one who wore a poncho made out of fur that she probably wrestled off a polar bear.

Most Guardians created their clothes just by thinking of them—but Jake wouldn't have bet against Irena's being real. "If you open up a little, I'll project it to you."

She hesitated before nodding. Jake focused on a few remembered images from the movie. After a second, Irena looked to Alice. "Flying monkeys?"

This time, it was Alice who shrugged. "That seems accurate."

"We need to have a movie night," Charlie said as she took the seat next to Drifter. "We'll set it up at my place." She glanced at Jake. "Maybe Pim and Becca would like to come up from San Francisco."

"Yeah. They probably would." The movie wouldn't be a novelty for the other novices, but going anywhere but Caelum or the Special Investigations warehouse would be.

He looked up, spotted the bronzed-skinned Guardian walking into the lounge wearing a pair of loose pants and a button-down shirt, his black hair shorn almost as short as Jake's. The Doyen. Jake nodded a greeting, got a nod in return.

Charlie went over to Michael with a wide smile before going up on her toes to kiss his cheek. The Guardian had to bend down—though not as much as when Charlie kissed Drifter. "Michael."

Alice paused for an infinitesimal second with her wineglass at her lips. No wonder. The Doyen was even less sociable than the Black Widow was; but considering that Michael and Charlie had had some connection when they'd jumped to Hell the last spring, Jake wasn't completely surprised.

He *was* surprised by the way Michael seemed to avoid looking at Alice. Not ignoring her, exactly—but when he said his greetings, he moved a little faster past her than he did everyone else.

Finally, he looked at Charlie again. "Your sister is well?"

It wasn't, Jake knew, just a polite question. Charlie's sister, Jane, was engaged to the demon Sammael. No one at the table had slain him yet—and thanks to a bargain, Drifter *couldn't* slay him—primarily because the demon was also bound to leave any Guardians that Charlie cared about alone.

But since Sammael also headed Legion Laboratories, and the organization protected and employed many of Belial's demons, Michael kept tabs on Jane.

Charlie gave a half smile, and shrugged. "She's all right. You know."

Yeah. Way to bring a girl down at her party. At least he wasn't
the only dick, then.

Michael smiled slightly. "I do. I've brought this for you."

At first Jake thought it was a Scroll—one of the texts from the
Caelum archives. But it was a rolled-up sheet of music, instead.
An original composition of some kind—and by a guy Jake hadn't
heard of but who was apparently good enough that Charlie was
half in tears.

Okay, so he *was* still the only dick.

Alice was smiling, too, until she looked from Charlie to the
Doyen. "Michael," she said, and her lips firmed, her spine stiffened. "I fear the Marrakech Gate might have been found out."

He inclined his head. "I will warn the others."

"And," she said in a lower tone, "I have been contacted by one
of Belial's demons. It would be useful to me if I could learn more
about the prophecy."

"I see." He looked to Drifter. "If you have anything more to
share with Alice, you may feel free to do so."

"All right," Drifter said, frowning a little at her.

"Thank you. I must go; I wish you all well. Charlie, congratulations." Michael turned and left, and a moment later Jake felt the
light touch of the Doyen's teleporting Gift.

Jake resisted the urge to shake his head. The Doyen made
jumping look easy, but he was God-knew-how-old.

"Count me in on that movie night—and I'll bring the novices
up from San Francisco," Selah said, rising from her chair. "Lucas
and I have to go as well, Charlie. Does anyone need a ride?"

Irena shook her head. Alice looked to Jake.

"May I impose on you after I speak with Ethan?"

"Bumpy," he reminded her.

Selah's cupid's-bow mouth curved. "It might help if you teleported with your eyes open."

"I do—so that I can see what's coming at me. They're just
closed when I land."

"Perhaps you shouldn't be so quick to leap," Alice said in the
prim tone that made the back of his neck tighten, "if you are not
prepared to face the consequences of it."

For some reason, Drifter and Selah both grinned. Jake did,
too, but his showed more teeth. "Golly gee, Alice, I've never
thought of it that way before. That'll change everything for me."

"How fortunate that I am here, then."

"Oh, yes. With words of wisdom like that, you'd have made one hell of a—" He bit it off. Not mentor. He wouldn't go there.

She raised her eyebrows.

"Paratroop instructor," he finished. Fucking stupid.

"Oh, dear. Leaping from an airplane? How unseemly. My skirt might blow up over my knees." With that, she dismissed him, turning to Marsden and Selah.

Jake watched her, tried not to picture her spindly legs sticking out from billowing black fabric. Maybe they weren't bony, though—when she'd been fighting, a ballerina couldn't have matched her grace. Instead of thin and knobby, her legs might be slim, strong. And her skin would be the same smooth, dusky gold as her hands, her cheeks.

Jesus. He must be crazy, imagining the Black Widow naked. She probably bit off the head of anyone brave enough to get into her bed. A guy would need balls of steel . . . or no balls to lose. Like a woman—

His gaze moved from Alice to Irena, then back to Alice. And that was enough for his dick to take over, making him desperate to see, to know. He'd have crawled under the table if he thought it'd get him a look at her legs.

Hell, he'd have settled for a glimpse of her flippin' wrist.

"Jake? You here?" Charlie waved her hand in front of his eyes.

He vaguely realized they were looking expectantly at him, that Selah and Marsden were gone. And that he'd been staring at Alice for at least a few minutes.

Someone must have asked him something, but he didn't care enough to find out what.

He met Alice's eyes. "I'm wondering how you fight in that skirt."

"You plan to spend any time in one, Jake? Maybe you ought to consider taking her on as a specialist," Drifter said over his whiskey.

"I might." Jake held her gaze. "Do you have to cut it open to kick? Or do you change clothes when a demon shows up? The time wasted could be dangerous."

Irena added her curious stare to Jake's. "That is true, Alice. And you used to wear that redingote and trousers, so that it freed your legs. You no longer do."

"Because it is no longer necessary. This has plenty of give, and I can move freely." She tugged on her sleeve. The silk stretched, then snapped taut against her arm when she let it go.

"It's spandex?"

Jake would've laughed at the horrified note in Charlie's voice if he hadn't been so gobsmacked.

"It's the spider silk." Freaky as hell, but badass. If the strength of the woven material was anything like what he'd seen up in Caelum, her dress would be like armor. "Hot damn."

Drifter frowned. "The what?"

"From the spiders. In her quarters."

Drifter's brows shot up, and he turned to Alice. "You got some living up in Caelum?"

Alice nodded.

"Well, hell. I figured all the talk of spiders and vampire blood was just the novices saying the same fool things about you that they always do."

"No," she said. "That one is true. I asked Selah to bring the first few widows not long after the Ascension."

Drifter seemed to consider that. "All right, then," he finally said.

He was going to leave it there, but Jake wouldn't. No matter how much it cost him.

"So everything you're wearing is made of the same stuff?" And in the temple, it had been smooth and warm under his hands. "Even your bloomers?"

Irena broke out with a loud laugh, startling the humans around them. Charlie groaned, and Jake tossed a five-dollar bill on the table in front of Drifter.

A human couldn't have tracked the speed at which Alice reached over, pinched the money, and sat again. Jake's body tightened, but he forced his mind out of her skirts. Tried to.

When she moved quickly, everything rigid became supple, her body long and fluid.

"They aren't made of spider silk, novice. I weaved them from the legs of those widows who have passed," Alice said, her back straight now. "For when one is a Guardian, loyalty is the utmost virtue. And so I keep my friends close—even if they itch."

"You've got itching down below?" Jake leaned in and lowered his voice. "They've got powders for that now."

Alice smiled. Her teeth, he saw, were sharp again.

"Oh, Lord." As if sensing disaster, Charlie spoke up, asking Alice's opinion on the materials the decorators planned to use at the theater.

Jake sat back, studying Alice.

Spider legs and loyalty. She'd used the same tone that'd gotten his back up before, but he'd have bet his left nut that her moralizing platitudes were a joke.

Half the time, anyway. Or only around people she was tight with—not the fucking new guy.

But when she unbent a little, the Black Widow wasn't half-bad.

And where had he gotten the impression that she was dried up, spinsterish? As angular as her features were, they weren't pinched or heavy. Her dark brows, her straight nose, and her direct gaze gave her a no-nonsense look, sure—but there was also something dainty about her mouth, her pointed chin.

When he looked past the severe braid and rigid posture, she appeared about the same age Jake did. Early twenties, maybe. Not more than twenty-five.

It was the dress, he thought. And he didn't usually notice the thickness of a woman's lashes when the disapproval in her eyes was driving icy spikes into his brain.

Those lashes flickered in response to Irena's voice. Alerted by that unease, Jake realized Irena was addressing him, caught the tail end of her question.

"—have begun your specializations?"

"I'm on swords. With Alejandro." He checked his watch. "I'm meeting him at midnight."

Every day the same: four hours with Alejandro, six hours in San Francisco, ten with Drifter, and the rest in personal study. Now that he'd come across Alice's collection, most of those personal hours would probably be spent in the Archives.

"Alejandro? That is good." Irena nodded abruptly, and Jake wasn't about to ask why her tone suggested otherwise. "He was born to wield a blade."

Charlie looked at Drifter. "You're good with a sword, though. I've seen you."

"Damn good," Drifter said. "But I'm more of a fists-and-pistols man."

"Hugh taught both of us the basics of the discipline, Charlie," Alice said. "But when we specialized with Alejandro, I daresay we learned more in one year than the previous sixty."

"That we did."

"Jake will, as well." Alice's gaze rested on him. "I have already seen Alejandro's influence in the way he holds his blade."

Charlie flashed a grin at Drifter. "Alejandro used to freak me out, you know—the first couple of times he came in here to visit you. There's that devil goatee thing he's got going on, and then he's all dark and quiet and staring. Like it hurts him to smile."

"He's a good man," Irena said softly.

"Yeah." Jake glanced at Alice, and got his money ready. "It's other people who creep me out."

And if he told himself that enough, maybe he wouldn't think about stroking her mouth open with his tongue. He must be desperately horny to be thinking of it now. But he sat anticipating her reply, completely focused on her lips as they softened and parted.

Her forked tongue flicked. A cobra swiftly uncoiled from her mouth onto the table, and struck at Jake's face.

A second later, Jake opened his eyes and looked up at the stars.

Yeah. He'd probably deserved that.

CHAPTER 5

Oh, dear, Alice thought as the empty chair across the table began to tip backward.

Without glancing that way, Ethan reached around Charlie's shoulders and steadied it. "He needs to be controlling that."

Irena's knife had appeared in her hand, but she vanished it just as quickly. "Was that a cobra?"

When Alice nodded, Irena threw her head back, howling with laughter.

Charlie blinked. "What just happened?"

Alice had used enough force that the other two Guardians had seen it, but a vampire couldn't receive images.

"Alice puked a snake all over the table," Ethan said.

"For heaven's sake, Ethan." Alice grimaced. "You make it sound so revolting."

"I ain't ever come across anyone who could make it look pretty."

Alice waited as a waiter set a basket of fried onion rings in front of Ethan, then Irena's plate, heaped with seafood and potatoes. After the waiter's brief hesitation, Charlie pointed at Alice, and he put Jake's hamburger next to her wine.

"Perhaps I shouldn't have done it," Alice said once he'd moved on. Irena's laughter had faded to a low chuckle, but Alice hadn't missed the curious glances it had brought their way. "Someone might have seen him disappear."

Irena liberally salted her potatoes. "No one did, Alice. If they had, we would have sensed it."

"Even if they did see it, they'd talk themselves out of it. No sane person would believe it for long." Ethan didn't reach for his food, but studied her face with a slight frown. "And I've never seen either you or Jake grate on another body so much, or him run his mouth on purpose like he was. You two have an altercation I should know about?"

"No."

"One I shouldn't know about?"

Alice smiled and shook her head.

"He is an odd one," Irena said. "He should be irritating, but I only want to rub his head."

Alice did, too. Her fingers curled into her palms.

"And he's got a good brain in it. Picks up everything I have to teach him right quick. Aside from his specializations, there ain't much left that he needs but experience." Ethan clenched his jaw, and Alice recognized the worry he projected. It was the same worry she'd often had for her own students. "He's just too damn young to be getting it by going up against demons."

"Someday I'll get used to the idea of sixty years old being young," Charlie said.

"Well, some of it's maturity. You've earned yours by the bucketful." His gaze warmed when he glanced at her, and when he looked back at Alice, his eyes were glowing amber. "Jake, now— a year ago, I couldn't have said the same. But what happened to Charlie hit him hard."

"As it should," Irena said.

Ethan shook his head. "He'd been out of the warehouse less than a day when Sammael went after them. That the demon got to Charlie is on me."

"And which Guardian would ever see it that way, Ethan?" Alice asked. "If it had been us, newly returned to Earth and untried in combat—and failing our assignment?"

"Not a one, I suppose. Still, it ain't on him."

"But don't take the responsibility away from him, either. Particularly if it forces him to be more careful in the future." Alice drew in a breath, scenting the fried potatoes and hamburger sandwich. How very wasteful it would be, should they go uneaten. She pulled Jake's basket closer. "It is just as damaging to be overprotective."

Ethan heaved a frustrated sigh. "Yes."

Charlie's fingers moved over Ethan's fist, and she squeezed before letting go.

And a single touch soothed his worry. It was absolutely lovely—and if Alice hadn't already been fond of Charlie, she would have been then. "And you remember when we were his age, Ethan. Our mentors despaired we would ever be mature enough to return to Earth, yet we survived."

"*We?* Way I remember, I just got dragged into whatever you were doing. So it seems to me they was mostly worried about you."

"That is true," Irena said.

"There, you see?" He turned to Charlie. "I never seen anyone so inclined to study and practice, but also so inclined to give our mentors shit for it. She'd screw up her face like she'd been sucking lemons, then repeat every bit of advice they gave to us, or start reciting passages from the Scrolls."

"Come now, Ethan. Lemons?"

"Hugh once described you as a 'challenge,' Alice," Irena said. "He was being kind."

"Oh, dear. Thank you so very much for your aid."

"And she'd start in on me for saying 'ain't' or 'shit'—then go transcribe the kinky books in the Archives and pass them out as instruction manuals. I still got one."

A rolled-up sheaf of paper appeared in his hand, and he gave it to Charlie.

"Ethan, no," Alice protested, laughing.

Charlie peeled back a page. Her eyes widened. "Oh, Lord." She glanced at Ethan, a hint of calculation in her expression. "So that's where you learned that."

"You hush." Embarrassment tinged his cheeks, and he pulled it out of her hands, vanished it.

"Thank you, Charlie," Alice said. "That was very well done."

"It was, wasn't it?" She smiled up at Ethan. "I'm surprised, though—that stuff like that is up there."

"I've heard tell there was just the Scrolls, once. But then Guardians started bringing back books and newspapers and such for the rest of us. That was before my time, though." Ethan looked to Irena, who frowned.

"It was not long after the printing press," she said. "But I am unknowing of the exact date. And always there have been scholars who recorded their histories, or their experiences on Earth. A few poets."

"Most of them tedious." Alice studied the giant hamburger, wondering how best to eat it. She rarely consumed food and had never attempted anything of this size before—but following the example of the humans around them meant she'd have to unhinge her jaw with every bite. It simply would not do. "Irena—would you please?"

She pointed to the knife and fork lying unused next to the other woman's plate. Irena pushed them over, then resumed eating with her fingers.

"And the Archives are sadly lacking any mention of the one thing about which I would be most interested to learn: Belial's prophecy." Even halved, the sandwich was too large. Alice made another cut, another, yet another . . . and made herself stop. "Ethan, I regret the necessity, but I must ask if there is anything you haven't shared with us."

"I reckon there is." His lazy drawl didn't deceive her; Ethan pretended to be slow, but his mind was always two steps ahead. "But I don't suppose you'll be sharing why it's such a necessity."

Alice looked down, managed to cut a bite-sized piece from the bun.

"Goddammit, Alice. It ain't a stretch to figure Teqon is giving you trouble again. But your husband's dead by now, so it can't be about him. You got others in your family line to worry about?"

He'd pressed. She hadn't prepared for that. It was a minor miracle that she prevented her hands from shaking, that she didn't drop her utensils. That she held her shields, concealing her dread and terror.

"No, I don't." Anticipating his next question, she added, "And I do not fear for my life at this time."

Just her soul. Just the few friendships she'd created in the past century.

"But if you need help, you'll ask for it."

She met his eyes. "I just did, Ethan."

His jaw hardened, and he turned to Irena. "You know what this is about?"

"I do." Irena delicately flaked a selection of fish from her fillet. "And I will tear your spine from your body if you do not provide Alice what she asks."

Charlie's shock ripped through the room. "What the—"

Ethan touched her arm. "Don't fret, Miss Charlie. That's just Irena's way of easing my mind, saying she'll go to any lengths to help." The corners of his eyes wrinkled with his faint smile. "All right, Alice. So long as you've got someone in your corner."

"Thank you." She prayed whatever he had to tell her was worth knowing—and that Irena wouldn't mention her intention to take Alice's head if Teqon couldn't be appeased. "So if you will explain—"

She paused; Ethan was shaking his head. "This ain't the place. We need a bit more privacy, considering that it involves Michael."

Something in her chest twisted. "Oh."

"Fact is," Ethan continued, "I don't suppose you need me to tell you. You're heading out with Jake once you're done here. He can fill you in."

"You've told him?"

"Course I did." Ethan seemed surprised by *her* surprise. "Jake's out there risking himself with me, and his eyes are as sharp as any I've ever seen. So I figured he ought to know what all is grabbing my attention, and why I've been looking at a few things the way I have been." He leaned back in his chair. "Besides, I don't think I'll have a private moment for a couple of hours. Charlie and I have to head on over to the theater, pick out curtains or paint colors or something."

"I see," Alice said, certain she did. Beside her, Irena stiffened as an excited buzz swept through the restaurant. Not sensing any alarm from the humans—just admiration and disbelief—Alice didn't glance away from Ethan. "How heartless you are."

He grinned. "I'd have made it easier on you if you'd told me what your trouble was. Now, I figure you might want to stock up on those itching powders." He raised his voice a little. "When you get done playacting, Jake, maybe you'll tell Alice about the trip to Hell that Charlie and I took."

Charlie's gaze shifted over Alice's shoulder, and she let out a thin, strangled sound. Then she dropped her head into her hands. "Please don't kill him, Alice. This is my fault."

Charlie's warning kept Alice from calling in her weapon when an unfamiliar man gripped her hand.

Jake. His psychic scent was unmistakable.

He tugged her up against his chest, wrapped his arm around her waist, and said loudly, "I just couldn't wait to see you again, babycakes."

She'd had a response forming on her tongue, but the sheer absurdity of his greeting rendered her speechless.

He smiled with lips that were almost feminine, despite the thin mustache and goatee he now sported. His dark hair had the long, careless wave of a poet's. Handsome, but it was a refined, androgynous beauty.

Why in heaven's name would Jake trade his strong, boldly formed features for this? His smile was much more appealing when it forced a curve onto his chiseled mouth.

"You ready to go, babycakes? We've got booty to plunder." His gaze bored into hers, and his palm slid low on her back. His head slowly descended. "And I intend to plunder all night long."

Booty? Ah, yes. A pirate. Now she recognized the actor from movie posters and merchandise that she'd seen marketed to teenaged girls.

"Is—" She averted her face, and his warm lips landed on her jaw. Undeterred, he began to nibble. Oh, dear.

She would not shiver, Alice told herself. She would not.

"Is this necessary, novice?"

His deep voice was suddenly his own, soft against her ear. "Play along; it'll make Charlie happy."

Considering that the young vampire was repeatedly thumping her forehead against the table, Alice thought that whatever Charlie had asked of him, this wasn't precisely it.

Irena rose to her feet. "Well then, Alice. You are getting what you need, and so I'll leave you to it."

"But—" Dismayed, Alice tried to turn, but Jake held her fast. Tossing him across the room would create a bigger scene than they already had, so she merely looked over her shoulder. "Won't you wait to hear?"

"If this information regards Michael . . ." Irena shrugged, and pulled her white hood up over her hair. "I will not influence your decision, Alice, because the action you take will determine mine. So seek me out when you decide to act. Be well, Drifter, Charlie." She smirked. "Jake."

"Bye, Irena," he said cheerfully.

Alice faced him again. It would be snakes and spiders and

leeches this time. And squirming maggots. Devouring one another.

He wasn't looking at her, however, but studying the table with an amused expression. "So this is what happens when you get your hands on a man's meat."

The mutilated hamburger. Oh, the images she could create from that. She glanced down.

Alice's hand flew to her lips, stifling her shriek.

A circus clown's head stared up at her from the basket, his mouth stretched in a horrid red grin. Less than a second later, the illusion vanished. Jake released her and stepped back.

Blast, blast, blast! He couldn't have missed how her heart had jumped, the gasp she hadn't smothered.

"I told you he learns real quick," Ethan said mildly.

She looked up. Jake's grin was as wide as the clown's had been. "Gotcha, babycakes."

❧

Certain that whatever came out would be more laugh than cackle, Alice didn't unclamp her lips until they were halfway across the lake, heading east toward Ethan and Charlie's home. Jake probably thought her silence came from anger—which was just as well. If he feared retaliation, he might tread carefully.

Except he looked more pleased with himself than wary. And more *himself*—at some point during the flight, he'd reverted to his natural form.

"I guess this means we're at war now," he called over the rush of wind.

Alice held her hand out long enough to sign, *How juvenile that would be, novice*—then resumed plotting her next attack.

Guerrilla tactics would be most effective. Unexpected, brutal, and launched from familiar terrain. The Archives, perhaps. Or, considering how many decades of experience she had over him, the practice field or the sky.

Perhaps he expected *that*, though. Jake never flew ahead of her, even when she slowed and offered the lead. He allowed her the altitude advantage, and maintained his flanking position at eight o'clock—about forty-five degrees behind and to the left.

She glanced over her shoulder and frowned. His wingspan was longer than hers.

He caught her look and made a signal she'd seen thousands of times, while practicing countless hours of flight formation. Automatically, she altered her course, flying straight up.

It hadn't been raining, but the clouds piled thick. She broke through and hovered, the gentle wind teasing the hem of her skirt. The whisper-light silk was heavy now, saturated by the vapor and clinging to her legs, but there was no point in vanishing the moisture. She'd have to descend through the clouds, eventually.

Jake slipped through the surface, the vapor swirling and closing behind him. Mist coated his face, and he wiped it away with a swipe of his hand. He was chewing on his toothpick again.

"So," he said, hovering in front of Alice, his wings beating a steady rhythm. "Charlie and Drifter's trip to Hell."

"Here?" The clouds drifted by below their feet. They were high above the lake, and a psychic probe didn't reveal any demons or Guardians near enough to hear or to see them signing . . . but there were ways to be certain no one *could*.

Three of the demonic symbols—*silence, surround, lock*—scraped near the entrance to a room or building and activated by drops of blood prevented anyone from entering and every type of communication. Even someone watching their hands wouldn't be able to understand their gestures.

"I assumed we would use the shielding spell around the house," Alice said.

"This'll work."

"Yes, but—"

"I'm not such of fan of being stuck behind the shield. Not when you can't hear or sense what's coming. I've learned to avoid it, if I can."

Because that was how the demon had tricked Jake before capturing Charlie, Alice realized. Jake hadn't been able to determine through the shielding spell whether the shape-shifted demon was a human. But his mistake was one many Guardians might have made, no matter their experience—when a demon was in human form and his psychic shields tight, a Guardian and demon could pass on a street, each unaware of the other. And they'd only had knowledge of the shielding spell for less than two years.

"Then it seems you have only learned to avoid the situation, instead of learning how to prevent the same outcome," Alice pointed out.

"Ya think?" His face was suddenly expressionless, his tone flat.

What in heaven's name had offended him? Surely he hadn't interpreted her statement to mean that she thought he was too fearful of being in that situation again.

A gust of wind buffeted her toward him. She steadied herself, and tried again. "I don't intend to suggest that you are a coward for avoiding—"

"This'll work, Alice."

"But I didn't—" She was on the verge of flitting her hands like a silly goose. Slowly, she brought them in. "Very well then."

His gaze slid down her form, paused at her legs. "Unless your spider is getting cold."

"Lucy?" The widow was curled up in a watertight pocket sewn into the lining of her skirt, cozy from Alice's body heat. "No. But thank you for taking her comfort into consideration."

His brow creased for an instant. It cleared when he shook his head. "Okay, here's the thing: you know Michael was teleporting around Hell last spring, searching for the prison that Lucifer had kept the nephilim in, right?"

"Yes, that is what Selah told me. Also that Michael found it." And discovered that Lucifer had let all of the nephilim go—over one hundred released to Earth. A frightening number. More than two to every Guardian left after the Ascension—and that was including novices.

"Yeah, well, what she probably didn't know was that Michael had to take Charlie and Drifter down Below, so that they could open the prison."

"It was shielded?" It must have been, or Michael would only have taken Ethan, whose Gift allowed him to open any lock . . . except for the lock cast by the shielding spell. For that, Ethan needed Charlie, and her rare tendency to sense psychic energy as sound, rather than a scent, a flavor, or physical touch.

"Yep. And as they were getting ready to go, Belial shows up. He tells Michael the prophecy will be fulfilled, that his followers will return to Grace—well, let me send you the image Drifter gave me."

Alice nodded, then instinctively squinted her eyes. Michael had been standing in front of a large black building, facing Ethan. His wings were folded behind his back, and his sword dripped blood. Between Michael and the building, a figure shone with brilliant light: Belial.

It was said the demon had retained his angelic form, and Alice didn't doubt it. She had the impression of multiple pairs of wings, of beauty so great it was painful to look upon.

Alice had seen him almost two years ago, in the short battle against Lucifer that had led to Michael winning his wager and the Gates to Hell being closed—but she couldn't *see* him any better through Ethan's eyes than she had in person.

The image vanished. Jake rubbed at his eyes. "Flippin' fuck. That hurts my brain."

Hers as well. And left her confused, wondering what had been so shocking that Ethan had kept it to himself. "So, apparently this means that Belial believes in the prophecy—and he confirmed that the prophecy exists."

Unless, as demons often did, Belial had been lying. But what would be the point of lying about it to Michael, who had dismissed the prophecy's validity?

"Yes, and Michael's response was to call it a bunch of bullshit." Jake gave his head a hard shake. "Well, not in those words. But the gist, you know."

"I do. But was that all that was said?" A wet tendril of hair blew in front of her eyes, and Alice lifted her arms, quickly weaved it back into her braid. "Jake? Was that all?"

She sighed when she realized that his gaze had unfocused. At the restaurant, she'd noted that he had a tendency to drift off in the middle of a conversation. Now she had to repeat his name several times before he snapped to attention.

"Yes, Alice. Yes." He chuckled to himself, then just as quickly sobered. "No, that wasn't all. Because that's when Belial said that Michael should have known Lucifer would release the nephilim, because he—Belial—had taught Michael to think like Lucifer."

Alice blinked, certain she'd misheard. "Belial *taught* Michael?"

"Yep." The answer was grim.

"Taught him where? When?"

"Dunno."

"But he—? And how—?" Alice closed her eyes, tried desperately to order the questions spitting through her mind, to suppress her revulsion.

Taught by a demon.

She trusted and loved each of her mentors. To imagine Michael having a similar relationship with a demon—even a demon who was Lucifer's enemy—made her feel as if a sickness had taken root inside her, putrefying her body and emotions as it spread.

But surely it hadn't been the same. Surely, whatever Michael and Belial's relationship, it couldn't be compared to what she'd shared with her mentors.

Alice took a long breath. "What did Michael have to say about it?"

"Just that any association he might have had with Belial was long past, was nothing as Belial imagined it had been, and was best forgotten."

That resembled what Michael had said about the temples. She met Jake's gaze, saw the same realization there.

His eyes narrowed. "Think it's connected?"

"I don't know. I cannot even—" She shook her head. "Why didn't Ethan tell the rest of us?"

To her surprise, Jake shape-shifted into Ethan's tall form. And she had to smile when he drawled, "Well, I reckon there's no need to go about causing a fuss just yet. It may be that Belial was lying, hoping that every Guardian would be looking at Michael all suspicious-like, and that it might have us squabbling with one another instead of putting a world of hurt on Belial's demons like we oughta be. So we'll wait until we figure the truth of it before telling the others."

Alice nodded thoughtfully. It was similar to one of the reasons Guardians hid their existence from humans. Not that they didn't deserve to know the truth—but that the repercussions might be far too dangerous.

"And it does not change what Michael is now," she murmured. A leader, a healer, the most powerful warrior—Michael was the heart of the Guardian corps.

"That it doesn't, little lady."

Alice lifted her brows.

Jake grimaced, and was suddenly himself again. "Yeah. That was more John Wayne than Drifter. Anyway, I'm guessing that even if it isn't a lie, Michael is thinking the same thing as Drifter: that at this point—after the Ascension, the nephilim popping up—it's better not to have division in the ranks. Especially over something that could be nothing."

Yes, and especially now. The minor grumblings that had begun after Michael appointed Lucifer's daughter as the head of Special Investigations might escalate.

Michael had never suppressed opposing viewpoints, had never reprimanded anyone for dissention. She remembered several instances when he'd called for debate over the Guardians' role during human wars, the heated discussions that had followed. But even when Guardians acted contrary to the consensus they'd reached, Michael hadn't disciplined them. As long as the Rules had been followed, as long as the Guardians hadn't hurt humans or denied their free will, Michael allowed the Guardians to act according to *their* free will.

So he likely didn't want to create tension over a matter that had no bearing on problems the Guardians were facing today. It was, Alice thought, the decision she'd have chosen, too.

"So," Jake said, his gaze steady on hers. "That help at all?"

Perhaps discovering that Michael had a dark secret might have helped—it could have let her consider the unthinkable. But this had only served to remind her of what a fine Guardian he was.

And there was nothing to use against Teqon.

"I don't think so." Alice gathered her skirts in her fist, holding them bunched and tight against her thigh. "But thank you."

She dropped through the clouds, and heard the snap of Jake's wings as he dove after her.

He couldn't have been far behind when she broke through the mist and leveled out, but she didn't see him when she glanced over her shoulder. Wondering if he'd looped around, she looked down—just as he flew in beneath.

"You don't give a guy a chance to say 'You're welcome,'" he said, facing her with his hands laced behind his head and his ankles crossed.

"I'm sorry. I—" Alice broke off, marveling that he hadn't rolled over yet. Flying on one's back was tremendously difficult. Instead of beating in a smooth sweep, their wings had to perform an awkward rowing motion while in vertical alignment. It was easy to roll and to fly upside-down for a short period, but after a few seconds Alice—and every Guardian she'd ever seen practice it—lost her balance and went spinning out of control. Yet Jake had maintained a smooth course for several hundred yards now. "You're *very* good at that."

He grinned. "I can even carry weight."

"Most impressive."

"Yep." Though he was still smiling, the humor had left his eyes, the intensity of his stare had deepened. "Wanna ride?"

Her gaze fell to his waist. His damp T-shirt molded to an abdomen that was as tightly muscled as his backside. She had no doubt he could support her.

And she wanted to. Wanted to close her eyes and feel the wind against her face, that incredible sense of freedom—and have it come through no effort of her own.

It wouldn't even require trust. If he faltered, she could save herself.

But she wouldn't be able to escape the intimacy of such a position.

Alice shook her head, and increased her speed. She half-expected Jake to keep pace beneath her, but he simply rolled into his flanking formation. Shortly, they came over Charlie's large lodge-style home at the edge of the lake.

A dock extended out over the water, and stairs led up to the house. Trees provided cover near the rocky shoreline.

Alice caught the side of her skirt again, and quickly descended. She'd barely touched down on the shore when a loud splash sounded behind her, a body hitting water at enormous speed.

Jake.

She whirled, scanning the sky. No demons. She pushed her Gift in a wide sweep, touching hundreds of spiders, building a sensory map of the immediate area. Nothing unusual moved through the trees, no one appeared as a bright spot of heat.

Jake hadn't been attacked, then . . . but had dove into the lake.

His head broke the surface an instant later. His gaze never left her legs as he strode out of the water.

Alice looked down. Nothing showed. Her boots were laced to mid-shin, and although she'd pulled the hem to her knees when she'd gathered her skirts, her opaque black stockings concealed her skin.

Without a word, Jake passed her, began climbing the steps. His sopping T-shirt vanished.

Oh, dear. Lean and tall, with his wet jeans riding low, Jake looked every inch the young soldier he'd been as a human. Alice averted her eyes, her breath coming faster. It was fortunate that she'd settled her nerves during her bath.

She had a weakness for a man's strong back—had ever since she was seventeen, at her father's dig in el-Amarna. In the

Egyptian heat, the men working had often taken off their shirts. The first time she'd seen Henry, he'd been among them, and the dust had turned their skin the same worn yellow. But when he'd washed, it had been the palest gold, and Alice had thought it the most exotic, beautiful color she'd ever beheld. So unlike the florid color of the other British men in the sun—those few who would remove their shirts. Jake, with his deep tan, was almost as dark as some of the Egyptian men.

And her tastes had expanded since then.

"It's the Enthrallment," Jake said suddenly. "It still hits me sometimes."

Alice studied him as he crossed the deck. Enthrallment came upon novices in their first years after returning to Earth, when their heightened senses were overwhelmed by the variety and scope of the scents, sounds, sights. But it usually sent the psychic scent into a spin, like inhaling too much hashish or whirling about in a circle. Jake's was steady—and remarkably solid.

"I see," she said doubtfully. "And cold water shocks you out of it?"

It never had her. Only lying perfectly still, trying to sense nothing.

"No." Jake opened the French doors, stopped to disengage the security system. The water vanished from his jeans. An overlong knit sweater appeared in his hands, and he pulled it over his head, tugged it down in front.

She caught a thread of frustration from his psychic scent before he blocked it.

How strange he was. Alice followed him through the house, wondering what had sparked his arousal. Certainly nothing on her person; he'd made that perfectly clear earlier. And every day, he saw women exposing far more than a stocking-covered shin.

Perhaps it had been her boot heel, then. She liked it very well herself. The elongated hourglass mimicked a woman's form, and provided a wide base for stability. And she'd coated the soles with silken webs for traction and softness; her steps barely made a sound on the wooden floors.

Pretty and practical. Hardly erotic, but maybe he was one of those men who could hold a teacup in his palm and become excited by its shape.

She entered the tech room behind him, and felt a movement in her pocket—Lucy, overcome with a sense of urgency, the need to find a new location for her web.

Alice pressed with her Gift, felt the spider's body, heavy and full with children. *Soon, Lucy.* The spider wouldn't understand the words, but the calm, soothing tone relieved the widow's unease.

Jake moved to a long table holding more computers than Alice had seen in one place. The room was all of plastic and metal, and spotlessly clean.

"I've got your pictures from Tunisia," he said, bending over one of the keyboards. "I don't have any printer here that can handle the size you've been blowing them up to, but I'll send them out, pick them up tomorrow."

She turned away from the wall of security monitors that recorded the exterior of the house. "That isn't necessary. I can—"

"I'm ordering copies for me, too. It's just easier to do them all at once."

"Oh. Very well then."

He glanced over his shoulder. "This demon you're looking for—Teqon? You're in luck."

"Oh?" She joined him at the table.

"Yep. After SI hacked into Legion's server, some of the demons changed locations, their human aliases. Not him, though. He's living in Cairo."

Egypt. The climate would suit Lucy. "Do you have an address?"

"Yep. Do you need a ride?"

"Yes." She couldn't take Lucy though the Gates, so she would have to fly halfway around the world. "But you must leave immediately upon our arrival."

"My Gift doesn't always work that way—and I don't think your little Lucy can make me jump." He straightened and looked at her, his gaze assessing. "Those demons at the temple were only planning to torture you."

"Yes."

"So you're assuming that Teqon won't try to kill you."

She took a step back, crossed her arms. "Yes."

"What if you're wrong? You can't trust a demon, can you?"

Blast. He knew he had her there. She shook her head.

"So I'll just hang around and watch your back." His lips didn't curve, but Alice was certain he was smirking inside. "And this way, you're looking before you leap, being prepared—all of that smart Guardian stuff."

The wretch. She opened her mouth, closed it. Admitting defeat, she urged Lucy out of her pocket.

Jake grinned and held out his hand. "Have you been to Cairo?"

Alice scooped up the widow and placed her in Jake's palm. "I was raised in the city. Why?"

"I haven't been. So I've got the idea of it in my head, the location—but nothing specific. It'll help if you focus on it, too, and give me a good anchor."

She nodded and looked up into his face, attempted to call up an image from one of her recent visits. Perhaps of a jewelry stall in the marketplace, one that sold figurines and scarabs of lapis lazuli—Jake's eyes were the same deep blue.

Strange that she hadn't noticed before.

His fingers laced through hers. "And maybe you'll tell me why you're jumping into a demon's parlor."

❧

Flippin' hell. He'd teleported, no sweat—but this wasn't Egypt. They'd landed in a freezing attic, somewhere.

Jake let go of Alice's hand. Not wanting to see her disappointment, he didn't look at her—just pulled out his GPS.

The attic was big, but there was nothing unique about it. Wooden rafters. The style of the dust-covered chairs and tables suggested France or England—maybe the United States. Stars shone faintly through a small, high window, told him it was in the northern hemisphere. The sky was lightening with the approaching dawn. Definitely Europe.

The GPS said Manchester, Great Britain.

He glanced toward the other end of the attic, then stared. Jesus. Cobwebs filled the corners, hung like dirty veils from the rafters and between the posts of a huge, molding bed. And if that creepshow wasn't enough, restraints were tied to each post, and leather cuffs rotted against the sagging mattress.

"Leave," Alice whispered beside him.

Jake frowned, turned to look at her—then had to focus over the images of Cairo that suddenly flooded his head.

Her eyes were closed, and she was shaking. "Leave now!"

He grabbed her hand, pulled her in tight. And pounded his Gift as hard as he could.

CHAPTER 6

An uncontrolled jump—and one bitch of a landing in a narrow alleyway. Jake barely had time to register the feel of Alice sprawled beneath him before she elbowed him off and scrambled up onto her knees.

Lucy sat in her hand, and Alice was whispering to the spider—but Jake thought she was trying to calm herself, too.

And he felt like shit now, dammit. "Look, Alice, I screwed up on that jump, and—"

"I put it there." She stood, her face and back stiff. "I didn't control my thoughts, and put that location into your head. But we are here now, and it is forgotten."

Yeah, right. That's why her heart was still beating like a jackrabbit's.

They'd jumped just after he'd asked her what the deal with Teqon was, and her thoughts had leapt to that location. But why would a woman raised in Egypt and with an American father think of England?

That creepy attic hadn't been touched in the past twenty years, since Alice had returned to Earth from Caelum. Whatever took place in that attic had happened when she'd been human.

So the question was: Had that bed been hers, or had it belonged to someone she'd known?

He watched her, but hadn't a clue to her thoughts. Her emotions were blocked, and her expression was carefully neutral as she took in the tenements rising high on both sides of the alley, the rickety carts, the drying clothes strung over their heads.

"We are obviously in the eastern part of the city," she said. "How far to the demon's home?"

He consulted the GPS. "About half a kilometer southwest."

"Shall we walk, then?"

Jake got to his feet, slapped the dust of the alley floor off his ass. He sniffed, and slapped harder. It was more than dust.

"You will need to change your clothing, anyway," Alice said. Her robes and head scarf from the temple were back, and she'd darkened her skin and eyes. "A white man is still noticed in these older sections of Cairo, especially among the street children."

So he needed to look local. He shifted into the first form his mind grabbed hold of, and Alice's mouth flattened.

"You still look foreign."

He knew from news feeds that his loose jeans and button-down cotton shirt were unremarkable, so it must have been his face. "But it's Omar Sharif. You know, from *Lawrence of Arabia*."

She frowned. "Is that an Egyptian actor?"

"Yeah, he's from—" Okay, he wasn't sure. And maybe he'd put a little too much Peter O'Toole into it, anyway. "Forget it."

He tried another. Alice raised her eyes to the heavens, then strode to the mouth of the alley.

Jake followed her, fighting his grin. "Come on. It's Yul Brynner. You should have stars in your eyes."

"Are you trying to put stars in my eyes, novice?"

"Do I look crazy?"

Damn. That probably hadn't been the best response—because he *did* want to see something in her eyes besides disapproval.

Better yet, he wanted them closed, her skirts up around her waist, and her dancer's legs wrapped around him. Those black stockings and witch boots were optional.

Yeah, he was flippin' insane.

She stopped, faced him. "You look like an overly handsome man who will bring attention to us, and alert the demon of our approach before we arrive."

Screw this, then. Jake shifted back into his own form, then did what she had, simply darkening his skin and eyes.

Alice's lips thinned. "That hardly solves the problem."

She stalked out into the street. Jake weaved through the busy foot traffic after her, pretty damn sure she'd just called him handsome. Maybe overly handsome.

Hot dog.

"At the very least, grow your hair out," she said when he caught up. "And a heavy mustache. Roll up your shirtsleeves, and wear a watch. A cheap one, so that you do not attract thieves."

He studied the men sitting outside a café, and walked around an exhaust-belching bus to conceal the transformation.

She eyed him critically, then nodded. "How is your Arabic?"

"Nonexistent."

He could've sworn that relief flashed over her prim expression, but her reply was pure sourpuss. "I suppose you focused on the Romance languages first. The novices from America and Western Europe so often do, as those are the easiest for them to learn."

"That's true," he said, refusing to be baited. He'd have bet anything that she wanted to piss him off so bad he'd leave. "I did pick those up first."

Before working his way west across Asia. Arabic and Swahili were up next, but he wouldn't say so. He was starting to enjoy watching her bloomers twist into a knot.

"Arabic is spoken by a quarter of a billion humans, novice. You should make an effort to learn it if you plan to be active in this region."

"Golly gee, Alice. You're right—I should get on that. Maybe you'll volunteer to tutor me."

She slanted him a narrowed look. "I don't think so."

Dangerous ground, but he stepped on it. "Do you tutor anyone now?"

"No. How much farther?"

Yeah, now he was pissing *her* off. Even in these twisting streets, she could estimate distance as well as he could. He made a show of checking his watch and glancing up at the sun before pulling out his GPS. "Okay, yeah. We've been walking about one minute. So, go figure, we've still got a little less than half a kilometer to go."

She pulled in a breath through her teeth.

He had to hand it to her; that was pretty brave. A brown haze filled the sky, so God knew what she'd just sucked into her lungs while controlling her temper. Even a Guardian might choke on it.

And it did sound as if she was strangling when she said, "Thank you, novice."

Jake grinned at her back as she set off at a walk again—smoothly now. Trying to appear inconspicuous, probably, but she still didn't look completely human. She hadn't increased her pace to an inhuman speed, but she was practically gliding, as if her limbs were weightless beneath her robe.

Her legs. Jesus. He needed to get his head from under her skirts. Which meant he was going to take a flying leap into a minefield.

"So," he said, catching up. "They all Ascended, and because of that, you don't take on new pupils. Tell me, Alice—is that avoiding the situation, or learning to avoid the same outcome?"

Yep. The look she gave him should've made mincemeat of his dick.

Should've, but didn't. "You could take me on, get back on that horse, try riding again," he continued.

"How brave you are to offer, novice. And how generous."

Mincemeat, and her tone could've frozen the rest. "Yeah, I'm all heart. But you wouldn't have to worry about me—I don't intend to Ascend anytime soon. And if it makes you feel better, every single person in Caelum that I had sex with decided to Ascend, too."

"Oh, dear." She stopped and looked up at him. "You're so terrible?"

"So good." He grinned. "Everything after me is a letdown—the only thing better is Heaven. So off they went."

"And there is your optimism again." Her lips curved, but she quickly firmed their line and moved past him. "But as I also have no intention of Ascending, I'll be certain to avoid *that* situation, as well."

Yeah. He'd figured that. But a man could hope.

❦

He wasn't going to leave. Alice fought through her rising guilt as they neared Teqon's residence. She shouldn't involve Jake in this, in any way.

What an excellent Guardian he made; choosing to stand beside her, though she gave him ample reason to go. And he'd served as a welcome distraction through the streets, so that she'd had no time to despond over the upcoming confrontation. Instead of arriving at Teqon's door weakened by doubts and fear, she was fueled by antagonism and no small amount of frustration.

How could she like Jake so well—and yet want to take her blade to his tongue so that he'd never speak again?

Not that it would matter; a Guardian's tongue would grow back.

Conceal yourself, she signed as they rounded the final corner. *I truly don't think my life is in danger, but he might try to make an example of yours.*

Jake appraised her silently, then nodded. *I'll be listening.*

She walked briskly across the small square, surprised that Teqon didn't reside in the more modern and expensive part of the city. Demons were so aware of appearances, and preferred to surround themselves with power and wealth. But perhaps Teqon had chosen it because the disparity of wealth was more obvious here; squalor was a constant neighbor, the gap between them wider.

Her gaze swept the area as she waited for an answer to her knock. A young beggar girl now sat where Jake had been standing. He would have no trouble hearing everything inside Teqon's house.

Footsteps approached on the opposite side of the door. A human, or Teqon? Though Alice revealed herself when she used a psychic probe to find out, at least she was prepared to face the demon when he opened it.

He'd silvered the hair at his temples, but he still appeared as young and handsome as any film star. More so, perhaps. His lashes were so thick and black that the first time she'd seen them, she'd wondered if he'd lined them with kohl. He was tall, as demons so often made themselves. His business suit of dove gray silk had been tailored perfectly to his form.

But then, through his connection to Legion Laboratories, Teqon was now—as he had only pretended to be when she'd met him—a man of importance and money.

Alice shifted into her own features, and vanished the robes over her dress. "You have not changed at all, demon," she said in Arabic.

As she'd hoped, Teqon responded in the same language. "But you have, Mrs. Grey. You are stronger, faster, immortal—and I believe you owe me thanks for it."

"I owe you only one thing, and gratitude it is not."

He stepped back, holding the door open. "Then come inside, and we shall discuss how you will pay me."

His house was of wood and marble, with rich, colorful fabrics upholstering the furniture. There were humans in the house—servants, Alice guessed. A wife, perhaps. Though they could have no children of their own, some demons augmented their masquerade by marrying into human families.

As she'd expected, the main rooms of the house opened up to an interior courtyard. A fountain bubbled near its center—there would likely be vegetation, shelter, insects.

"Shall we speak in the courtyard? I prefer to feel the sun."

Teqon gave her a mocking smile. "And there is no roof, so you might escape."

"If I must."

The demon turned his back on her as he led the way outside. Rage and shame burned in Alice's throat. Any other demon would have been in pieces on the floor after offering such an easy target.

She swallowed it down, and sat gingerly on the edge of a stone bench. Jasmine spilled over the giant urns at each end. Behind her, a date tree bent under the weight of the fruit on its branches.

Alice smoothed her fingers over her skirts. In the hollow of her knee, she felt Lucy anchor a dragline and begin to descend along her calf.

At the fountain, Teqon turned to face her, a frown marring his handsome features. "I do not remember you being so rigid, Mrs. Grey. I chose you because you chafed against structure—against authority. It made you more likely to carry out your task."

"After one hundred and twenty years, perhaps I have been chafed smooth."

"I doubt it." He slipped his hands into his pockets. "You must have received my message."

He did not, she noted, ask about the demons who had delivered it. "I did."

"And you intend to follow through."

It wasn't a question. Because she hadn't attempted to slay him, he must have been certain of her answer.

"Is there nothing else you want? There must be something that would make you reconsider."

"And release you from your bargain?" Teqon laughed, a short and hard sound. "No."

"What of the prophecy?"

His dark eyes began to glow crimson, but his hard smile remained. "That prophecy is all the more reason to fulfill your part."

Lucy reached the ground, and Alice felt the widow's indecision. Alice hesitated, too, for just a moment. But she had nothing that might sway Teqon now, and she doubted he would deal on speculation. Their interview here was at an end.

Alice stood and lightly opened her Gift, urging the spider toward the date tree. *Be safe, little one.*

Teqon's hand was around her throat an instant later. Her boots left the ground as he lifted her.

"You used your Gift." His fingers shape-shifted, became talons. "What *is* your Gift, Mrs. Grey? What have you done?"

She pushed Lucy faster. *Climb. Climb and hide.*

The demon tried to dig his claws in. His eyes widened with surprise and anger as they scraped across her collar without tearing through.

He settled for crushing her throat. Pain screamed, left her dizzy.

"Is it impervious to everything?" Teqon studied her dress, then casually slipped a dagger between her ribs. Something inside tore, collapsed.

Alice beat back her panic, and the black wave that threatened consciousness. He hadn't aimed for her heart. Just her lungs. He wasn't going to kill her. He couldn't risk killing her.

He smiled. "It's not."

She only needed to break his hold. Needed to focus through the agony, and call for her weapon so that she could cut through his arm.

"Let her go, demon."

Oh, dear heavens. Jake. He'd teleported behind Teqon, his sword against the demon's neck.

Teqon tightened his grip on her throat, gave her a shake. He spoke in English, just as Jake had. "Do you think slaying me would save her, Guardian?"

Alice recognized the victorious glint in Jake's eyes. It was an easy kill. Jake had the advantage of surprise, of Teqon's neck already on the edge of his sword, of Alice being in a position that—though she was injured—wasn't mortally dangerous.

And any other time, she would have told him to take it.

Alice lifted her hand and signed, *Don't kill him.* When Jake frowned and the edge of his blade drew blood, she frantically added, *I beg you, please.*

His jaw tightened, but he moved toward her, keeping his sword at Teqon's throat. His arm circled her waist. "Let her go."

Teqon unclenched his hand, and Alice's head fell back against Jake's shoulder—her muscles too damaged to hold it up.

"Only because she cannot serve our purpose if she is dead. We are fated to take the throne in Hell and return to Glory—"

"Yeah, yeah. Save it," Jake said, backing up. "I've heard it before from your buddy Sammael, and thought it was bullshit then, too."

"I wonder if you'll say that when I take your heart, fledgling." Teqon's gaze shifted to her face. "You will pay your debt, Mrs. Grey."

With a shudder, she called in the demon's heart from her cache. It was still as warm as when she'd cut it from his chest in the temple.

She tossed the organ, and it landed with a plop at Teqon's feet.

Its blood dripped from her fingers as she signed, *I will include one hundred twenty years of interest, and I'll collect it from all of your associates. There will be no one left to return to Glory. Reconsider, demon.*

He shook his head. "Never."

"Are you done?" Jake's voice was cold and flat in her ear.

Yes. She gripped the hand at her waist. His Gift punched through her, and sent her spinning again.

She was bound.

Around them, sunlight filtered through a jungle canopy. The air was thick as sweat. Jake didn't know where the fuck they were. Didn't care.

He didn't wait until Alice steadied, could barely contain his anger. She didn't flinch when he leaned over, his face an inch from hers.

"You went in there, knowing that if he killed you, you'd be trapped in Hell for *eternity.*" Trapped, because she'd made a bargain, and obviously hadn't fulfilled her side of it. But hadn't said a thing, though Jake had been outside, ready to charge in if things got too fucking hot. "Knowing that if *I* had killed him, I'd be the one sealing your goddamn fate. That as soon as you died, you'd be down Below with your fucking head frozen into the ground. Because you didn't say a fucking word to warn me."

Her blank expression didn't change. And she couldn't talk, because the demon bastard had crushed her goddamn throat.

I told you he wouldn't kill me, she signed with bloody fingers. *And you heard; I still serve a purpose.*

"What fucking purpose?"

His shout echoed through the trees. Birds startled, took wing. A monkey screeched in the distance.

Alice's lips pinched together. *A Guardian who loses his temper risks losing all.*

He about lost it then. Jake spun away from her, his jaw aching with the force of his clenching teeth. Yelling at her didn't help. And, Jesus—he could smell the blood that had poured down her side. The wound was sealed and healing, but it must still hurt.

He'd been thinking of getting to a Healer. Instead he'd teleported here, ended up in bumfuck—

He registered the trees, the river. Recognized them.

Oh, shit. Of all the goddamn bad luck. He'd gone for a healer, all right. A dead one.

Bobby Wolk. The medic had carried a picture of his girl in his jacket over his heart—wrapped in plastic so it wouldn't get wet. Out here in the boonies, everything had gotten wet, started to rot.

And not two yards from where Jake was standing, a land mine had once been hidden beneath rotting leaves. Shrapnel had ripped off half of the medic's chest, his face, shredded the picture of his girl.

It had been quicker than what the rest of them had faced.

Jesus. Jake rubbed his eyes, said quietly, "Whose heart are you bound to deliver?"

It had to be a heart. That much had been clear when she'd thrown the demon's at Teqon's feet.

She didn't answer. Couldn't, since he wasn't looking at her. It didn't matter, though. Despite Teqon's threat to Jake, there was only one heart that any demon would care about having.

"Michael's?"

He turned as he said the name, and caught the way her eyes closed, as if she was trying to block out the truth. Even expecting it, the confirmation stunned him.

"Jesus," he whispered. " 'Loyalty is the utmost virtue'? How the hell could you make such a bargain?"

She looked at him. Just stared at him, her eyes huge. Her mouth, her fingers didn't move. Bruises mottled her throat.

Jake shook his head. Wanted to be sick. Or to kill something. He faced the river instead, and began walking. He wouldn't look back.

"There's a Gate twenty-eight miles south," he said. "Try to make it there without betraying the rest of us."

CHAPTER 7

Two hours into the weekly poker game at the Special Investigations warehouse, Jake was out three thousand dollars—and having a difficult time giving a shit.

Just as he'd hardly noticed when, thirty minutes after leaving the Black Widow behind in Vietnam, Alejandro had stabbed a sword through his thigh. Throw in Drifter's fist and a cracked cheekbone, and a sick tension in his gut that wouldn't go away—and Jake had one creepy Guardian as the reason behind his clusterfuck of a day.

He just couldn't get her face out of his head, the vision of her haunted eyes.

And her goddamn bargain.

"Jake, sweetie." He glanced up; Pim was smiling at him across the table. If her legs had been long enough, she'd probably have kicked his shin beneath it. "Get your head out of your ass and ante up."

"And don't even think about leaving this table," Mackenzie added, glancing up at Jake through bangs that reached his black-lined eyes. Since he'd been added to a team that traveled to various vampire communities, warning them about nephilim and demons,

Mackenzie had been playing up his Goth look. "You haven't had a streak of luck this bad since . . . well, ever. Not since I've been working here, anyway."

"Oh, like you'd ever win without a hammerspace and speed, vampire." Becca stuck her tongue out at Mackenzie, but a second later the gesture changed from a childish taunt to a suggestive wag.

"Jesus, Becca. Put that back in." Jake tossed his chips in, cursing the day he'd become the flippin' den mother. After Drifter had moved in with Charlie and stopped coming to San Francisco as often, the job had somehow fallen to Jake. Now he was the one who oversaw the other novices as they played, giving them pointers—on using sleight of hand to pull in a card from their hammerspace, on noticing when someone else did, and honing their psychic abilities to sense someone cheating or bluffing.

Pim could've done it. She was almost as good a player as Jake was. Older, too—even if she hadn't been a Guardian as long.

Jake checked his watch. Another hour, and then he was on his own time.

"In a hurry to get somewhere, Jake?"

Ah, crap. Pim's cute face had taken on an innocent expression. Jake usually ended up paying someone a fiver after she got that look.

At least he usually got a laugh out of it, too. Pim loved gossip almost as much as she loved the testicle-withering teenybop music she was playing on the rec room's stereo, and when they'd been stuck in Caelum after the Ascension—two of only seven novices left—shooting the shit with her had been part of the reason he'd managed to stay sane. Though her sole goal in life seemed to be busting his balls, she was, as his granddad might have said, good people.

"Nope," Jake said easily. "Just wondering why it's twenty hundred hours, and no one is heading down to the corridor to relieve Jeeves."

Becca began dealing out cards, and she said, "Because—thanks to you and Pim—our security shifts are eight hours now."

Jake leaned back in his chair, staring at Pim. That must mean that they were putting her on active duty, just like he was with Drifter. "No shit? They're sending you out?"

"You're supposed to say 'Congratulations,' dipshit."

He frowned at Becca, then glanced back at Pim. Her smile did look a little smaller. "Well, yeah. Who are you heading out with?"

"Dru. That way I can learn my Gift faster, get practical healing experience."

Jake clenched his jaw, looked down at his cards. Dru had been on full status, what—fifteen years? And as a Healer, she didn't see as much combat as other Guardians who'd been out as long. "That makes sense."

Pim flashed him her *don't be an asshole* look. "I won't be out there the same way you are, because I can't get out of trouble as fast. So if a demon shows up, I'm supposed to let her handle it. I'm just there to observe for now."

"Okay, yeah." Still bad, but not *as* bad. "So you'll still be training here?"

"And with Dru. When you took us to Caelum the other day, that was her seeing how we'd mesh. Then we came back here to talk to Hugh and Lilith, and made it all official with Michael this morning."

"Right on."

"Yeah, it's all good." Pim's innocent look returned, and she looked over at Becca. "Jake went into the Black Widow's lair. Dru and I left before he came out."

"Damn." Becca pulled a face. "If we'd known you were that desperate, Jake, we could've paid someone to give you a pity screw."

"You had sex in the library with the Black Widow?" Mackenzie looked up from his cards. Jake thought the only reason the vampire didn't give him a high-five was because of Becca's sudden glare.

"It was at her place," Pim said.

"She has a place?" Becca's expression was blank. "I thought she just lived in the Archives."

Jake stared at his cards. Not even a pair. He threw in more chips, anyway. "It's in Odin's Courtyard."

Mackenzie looked up. "Odin's?"

"There's a big ash tree, like what Odin hung himself from—to gain wisdom," Jake said. And it sounded like a hell of a painful way of getting smarter. He preferred the easy method: opening a book or turning on a computer—or fucking up and paying for it. "But it's marble. Like everything else."

Mackenzie wouldn't ever see it. Vampires could be teleported to Caelum, but—because the sun never set—only into closed rooms.

"So why didn't you know she was there?" Mackenzie looked at Becca. "You told me everyone knows where everybody lives."

She shrugged. "It's all the way up in Boreas—which is empty now. No one heads there anymore; mostly they stay in Zephyrus and Notus, but I haven't seen her there. So I assumed she was at the Archives, or close to it. Somewhere near the center temples."

And, thanks to that, Mackenzie looked more confused now than he'd been before. Leaning forward, Jake pushed aside the pile of chips and put a blue one in the center of the table. "This table's Caelum, right? You've got Michael's temple here, and it marks the central areas, with his quarters, the Archives, and the general meeting places."

"And the freak courtyard," Becca said, her dark eyes widening. "All of the archways leading into it are Gates, so you can't walk through them—you'd just end up on Earth. And if you fly over them, thinking you'll go over the top of the buildings around it and land inside . . . it's not there."

"Dun dun dun," Pim intoned dramatically.

Jake shook his head. "I teleported in. There's just a fountain— and you can walk out beneath the arches, no problem."

"What?" Pim stared at him. "You didn't tell us?"

"You'd built it up into the dark altar that Alice sacrificed all of her novices on," Jake said. "I didn't want to ruin it for you."

"*Alice?*"

Jake ignored her speculative glance, looked over at Mackenzie again. "And there's no real east, west—because the sun doesn't move, and a compass just spins. But there are these four spires we use the same way, like points on a compass, and they're the name of the Greek winds. So the north quarter is Boreas, then there's Eurus, Notus, and Zephyrus in the west," he said, moving clockwise around the table. "Odin's Courtyard is way up here near the edge of Boreas."

"Got it." Mackenzie nodded, then folded his cards. "And I need to meet this Black Widow sometime. If she doesn't have acid for blood and little kids in her oven, I'll know Guardians are liars."

"We never lie," Becca said with a straight face and moved the chips back to the center of the table. "So what *did* you do in there with her?"

"Nothing," Jake said.

"Nothing? That's all you're going to give us?" Pim sighed.

"You've been so closemouthed lately. Alejandro's rubbing off on you, Jake."

"And not in a sexy way," Becca agreed.

Pim propped her elbow on the table and put her chin in her palm, staring off dreamily. "I wonder if I'll rub up against Dru in a sexy way."

Mackenzie was suddenly very still. Good man. When women went there, a smart guy knew to stay quiet and let them keep going.

Pim, Drusilla, and rubbing. If those magic words didn't cure the rotting ache in Jake's stomach, then there was something very, very wrong with him.

"You think she swings that way?" Becca asked, and Jake decided to toss her into the mental mix, too.

A moment later, he pinched the bridge of his nose, tried to beat back his frustration. Everything in his head was sexy as hell, but it wasn't working.

Pim shrugged. "If she doesn't, I can always go back to my human form." She grimaced. "Only taller. And *bigger*."

"Oh, God. Do not want." Mackenzie shook his head as if to rid himself of that new image, and Pim laughed. "Anyway, is that a good idea—hooking up with your partner?"

"No," Jake said.

Becca frowned at him. "I know I'd feel a lot better if I was out there with Mackenzie instead of being cooped up here."

"I'm just running into other vampires, baby," Mackenzie said.

"Yeah, until you hit a community being run by a demon. Or the nephilim show up."

Jake tossed his cards down. "And then what would you do, Becca? With no Gift and only five years of training under your belt, your head would be stuck on a pole next to his."

"Fuck you, Jake." Becca leaned forward in her seat, an angry flush burnishing her cheeks. "You've been nonstop with your negative crap since you went active and fucked up in Seattle—"

"Becca," Pim said softly.

"—and tonight, you sit there like something's crawled up your ass and died there. Don't take that shit out on us."

Jake stood, placed his hands flat on the table. "Golly gee, Becca—what do you want me to say? That it's pretty out there? That it's easy?"

"Pretty? Easy?" She sat back, shaking her head. Her anger disappeared as if she'd clicked it off. Jake wished he could do the same. "You're out there, being a Guardian. Saving people, helping them. Doing what we're supposed to do. Pretty and easy isn't the point, retard."

Jake stared at her. *Being a Guardian.* It wasn't that simple. Nothing was that simple, but it cleared a path for him. Unwound some of the tension in his gut. "I love you, Becca."

She rolled her eyes. "Duh."

He grinned, and pushed away from the table. "I'm out."

Behind him, he heard Mackenzie grumbling, Becca's sarcastic attempt to soothe the vampire, and the scrape of a chair. A second later, Pim caught up, her short legs working overtime.

"So when you're a guy, you want to be tall," Jake said. "But as a chick, you're just high enough to—"

"You don't want to finish that."

She had a point—he'd already lost too much money that night. And a glance at her face told him that even though she'd said that with humor, she was nervous, too. He stopped walking. "What?"

Pim gave him a tight smile, and pulled him into one of the empty offices.

I need a favor, she signed. Her fingers clenched before she rushed through the rest. *I want to know how my brother is doing. But I don't know how to access anything but Google, and he's not showing up in any of the searches I do.*

Whoa, boy. Jake slid his hand over his head, the sick feeling rushing back in. Different, but tearing him up just as much.

The custom of training in Caelum for a century wasn't just about obtaining enough skills to fight demons. It forced them to leave human relationships behind. After a hundred years, family members, friends . . . most of them would be dead.

But she, Jake, and the other novices had come back early. And instead of finding out how their families lived and died through historical records, they had to accept knowing their loved ones were out there—and still living.

Maybe.

Jake let out a long breath, then signed, *Are you sure?*

Yes. I don't need to see him. I just want to know he's okay.

And if he's not?

Lie to me. Her round face was serious.

Jake nodded. *I need everything you can give me about him.* He smiled when a paper immediately appeared in her hand.

She passed it to him. "Have you looked up yours?"

"No."

"Do you think about it?"

The image of a farmhouse in Kansas flashed in front of his eyes. "Every day."

"And you chicken out?"

"Nope." He vanished her brother's information into his hammerspace, and thought of an attic in Manchester. Teqon had called Alice "Mrs. Grey"—and Jake knew she'd been transformed about the same time as Drifter. "I just always find something that needs to come first."

❧

For almost two days, she'd been on the verge of screaming. Alice could feel it in the back of her throat, balanced on the cusp of her determination. Only her will, she thought, kept it from tumbling over into despair, and producing a howl that might have terrified a hellhound.

Her will, and a healthy measure of distraction. The new site she'd discovered wasn't as carefully constructed or as exquisitely decorated as some of the others—but it was *different*.

A burial chamber. She was almost certain of it.

By the light of the halogen lantern she'd set on the dais in the center of the room, Alice carefully scraped paint and stucco from the chamber wall into a sterile beaker. She'd been down on the stone floor so long, her knees had actually begun to ache. All she needed was for her back to pain her, to cover herself with dust and perspiration, to be surrounded by the murmurings and discussions of the diggers, and she might have been young again, crawling around the temples at el-Amarna, making rubbings of the hieroglyphs and figures carved nearest the floor.

But it was cold, clean, and silent here. There was only the rasp of her scalpel, and the sandy trickle of stucco into plastic. The slow beat of her heart. And . . .

Alice stilled her hand, listening. There it was again—another heartbeat, almost directly behind her.

She vanished the scalpel, instantly replaced it with her naginata. In the same movement, she stood and whipped her weapon around.

And froze with the point of her blade at Jake's throat.

Oh, dear heaven. She met his eyes, then her gaze dropped to

the blood trickling the length of his neck. The tip of her weapon had pierced his skin.

She vanished it, turned back around. The beaker had fallen to the ground. Her fingers shook as she picked it up, and the scalpel trembled when she called it in again. "That was—"

"Stupid, yeah. I forgot how flippin' long your weapon is." Jake lowered himself beside her in that easy way men had—balanced on the balls of his feet, his knees wide, and his elbow resting on his thigh. He reached out, rubbed the surface of the fresco with his thumb. "So . . . what do you want me to do?"

Alice stared blankly at the painting, uncertain how to interpret his question. Uncertain how to interpret his quiet focus on her, and his lack of anger. Uncertain, even, as to why he was not after her head with his sword.

She wouldn't have let him take it, but she wouldn't have blamed him for the attempt.

A glance confirmed that he was looking at her, waiting for her response. And she decided that she didn't want more uncertainty. She had enough.

"I want you to leave," she said.

And the wretch laughed. Disbelieving, she watched him rock onto his backside, brace his hands on the floor, and stretch his legs out. "No can do, Alice. I'm here, and I intend to stay."

His unbuttoned, long-sleeved shirt fell open with his movement. Beneath it, he wore a black undershirt, and emblazoned across the chest was a red tongue sticking out of an open mouth.

It could have been an analogue to his response, she thought. "If you don't intend to listen, why bother asking?"

"I asked the wrong question. Well, not exactly. I didn't lead up to it the right way."

He hadn't led up to it at all. Alice leaned forward, began scraping again. He was too blasted stubborn to take the gesture as a dismissal, but she found some satisfaction in performing it. Perhaps she ought to take a cue from his shirt, and weave "leave me be" across the back of her next dress. And add an image that would drive the point home.

There was a tug at her hair. Startled, she glanced over her shoulder.

Jake was holding the tail of her braid up, and peering intently at her back. "Wait, don't move—" He sighed, and his gaze lifted to hers. "Was that a donkey?"

Oh, dear. She'd projected that? Perhaps she'd driven the point a little too hard. "A mule."

"And it was sucking its own—"

"Yes, well." She yanked her braid out of his grip. "I had to amuse myself while you were leading up to whatever it is you imagine I'll want."

"And *that* amuses you?"

Alice looked away from his grin. Her psychic shields were weak, her emotions swinging wildly. She fought the sudden urge to bury her face in her hands, to let herself cry and scream. Fought, and realized it wasn't that she wanted him to leave. *She* wanted to disappear.

Just wanted to go away . . . for a while.

"Hey," Jake said softly. She watched his shadow on the wall darken as he came up on his knees beside her.

He didn't try to touch her. Thank God for that. She felt like a riotous mess encased by tenuous threads, and she didn't know if a touch might have her erupting or collapsing in on herself.

Either would be worse than her current misery: that he was witness as she barely held it together. And so she had a little something to be grateful for.

But she would be even more grateful for a distraction—anything that would turn both their minds away from her humiliating state.

"Please." She retrieved her scalpel. "Go on."

"Okay." He drew a deep breath, but it was still another minute before he said, "Here's the thing: I never wanted to head off to war. I wanted college—wanted this, actually."

His fingertips slid across the fresco, and Alice felt the silent pull of his fascination, his almost-buried longing. Though she couldn't fathom where he intended to take her, what leap he was making—she understood that yearning.

Slowly, she capped the beaker, then angled herself to study his profile as he continued.

"And when college fell through—because of money, and some shit grades after I shammed my way through school—I worked my ass off getting the car I wanted, and I planned to drive myself right out of town, find a job on a dig wherever and however I could." He ran his hand over his head, glanced at her. "Then I had to go up in front of the draft board, and came close to making a run for Canada. And thought about proposing to the girl I was bang—*dating*, because there was a marriage exemption then."

And he wouldn't be pressed into service, she realized. "You were frightened that you'd be killed?"

He gave a silent little laugh. "Way things turned out, I should've been." His smile lasted for another second, then he shook his head. "And, yeah, that was part of it. But most of it was I just didn't believe in anything we were doing over there."

"But you didn't leave America or marry her?"

"No. I ended up with a list of reasons to go—but it came down to just a few. I knew how everyone in town would be looking at my grandparents if I took off for Canada. A small town like that . . . and there'd already been enough talk. My mom ran off when I was just a kid, and my dad was the town drunk." A dull flush tinged his cheekbones, and he abruptly stood. "Anyway, they'd have been okay with whatever I did, but it would have been hard on them. And getting out of a draft wasn't a reason to marry someone, either. Especially Barbara, because she was a great girl—but she wanted to spend the rest of her life right where she grew up. One of us would have gotten screwed."

His discomfort was acute, almost like a physical pain. Alice looked away from him, but she heard the slide of fabric against skin as he shoved his hands into his pockets, his slow tread as he crossed the chamber. She couldn't conceive why he was baring himself in this way. How could it possibly be relevant to what he'd discovered about her bargain?

Yet he must think so—and even though he obviously thought what he exposed was something shameful, or perhaps foolish, he was determined to share it.

But Alice wished that he wouldn't. She didn't want to see this side of him. Didn't want to know that he'd made these choices with the grandparents he'd loved in mind. Didn't want to think of all the people she'd known—men, women—who would have used another person to secure their own future, married another person without considering his or her desires and needs. Without ever seeing who that person was instead of what they wanted that person to be.

Jake had managed to distract her, but she hadn't wanted understanding and admiration to follow. Yet she knew that even if she asked him to stop, he'd continue.

She was too intrigued to ask him to stop now, anyway. "So you went, though you didn't believe in it. I'm not condemning you," she added when his shoulders stiffened. "I'm simply curious."

He shrugged. "By then, I'd convinced myself that I might be wrong. I was nineteen years old—so what did I know? And the only way to find out for sure was to go. It wasn't the fighting, wasn't going into service. I'm not a pacifist. If I was, I wouldn't be doing this now."

"No." A Guardian couldn't keep his weapon sheathed, and expect to survive. "Were you wrong?"

He faced her, his expression clearing—and, she thought, taking on an unexpected amount of amusement. That boundless energy seemed to roll through him, and he strode to her side, went down on his heels again. "It's probably best not to get me started. What I will say is that I felt sick to my stomach all the time. Not so bad when I was in Basic, but once we shipped out, it was just—" He made a fist in front of his abdomen, then twisted his wrist. "All the time. Then you get out in the boonies, and it's worse, because you're scared on top of it—and wondering what the hell you're doing out there. Then there's the other times, when it's half-fun, because the guys you're with are ranging from ice-cool to batshit crazy, depending on the day and how you look at them. Mostly, you're just trying to stay alive. And you're doing whatever you can to make it right in your head, even if means making demons out of the other guys, joking about it any way you can. Then you kill one and you're puking your guts out."

He stopped, and his gaze leveled on hers. "I don't do that when the demons are real," he said.

"No." She smiled faintly. "I noted that you employ other methods of celebrating when you slay one."

And the memory of that spontaneous kiss seemed to weave silk threads within her chest; his slow grin pulled them tight.

"I went too fast," he said. "It was sloppy."

"Yes, well. First times usually are." Oh, dear—how breathless that sounded. And her heartbeat had not quickened, but it was pounding unusually hard. She firmed her lips and replied, "*Decapitations* usually are. With more experience, you will know to expect some messiness."

He turned his head to the side, his jaw clenching. Then he stood and moved away again.

She watched him, absurdly grateful that he was no longer close. What a ninny she was. She shouldn't let him have this effect on her. Nothing would come of it—and unreciprocated sexual attraction was a distraction she *didn't* need.

Perhaps she'd been in this room for too long. When he'd finished with this, she'd ask him to take her to Caelum. A hot bath, time to settle her nerves—then she'd be ready to return to work here.

For now, it helped to recall how easily he'd dismissed her as a real woman. That memory did not loosen the threads in her chest, but bound them. Still, the purpose was served—her voice was neither breathless nor prudish when she asked him to continue.

He looked at her over his shoulder, nodded. "So one night, we were assigned a simple extraction from a village, just escorting an officer out—but it all got fucked up. And next thing, we're on our knees, and they're deciding whether to shoot us or to use us for leverage."

"They must have chosen the second option."

"Yep. They took my communications equipment, stuck us in a cage. Bamboo, but strong. And the second night was when all the really bad shit went down." He paused to examine an empty, horizontal niche that had been cut deep into the wall, then turned to face her. "We heard the first screams coming from the perimeter of the village. Women, men. Machine gun fire, but it never lasted long. Then there were just more screams, kids and people running everywhere. Every now and then we'd see something going past the cage—but so damn fast we didn't know what the hell it was. Then it came right up, splintered the bars just by squeezing them."

Oh, dear heaven. "A nosferatu?"

As strong as a demon, but bloodthirsty—and without the Rules to govern them. Both demons and Guardians would hunt nosferatu down, kill them on sight. Fortunately, they were easy to identify—the hairless, pale behemoths couldn't shift their shape. The monsters usually stayed hidden away in caves, but when one did venture out, it could easily massacre hundreds of humans in a single night.

"Got it in one," Jake said. "Of course, we didn't know *what* it was. And it came into the cage . . . just ripped our lieutenant to pieces. But it left the rest of us alive."

Her brow furrowed. She'd been certain he was telling her how he'd been killed: the sacrifice he'd made of his own life to save another's—the sacrifice that allowed him to be transformed into a

Guardian. They'd all done the same; it was the one act that linked them. "And you escaped the cage?"

"Got out of there as fast as we could. It was nearing dawn by then, too, so we could see what had happened. Everyone, torn apart." He swallowed hard, shook his head. "Everyone but the kids."

Alice squeezed her eyes shut, tried not to imagine. "Don't tell me what it had done to them."

Jake was silent for a second; then he gave a short laugh. "No. I mean, it left them alive, too. It didn't do anything *different* to them. But it also destroyed all of the communication equipment, anything I might have used to call in help. The nearest village was ten clicks south. We, uh, ended up deciding to take the kids there."

She studied his face, thought about what he probably wasn't revealing. A team of soldiers could have traveled the ten kilometers in a relatively short time. But if they had—and even if they'd made contact and a helicopter had come in to retrieve them—she knew there was very little chance help would have been sent to those children. "How long did it take to decide?"

"I prefer to think the guys who wanted to leave the kids behind just went temporarily crazy." His smile was grim. "So it took us half the day to get that settled, to round up the kids and as much ammo and munitions as we could carry, and get out of there. And with most of the kids holding toddlers or babies . . . we didn't get there by nightfall."

Alice breathed a small sound of dismay.

"And it started grabbing us. Not the kids. There were eight of us left after the lieutenant—but it didn't mow through us like it had the village. It'd pick our guy up, then take him out where we could hear what was happening to him. And we were moving those kids as fast as we could, but when the screams stopped, that was when we knew to huddle down and keep watch for it again. Our grenades were useless. By the time we'd throw them in its direction, the damn thing would be around the other side of us. And even when we got lucky enough in our aim to shoot it, it just kept on coming."

He met her eyes, said evenly, "I was scared. No—beyond scared. For myself, for the other guys, for those kids. Nothing else I'd seen over there came close."

Did he think he shouldn't have been frightened? "Understandably so."

"Maybe. But the thing is, that sickness in my gut was gone.

We were losing our men, we had no fucking chance against this thing—but what we were trying to do was exactly right." He gave a quick, self-disparaging smile. "Of course, that was the only thing that was clear. I was thinking the craziest shit, making all these deals with God, the devil. Buddha got thrown in, too. Thor and Superman. I honestly would have done just about anything to get out of there—and worried about the consequences later."

She looked down at her hands. If only her circumstances had been as noble as saving a group of children. But willful ignorance could not be so easily excused. "I can imagine," she said quietly. "And then?"

"It took Thompson—which left just me and Pinter, the FNG. So—"

"FNG?" Alice glanced up. "A weapon?"

He crossed the room, laughing to himself and shaking his head. "The fucking new guy. A month before that, I'd been promoted to spec-4—a communications specialist—but I still had the title. So it was a good day when Pinter came along." Jake lowered himself down next to her again. "And he was the only one who got out of there. Maybe. Could be, he got wasted the second he and the kids made it to the village. Dunno."

"Because you didn't make it."

"Nope. Because by then, we'd figured out that it was choosing us by age—or rank, maybe. Working its way down, and just playing with us before it went after the kids. So after it got Thompson, I knew I was next. And a part of me was hoping that Thompson wouldn't ever stop screaming." That flush covered his cheeks again, but he didn't look away from her. "But it wasn't just dying that scared me. I had a pretty good reason to get back home in one piece. But I knew it wasn't going to happen—and that somehow, I was going to have to take that thing out with me. So I wrote a letter to my girl, had Pinter and the kids huddle up, then went out to wait for it."

She tried to interpret the smile that began to form on his lips. Half pride, she thought, and half disbelief—or embarrassment. "What did you take with you?"

"A grenade," he said, then grinned before he stood and moved to the middle of the chamber, hopping up on the dais behind the lantern. His shadow loomed across the ochre-washed wall. "But just as a diversion. Because Thompson had tried that, and the nosferatu swatted it out of his hand before it went off. But I had two land mines—and I dug out a hole for them and covered them up. And when Thompson stopped screaming, I stepped on them."

"But didn't they—"

"Nuh-uh. Because they had mousetrap detonators—pressure release—that could be rigged so they don't blow until you lift your foot. So I'm standing there like this—" He spread his legs shoulder-width apart, hunched his shoulders, and widened his eyes. "Shaking like crazy. And thinking how stupid it would be if dawn came before the nosferatu did, and I was stuck there the whole flippin' day."

Alice's startled laugh pealed from high in her throat. "Yes," she agreed, nodding. "That would have been unfortunate."

"Yeah, but it didn't happen." He abandoned his stance, and shrugged. "The nosferatu came, I went boom! And it did, too. Then there was Michael, showing up and asking me to come be a Guardian. And I thought, 'What the hell.' Better than singing in Heaven. Or Hell, if I was headed there instead."

"Yes." The vestiges of her laughter fell away, and she sighed. "Jake, if you told me this in order to lead up to Michael, and make an argument about why I shouldn't kill him—"

"No. That's not it. Because after I got over being pissed, I realized what you were doing at Teqon's place. Trying to get out of your bargain, right? You don't want to kill Michael any more than I do. That's why you told Teqon to reconsider, and threw that heart at him. Which, by the way, was both badass and creepy."

"It got my message across."

"Yeah. Which is why I'm here."

"It is?" She was utterly lost.

He stepped down from the dais. "I know what it's like to be stuck, when you've only got two or three really bad choices. Or no choice."

"Oh. I see." Her back stiffened. "Thank you for coming to offer your sympathy."

"Ah, there you go with the porcupine again. But I'm not here out of pity; I'm here to help."

"Help?" She stood in a quick movement, and her voice had a sharp edge. "There is nothing that can be done—I will either decide to fulfill my bargain, or I will not. So you are better put to use elsewhere."

"Gee, it's too bad you think so. Because I'm putting myself to use wherever you are. It'll be a good experience for me."

"So you said before," she reminded him tightly, then held up her hand when he opened his mouth. "No. For one, you are training with Ethan—"

"Nope. I popped over to Seattle before heading here. And I told him I'd be working under you for a while."

Oh, dear heaven. Had Jake told him of the bargain? "He agreed?"

"I would've come even if he hadn't. As it was, he just asked, 'This about that demon?' And I said, 'Maybe,' and he said, 'All right, then.'"

"The traitor," Alice muttered.

"Not from where I'm standing." Jake's gaze was steady. "Look, Alice. I'm the only one available to you. Before the Ascension, you had more options. Maybe Irena or Drifter could've taken more time away from their assignments. But now there's just me. And I'm going where I feel I'm most needed, and where I can offer the most help."

"But there is nothing—"

"*Help*, as in finding out more about the prophecy. And if that means we take that list of Belial's demons and threaten to cut out their hearts one by one unless they spill everything they know about it, that's what we'll do. And we'll find something that Teqon will want."

Alice slowly closed her mouth. The idea held promise, and was something she'd considered before and discarded—she couldn't have attempted it alone.

Not that it mattered. "Teqon said he wouldn't accept any alternative."

"And he's a demon, which makes him a liar. But if that fails, we'll try something else."

Ever the optimist. And she was tempted to accept.

As if sensing that she wavered, he pressed, "I don't have enough experience to head out on my own yet, but I'll get more doing this with you than I will with Drifter. So you'll be helping me, too. And if you don't agree . . . well, I'll just find you by teleporting wherever you are. I might anyway, if it means I keep landing in places like this. Are we underground? In a hypogeum?"

"Yes." She sighed. "You're incredibly stubborn."

"I know." He hooked his thumbs into his pockets and seemed to try very hard to appear chagrined. "It's a fault."

"Yes, well—I hope you don't intend to immediately set off

hunting demons." She pulled in a measuring tape from her cache and tossed it to him. "We need to find the dimensions of the chamber, then create a visual record. Do you want to sketch or to photograph?"

He caught the tape. "You're a goddess, Alice."

"I know." His smile did silly things to her insides, so she turned away, seeking another distraction. "I am Zorya Polunochnaya. Patient and wise."

Or she would try to be.

"Isn't that the crone?"

She speared a glance over her shoulder, felt her stomach tumble a little more, and pointed at the wall. "Measure. Now. Or I will smite thee."

CHAPTER 8

The next two hours passed more smoothly than Alice had anticipated. As she finished the details on her last sketch, she mused that it boded well for when they moved against any of Belial's demons.

She glanced at Jake, who was crouching in front of the dais. Muffled rock music came from the tiny speakers in his ears. He'd been efficient and, once they'd split up their tasks, hadn't needed to ask for direction. And though she couldn't ignore his presence, she'd been able to focus on the work, and let her emotions settle.

And become aware that the uncertainty she was feeling now hadn't just been over Teqon, and Jake's sudden appearance. It was this chamber.

All of the sites had been mysteries, had offered more questions than answers. Yet this one simply didn't *fit*.

But why? Was it just the difference of being a burial chamber? Her gaze skimmed past the entrance, open to the long, narrow shaft that led aboveground, to an olive grove in the Italian countryside. The Etruscan frescoes on the walls were of the same scenes she'd seen before—and the technique of plastering stucco over stone before painting them had been used once in India. The dais was nothing more than a limestone slab, but she'd seen many of those before, too. Not in any of the temples—but many sarcophagi rested on similar stones in other, human-made chambers. The red ochre staining the walls and ceiling was common to many burial sites, as well.

Jake stood, yanked the wires to his headphones, let them dangle from his fist. "This place is a mess. Like a couple of guys from different eras came in and slapped it together as fast as they could."

There was her answer—and he managed to surprise her, yet again. "Yes," she agreed. A muddle of styles and influences. "There's no coherence."

"Yeah. They're just pulling sh—*stuff* in from everywhere. But not the materials, because look at this." He used the toe of his boot to tap the side of the dais, then pointed at the long, low niche in the wall. "The grain in the stone matches. So they just cut out the block, and plopped it right here in the middle."

"Then didn't cover the hole it left, though it disturbs the symmetry of the room."

Jake nodded, then turned toward her. "But here's the weird thing: they're the same size. Exactly. If we slid that baby back in, we wouldn't see more than a hairline crack."

Alice blinked. "Are you certain?"

"Yep."

Impossible. That left no room for a tool to cut the block from the face of the stone. And even a Guardian couldn't vanish a portion of something into his cache; an object had to be vanished in its entirety. Unless . . .

"It could be a Gift," she said. And thinking of it, she pulsed her own. "I've seen Irena do something similar with a piece of metal she was sculpting. And before the Ascension, there were a few who had an affinity with stone, but I never saw how they . . . Oh, dear. Five people have just come into the entrance shaft and are walking this way."

"Humans?"

She pressed again, sensed the heat of their bodies. Not hot enough to be demons, not cold enough to be nosferatu or vampires. "Yes."

Frowning, he walked to the chamber entrance. There was no door to close it. Alice sighed, then began vanishing her things. She could hear voices now, indistinct.

Jake backed up a step. When his sword appeared in his hand, Alice called in her naginata.

They aren't speaking Italian, he signed.

Alice leapt over the dais, was beside him instantly. The voices were distorted down the long, zigzagging corridor—and the five had already moved past the first bend. She had no spiders waiting there.

She listened, then met his eyes. Though she didn't know the language, she recognized the rhythm, the sound.

Demon tongue, she told him. The Old Language.

Teqon? Would he have found you again, sent more?

Had she mistaken the temperature? She stared down the darkened corridor. Oh, bother. If it was a demon, she'd already revealed herself by using her Gift.

She shot a psychic probe out, swift and pointed as a bolt from a crossbow. And quickly raised her shields again, her skin crawling.

The voices fell silent.

Demon? Jake asked, studying her.

I don't know, she signed. *Dark. Strong. I haven't felt it before.*

His face hardened. Though he aimed it away from her, she felt the blast of his own probe.

I've felt it, he signed. *Nephilim. Which means we get the hell out of here.*

She hesitated, and Jake shook his head, a slight smile on his lips. *Don't even think about it, oh goddess of mine. We've got vampire blood, so we could take one on, maybe two. Five, and we're toast.*

He was right. And this time, he had the experience and knowledge. He'd faced the nephilim alongside Ethan and Alejandro on two separate occasions, whereas she'd never seen one.

But she despised the thought of them coming into this chamber—these sites were *hers,* blast them!—and wanted desperately to know how they'd found it, what they planned to do here.

"Alice," he said.

"Of course." Her nod was stilted, and she held out her hand. "Of course. Let us go."

Immediately, his Gift kicked through her. The walls remained solid around them. His fingers tightened on hers, and he tried again. And again.

A red glow appeared at the end of the corridor.

"Shit." Jake pulled her back, to the opposite side of the chamber. His Gift slammed again, with enough force to push her off balance. He caught her around the waist and dragged her up against him, pressing her cheek into his neck. "Hold on. I'll get us out. I probably just need to see what's coming at me."

Alice vanished her weapon. He would succeed, she thought. But if it was at the last second, an uncontrolled jump and landing, she didn't want to accidentally take his head off with it.

Jake's arm tightened around her. The nephilim's footsteps were approaching—fast, even to her quickened perception. Careful to keep her skin against his, she turned her head, tried to watch from the corner of her eye.

The nephilim were almost at the entrance. Red skin, black feathered wings. The males wore only plated skirts; the two females had similar armor, topped by a filigreed breastplate. Their swords were stained with rust—or dried blood.

Alice's fingers clenched as she prepared to call in her weapon again.

Jake lifted her, and the world spun.

Her shoulder hit rock, and Jake swore. Then his body was hard beneath her. She scented blood, heard the scrape of a knife. She raised her head—tried to. Only three or four inches, and then she rapped it against stone.

Disbelieving, she looked down into his face. He'd rolled them into the niche carved into the wall. And she could no longer hear the nephilim's footsteps. Just her heartbeat, and Jake's.

He'd activated the shielding spell, she realized. He'd scraped the symbols into the stone, then used his blood to seal the opening of the niche.

"*Goddamn.*" His embarrassment seared her psychic blocks.

"We are alive, novice," she said, and turned her head to watch the nephilim race across the chamber.

She couldn't stop her flinch when one stabbed his sword toward the niche's opening, but the blade skidded across the invisible shield as if he'd tried to impale steel. Slowly, she loosened her hold on Jake, shifting her body to the rear of the niche. She only managed to lever herself onto her side, her thigh over his and still half-lying on him, but it wouldn't be as distracting as straddling his hips.

"I wouldn't have thought of this," she added as an arrow splintered against the shield. "I've never used the spell. I'd have been dead now if I was alone."

A female nephil hacked at the stone with an axe. Chips flew, but the shield would hold its shape around their small space even if the nephilim managed to chisel an opening in the rock above them.

"Next time," he said, "I'll set the shield at the chamber entrance."

"That would have been ideal," she agreed.

"I avoided the situation." His wry grin seemed to dare her to say *I told you so.*

"Yes, well. Typically, I steer clear of being trapped in stone niches the size of a sarcophagus, with nephilim waiting to let their axes take bites of my skull. But we all eventually find ourselves in those situations we avoid, and must make the best of them—which you did. Can you teleport from inside the shield?"

"Yes. Want me to try, or wait?"

"And see what they do?" At his nod, she said, "That would also be ideal."

To her surprise, what the nephilim did was hold a short consultation—then vanish their clothing.

Demons in their original form had no gender; they adopted genitalia after shape-shifting into human forms. But perhaps because these nephilim possessed human bodies and could only shape-shift between their human and current forms, they'd had to adopt the sex of their physical host, as well.

"Nephilim orgy?"

Alice would never admit that she'd been wondering the same thing. "If so, the males need encouragement. I have seen slugs with more vigor."

She felt his gaze on her, but continued watching the nephilim. They abandoned their assault on the niche, and arranged themselves in a circle around the dais. Their black wings were spread, their wing tips touching.

Those black feathers sent unease rolling through her. Of the Guardians, only Michael had similar wings. The rest of them could mimic a demon's leathery wings, the nosferatu's more membranous ones, and create their own of white feathers. But no one could copy Michael's, or the way in which his amber eyes could become wholly obsidian.

The crimson glow had left the nephilim's eyes, leaving only black.

Their appearance had also apparently turned Jake's thoughts to the Doyen, but in a different direction. "Does Michael know of your bargain?"

"Yes," she said flatly, but of course her tone did not dissuade him.

"And?"

"And I am to do as I must, with the understanding that if I choose to fulfill it, Michael will do as *he* must."

"Kill you."

"Defend himself."

"Kill you."

She shrugged as best she could in the cramped space, and felt the ice-tipped spear of his anger.

"Would you try? Assuming you *could* beat him."

Little chance of that. Challenging Michael would be more difficult, she imagined, than taking on five nephilim. "I like to think I wouldn't."

Once upon a time, however, she'd also thought she wouldn't have made a bargain with a demon.

"But if it came down to it? His life or your soul?"

Her chest was in knots. In truth, she didn't know if she'd stop herself because it was *right*, or because there was no point in following through. "If I did fulfill the bargain, I would no longer be frozen in Hell when I died, and no dragons would be devouring my body in the Chaos realm. But if I murdered him to save myself, wouldn't I be bound for Hell, regardless? Unless I atoned for that—but how could it be forgiven, to cold-bloodedly plan his murder? And so the only difference would be the nature of my torture."

Jake shook his head. "You don't know that. We don't know how humans and Guardians are judged in the afterlife. That's not our role."

So he could recite from the Scrolls when it suited him. "No. But I know how I would judge myself." And that was all that mattered while she was living. Her opinion—and the opinion of the few who held small pieces of her heart. "So I would create another alternative."

"Like what?"

"Like not dying, and trying to make immortality last as long as eternity," she said, avoiding his gaze. The nephilim's mouths were moving in unison. "They are chanting now."

Jake was rigid beside her, but he did not pursue it further. Silence fell between them, as if they were listening to the chanting they could not hear. The tension slowly left his form—probably from boredom. With no room to prop her elbow, she allowed herself to relax against him, watching the nephilim with her cheek resting on his shoulder.

They got along best, she mused, when neither of them spoke.

After twenty minutes, however, with the nephilim not having so much as ruffled a feather, her thoughts began to wander. To his leg, most often, and the muscled thigh lodged between hers. It would be very easy to rub against him.

Very, very easy. Her forehead creased as she contemplated it. If she went slow enough, he might not even notice—or just assume it was the restless movements that any woman made when she was stuck between an attractive man and a wall.

An inch, she thought, over the course of an hour. She could entertain herself and relieve tension at the same time. And the rubbing would not ignite her senses half as much as the excitement of hiding her reaction, the anticipation of reaching her goal.

By the end of the hour, she would be so focused on it, her arousal so high, she'd very likely attain orgasm. From an inch.

Her lips pressed together to muffle her laugh as she pictured it—and then she bit back her gasp as Jake shifted slightly, against flesh sensitized by her imaginings.

Needy flesh, aching now for another stroke, however small.

She went utterly still, not daring to breathe. How foolish that had been, teasing herself, pretending that she could perform such a mental exercise without evoking a physical response. Now she was inflamed.

Her eyes followed the movement of Jake's hand as it rose to his mouth, then she looked away. Still, she heard the soft click of his toothpick against his teeth, the slide of his tongue against smooth wood.

If only the nephilim would do something.

Jake made a quiet, frustrated noise and moved once more. The breath she'd held hissed through her teeth. She felt him turn his head, and his gaze on her before he looked out at the nephilim again.

"This is the most boring orgy ever," he announced.

And yet she was more aroused than she'd ever been upon witnessing one. "I will defer to your judgment, novice. You are likely more familiar with boring orgies than I am."

For a few seconds, she held out hope that her response had silenced him. Then he said, "And if I hadn't already known nephilim were evil, I would now."

She bit, despite herself. "Why is that?"

"Because they arrange themselves so all we get is an ass shot of that male. Then, between their angle and their wings, they cover up the chicks."

And that was the shape of things, she thought wryly. She was all but sprawled atop him, inflamed . . . and he was hoping for a glimpse of nephilim breasts. "Perhaps they aren't so evil, novice. I have been enjoying the view."

He was quiet again. She heard the distinctive crinkle of paper money, then he turned his head toward her and said, "What really needs to happen is that one bends the other one over, and gives it to her so hard that the only thing coming out of her mouth is—"

Her gasp cut him off as the nephil suddenly lifted his stained sword and buried it in the stomach of the male to his left.

"Oh, dear God!" Alice dove across Jake's chest.

His hands clamped around her waist before she breached the shielding spell. "Hold on, goddess."

Her fingers clenched on his shoulders, and she suppressed her automatic response to defend the weaponless male. Given the opportunity, she'd have stabbed the nephil, too. "What are they doing?"

The injured male wasn't fighting, but kneeling on the dais. Still chanting, the nephilim moved in measured steps around him, their swords flashing. Between wings and arms, she saw the symbols they were carving on his crimson skin, the blood dripping to the floor.

"A ritual?" she wondered aloud.

"That, or a sacrifice." His face hardened as he took in the macabre dance. "Sick."

"Yes." And looking made her feel a part of it, unclean, but she forced herself to watch. "He's not healing."

"Because of the symbols?"

"I don't know. Could vampire blood be on the swords?"

Jake shook his head. "They get vamp blood in them, and they can't stay that size. They start to shape-shift back to the form of their host. Their red skin looks human again for a second or two. But they still heal fast."

More symbols, more blood. Alice scooted down Jake's legs, raised her body as high as she could, and called in her sketchbook. The only place to put it was on his chest.

She had to twist her arm awkwardly between them. Her elbow dug into his stomach, and the already taut muscles hardened to steel. "Sorry."

"Don't be," he said, and then the scratching of her pencil filled the niche. Within seconds, she had the outlines of the nephil's front and back, and the position of the symbols visible to her. "I've got a creepy feeling about this, Alice. Bad creepy, not good creepy."

So did she. "I can't see all of the symbols," she said in quiet frustration.

"Maybe they'll leave the body when they're done with it. Or maybe we should start shooting them now."

Though nothing could penetrate the shield from outside, anything could exit it. Yet bullets and crossbow bolts would barely affect the nephilim.

But, she realized, Jake wasn't proposing that they try to stop them from killing the nephil. He wanted to interrupt the ritual.

"Yes." She nodded, and vanished her sketch pad. He'd already called in a semiautomatic pistol. No silencer, she saw, and prepared for the pain in her ears, but he thrust the tip of the barrel through the shield. She heard the click of the firing mechanism, but the explosion was on the opposite side of the shielding spell.

Jake hit the first female in the side. Not more than a flesh wound, and not so much as a flinch from the nephil. She healed almost instantly.

"Perhaps it would—"

"I'm going for blood splatter," he said.

How . . . brilliant, in truth. Blood was the key to rituals, to activating spells. Mixing it could potentially do more damage to the nephilim's ritual than their weapons would.

Alice smiled and called in her own gun. It was, she noted with satisfaction, larger than his. "You are quite adept at locating unusual holes."

A chink in armor, a weak spot in a plan, a course of action— obvious or unexpected, she had a feeling he could find it.

A laugh shook his body. "I'm even better at stuffing—"

"Your filter, novice." She slid the gun barrel past the face of the niche, began to squeeze the trigger—and the pistol kicked in her hand. The nephilim stumbled before standing upright again; the one on the dais lay motionless. "What in heaven's name . . . ?"

Jake cursed and pulled his gun back inside the shield. She tried to do the same, but couldn't until he took it from her. His blood had set the spell; only Jake—and any inanimate object he held—could return through the shield from outside.

"Something hit us," he said. "Look at the ceiling."

A crack ran through the spiraling pattern of red ochre. Chunks of limestone rained down. "An earthquake?"

"We'd have felt that in here. I'm thinking whatever they were trying to do, they did."

That kick she'd felt had been a surge of power, then. In the center of the room, the nephilim vanished the body and blood. Like the ceiling, the dais had cracked. Two nephilim took hold of each end and tossed the stone slab to the side.

Not so remarkable. She could have moved it.

Would have moved it, if she'd known there was an opening beneath. The nephilim stepped over it, fell out of sight. Into another chamber?

"Blast," she whispered, shaking with anger, with disappointment. "Blast."

"Hey." His hands firmed on her waist. "There's a good chance they opened it with the ritual, and there was nothing to find before they did. Now we've got something to look at when they leave."

"I know it." She closed her eyes. How long would the wait be this time?

"Alice."

Only seconds. One by one, the nephilim leapt out of the lower chamber. The last carried . . .

Alice caught her breath. "Is that a Scroll?"

The rolled parchment was identical to those in Caelum's archives—and the nephil held it in his hand, though it would have been safer vanishing it into his cache. But only Michael could vanish the Scrolls.

"Looks like. What are the odds that I could snatch it from him and get back in here without getting killed?"

"Very low, novice."

"Yeah." As the nephilim passed out of the main chamber into the shaft leading outside, Jake slammed his foot against the end of the niche, his psychic scent boiling with frustration. "Damn it all to flippin' hell."

❦

They dropped into the chamber together. Jake fell to his knee, swept his pistol in a semicircle. His side was clear. Round room, completely empty. Behind him, he heard Alice's quick pull of breath, his name in a shocked whisper.

He pivoted. She was all right, he saw instantly. Standing with the naginata slack in her hand, and staring at—

Holy hot hell.

A skeleton was pinned to the wall, held up by a sword through its ribs—and two iron stakes at the apex of each outstretched wing. Three demonic symbols were carved into the stone above the skull.

He glanced at Alice; her eyes were wide as they met his. Wordlessly, she shook her head.

Yeah. He was that lost, too—could barely organize the questions streaming through his mind.

A skeleton wasn't so unexpected. It was a flippin' burial chamber, after all. But those wings . . .

He forced himself to focus. "Those wing bones aren't demon or nosferatu," Jake said.

"Unless a demon shape-shifted." Alice moved closer to the skeleton, bending to examine its right hand. "And look how the fingers are curled. They must have been set like that after death. Holding the Scroll?"

"That's my guess. Someone was delivering a message." His gaze lifted to vacant eye sockets, then to the symbols above. "More than one."

And the nephilim apparently hadn't cared that they would see it. Or, not realizing that Jake could teleport, they were waiting outside—intending to kill Alice and him when they finally emerged.

"Yes." Her camera replaced her weapon. "Let's do this quickly."

❦

Alice didn't immediately pull away from him when they teleported into the tech room at Special Investigations. Jake watched her close her eyes, fight the dizziness.

Holding her steady was a pathetic excuse for getting his hands on her again, but he used it. He already knew the shape of her waist, her lower back. She'd probably hit him if he went for ass. Lightly, he settled his palms on her shoulders. His thumbs rested in the silk-covered hollows above her clavicles.

Slender, angular—but not bony. Except for her elbows. And even those, he wanted to cup in his hands. Undo the tiny buttons that climbed her sleeve. Rip her dress off, or just lift her up on one of the computer desks and yank down her bloomers.

Did she wear bloomers? He couldn't recall the outline of anything beneath those skirts, no ruffles or panty lines. Maybe she went bare. Maybe she was, right now, wearing nothing but her stockings and boots beneath those skirts.

Hot damn.

But it didn't matter. Whether he had to tear them off first or could just dive in, he wouldn't come up for air until she begged.

No, no. While begging, she'd probably call him "novice." Not the best thing for a man to hear at that point. Far better if she was quiet when she came.

Or screaming. Screaming was good, too.

He looked down, met her icy blue stare, saw the prim set of her mouth.

Yeah. None of that was ever going to happen.

He'd been in that hole with her for too long. Just because she'd gone soft against him didn't mean she had any intention of letting him play drill sergeant and give her a tongue-lashing.

He removed his hands from her shoulders, shoved them into his pockets.

Alice lifted her chin and surveyed the room over the length of her nose. "This will not do at all, novice. We need more space."

He couldn't argue with that. But when he turned and told her to follow him, it was still an effort not to kick one of the chairs on the way out.

Goddammit. For a while, from the time he'd jumped into that chamber and up until they'd jumped here, that giant stick of disapproval hadn't been up her ass.

Now it was back.

And there was nothing to do but see how far up it would go. As they walked down the corridor leading from the tech room to the main offices, he rapped his knuckles on a utility door.

"A closet," he said when she glanced at him. "In case you

change your mind, decide to go for tight quarters. You seemed to like it. Enough to cuddle, at least."

Yep. All the way up her spine, and branching out into her shoulders.

"I'll let you poke me again, too," he offered. "Maybe with your knees, next time." Spread, on his shoulders, while he licked and licked.

"I don't think so, novice."

"Ah, come on. You know the thought of stabbing me with your bony parts makes you hot."

He stopped in front of Hugh and Lilith's office door, and she took another step before doing the same. Her mouth was a tight line, her arms folded across her chest.

He was such a dick.

So she wasn't looking for a quick bang—or a long one. He should have been able to deal with that. Hell, he wasn't looking for one, either. He'd done the orgy thing, thirty years of mindless fucking, and had been getting tired of it even before the Ascension.

But why was it that when he started wanting a little more, it was with the Black Widow? Jesus Christ. Sexy, funny, smart women lay thick on the ground—and most weren't struggling with whether to kill a Guardian or to flippin' save themselves. At SI alone there were at least a dozen smoking-hot women, and they might have starred in his fantasies now and then, but sex wasn't worth fucking up his friendships with them.

Yet here he was fucking everything up with a woman he couldn't stop thinking about, and it wasn't just the bang he wanted. But damn if he knew what it was about her that was getting to him.

Hell, maybe it *was* her struggle with her bargain. He couldn't say he knew many people—men or women—who had to carry a burden that heavy. And if their souls were on the line, how many people would have just taken the easy route?

Yet Alice hadn't. And by trying to do the right thing, she'd hooked his interest. Too bad she didn't want him hooked.

He shook his head. That still didn't explain the level of dickery he'd sunk to. This wasn't the first time a woman hadn't returned his interest. But he'd never taken it like this before. Had never taken it *out* on someone like this before. And he'd never been so disappointed that he couldn't get through. That he couldn't even see a possible opening.

He pushed through the office door without knocking, thinking that if he'd been born eight hundred years ago, when men didn't wait for permission before grabbing a woman, he'd have had Alice up against a wall already.

Like eight-hundred-year-old Hugh had Lilith up against a bookcase.

"Gee," Jake said, and his life flashed in front of his eyes. Lilith was going to kill him. "I need you in the main conference room. And a lock is a real swell invention."

He closed the door, let out a breath, and began to pray. They'd still had clothes on. Maybe he wasn't dead. She might just order her hellhound to eat his liver.

Something bumped against his ass. He had no hope it was Alice, so it could only be Sir Pup, prodding him with one of his giant noses, on one of his three giant heads. When Jake turned around, the hellhound appeared mostly dog—which was the reason Jake didn't teleport. If Sir Pup had been in demon form, standing as tall as Jake and sporting barbed fur, scales, and eyes glowing with hellfire, nothing could have kept him there.

"Look, I'll make you a deal," he told the hellhound. "She offers you any body part, and I'll counter it with double the weight in raw, bloody beef."

Sir Pup grinned at him with his three sets of razor-edged teeth.

Jake didn't know if that meant the hellhound agreed, or if Sir Pup was just anticipating the taste of his liver. "Triple the weight. And you probably don't want to go in there," Jake added when the hellhound shouldered closer to the door. "What they're doing isn't safe for young, impressionable minds."

Alice's laugh might have been in response to his warning or the way the hellhound did a doggy version of an eyeroll—Jake wasn't sure. But he wasn't going to ruin her lighter mood. He concentrated on not being a dick on the way to the conference room.

Which meant he didn't say anything until they were standing inside, studying the large oval table.

He glanced at her. "The room's big enough?" When she nodded, he vanished the table.

Alice took the chairs, then began calling in bones one at a time, swiftly arranging them on the floor.

The skeleton had fallen apart as soon as they'd touched it. Despite being forced to replace each bone individually, she only had to consult her sketches twice. Within a few seconds, the skeleton had been restored, and Jake had been treated to a display of grace that made him want to pound his head against the wall and howl his frustration.

He kept his mouth shut, and called in the sword and iron stakes. Then held on to both when he heard Lilith and Hugh come in.

Lilith's dark gaze swept the floor, ran over Alice, landed on Jake. "I might kiss you, puppy," she said, striding toward him. "Or make Hugh do it. Because *I* should kick your ass for jumping to Hell. How did you get it away from him?"

"Who?" Jake waited for it to make sense. Lilith usually did. "What? I didn't go to Hell."

She pointed at his hand. "You have Michael's sword. Belial had it before the Gates to Hell were closed. Where did you get it, if not there?"

Astonished, he lifted the sword. Longer and wider than most of the swords he practiced with, and forged of bronze, he thought it was similar to the one Michael had used to slay the dragon, but he didn't know if it was identical. He'd rarely seen Michael's, and half the time, it had been on fire. But Lilith was more familiar with it—had even wielded it.

Beside him, Alice shook her head. "No. Look at the blade."

"May I?" Hugh held out his hand, and Jake passed it to him. The overhead lights reflected off his eyeglasses as Hugh angled the sword, studying it. "It's rather dinged up, isn't it?"

"Yes," Alice said. Her gaze warmed as she looked at Hugh, and Jake felt a little twist in his gut.

Stupid. Everyone who'd trained under Hugh loved him. Lilith had come over from the dark side because she loved him. If Jake batted for the other team, he'd have made a play for Hugh in a second.

It'd probably have been easier than making a play for the Black Widow. And smarter than wishing she'd look at him like that.

Lilith appraised her quickly. "You're the Black Widow. The novices speak of you."

Though Alice's tone was neutral, Jake thought he saw a hint of curiosity in her expression. "And you are Lucifer's daughter. *Everyone* speaks of you."

That obviously didn't displease Lilith. She was smiling when she looked to Hugh again.

He carefully tested the edge of the blade with his thumb. "Dull." And Michael's sword could cut through stone.

"Damn," Lilith said softly, then turned to the skeleton. "A friend of yours, puppy?"

"Nope. My guess is, he's been dead longer than you've been alive—five hundred years longer."

That surprised her. "Twenty-five centuries?"

"Yep. We'll run a few tests to determine the date of death, but judging by the chamber we found it in, the latest styles there, we're looking at around fifth or sixth century BC. And there's no telling how long he was alive before that."

Lilith crouched next to the skeleton. Her black hair slid forward over her shoulder when she leaned closer, and she hooked it behind her ear. "Where did you find it?"

"A hypogeum in Italy," he said, then looked to Alice. She would know exactly where; he hadn't been outside the chamber. "There might be nephilim still there."

"Nephilim? Wait a moment," Hugh said, and flipped the sword around, presented it to Jake. "Best if you only have to tell us once, and we'll get a team ready while you're gone. Can you find Michael?"

Jake took the sword, vanished it. "If he's not blocked."

Theoretically, his Gift could take him to anyone he knew, as long as they hadn't completely shielded their psyche and weren't behind the shielding spell. Selah could; Michael could.

Jake had a little less luck with it. He assumed the only reason he'd found Alice was because she pulsed her Gift so often.

Lilith glanced over her shoulder. "Do you need help, puppy? Sir Pup is hungry."

He met Alice's eyes. "Nope," he said, and imagined her watching Sir Pup pounce on him—imagined her hearing his girly scream.

Jumping was as easy as pie.

CHAPTER 9

Michael was in the middle of the freak courtyard, wearing the loose white shirt and pants that reminded Jake of his granddad's pajamas. They only lacked stripes.

Better than the toga, though. Jake didn't understand how any man could run around in one, but maybe it was about morale. Nothing inspired a guy to keep training like knowing someone in a sheet could kick his ass.

Though Jake jumped in behind him, Michael didn't spin around and almost chop off his head as Alice had done. The Doyen continued looking at the fountain, the obelisk in the center and the eerily perfect arc of water that fell without a splash into the pool below. He glanced over when Jake moved even with him.

Jake was trying, as he had the last time he'd been here, to read the writing at the bottom of the obelisk. It was small, but it wasn't *too* small—he should have been able to make it out. "Is that messing with my head?"

"It is Caelum, and her sense of humor. You cannot read it unless you are in the water."

"Huh." He looked a second longer, wondering if he should be

creeped out that Michael spoke of the realm as if it were alive. "Another time, then. Alice and I found a dead Guardian, a sword that Lilith thought was yours, and a few nephilim in Italy. They want you back at SI."

"Then I shall go."

"There is one other thing first," Jake said, and when Michael didn't disappear, he took that as a sign to continue. "Alice needs me more than Drifter does, so I'll be helping her from now on. Until she gets out of this bargain."

Michael studied him for a long moment, then inclined his head. "Well done, Jacob Hawkins." He smiled faintly. "If you are assisting Alice, should I be more wary when you teleport in behind me?"

Jake shrugged. "I'd say no—but the truth is, it'd be a great boost for my ego if you were."

Michael disappeared a moment later, and Jake stood, listening. Michael's laugh echoed in the courtyard of stone, but no other sound did.

If Caelum did have a sense of humor, she used Michael's voice to express it.

❧

Jake took a trip to Mongolia and Kansas before finally arriving back at the SI warehouse. He teleported in between Irena and Alejandro, at the feet of the skeleton. At the head, Alice stood next to Drifter and described the nephilim's ritual.

Jake only half listened. The conference room was full; Selah must have been busy assembling the team that would return to Italy and search out the nephilim—ten Guardians who were usually active in the field surrounded the skeleton. All of the novices were here, but no vampires; the sun was up over San Francisco, so they were in their daysleep.

He met Pim's eyes. She flashed him a wide smile and a thumbs-up before looking down at the skeleton again, her face solemn.

Michael's expression was equally grave as Alice concluded with a description of the skeleton's position on the wall and the symbols written above. And when she finished, they all looked to him.

"His name was Zakril," he said softly. "He was a Guardian, one of the first. And he was a friend."

Damn. Jake saw Alice's sudden discomfort in the way her spine stiffened, thought it was the same as his. Until that second, they'd just been bones on the floor.

Michael glanced up at Alice and shook his head. "I am grateful that you brought him here. I did not know what had become of him after he took leave from the corps."

"He'd left the Guardian corps without having to Fall and become human again?" Lilith arched her brows. "You're such a pushover, Michael."

Beside Jake, Irena had tensed. "We are allowed time away from our duties if we need it, demon."

Her hostility was almost palpable—and wasted on Lilith, who didn't have psychic senses anymore, and who probably didn't give two shits.

"I'll remember that when I schedule in vacations," Lilith said, and looked at Hugh, who nodded toward Jake. She turned to him. "Your doubts, puppy. I want to hear them."

No use questioning how Hugh had known. The man could read body language so well, he could determine when even a demon was lying.

Jake met Alice's eyes, and saw the curiosity there. "These sites were probably built by Guardians. The chamber—with Zakril in it—was sealed by Guardians. That dais covering it wasn't cut with a tool, but a Gift," he explained. "And Zakril was a message. I don't know who the message was for—but even if you're at war, you don't use the body of your own man to send it."

"Yes," Michael said. His eyes were obsidian now, making it almost impossible to determine where he was looking, but Jake felt the weight of that dark gaze.

Not an oppressive weight, though, so he continued. "Was Zakril a traitor, then—or was he betrayed?"

"Betrayed," Michael answered. "But it was done before he left Caelum."

Well, here we go then, Jake thought. His gut was roiling, he was going to piss everyone off, but it needed to be asked. "By you?"

He felt the muffled surprise and anger around him, yet every Guardian still turned to Hugh as Michael responded.

"No."

A wry smile touched Hugh's mouth. "That was truth. It has all been."

The relief in the room wasn't just Jake's. The tension left his stomach.

"What happened, Michael?" Irena asked, and as she spoke, she bumped Jake with her hip.

It was—he prayed—a friendly bump. He looked across the skeleton at Alice, but couldn't read her expression. Thoughtful, maybe. Or concerned.

He'd have preferred ice and disapproval to knowing that she worried.

Michael lowered himself to his heels, lightly touched Zakril's fingers. "We were divided. There were those who wanted to depose Lucifer, and take over rule of Hell."

"Hardly objectionable," Alejandro said. When Jake trained with him, Alejandro usually spoke Spanish; now, Andalusia rolled lightly through his English. "I would rather see a Guardian on the throne than a demon."

"Yes," Michael agreed. "If it would not have meant denying humans their free will, and freeing the nephilim from Lucifer's control." He looked up. "It is too long a story now, when there are nephilim to hunt. We will call everyone to a gathering in Caelum a week hence, and I will tell you all you need to know."

All you need to know. Not, Jake noted, everything they wanted to know. But Michael was already asking, "Alice, do you have the symbols? I will not be able to enter the site and see for myself."

Lilith narrowed her eyes when Alice pulled in her sketchbook. " 'She waits below,' " she read, then glanced at Michael. "She, who?"

"The one who betrayed him. But she does not wait. She is dead, by Zakril's hand." He stood slowly, shaking his head. "This was the scribbling of someone who believed in the prophecy, but hoped they could prevent it from coming to pass."

At the mention of the prophecy, Alice became absolutely still.

Jake watched her, considering the implications of it. What little they knew of the prophecy said that Belial's rise to power depended upon the destruction of the nephilim—who would be equally invested in seeing that the prophecy wasn't fulfilled. And although their goals were different, what interested the nephilim might also interest Teqon. "So this particular message—'She waits below'—was for the nephilim?"

And if so, hopefully Michael would reveal at the gathering how these Guardians and nephilim had become allies.

Michael nodded. "I believe it must be. Let us see if we can find them, and retrieve the Scroll. Irena, Alejandro—choose your teams, and make certain you each have vampire blood available. We will go in three groups."

One to each teleporting Guardian. Flippin' fantastic. And it wasn't a surprise when Alejandro gave Jake a nod, including him on his team, but Jake was almost knocked off his feet by the hearty clap Irena landed on his back.

"Now you are in all the way, yes?" She grinned at him, and then strode past Alejandro, giving the tall swordsman the same Death Stare she'd given the women at Cole's.

What the hell? He briefly met Alice's gaze again before she turned to speak with Hugh. Jake watched her sign a greeting, and their short embrace. They hadn't met, he realized, since Hugh had Fallen in the early 1990s and began living as a human again.

Jake began to look away, giving them privacy, until Hugh signed to her, *If I hadn't known it was you, I would have thought it was someone wearing your face.*

Surprised, Jake glanced at Alice. Because Guardians could shape-shift, they learned to identify one another by mannerism as well as physical features. For Hugh to make such a statement suggested that, in less than twenty years, Alice's had completely changed.

I have been told it is not so noticeable when I move quickly, Alice replied. *And if I make a conscious effort, I can still move as humans do.*

When Hugh only looked at her, she lifted her chin and pursed her lips. "Everything that we touch, everything that touches us— it all leaves its mark," she said, mimicking Hugh's voice, then smiled as he laughed.

I connect with them often, she continued. *I am always pushing myself into them; I suppose it is only fair that they leave something in me. And I do not care that it appears odd—truly, I don't.*

No. You wouldn't. Hugh studied her for another moment. *And they no longer frighten you?*

She swept her hand at the floor, indicating the bones. *I found that their usefulness and my gratitude eventually trumped my terror.*

Jake did look away then, his jaw clenching, his chest tight. The Scrolls stated that a Guardian's Gift reflected some part of their human life. His was easy; Jake had spent most of his wanting to be anywhere but where he was.

But Alice had been saddled with spiders? And it was a leap—he knew it was one hell of a leap—but now he had that attic in his head again, that molding bed . . . and those cobwebs.

Somebody restrained there wouldn't have been able to move, no matter what was crawling on her.

"And I see that I will not have to ask if you are prepared, Jake. You look as if you might tear apart the nephilim with your teeth." Alejandro's glove disappeared when he held out his hand. "I suggest a sword; leave the chewing to Irena."

"Yeah," Jake muttered, and took one last glance at Alice as she joined Michael's group.

And it was, he realized, getting much, much easier to follow her.

❧

After six hours with no sign of the nephilim, Alice's hope—then frustration—had distilled into resignation. When dawn began brightening the sky, Michael sent out word that they were to return to their duties while he continued to search the area.

Though Alice had walked through the hypogeum again after they'd teleported to its location, looking for anything she'd missed the first time and making certain the nephilim hadn't returned, she broke formation and flew in that direction—and then was saved an hour's trip when Ethan and Selah appeared in the air beside her and they teleported to the site together.

Birdsong filled the olive grove; a light wind rustled the leaves. Jake was kneeling in the grass next to the open shaft that led to the hypogeum, muttering to himself. When Ethan cleared his throat, Jake stood and held his hand out to Alice, palm up.

"A little help?" he asked, and she saw the wolf spider hatchling clinging to his thumb. "I'm afraid I'll squish him if I push him off."

"They are more resilient than that." Alice held his hand still with her right, and aligned her left palm with his. A nudge of her Gift forced the hatchling to move—and revealed that there were no longer any spiders in the corridor beneath their feet. Startled, she looked at the ground. The shaft opening was still there. "Did it close up while we were away?"

"No." Jake met her eyes. "I found them all, brought them out. Just in case."

"I see." She let go of his hand, walked to the nearest tree, and took a long time settling the hatchling at the base of the trunk. Behind her, Ethan and Selah told Jake about their group's search, and when Alice's heart was not pounding so hard, she returned and relayed the same about Michael's group.

"We struck out, too," Jake said when she finished. "Not even a demon or vampire, let alone a nephil."

"Well, we ain't going to be sensing them once they get into human form and start blocking." Ethan's hat cast a shadow over his face, deepening his frown. "My feeling is, if there's no vampires around—not in all the area any of us searched, including the cities—that it's a sign the nephilim are staying in this region. Or have been visiting often, knowing where this site was going to be, and waiting for it to show."

A line of worry etched between Selah's brows—and little wonder, Alice thought. They'd known large communities of vampires had been killed by the nephilim, but there'd been no indication that the smaller, more rural communities were in danger. But if the nephilim were quietly slaying those vampires as well, Lucas and the vampires in Ashland would be under the same threat as Seattle.

"The first vampire massacre was in Rome," Alice said. This grove was a few hundred kilometers southeast. "And the next in Berlin."

"Have you found any sites in Germany?" Selah asked.

Alice shook her head. "Nor in the western United States. But I find most by luck—traveling to the right region at the right time."

"You won't be limited by the Gates or travel time now," Jake pointed out. "We can pop around as many places you need to, hit them once a week. Or once a day."

"That will be more convenient." Noticing the subtle shift in Ethan's expression, in Selah's psychic scent, she added, "It must be nearing sundown now in Ashland and Seattle. If you wish to go, I will ask Jake to return with me to San Francisco. I'd like to finish with Zakril tonight. Michael has requested that we give the remains to him after we've gathered what we need for the tests, and I see no reason to delay."

Ethan looked to Jake. "That work for you?"

"Yep. We might take a detour, but we'll get there."

Ethan shook his head. "I'm meaning, does it work for you to give back the skeleton? You figure Michael's hiding anything—and if that skeleton disappears, maybe something important goes along with it?"

"Hiding something? Yes. Something we need to know, and that isn't any different than the secrets we all keep? Dunno." Jake rubbed at the back of his neck. Uncertain, Alice thought. And uncomfortable at being reminded how he'd questioned Michael before.

Yet it had been *right* to do so. He'd raised doubt, but in doing so had forced Michael to clear it.

His hand dropped to his side. "Yeah, it works for me." He met Alice's eyes. "And you?"

"Yes."

"We will go then," Selah said, and stepped closer to Jake, her blond hair fluttering around her shoulders. She rose up, kissed his cheek. "And congratulations. It came sooner than we expected, but we all knew it would come—and you are the first since the Ascension."

Jake's brow furrowed. If it hadn't amused Alice so much, she would have pretended it was the pink light in the sky that put the color on his face. "Uh, yeah. Thanks. But I have no idea what you're talking about."

"That's because you were gallivanting around when Michael first showed up at SI, and missed him correcting Alice when she referred to you as 'novice,' " Ethan said. "Seems you did something that makes him consider you a full-fledged Guardian now."

"I did?" Jake ran his hand over his short hair, his eyebrows drawing together. Then his gaze settled on Alice, his irises like rings of polished blue stone. "Hot damn. So that was the 'Well done, Jacob Hawkins' thing."

Jacob. Behind her back, Alice tried it out over her fingers, liked the feel of it.

"That sounds about right." Ethan nodded. "I ain't kissing you, though. We'll probably have a little shindig for you at the gathering—"

"Drifter!"

"—so pretend you're real surprised." He grinned and held out his hand to Selah, who was scowling at him. "You going to drop me in a volcano now?"

Alice didn't hear her reply. They disappeared, and Ethan was either falling into burning lava or safe on his deck in Seattle by the time she dragged her gaze back to Jake's, found it leveled on her face.

Had he been watching her during that entire exchange? And if so, he'd been thinking . . . what?

She did not like being in this uncertain, self-conscious state, yet he'd taken her there again. "What is it?"

"I'm just wondering—if 'novice' is out now—what you'll call me when you want to remind me of my place."

He thought she'd intended to put him lower than her? Her fingers curled, but she stopped herself from denying it. Using his rank as often as possible was about distance, not status. First names felt intimate. Yet revealing *that* would bring him closer—by however small an increment—simply through understanding.

"Hawkins, I think," she replied.

"Hawkins." A muscle in his jaw worked. "And my place, I'm guessing, is over here."

So he *did* understand—or had just realized. "Not necessarily," she said. "I'm quite capable of adjusting my own position if I do not like where I am."

His eyes narrowed speculatively. "So if I came over there, took a victory dance like I did in Tunisia, you'd just stand still and let me? That is, you would if you liked it."

Alice's back stiffened. What a wretch he was to tease her about this. When he irritated her, when he shoved images of gruesome clowns into her mind, she could at least respond in kind. But at some point in that niche, she'd revealed her attraction to him—and when he threw it at her, she had no ammunition to volley in return.

She could only pretend that, although he'd hit his target, it had little effect. "In these circumstances, I suppose I would stay still. I should hate, after all, to be the damp rag on your celebration."

"Would you?" He crossed the distance between them quickly. Alice drew in a short breath, but he didn't touch her, didn't swing her up, didn't kiss her. In a tight, low voice, he asked, "So you'll let me?"

To say no, to deny him whatever satisfaction he gained in using this against her, was also to retreat. If she backed away, he won this.

How strange that she had no idea what would be won. Maybe it was only her pride. But if there was only a tattered scrap left, it was well worth fighting for.

And if she managed to convince him that she was impervious, perhaps he would no longer use this part of his arsenal.

"I will if I must," she finally said, and closed her eyes. "I shall bear it by thinking of England."

He was not breathing. Birds twittered, the breeze brushed her skirts against her legs, and the pale morning sun warmed her face. But Jake was not moving.

Perhaps this had been a joke. If so, she hoped that she had ruined his punch line.

And indeed, when she opened her eyes, there was nothing in his expression that suggested he was laughing—or even that the battle she imagined earlier was *between* them. As he stared at her mouth, the battle seemed firmly lodged within him instead.

"Jake?"

His gaze snapped up to hers, and held it. Then he shook his head. "Forget it," he muttered. His shoulders rigid, he turned and walked away. "Just forget I asked."

CHAPTER 10

Had she thought they got along best when they didn't speak? She'd been wrong. And the companionable hours they spent in the hypogeum had apparently been a fluke.

As they finished with the skeleton—and then teleported to the Archives in Caelum to search through her files for any clue to what the Scroll might have said—she and Jake were silent but for the occasional question or comment about the work.

And it was *irritating*. How polite they were! He sat at the opposite end of one of the Archive tables, surrounded by pictures and reference books, his music playing in his ears and his laptop computer open in front of him. He tapped constantly at the keyboard. Tapping tapping tapping. Remapping the sites, recording their dates, trying to determine the route of the Guardians who'd built them.

As if she hadn't already done that. Not on a computer, perhaps—but it lay in her notes, somewhere.

Yes. Absolutely irritating. And maddening, to find nothing useful here. To be always aware of him. To glance up and see that even if he was looking at her, his gaze was unfocused and his thoughts obviously elsewhere.

And when her laptop began to blink its familiar warning, she was doubly annoyed by the realization that his battery lasted longer than hers.

Well, she would rather feed her entrails to pigs than change it in front of him. She snapped the lid closed, began arranging her notes. If she did not pay attention to what she put in her cache, she would never find it again.

"You're taking off?"

"I must attend to a few chores," she lied. But perhaps she would go to her quarters, set the shielding spell, and scream and scream. "And it is time for you to leave for your session with Alejandro, isn't it?"

"Tonight, yeah, in a little while. Tomorrow? Nope."

Alice frowned and looked up from her notes. "Surely you are not stopping your sessions now that you've been given full status."

"Nuh-uh." Jake had tipped back in his chair, his hands laced behind his head. His T-shirt was mocking her again; when she finally deciphered the stylized letters, she realized that they spelled "kiss." "I'll still be getting an intensive session a couple of times a month from Alejandro. But everyday practice, I'll get with you."

"Alejandro will teach you more about fencing than I can."

"Yeah, but if we're going to be working together, shaking down Belial's demons, it makes more sense for us to get a good feel for each other first. Find out where you're strong, where I am. And where we need to compensate."

She could not argue that. "Very well, then."

He let his chair rock forward. A second computer appeared beside his first, and he began tapping again. Alice drew in a long, calming breath, and vanished everything from her end of the table.

She did not get up, however, but let her gaze run over the cases of books and Scrolls. When she was amid the long rows of marble shelves, the scent of bindings and paper and parchment, her bargain usually felt very far from her.

It didn't now. Not when the prophecy and her work had become so unexpectedly entwined. And yet, after twenty years and seventeen sites, she still knew so very little.

Too little. It was the same lament and frustration that everyone she'd ever known who had studied an ancient site felt, and she'd always laughed at them for asking too much. Awe and discovery should have been enough. She could have laughed at herself for succumbing to the same.

Would have laughed, if her life and soul hadn't depended on finding the answers.

Maybe a cackle would do, however. She narrowed her eyes at Jake. My, wasn't he so very comfortable down there, with his music and his computers. Here she sat, prickly and despondent, contemplating the terrible fate that awaited her, and he was . . . no longer tapping, but using a controller of some kind.

"Are you playing a *game*?"

"Yep. DemonSlayer. I'm almost—" He made a dismayed grunting noise. "Dead."

Alice stared at him, and he flashed a grin at her over the top of his computer screen.

"Hey, it's personal time. It's either this or porn. And this takes my mind off . . . other things."

"I see," she said. She didn't, though—and now she was trying to fit this into what she knew of him. "So you are a geek."

His controller clattered to the table, then disappeared. So did his computers, giving her a clear view of his dumbfounded expression. "A what?"

"A geek. It means—"

"I know what it means. How do *you* know?"

She lifted her chin. "I'm not completely ignorant of contemporary culture."

The most convenient locations to charge her computer batteries were human libraries—and even she found herself tempted by magazines and the Internet.

"Just mostly ignorant," he countered, and she decided it wasn't worth arguing. She'd lose. And it gave her some pleasure that he was looking disgruntled now. "Anyway, I'm not one. I'm not dedicated enough."

She hadn't known there was an element of commitment to it. "What are you dedicated to, then?"

He looked at her longer than the question warranted, but it wasn't until his voice lowered that she realized he'd taken it more seriously than she'd intended. "Being a Guardian. A *good* one. This." He tapped his fingers against the photographs on the table. "And helping you."

It was as if he rolled her wretchedness over, like a pitted dark stone—and revealed something sparkling beneath. His eyes were the most striking blue, her heart was pounding, but still she managed to ask, "And what if being a good Guardian means that you cannot help me?"

"I'm hoping it won't be an issue."

"Optimism, once again." Yet she appreciated it; she had so little of her own. "I will try to keep it from becoming an issue."

He nodded and released a heavy sigh, sliding his hand over his head. Her gaze followed the movement, then returned to his when he paused.

He let out a short laugh. "Go ahead."

"What?"

Jake stood, strode the length of the table, then crouched beside her chair. "Rub it." When her mouth fell open, he shrugged. "Women want to. I don't know why, and I don't think anyone asks Michael as often as they ask me. Maybe it's the puppy thing. Dunno. But feel free."

She curled her fingers. Unto death, she would deny how very much she wanted to. "That's ridiculous. I could shape-shift and have my own hair as short in an instant."

"You could." He grabbed the front legs of her armchair. Wood scraped over marble as he hauled her around to face him. "But then you'd have to redo your braid when you shape-shifted back."

Oh, dear. She was either going to laugh or throw herself onto his head. But, she reasoned, there was no need to *admit* she wanted to. "It does seem an unnecessary effort when yours is right here."

"That's right, goddess. Talk yourself into it. I'll just sit and try to keep myself from jumping your bones."

Some of her amusement dissolved. She wished he wouldn't watch her, but she couldn't order him to look away. Thank heavens he closed his eyes. He was probably imagining that her widened fingers were creepy spider legs, she mused, and pushed their tips from his hairline to the back of his head, until she was cupping it in her palms.

That was all she'd meant to do. But his short hair was so surprisingly soft—she'd thought it would be as coarse as whiskers. She drew her fingers back up. Not rubbing, but stroking—yet Jake didn't object. He bent his head over her lap, and the hollow at the base of his skull was revealed to her, looking oddly vulnerable despite the severity of his haircut, the strength of his neck. She trailed the pad of her thumb through the hollow. Like silk on the downstroke, and slightly abrasive coming up.

A shudder wracked his body. Alice froze, but he didn't move. He was still looking down, a hand on each of the chair's front legs, and his muscles were as rigid as hers when he said, "You're not wearing your boots."

She resisted the urge to curl her toes, to pull them back beneath her skirts. Her stockings were adequate covering. "I vanished them an hour ago."

And if she'd been alone, she'd have tucked her legs beneath her as she worked. She'd have let her spine touch the cushioned back of her chair.

His hair skimmed deliciously beneath her fingers when he lifted his head. Her breath caught, and his eyes locked with hers. They burned, as if lit from behind by a blue flame.

Were hers? Oh, dear heavens—did hers look the same? It felt like they must.

His breathing was harsh and shallow. "Alice. I'm trying very hard not to." His jaw clenched and released. "But I'm afraid I'm going to jump—"

Jake disappeared—and took her chair with him. Alice cried out in surprise, but it was cut off as her bottom thumped against the marble floor. Pain shot up her tailbone.

Oh, but she would kill him. Alice stared at her skirts hitched up around her bent knees, and hastily closed her splayed legs. Kill him, and then . . . and then . . .

She didn't know what. Shove his head between her thighs and rub herself raw, most likely. She contemplated that, and couldn't decide whether to laugh or to slide her hands down and use them as a replacement.

But what a strange picture she would make if he returned to find her settling her nerves on the floor—or if anyone else should happen by.

No, she thought. That would not do at all. So perhaps she would go home and attend to a few things after all.

❧

Goddamn. Jake lay facedown on a wooden floor, his cock painfully stiff beneath him, his hands still locked on the chair legs.

Alice was going to kill him. Or feed him to her giant spider.

And had she really looked like *she'd* wanted to eat him? Sweet floating Moses, let it be true.

But maybe it had just been wishful thinking. And it would be best not to think that way at all, or he'd end up humping the floor instead of figuring out where the hell he'd landed.

The room smelled clean, powdery. Beside him, ruffled white cotton hung over a knotted rag rug. Dust bunnies and a ratty stuffed bear lurked in the darkness beyond.

A bed. Oh, shit.

He listened, and rolled over onto his side, came up on his elbow. The racing heartbeat and the quick, shallow breaths had the same effect as an ice bath. A psychic probe told him it was a kid. Awake, and scared as hell. Shit shit shit. He could try to leave . . . but freaking a kid out and then taking off didn't feel *right*. An adult might talk themselves out of whatever frightened them; a kid, not so much.

The bed squeaked. Jesus, who should he look like? What did kids watch on television nowadays? He had no flippin' clue.

Too late, anyway. A pair of wide blue eyes peeked over the edge of the mattress. Maybe four or five years old. Her long brown hair was in two braids, and they dangled toward him.

Kansas again. But this time, he hadn't brought the Wicked Witch.

"Hey, Rapunzel," Jake whispered. Soft and easy, so she wouldn't take off screaming for the two other women in the house, whose minds were heavy with sleep. "Did you lose your teddy bear?"

Her braids swayed as she shook her head.

"But there's one right here under the bed. Want to see it?" He vanished the bear into his hammerspace, then made it appear in his left hand.

The girl blinked.

"Just a little magic," he said, and turned the bear's face up. One of the eyes was missing, and stuffing puffed out of the hole. "Ouch. Something under there got him, huh?"

Her eyes went impossibly wider. "Monsters?"

Ah, damn. *Real slick, dickhead.* "Nope," he said quickly. "I used my magic, made them all go away. Teddy here helped; check out his sword." Jake called in a dagger, held the handle against Teddy's arm, waved it around. The giggle told him he'd done something right. "Yeah. We'll just get rid of this, though. He'll make it appear again if he needs to protect you with it. But I'm pretty sure they're gone for good."

He vanished the knife, lifted the bear. Her fingers brushed his when she took it, and something clamped tight in his chest. "So, Rapunzel—do you have a name?"

She nodded but didn't answer, and used her pinkie to poke the stuffing back into the bear's head.

"Ah," he said. Now he just needed some candy, and he'd be a pervy asshole. "That's right. You can't tell me, because I'm a stranger."

The look she gave him told Jake he'd just said something stupid. "I know who you are, silly."

The clamp grew tighter. Facing a demon would be easier than this. Facing Alice right now would have been easier than this. "Is that right?"

"Your picture's *always* on the fireplace. Even when it's Christmas, and I want Princess Mandy to sit there and watch me open presents."

Judging by her cross expression, that was an offense of the highest order. "Sorry."

She shrugged. "Grandma said you'd know my name. That you're in Heaven, and you watch us, and you know me."

His heart squeezed into pulp. "What are you thinking, I don't know you? Close your eyes for one second." She did, and he'd searched through the room and was back before she opened them again. Some things never changed—names written on Sunday school papers, in permanent marker on winter boots and coats. "You're my granddaughter, Lindsey Hawkins."

She shook her head. "*Great* granddaughter."

"That's what I meant—*great* granddaughter." And he was a great grandfather. Jesus. He didn't want to do the math, calculate probable ages, because that meant they'd only been kids, too. Two generations, just out of high school. He sat up. "Now, are you going to tell me why you're awake so late?"

Hugging the bear to her chest, she said, "Just got scared."

"Of what?" When she only looked at him, he guessed nightmare. "Okay. You want me to hang around here until you go back to sleep?"

"Yes," she said, and smiled. "I like your chair. Is it from Heaven, too?"

He glanced over at the armchair. Gold silk; a tall, bowed backrest; intricately carved gildwood; fluted, scrolled legs. Not fit for an angel, he thought, but a goddess. "France, I think."

"Grandma has one like it. Not the same though. Hers is puffier. Are you going to see her?"

His chest, his throat were aching—but his gut was all right. He reached out with his mind again, focused on the elder of the two sleeping women. If she was dreaming, they were good dreams. He didn't feel any fear in her.

And Barbara had given her his last name, even though he hadn't made it back, hadn't given her anything but a promise he wasn't able to keep. He swallowed over the constriction in his throat. "Probably not tonight, Lindsey. But pretty soon."

"I'll tell her you scared away the monsters."

"Okay."

When she lay back against her pillows, he moved to the chair. After vanishing his boots, he propped his feet up on the end of her bed, and recognized the blue patchwork beneath them. "This quilt used to be mine, you know. *My* grandma made it for me."

"I wanted a pink one."

Jake grinned, and settled in to wait. "Sorry."

✺

Alice was in the widows' room when she heard the "flippin' hell" from the next chamber—her bathing chamber. She glanced down at Nefertari, standing at her knee, and sighed. More than five hours had passed since Jake had left her in the Archives; though she could have justified sending Nefertari out in those first minutes, when Alice's blood had been simmering with frustration, using the tarantula now would just be petty.

Still, she kept Nefertari by her side as she entered the bathing chamber. The humidity was still high, but aside from the large porcelain tub, the room was empty.

Jake turned to face her, his expression unreadable, a toothpick motionless in the corner of his mouth. This time, his clothing did not offer a clue; the logo on his T-shirt named a mythological river in the Greek underworld.

How very strange he was.

And his greeting didn't make her alter that assessment. "I've had an interesting day so far. But good. How about you?"

She crossed her arms, wondered if she would ever understand him. "It has been acceptable."

A lie. It had been remarkable. She'd thought of him as she'd bathed, remembered the glowing of his eyes—and an activity that had become a chore in the past seventy-five years had regained excitement, ardor.

But she was uncertain how to respond to that yet.

"Only acceptable? That's too bad. Do you know what it smells like in here?"

Baffled, she drew in a breath. There was, perhaps, a very slight odor. Not soap or shampoo, because she didn't need to use them, and perfume might give her location away when she stalked demons or nosferatu. And it was not *her*, either, because Guardians' bodies had almost no scent.

"No," he said, and removed the toothpick from between his lips. "It's psychic."

Alice frowned and reached out, felt nothing—then abruptly shielded as she realized what he'd sensed.

With enough time, with enough intensity, a location could absorb the psychic energy from the people around it. But it dissipated quickly; within a few days of the Ascension, all of the empty quarters in Caelum had been erased of their former inhabitants.

She used this room not just for bathing, but to settle her nerves—and she'd used it almost every day for over a century. But she couldn't detect what her psyche had left, because it was hers . . . and only hers.

"Yeah," he said, and was in front of her an instant later. His grin was slow and, Alice thought, as cocksure as any she'd ever seen. "Did you imagine it was me?"

How dare he! Outrage bloomed though her, fierce and dark. "You presume too much, Hawkins."

"Probably," he said. "So let's forget I asked."

His mouth covered hers, as quick and unexpected as the first time. Alice gripped his arms to steady herself, kept her lips pressed firmly together.

He made a disappointed sound in his throat and pulled her in harder against him. His mouth moved more roughly now, more insistently, but she did not soften, even at the touch of his tongue.

Abruptly he let her go, turned away. *Be silent,* she told herself. *Dismiss it completely.*

But his muttered "fuck" shattered that intention.

"What did you imagine?" The cold anger in her voice sent Nefertari scurrying away, leaving a trail of urticating hairs. Just as well. If Jake left, too, better that it was because of her, not a blasted spider. "That I would melt at your feet? That I would beg for another kiss?"

"Yeah." He shoved his hands into his pockets. "I hoped."

"You arrogant, insensitive lout! Does playing with me amuse you so much? What are you attempting to gain—to prove? That you can turn the Black Widow into—"

"Jesus Christ! How screwed up is your head?" He faced her again, his expression thunderous. "I wasn't thinking of you at all—only how flippin' much *I* wanted to get my mouth on you!"

Stunned, Alice stared at him. Jake looked away, ran his hand over his head. Regret filled his psychic scent.

"You want to tell me it was stupid, go ahead. Or better yet, tell me something I *don't* know. But, Jesus—why else would a man kiss a woman except that he wanted to?" He glanced at her face, and stilled. "Did someone kiss you to hurt you?"

She couldn't immediately respond. Her mind felt like it was in heavy, heavy water as she reinterpreted everything he'd said and done over the past few days. He'd wanted to kiss her? When had the change come? And why?

But now there was rage gathering below his psychic scent, so she forced her lips to move. "No. I've never been hurt."

Her only complaint was that she'd been treated so very, very gently.

He let out a breath. "Okay. And you *have* been kissed before."

"Of course. And there is procreation." When his brow creased, she explained, "That's another reason for kissing."

"Ah." He rubbed at the bridge of his nose. "You know procreation isn't really about *kissing*, right?"

Her withering stare only seemed to entertain him, and the heaviness in her finally receded into puzzlement. "Why in heaven's name would you want to kiss me?"

He spread his hands. "Hell if I know."

That was reasonable, she supposed. She was the one woman he did not find physically attractive, yet he wanted to kiss her; she found many men physically attractive but did not want to kiss them. Only Jake.

The odd symmetry of it amused her. And a kiss would likely be pleasant.

"Very well, then. Close your eyes. It seems you are more apt to teleport if they are open." And if she did not maintain her composure, then he would not witness it.

His brows drew together, as if he doubted he'd heard correctly. Then he breathed, "Hot damn," and complied.

He seemed truly eager for her kiss. How bizarre he was.

And how very warm. The tension in his shoulders should have softened with such heat, she thought, but it increased when her palms curved over them. She rose up to her toes and brushed her mouth across his. Perhaps all the softness had gone to his lips—so hard a moment before, yet now they yielded easily.

Like petals, as written in so many sex manuals, but that did not seem masculine enough to describe Jake. A valve, perhaps, slowly opening.

Oh, my—this was *so* very pleasant, wasn't it?

His strong hands cupped her face, and she quickly opened her eyes to be certain his were still closed.

They were, thank goodness. He might feel her fingers tremble, but he would not see them. And she did not think *pleasant* should be making her shiver.

Very well, that must stop. She stroked her hands from his shoulders to the back of his neck, and her fingers did not shake so much when they searched out new skin, when they were tempted by the proximity of his shaved hair.

Jake angled his head, and licked deep into her mouth.

She couldn't halt the noise she made, couldn't prevent herself from pressing her body full-length against him and licking him back. And again. Oh, dear God. The need curling through her was not like a rosebud unfurling or an easy release of pressure, but a corkscrew, digging deep, preparing to pull open something that she'd put a stopper in long ago.

What was she supposed to do with *this*? With him? And why now, when intimacy of any kind could only make whatever decision she made so much more painful?

How softheaded she was. How foolish.

She pulled away, feeling absolutely wretched. And what a coward she was to avoid his eyes, but she could not bear to expose herself now.

"Jesus," he said, his breathing ragged; he strode to the bathtub and back. "Truce, okay? For five minutes. We don't talk about this, or why you just chickened out."

Only five? She would give him no choice but to allow more time than that. Stiffly, she nodded. "Very well. Come along, then," she said, and struck out for the stairs. "Did Alejandro return to Caelum with you?"

"Yeah, he did. But—"

"Let us find him, and then Irena. She assures me they are friends, but I warn you that it might prove unpleasant." And it would not make her shiver. "Yet necessary. How is your French? They speak nothing else to each other."

"Alice."

She blanked her expression, looked over her shoulder. "It is for a gift. Now is the best time to procure the measurements for it."

"The best time? Yeah, I bet it is." With a laugh that seemed half-amusement, half-frustration, he shook his head. "All right, goddess. Lead on."

♦

Doing the jitterbug in the middle of a courtyard in eastern Caelum wasn't so bad, Jake thought—but doing it as a victory dance probably bordered on dickery. So he only toe-stepped a little when Alice wasn't looking.

Alejandro was, as usual, quiet. Like Alice, he was in his customary black, from his tall boots to his long-sleeved shirt.

It was almost funerary enough to drag a guy's spirits down. But that would be like focusing on Alice pulling away from him instead of thinking about how she'd almost fried his brain with that kiss, so Jake shook his head and changed into a red Grateful Dead T-shirt.

He probably hadn't needed to bother. Irena emerged from one of the buildings, her auburn hair brilliant in the sun, her blue tattoos patterning her arms like cobalt snakes, and her green eyes flashing. The leather vest and leggings were brown, and her smile reminded Jake of a big, hungry tiger.

Alice signed to Irena, but her body obscured his view of her hands. When she finished, Irena looked over at Jake, sized him up, and nodded.

"*Oui*," she said, then glanced at Alejandro. Unlike her English, her Parisian French held almost no trace of an accent as she continued, "What will best serve him?"

"Two swords of equal length." Alejandro turned to study Jake, and stroked a forefinger down his goatee. "They should have a light weight and long reach. He is a fox, not a bear."

"You would have all of them be foxes. Show me," Irena commanded. "And I will determine for myself."

Alejandro inclined his head. "Jake, your swords. Alice, if you please? Use the weapon of your preference. Defend yourself to begin, and then attack."

Alice's naginata appeared in her hand. Jake called in his swords. Her gliding step returned, and a smile formed on her lips.

"I need to see her blood, Jake," Irena called. "If you hold back, the balance will be off."

"Isn't 'making sure that I don't kill her' holding back?"

Irena snorted. "Do you imagine you could? I see I will have to factor in your inflated ego, and weight your swords more heavily."

Jake knew how fast Alice was, how deadly. He'd seen it in Tunisia. No, this was a delaying tactic, because now that he realized what Alice had meant by a gift, he was thunderstruck.

Customized weapons, forged by Irena and strengthened by her Gift.

She'd created the swords he had now. The Guardians' armory was filled with weapons of all shapes and sizes—but they couldn't compare to a pair made *for* him.

But he would have to thank Alice later. Though Alejandro had put her on the defensive to start, she didn't wait for Jake. Her blade streaked diagonally toward his chest. Jake crossed his swords, caught it, twisted. She pivoted, her skirts flaring. The naginata's metal pole whacked his knee, almost brought him down.

"*Arrêtez!*" Irena strode forward, took his right sword. She ran her palm up the blade; her Gift slipped through the courtyard like a caress. When she returned it, the blade had a curve to it, and one of the edges had been dulled. She performed the same action to the second. "Mind your new cutting edge, and adjust."

"You will create a saber?"

Maybe it was just that he was used to hearing the swordsman speak in Spanish, and he was imagining the nasal disdain in Alejandro's voice—but Jake didn't think so.

"A shashka. He has no subtlety; an *espada ropera* will not do. I work with what they are, Olek, not what you wish them to be. Begin again, Jake."

Grateful to focus on anything but the brittle tension building between the two Guardians, he engaged Alice—and noted the difference immediately. Slower than Alice, he caught her strikes later, closer to his hands. But with the curve, he could apply greater force, pull the blade through in a longer movement, and keep their weapons in contact for a greater amount of time— effectively slowing her, as well.

Until Alice's blade slashed across his cheek. Irena shouted for them to stop, made more adjustments. Then she returned to Alejandro's side, and they continued to trade barbs at almost the same rate he and Alice drew blood. More alterations were made. Alice switched her naginata for a whip that she used to tear his swords from his hands. Eventually, she called in her sword—only one, and she used a smooth, two-handed technique that was as efficient as everything else she did.

More than an hour passed before Irena finally brought them to a halt. She took his swords, carried them to Alejandro. Her voice sharpened. "You will set them now."

Alejandro's jaw clenched, but he obediently clasped the hilt of each sword. His Gift wasn't like most—an outward punch, a burst of power—but seemed to suck energy toward him. The swords didn't catch fire, as Jake had seen other objects do with Alejandro, but heated until the steel glowed dull orange.

Alejandro and Irena didn't look away from each other, and the crackle of antagonism almost drowned out the scent of Alejandro's burning skin, the curl of smoke from his palms.

Jake glanced at Alice. *Friends?* he signed quickly.

She sighed. Strands of dark hair had escaped her braid, some curling softly, others standing up wildly. He wished he'd cut the ribbon at the tail of it, so that the braid would slowly unwind.

I suppose they try to convince themselves, she signed, then dropped her hand to her side when Irena turned. She'd taken the swords from Alejandro, but hadn't waited for the metal to cool; Jake heard the sizzle from her hands, even as her Gift ran a final caress down the length of the blades.

Yeah. All of the older Guardians were mostly just crazy.

When Irena presented the swords to him, they were only warm. "These are temporary. There is not quite enough metal in these, but to introduce any foreign steel would weaken them. I will make two that are heavier, stronger. Until then, these will serve you well."

His thank-you was probably not enough, but when Irena rocked back on her heels, an expectant look in her eyes, he realized that wasn't why she'd done it.

"I promised her a few minutes with Zakril's sword," Alice said.

Jake smiled wryly, brought it out of his hammerspace. Irena's Gift was sliding over it even before he placed the sword in her hands.

"It is so old, I expected it would be crudely formed," Irena murmured. "But the folding is incredible. It accounts for the length. Bronze should not be so strong."

"Yet it has been scarred." Alejandro joined her, and they appraised it together. Without, Jake noted, a trace of their earlier hostility.

"Yes. But not easily. It is time that has done it." Her green eyes were bright as she looked to Alice, then to Jake. "May I restore it?"

Alice lifted her brows. "I have no objection. There is nothing it can tell us now that it cannot if it is polished."

Jake shrugged. "Go for it."

Irena's Gift was a slow, sensuous glide as she pinched the edge of the wide blade between her thumb and forefinger, drew them up to the point, then back down the opposite edge. Alejandro stood utterly still.

Yeah. Just friends, my ass. Jake bit back a laugh and averted his gaze until it landed on something he'd rather see. Alice's mouth softened as she watched. Her lashes fell, and she looked away, her lips in a subtle curve.

Not embarrassed, he thought. *Amused.* She slanted a quick glance at him, caught his gaze on her, and her smile widened. He grinned in response, shook his head.

Friends, he mouthed.

Alice smashed her lips together as if to stop her laughter, but her expression changed to wide-eyed innocence when Irena said, "There. It is finished." She and Alejandro admired it for another minute, and then she passed it to Jake again. "Thank you."

Jake almost made a smart-ass remark, thought of Irena's polar-bear parka, of Alejandro's rapiers, and reconsidered.

Alice waited until Irena had returned to her quarters, until Alejandro had walked out of sight, and they'd flown almost to Odin's Courtyard, before remarking, "You displayed extraordinary control."

"With my swords?" He knew that wasn't it, but he still wanted her to say it.

"Your tongue." She blinked, then hastily said, "Your filter. You lost neither your money nor your life."

"Yeah," he said. "Thank you for the swords."

"Yes, well. Once, the number of Guardians made it impossible for Irena to customize a weapon for each of us. Now, there is no reason she cannot. And Ethan already revealed the surprise we'd planned for the gathering, so there was no reason to wait."

"Nope." No reason to wait at all. "When we land, I'm going to kiss you again."

She listed to the side, then began to pull ahead. "Surely that isn't necessary. A thank-you is enough."

And that wasn't a no. He caught up to her. "It's not about thanks. It's about my tongue, and exercising extraordinary control."

For two beats of her wings, she didn't speak. Her gaze was focused straight ahead, and Jake felt the familiar disappointment begin to harden in his gut.

"I can't," she finally said. "Surely you must see that."

"You know, I really don't." He only saw her set face, the collar that he wanted to unfasten one button at a time, until he'd stripped that dress all the way off.

The Black Widow.

The thought exploded through him, struck like shrapnel into his chest. "Jesus Christ. You can't seriously be staying loyal to Henry Grey?"

Her wings snapped vertical. She drew up, her face pale, her eyes cold. "You cross a line."

"Yeah. I do." And he wished to hell he'd managed to dig up more than her husband's name by now. "Are you?"

"Don't be ridiculous. He's been dead eighty years."

That didn't mean shit. Thousands of people remained true to their spouses decades after they'd died.

But if Alice was one of them, would she have kissed him?

He didn't think so. And if she thought staying loyal to Grey after his death was ridiculous, then any obligation she felt must have died with him. The date was too clear-cut; Jake would bet love had disappeared before that.

Her sigh made him conscious of how long he'd been studying her, working it through. Enough time, at least, for the color to return to her face, for her shoulders to droop.

"Jake." When she met his eyes, there was the same haunted expression he'd seen before. "Surely you must realize that there is scarce hope for me."

"No. I don't realize." He was hoarse, and he used anger to combat the fear gripping his throat. "But if you're doomed anyway, why not grab on and ride?" He felt, for an instant, the yearning in her psychic scent. It pissed him off more. "But hell if you'll stick your head out of your hole, right? If I hadn't butted in, you'd be hiding, avoiding any contact, waiting for the end. And why not? It's not like you're alone. You've got your spiders to worship you."

She laughed, a thin and withering sound. "My, how imaginative you are! They are *spiders*. They feel no more for me than a roach feels for a human who drops a crumb."

"Oh, *now* I see. You die, you're tortured in Hell forever—but they won't care. Won't be hurt if you never come back, won't ever feel betrayed when you give up. And that makes them even safer, doesn't it?"

Alice averted her face. Jesus. Now he was just being an asshole. Was just spitting his own failures and fuckups out on her.

He had to dial the anger back, even if it meant Alice would see that it scared him shitless to imagine she wouldn't escape her bargain.

"Yes," she said quietly. "It does."

Shocked by her admission, Jake didn't immediately follow her when she flew around him, continuing on. Her psychic scent was both stiff and vulnerable—just as when he'd found her in the hypogeum and she'd projected a mule onto her back. The cracks in her armor showing, after being under pressure for too long.

"Hey." Christ, he was always going after her. Maybe one day, he'd figure out why he was incapable of just letting her go. For now though, he'd follow his gut.

Jake slipped under her left wing, rolled onto his back, caught her mouth with his.

She stopped in midair, but didn't pull away. And she didn't deepen the kiss, but her hands cupped the back of his head, held his lips to the softness of hers.

"You are mistaken," she said. And only Alice, he thought, could sound so prim while her mouth was on a man's. "I haven't given up. I am still trying—but I also must be realistic about my chances."

"If realistic means that you're already seeing yourself screaming in Hell, what good is it? Screw realistic."

He felt her lips move into a smile, but a shuddery breath

passed between them. A brave face, he thought—with fear behind it, as if she was imagining, even now, the tortures that waited Below.

But he'd follow her there, too. He knew fear. He was on intimate, naked, well-lubed terms with fear. Nothing Hell had to throw at him would be worse than what he pushed into his own head on a daily basis. He'd go after her and . . .

Holy shit. He opened his eyes, waited for it to sink in, but it didn't sink. It shot through him. *When in the holy flippin' hell had he begun falling . . .*

❧

. . . *ass-over-head for the Black Widow?*

The lights were gone. Feathers brushed his face as Alice staggered to the side, her psychic scent spinning. The stink hit him. The godawful rot stink. And somewhere in the distance, the screams.

Closer, though, were the heartbeats. A dozen, maybe. And crimson eyes, flaring bright.

Oh, shit. In Hell—surrounded by demons. He and Alice were toast.

But being realistic never did anybody any good.

Jake called in his swords.

CHAPTER II

Alice didn't know how much time she'd lost. Seconds? A full minute?

Long enough for Jake's arms to be sleeved in demon blood. Long enough that he'd beheaded at least seven or eight. Long enough that he'd driven the remaining demons to the far end of the enormous room of black marble. The clash of the weapons didn't echo.

Two demons left—hadn't there been three a moment ago?—and Jake had them well in hand, like a centuries-old Guardian against two newly transformed novices. Alice told herself to focus, to search for the third. Her fingers rose to her forehead, as if she could press her brains into service. This couldn't be the effect of teleporting; the disorientation would have faded by now. Nor was it the stench.

Yet a bloated, putrid sickness invaded her limbs, her thoughts—as if her muscles and her mind had been fouled. Had it been her Gift? As soon as they'd teleported into the dark, she'd automatically reached out, but now she couldn't untangle whether this sickness had struck her before or after she'd pulsed it.

She reached out again, was immediately swamped by nausea.

Yes—it must have been her Gift. And she never wanted to know what her psyche had touched that could have produced this effect.

Blast it, Alice! Where is the third demon?

Not behind her. She was near a wall, her back protected. The light from the demon's eyes was not so unsteady now, did not flicker so much. The strange pattern on the floor began to take shape—waist-high rectangular stone blocks, laid out in nine long rows.

Not blocks, she realized. Sarcophagi. Symbols covered the black marble. Each stone lid was shattered.

She forced her gaze to move on, searching the walls, looking now for the source of the light. The quality of it had changed—rather than crimson, it was a faint orange red. Originating from outside? If so, that meant a door had been opened, for when they'd jumped here the room had been completely dark. And that the demon, instead of hiding, had escaped.

That would do just as well. They would likely be gone before he could alert anyone.

She looked at Jake again just as he cut through the final demon's neck. Headless corpses littered the rows of sarcophagi from the center of the room to where he stood now, almost fifty meters distant.

He turned, began walking toward her. Not cockily, though the bodies around him would have excused it, but with wary stealth, as if he was prepared for a demon to leap from behind a sarcophagus at any moment.

His eyes met hers for an instant. "Are you okay?"

Under any other circumstances, when their lives might not depend upon knowing each other's capabilities—and weaknesses—she would have lied. "I am not completely myself. You, however, did the work of five Guardians."

"Yeah." He kicked a head out of his path, turning as he spoke, checking the high ceiling. "Only because they were the equivalent of civilians, I'm guessing. I bet not one of them had picked up their sword in a millennium. Didn't stop 'em from trying to spill my hot Guardian guts, though. You have any clue what this place is?"

"The nephilim's prison."

He nodded. "Yeah. We both had the image of it in our head somewhere, didn't we? We'll have to thank Drifter in a second, when we teleport the hell out of here."

Alice's response was choked by surprise, fear. Around them,

the light whitened, brightened. Jake vanished his swords, streaking down the rows of sarcophagi toward her.

She sprinted to meet him. The light was blinding now, painful. Too slow, she thought. Against Belial, they would be too slow. Still, the command that boomed through the prison was not enough to make her stop.

The threat that followed it was. "I WILL KILL HIM UPON YOUR NEXT STEP!"

Alice skidded to a halt, her ears still ringing with it. Ten feet in front of her, Jake did the same.

But he wouldn't have, not to save himself. He'd have taken the risk, just as she would have if the threat had been against her own life. Unless—

She saw it in Jake's eyes at the same moment. Oh, dear heavens. Somehow, Belial had made Jake hear something different. The fudging of a single word, the pressing of a different meaning, and Jake had stopped to save *her* life.

A fudging, she thought—but that did not mean it had been a bluff. Belial might have killed them both, and why not? If Jake had reached her and they'd disappeared, it would be all the same to the demon. Death or teleportation; either way, they would have been beyond Belial's reach.

She glanced to the side, squinting, and made out the armored cadre of demons surrounding Belial. Saw the number of weapons leveled on them.

Another look at Jake told her he'd just seen the same. She held his gaze, saw the battle waged there between doubt and determination. If he could teleport to her side, touch her, and teleport away, it would be almost instantaneous.

But if his jump went awry, and he teleported *out* of Hell . . . he'd leave her behind.

On the heels of that realization was a second: that the only reason they were alive now was because Belial knew one of them must be able to teleport. With the Gates closed, Belial could use Jake's ability to travel between Hell and Earth . . . or to carry anyone Belial chose between the two realms. Perhaps even to Caelum.

And if Jake stayed to save her, he might be bound by a bargain and forced to serve Belial.

Her fingers tightened by her sides. Her lips formed the word. *Go.*

A streak of light slammed into her, tossed her. Pain shrieked the length of her arm. Alice twisted in the air. She just needed to land on her feet. A hand grabbed her ankle, whipped her around, smashed her facedown on a broken sarcophagus.

Blood filled her mouth, but the choking sounds were coming from behind her. Jake. She turned her head, and hands clamped over the back of her neck, pinned her feet and wrists. Terror ripped through her, then was swamped by rage. Her struggles brought more hands.

Belial issued a command in the demon tongue, and then spoke softly in her ear, his voice a soothing, sweet harmony. "Calm yourself. I promise you will see him. And he will see you."

Her rage slipped into ice when they brought Jake before her. There was more blood on him now, and the slices through his shirt and his jeans told Alice that the wounds were his. They'd used his sword to skewer his forearms together behind his back; a demon had his arm around Jake's throat, and his hand on the sword's hilt.

"Go," she said.

"He will not," Belial replied. "Not without you. As long as you are alive, he will stay. But I imagine the moment he touches you, he will attempt to take you. Your Guardians have done that very thing before: appeared, and taken away that which belonged in Hell. Fortunately, we have discovered a way to prevent it."

Belial moved in front of her, blinding, burning her eyes. "I cannot see him when you are between us, demon. Do you break your promises so easily?"

"I have broken nothing. It is your eyes, untouched by Glory, which are incapable of withstanding the illumination."

So he would pass blame, rather than admit to a mistake or make an adjustment. Lucifer, she was certain, would have said yes without hesitation.

Alice didn't know which would have chilled her more.

But neither could have chilled her as much as the sword that appeared in Belial's hand. Jake held its twin in his cache, but Zakril's could not flare to life as Michael's did, couldn't burn with white-hot flame.

Belial moved around to the other side of her. Alice saw Jake squinting against the light, then begin to furiously fight against the demon, against the blade through his forearms. Flesh and bone tore and snapped, and one of his hands was free.

Another demon joined the first, forced Jake to his knees. Then onto his stomach when he didn't stop resisting.

"I will not kill her," Belial said. "I will only make certain she stays in this realm."

There was a tug at the back of her dress, and a remark of surprise in the demon tongue. Then a line of heat ran down her spine as Belial sliced her dress open. Demon hands pulled the silk away.

Jake made an incoherent noise, a howl of fury that was cut off as a demon forced his head back, took his throat in a crushing grip.

She couldn't breathe. Couldn't get the breath to scream as the burning tip of Michael's sword sliced into her shoulder. Another cut, deep, beneath it. A stroke up, and around. A piercing stab, then a second above.

Belial stopped. "It is done. The symbols prevent her from being teleported out of this realm, Guardian. And if you leave, you will not be able to anchor to her and find her again." He stepped back; the hands holding Alice didn't let her go. "And now you will stand, teleporter, as there is something I require from you, as well."

Jake didn't move, and beneath the pain in her shoulder, the horror of what had been done, rose a fierce pride. *Yes,* she thought. *Make him force you, make him threaten. But never simply obey.*

"Stand," Belial repeated, "or I will sever her legs in two."

❧

Jake was on his feet before Belial had completed his threat. His arm screamed at the movement, but he focused past the agony.

Alice's gaze held his, her irises glowing brightly. Either she was losing it, or she was looking forward to handing out some serious pain to Belial's demons. Probably the second. And God knew, Jake was going to be right there with her. The symbols Belial had carved into her shoulder weren't bleeding—the sword had cauterized the wounds. But they weren't healing normally. The angry red should have been fading.

It all could have been worse, though. Lucifer would have just cut off her legs, and *then* threatened her arms. With Belial, they had some wiggle room. He would hurt them, but apparently not just for shits and giggles. Either Belial didn't enjoy causing pain—good—or, he just liked to hear himself talk and for others to heed him—not always so good.

He was talking now, and Jake was pretty certain it was leading up to the not so good. If the demon wasn't lying, this prison was at the edge of Lucifer's territory. Belial's army had moved in, had met little resistance, but their campaign hadn't finished. A small tactical strike against another holding remained, and Belial didn't want to delay it while escorting two Guardians back to his territory.

Which meant, Jake realized, that he and Alice were going to be locked up in here, with the bulk of Belial's army surrounding the prison while the demon led the final attack.

That wasn't so bad. But where was the catch—what did Belial require from him? A promise to stay? Belial might be arrogant enough to lock them in here, counting on Jake not to leave Alice in danger, but the demon wasn't stupid. All Jake had to do was get Alice under some kind of protection, teleport out and find Michael, then head back to the prison. They wouldn't need to anchor to Alice; they'd both already been here. And if he and Michael had to fight a few demons on the way back in—or an army of them—so be it.

Yeah. Jake would break a promise in a second. So there had to be a catch.

With luck, it wouldn't be a bargain.

"I know that Guardians cannot be trusted," Belial said. Jake had given up trying to *see* him. There was too much light, too many wings, and nothing to get his head around. Belial's demons looked like any other, though—red and scaly. "So I will leave twelve of my sentinels to see that you stay. If you teleport, they will kill the female."

So Jake wouldn't be taking off to get Michael. But he and Alice would be missed in Caelum, eventually—and as long as Jake didn't completely block his mind, Michael could still find him.

Of course, Belial wasn't *that* stupid, either. "The shielding spell will be placed around the prison, and keyed to my blood. No one will come to save you; and even if you teleport away, you will not be able to reenter this building."

Shit. He saw Alice's lips tighten. Yeah, Belial might not be chopping their legs off, but he was pretty damn good at crushing every hope they had. Probably because leaving his demons here and letting Alice and Jake figure it out for themselves wasn't as much fun as watching their reactions when he spelled it out.

"Six will guard the prison doors and the symbols that cast the shielding spell," Belial continued. "The others I will position around the room, near the ceiling so that if you lose your sense and decide to attack, you will not be able to reach them."

Wouldn't be able to reach them . . . ? Oh, Jesus Christ in Heaven. His wings.

Belial intended to cut off his wings.

Icy rage spiked through Alice's psychic scent. "Take mine, demon. You've already violated me. You might as well finish the job and take mine instead."

"If you flew toward the sentinels, they would see you coming; they would not see this one if he teleports to their side. But even if he manages to slay one sentinel, I will not leave him able to defend himself in the air."

Bullshit. "Then take my arms," Jake said. One was already half-gone, anyway. A clean cut might actually hurt less than whatever was going on there now as it healed.

Belial didn't answer him, but gave an order to the demons behind Jake. Yeah. Belial could justify it however he wanted, but this wasn't about defense, because taking his arms would be more effective than taking his wings.

But his wings were a symbol—and this was an attempt to demoralize them.

Not that he would allow it, Jake determined. The demons behind him let go of the sword through his forearm. Jake vanished it. No use trying to fight them. He knelt in front of Alice instead. His blood dripped onto her back when he flicked the sides of her dress closed, covering her.

It was something, he thought. One very small thing he could do for her.

"Now offer them willingly, Guardian, or I shall take *her* arms."

He gritted his teeth, then formed his wings, felt their comfortable burden. Alice made a soft sound, and her fingers flattened on the cracked stone lid. Jake shoved at the demon's hand holding her wrist. At a word from Belial, it was released.

"One thing's for sure," Jake said, and clasped his palm to hers, lacing their fingers. "His definition of 'willingly' is completely fucked up."

"I do prefer Michael's version of—" She clamped her lips together as his wings went numb, the weight on his back lightened. There were two thumps on the floor behind him, like overstuffed pillows whacked with a stick.

Pain ripped down the stumps of the wingframe. Sucking in a hard breath, Jake vanished what was left. The pain disappeared.

That had been faster than he'd expected—but then, he'd thought Belial would do it, and had been waiting for the demon to move. The strike had come from behind him, instead.

Easier that way, but he didn't exactly feel grateful.

They took away the fallen feathers, muscle, and bone. Of course they did. His wings could be reattached and heal in less than an hour—but now they would have to completely regrow. It might take two or three weeks. And they could only heal when he was wearing them, which meant forming the bleeding stumps again. That was going to really fucking hurt.

Once they grew to full size, he could shift them as small or as large as he liked. Until then, they were useless.

Jesus, his throat was tight. *Just a symbol,* he reminded himself. Feathers didn't make a Guardian. And so he wouldn't let it matter.

Alice's hand smoothed over his head. They'd finally let her go, Jake realized. And the demons were retreating now—except for the twelve sentinels. Their armor was much lighter than the other demons', which told Jake it wasn't often they were a line of defense or used for face-to-face combat. No, these sentinels would be the stealth: the ones that snuck up behind you and pulled your heart out of your back before you turned around.

"Demon!" Alice called out. Jake looked up; her striking face was washed in the painfully bright light, but her eyes were open against it. "There is a prophecy foretelling your rise to power in Hell. But if thwarting that prophecy means that I have to keep Michael's heart safe from you and all of your demons for the rest of my days, I will do it."

"Are you so certain it is not the Guardians who need to be kept safe from Michael's heart?" Belial's voice was faintly mocking. "For we are all made in the image of our fathers—and you were not safe from me."

Alice's fingers tightened, but she had no other reaction. She stared ahead until the light faded, and the silence that marked the shielding spell settled around the room.

"He might have been lying." Jake's rough whisper was like a yell in the darkness. Did the sentinels know any human languages? Did it matter?

"I know." She ran her fingers up over his hair, and for a moment, the soft rasp covered the sound of twelve demon heart-beats. "Well, then," she added, and though he couldn't see it, he knew her back had straightened. "Shall we get to work?"

❦

Over the next two days, Jake wasn't surprised that they didn't discuss Belial's parting remark about Michael. But they didn't talk about anything else that had transpired, or make plans for escape. Only about the site. But every time Jake tried to steer the sparse conversation in another direction, Alice mentioned how few batteries they had to power her lanterns, and urged him to hurry, to commit the prison's layout to memory.

And even with their Guardian speed, it was one bitch of a project. One hundred and sixteen sarcophagi, each patterned by different symbols. More symbols covered the walls, the ceiling, the floor.

They could have been processing any site on Earth—except that only the demons, Alice, and Jake showed up on their cameras. As in Caelum, apparently nothing in Hell could be photographed. Jake's sketches were shit, at best—and because they couldn't read any of the symbols, the only thing they learned was that one sarcophagus was missing from the pattern.

The sentinels didn't move, didn't breathe, didn't speak. They stood—or perched, if they were one of the six at the corners and middle of the ceiling—and watched.

Jake was sitting with his back against one sarcophagus, his feet stretched out toward another, and thinking about shooting one of the sentinels, when the lantern began fading. No big deal. They had laptops, cell phones. If they *had* to, they could shine their eyes like the demons did.

But Alice started to fret, flitting her hands. She came to sit next to him on the floor, muttering "oh, dear" like it was a one-hit wonder.

Yeah, he thought. Wasn't that just peachy? He went crazy for a woman, and she just went crazy.

He drew in a breath, and frowned. Alice had spent most of her time at the other end of the room, and since they weren't talking, he hadn't been breathing much. With all the rot around them, he didn't think he'd missed anything worth smelling.

Now, though, he could detect the faint, sickly sweet odor of infected flesh.

"Alice," he said quietly. "Is your shoulder healing?"

"Nooooo!" With a wail, she threw herself over his lap. When she began sobbing into her hands, he got it.

She was setting the demons up. Giving them this impression of a nervous, sickly wreck of a woman. Why, he had no idea—but she was working up to something.

And she was *good* at it. If he hadn't known her, he'd have been convinced.

He also thought that her parents had probably gone gray before Alice was out of her teens. Performances like this didn't just pop out of the ether.

But that infected odor was real, and his concern was genuine when he touched her braid. She wailed louder, and he had to bury his face against her hair. Oh, shit. He was going to crack up, and give her away.

She pinched the inside of his leg, hard. The sharp pain sobered him enough that when she lifted her tearstained face, he managed to keep his straight.

"I don't want to be in the dark," she said on a shuddering breath. "It frightens me so. I will go mad without light."

Yeah, right. But he let his concern ride up, so that it was all that showed in his expression. Those poker games were finally paying off. "Shh. It will be okay."

"We must escape from here." She began weeping again, laying her cheek on his shoulder. "But there is no way, is there? He said that I couldn't be teleported out of this realm, and I suppose that means I could be teleported *within* it—but we daren't even try with the spell up."

"No." Because if they were wrong, and she couldn't be teleported at all, Jake would leave her behind.

"But they will not lower the spell or let in light until he returns," she sobbed. "I just know it. We need to escape before that, or I am bound to go insane."

She gave his hand a squeeze on "bound," but he'd already picked up on her message. Hell, he'd been thinking about it for two days.

Belial could have forced him into an agreement simply by using Alice's life as the other half of the bargain. Something as easy as, *For as long as you serve me, I will spare her life.* But a bargain like that had a few loopholes—if anything happened to Alice, through Belial or not, Jake wouldn't be bound any longer.

Their time locked up here worked in Belial's favor. It gave the demon a chance to develop and word an ironclad bargain.

Jake would do it, to save her life—and they'd both be screwed.

"We need to get rid of the spell," he said quietly, and stroked the backs of his fingers down her wet cheek. "But I can't imagine how we'd get to the symbols, and survive. Not with all of these sentinels. Can you?"

"No, novice." Her denial was soft and sad, and his heart began pounding. "I cannot. And once we got out, we'd still have to make it past the army. Can you imagine a way to do that?"

He shook his head, and signaled he was lying in the same way she'd used. "No, widow. I can't."

"Then I suppose I must resign myself to the dark." She pulled back, and her eyes, bright and shining, met his. "Perhaps I shall occupy myself by weaving. It will settle my poor nerves."

But she didn't begin right away. First, she knelt in front of the lantern, and wailed again when it died.

❧

If Alice hadn't pretended that the darkness frightened her, Jake was pretty sure that twelve pairs of eyes would be lighting the room. Instead, the demons must have been tracking their movements by their heartbeats, the sound of their steps.

He'd bet anything that the assholes were enjoying her rapid, shallow breaths and the fear that occasionally leaked through her psychic scent. Jake mostly just enjoyed that that they were falling for it.

And, guessing that darkness was exactly what she'd wanted, Jake didn't pull anything out of his hammerspace to brighten it. He sat, formed his wing stumps, and gritted his teeth through the healing.

About fifteen hours after the lantern went out, the cackling started. Even knowing that it was an act, it lifted the hairs on his arms. And it apparently creeped out the demons, too. A few seconds after it ended, the sentinels flared their eyes. In the red glow, he saw Alice crouching on a sarcophagus, muttering into her gloved hands. Her waist-length hair was unbound. She cut a hank off and began to play with it: measuring it between her fingers, curling it into loops, then finally tying the ends together until she had a single, long strand.

The light disappeared, then blinked on when she began to run, cackling again. She passed Jake, a rush of wind in her wake, then leapt high into the air. Her fingers touched the ceiling, leaving a gossamer strand dangling almost to the floor. She landed lightly, sat, and cut off more hair.

They left her in darkness after that, and Jake lost count of the times the cackling and running were followed by that eerie muttering. He stayed where he was, sure that after what he'd seen, it wasn't a good idea to be walking around.

She'd been harvesting the spider silk for ten years. How much had gone into her dresses, and how much was stored in her hammerspace?

Judging by how long it was taking her, a hell of a lot.

By the time she began to skitter around the floor on her hands and knees, his wings were about as big as a cherub's. They probably looked pretty flippin' stupid—but at least they didn't hurt anymore.

He vanished them when she approached his row of sarcophagi. His legs were in the way. Jake bent his knees, expecting her to crawl by.

She climbed into his lap, cradled the back of his head in her hands, and kissed the astonishment from his mouth.

Her teeth nibbled lightly at his bottom lip, and Jake knew that he was missing something, knew that there was a message in all of this somewhere. But, hot damn, she couldn't really expect him to think? Not when she tugged his head closer so that she could tap her tongue against his teeth, then lick, and not when her thumbs were stroking that same rhythm behind his ears. Tap, lick, slow, lick, a slight hesitation, tap, lick, on and on, and the tease of it was going to drive him crazy.

It was going to . . . It was . . . *It was his name*. Morse code. J, A, K, E, over and over.

His hands were on her hips, and he squeezed her name back. He felt her open smile against his mouth, her silent laugh.

God. He'd thought he was falling for her? He'd been wrong. That had been nothing compared to the insane exhilaration he felt now. Nothing like his amazement that he'd been lucky enough to cross paths with this strange, brilliant woman.

And in a few seconds, he'd talk with her. But now, he let the moment roll over him, leaning in and taking a taste of her laugh. It faded from her lips, and she was kissing him back. No message there. Just the sweet clench of her fingers, the heat of her mouth.

It couldn't last, though. It wasn't the time, and definitely wasn't the place. And the slight perspiration on her skin wasn't from their kiss.

She was sick.

Something twisted inside his chest, painful and hard. The infected smell was almost gone, but the sword had left something in her. It had to be the sword—a Guardian's wounds always healed cleanly, and Guardians never became ill. But Michael's sword wasn't like any other weapon; when he'd impaled the dragon's heart with it, the metal had taken some of the dragon's power.

Jake had once heard about a Guardian who, before his transformation, had been cut by the sword, tainting his blood. The transformation hadn't completely taken hold, so he hadn't had all of a Guardian's abilities. Eventually he'd Fallen or Ascended—Jake couldn't remember. But he hadn't remained in Caelum.

And there was a vampire living in San Francisco who'd been tainted the same way—but instead of being weakened after his transformation, he was the strongest of his kind. Able to walk in sunlight and resist the daysleep. But the taint had also created in him one of the few anchors to Chaos—the dragon's realm.

What would it do to a Guardian who'd already been transformed?

Maybe nothing, he prayed. Maybe it just took longer to heal, for her body to fight it off.

He drew back, wished that he could see Alice's face. He repeated her name, then again, changing it so that the press of his thumbs was a dot, his fingers on the back of her hips was a dash, and a squeeze of both signaled a break between letters—streamlining the code so that it wasn't so dependent on intervals of time. A waste of superspeed, in his opinion.

Alice picked up on it fast, made hers a subtle right-and-left pressure behind his ears, and fit her lips to his again.

If we only sit quietly together, she explained, *they might suspect we are communicating.*

But not if we are making out?

Her laugh was a soft burst of air into his mouth. *Yes. Exactly.*

Okay, but listen—with you sitting so close to certain parts of my anatomy, I might not be able to prevent something from happening. Just so you know.

How unfortunate it is when one's body is so easily aroused.

Yeah. And they needed to stop talking about it, or his cock was going to demonstrate exactly how easy it was.

I am pleased that you agree. Because—if something should happen—I might not be able to prevent myself from rubbing against it.

Hot damn. But though his body was screaming at him to drag her forward over his happy-to-demonstrate dick, Jake checked himself.

Not the time. Not the place.

He ran his palms up to her waist before heading back to her hips. *How are you feeling, goddess?*

I can fight. I can fly.

Which told him that doing both was going to hurt her, but she'd push through it. *Okay,* he said, and adjusted his plan so that it wouldn't burden her as much. It'd be a little more humiliating for him, but he was used to that. *So how are we getting out of here?*

CHAPTER 12

By the time Alice crawled off Jake's lap, cackling again, she'd decided that he was quite possibly mad.

Surely that was the only explanation for the insanity that was his plan to get them past Belial's army. But for the moment, she would not think of it. She would lie perfectly still . . . and hope that this dizzying arousal subsided quickly.

She ought to have found another way to communicate with him. But she hadn't, and now she thought that it was fortunate that they'd decided to wait before their attack.

She fisted her hands to keep them at her sides, and listened to the pounding of her heart—and to Jake's. Something *had* happened, she was certain of it. At this moment, he was likely no more comfortable than she was. Dear heavens, it was almost like Enthrallment: her senses hyperaware, so that even the quiet and the dark rushed in upon her like the ocean. The ache in her shoulder was all-encompassing, as was the heaviness in her breasts, the tight heat below her womb.

She'd known frustration before. Yet that had had a different flavor, a yearning for something she didn't possess but knew existed, like spying a desperately wanted novel on a shelf too high to reach.

But this was worse. This was as if she'd been given leave to thumb through a few pages and had discovered it was everything that she'd hoped for—but was unable to finish the story.

And this was what her aunties had spoken of when Alice had been a young woman. It was what her mother had hinted passion should be—it was what had helped form Alice's fevered and romantic imaginings when she'd met Henry. But those dreams had been hotter than the marriage bed. There had been the warmth of love, but it hadn't been enough to thaw solicitous restraint and propriety. And there had been little help from Henry's family; he might have called her his delicate, exotic flower, but on English soil, she'd been a weed.

And Teqon's lies had been the manure that had let it all grow wildly out of control.

Oh, my. Those rarely visited memories were a cold bath—but only to her body. And Alice hadn't *needed* more anger and resentment to fuel her, but now that she'd sparked it, she would put it to good use against the sentinels.

With a vial of hellhound venom in her hand, she crawled toward the doors, where the six sentinels guarded the symbols. There were two spears to poison, but she would delay coating the spearheads until the last moment. Trace amounts of venom would slow the demons if it entered their bloodstream—or, in great enough quantities, paralyze them—but it had a distinctive scent, like a ripened peach.

Jake's heartbeat had returned to a normal pace. The wait before a battle was often the most harrowing part of it, but she couldn't sense any fear in him. She hoped he was reviewing the route he had to take through the sarcophagi—she'd made him repeat it until amusement had curved his lips and exasperation had hardened his fingers. He'd subjected her to a deep, toe-curling kiss that had ended only after she'd agreed to stop plaguing him, and to trust that he'd memorized it.

She did. But she still feared for him.

If he was moving at speed, one of the razor threads she'd stretched across the room could shear off a limb, or his head. The other webs she'd woven were sticky with adhesive as powerful as instant glue. Though they were not as dangerous as the razor threads, anyone running—or flying—headlong into them would become tangled in silk that was stronger than steel.

Jake sighed, signaling that there were two minutes left. Alice shifted into a demon form, mimicking one of the sentinels as closely as she could. The demons had been in the dark as long as Alice and Jake had—even a half second of confusion might make a difference.

And Jake's insane plan depended upon her using this form.

The more she considered it, however, the more she found that she could not argue with his reasoning. They could defeat twelve demons in combat. But against an army of unknown size and in unknown terrain, they only stood a chance by creating disorientation or fear—and with a head start.

And then sending beaucoup prayers to Heaven, Thor, and Superman.

Alice smiled into the dark. He'd said that with his hands, yet she could easily imagine the words in his deep voice, the laughter beneath. It was a sound she'd missed over the past few days.

And it wasn't through prayer that she'd hear it again.

She stood, familiarizing herself with the light armor she'd created, her movement and reach. The sickness was weighing her down, but he'd made her agree that they'd fight in tandem—that she'd avoid, if she could, a one-on-one confrontation.

Hopefully, Belial had ordered the sentinels not to kill them—only to subdue. If so, Jake and she would have a slight advantage: they'd slay without hesitation.

A half second here, a slight advantage there; they *had* to add up to enough. To consider any other outcome was impossible.

Perhaps that was why she felt utterly calm when she cackled the final time and uncapped the vial of venom. Jake would call in his weapon three seconds after her laughter began, coat his with venom as well. There was no stopping now.

Before one second passed, Alice had liberally doused the spear tips and poisoned the blade of her naginata with the remaining venom. She dropped to the ground. Her cackle hurt her own ears. Was it loud enough to cover the sound of her dagger slicing through the silk anchoring the spears?

It wouldn't matter. The threads she'd stretched like a bowstring and notched behind the spears shot forward. She heard the wet thunks, the shouts.

Crimson light flooded the prison. Her aim had been true. Two down—paralyzed.

Jake's crossbow bolts hit two more by the doors. A shriek sliced through the air above. Half of a leathery wing sailed in a flat spin over Alice's head, spraying blood.

Then Jake was at her back, covering her. His guns fired as she sprinted forward. Another screech tore from the ceiling, followed by the thump of a falling limb. A sentinel raced in from the side and hit a trip wire. A sticky web scooped him up, a fish wiggling in a net.

No, she thought. Her focus narrowed, the world contracting into sharp flashes of shape and sound. *Flies. Flies in my parlor.*

She lashed out with her Gift an instant before reaching the first sentinel. It was useless here, with no spiders, but the demons would feel the thrust of it—and they wouldn't know that nothing would come of it.

The demon hesitated, and one of Jake's bullets exploded through its left eye. Alice struck from that side. Her polished blade was a dance of reflected crimson light in her hands. It countered her weapon once, twice.

Jake darted by. His sword swept from the demon's left side to the opposite underarm—through the heart. Blood pulsed out from beneath his breastplate.

Jake's gaze narrowed over her shoulder. Alice whirled, calling in her whip. The crack of it was as loud as a gunshot. The razor threads at the end wrapped around the sentinel's neck.

Alice yanked. The demon was still running, still raising its sword when its head slid off.

She heard Jake's grunt of pain—saw the demon in the air with a crossbow. Too far away for her whip. She aimed at a silk thread stretched taut across the ceiling instead. It snapped like a cable, cutting anchoring threads, ripping through webs. Freed from its moorings, a razor web settled over the demon's horns like a mantilla. He lost his talons on both hands trying to tear it off, and his screech joined the ring of Jake's swords. Alice ran to assist him as he fought the last sentinel by the door.

She counted as she ran. One demon perched in the far corner of the ceiling, hemmed in by layers of webbing—apparently he hadn't realized he could cut through them yet. Three were caught in bloody bags of silk. There was the one that Jake had killed by slicing through its heart. Another had no head; and yet another, no fingers. Venom-coated bolts and spears had taken down four others. They were paralyzed, but for how long?

It only had to be long *enough*.

Jake turned, and she saw the bloodied crossbow bolt jutting from his sternum. The demon slashed with his sword; Jake stumbled back. Alice dove in, caught the sentinel through the knees. With a single, heavy stroke, Jake sliced through the demon's neck.

The doors, he signed, and ripped the bolt from his chest, tossing it aside. Her talons found the groove in the black marble, and she pulled. Jake cleared Belial's blood from the symbols, breaking the spell.

Oh, dear God. The pressure—the number of psyches outside—was almost deafening. So many voices. Screams. Bloated rot rolled over her Gift like a putrid corpse.

Jake stood at her back, watching the remaining demons. Alice braced her taloned, scaled foot against the left door, heaved with her full strength, and felt the stone beneath her hands slowly begin to give. Rancid, heated air rushed in.

With the spell gone, they could return to the prison—if they had to. But she would rather try to escape than wait, endlessly. Outside, there was a chance; trapped inside, there was none.

"The sword," she whispered, and held out her hand.

Jake placed Zakril's sword into her palm, and shifted. His clothes disappeared.

Alice looked at the shape he'd taken—a chubby, blond toddler with tiny feathered wings and a bleeding hole in his little chest—and decided that maybe praying *would* help. Heaven knew, they were going to need something like a miracle.

They might have had more of a chance shape-shifting to resemble Thor and Superman.

But there was no time to doubt. She fisted her talons in his thick golden curls, and lifted. Jake closed his eyes; his small body swayed. Forming a pair of demon's wings, Alice surged outside.

❧

Alice had known it would be horrible. It was, after all, Hell.

But even prepared for the stink and the heat, the first images almost overwhelmed her with dismay.

They were not outside, with the possibility of escape by air, but in a cave. The roof of the cavern seemed to be moving, and the pale light glittered as if dark crystals were trapped within the black stone. The floor sloped downward away from the prison, and the shadows told Alice that the source of light originated from across its enormous length. Between the prison and the cavern entrance, thousands of demons milled about—*Dear God, were there so many of them?*—with barely room between their shoulders.

She took it all in on her first step. The ground was soft, slimy. Her feet sank into it. She didn't glance down. Three demons approached, surprise in their psychic scents—and, she thought, horror as they stared at Jake's small body. Horror . . . not out of fear, but *concern*.

As if they were appalled to see a winged child injured.

Until she raised Zakril's sword. As one, they cried out and froze. Jake opened his small eyes. They glowed crimson, and his mouth drew back in a grimace full of fangs and blood. The shriek from his tiny body was an unholy sound of rage and terror.

The demons fell over themselves stumbling back.

Holding back her own scream, Alice wrapped her arm around his chest and launched into the air. From inside the prison, one of the sentinels called out.

Oh, dear God, dear God. She or Jake should have reset the spell with their own blood, preventing the sentinels from warning the others. Far too late now. She rose toward the ceiling, then shot toward the cavern entrance.

Shouts of awe and disbelief rolled across the floor on a crescendoing wave. Thousands of red eyes turned upward. Her heart and wings pounded furiously. They hadn't realized yet. The demons near the prison knew they were Guardians, but the rest had not yet heard.

A few more seconds, she prayed. Just a few.

But beneath the voices she heard the flap of leathery wings, like a colony of startled bats. Saw demons rising into the air, mobilizing.

"I need a ninety-degree, Alice, or you're going to get fried," Jake said, and it was a small voice that she could barely hear over the rush of wings. She glanced down, saw the missile launcher that he held horizontally in his chubby hands. The long tube was supposed to go over his shoulder, and the exhaust would blow out of the back. Impossible when she was behind him.

She rolled to the side, holding Jake out in front of her and facing the wall of the cave. When the launcher aimed down, Jake pulled the trigger. The backblast of fiery gas shot up toward the roof, illuminating it for a brief, horrifying moment.

So many legs. So many eyes.

Terror dug icy spikes into Alice's heart. *This wasn't a cave.* And there was a reason why none of the demons had been in the air before they'd come out of the prison.

She straightened out just as the explosion rocked the ground ahead of them. Demons scattered away from the plume of smoke and fire. She glanced behind them. Hundreds more were coming. Jake vanished the launcher, pulled in another.

She reached out with her Gift, and felt the response. The spiders were corrupted and fetid—but they were *hers*.

Swallowing the bile that rose in her throat, she razed them with her Gift like a scythe. They began to drop.

"Alice!" Jake's voice was deeper, his weight heavier. "Give me a ninety, now!"

"No." Her voice was thick with sickness, but she pushed her Gift harder. "Aim for the ceiling."

"What!"

"It's not a cave." She rolled, let him see.

It was worse, now that the spiders were moving. They had too many legs, their round bodies were misshapen, bulging, as if they'd gorged themselves beyond capacity. Each one could have filled her quarters with its size, and the roof of the cavern was covered in them.

Jake sucked in a breath. "Oh, Jesus Christ, please strike me blind!"

He flipped the launcher around and fired.

The missile ripped through the abdomen of one of the falling spiders. Alice dove to the side, barely avoiding its seeking claws. Below them, around them, the tenor of the demons' cries changed from anger to terror.

Faster, she urged the spiders, and began climbing higher. She dodged more claws, slipped between the trailing silk that sparkled with orange, like a flame trapped inside a diamond thread. *Be hungry.*

The missile exploded above. Charred exoskeleton rained down, more that was wet and decaying. Alice fought not to gag, and spun to evade another spider. Through the burning and the smoke, she saw the pocket of deep red.

The sky.

The suffocating bloat around her lungs eased. Jake let out a whoop as they shot through the hole in the carapace, but the sound faded into disbelief when he realized what they'd been inside.

"Holy shit. Those were flippin' *babies*."

"Yes." Alice didn't look at the giant corpse they flew over. "They'll be coming out soon."

"The babies or the demons?"

"Both," she said, and finally reached the head of the mother. The twisted, hairy legs stretched more than a kilometer in front of them. There was desert here, red sand studded with sharp boulders. Behind them, at a distance too far to calculate, a tower speared into the crimson sky. Lucifer's tower, she thought, remembering the descriptions she'd heard. His cities and the frozen field surrounded it. Somewhere, Belial had his own—smaller— towers, his own cities. She hovered, uncertain. "Where do we go?"

"Alice." Jake's voice was grim, and she looked in the direction he pointed. Not on the ground, but into the air. Alice's stomach fell as she made out the dark shapes. A company of demons flew in precise formation. The one at the front radiated a brilliant light. "Belial."

A psychic probe pierced her shields. Alice dropped several feet, gasping at the pain in her head.

Her arms tightened around Jake's bare chest. He was his full height now, but she knew he'd shift into a smaller size again if she had to fly quickly.

"He's seen us," she said. "Shall we run?"

"We wouldn't get far." Jake's hand clenched over hers. The pressure of his fingers felt oddly flattened by the scales that were her skin, as if a thin sheet of glass lay between them. "Alice—do you think Belial meant that you can't jump out of the realm, or that you can't jump at all?"

Did they dare risk teleporting? Jake was putting the decision in her hands. Her heart pounded. She stared at the quickly approaching light.

"Surely . . ." Panic lifted through her chest, almost flew away with the words. She battled it, and finished, "Surely he meant the realm."

"Okay. Think of Hell, then. Think of Hell . . . just think of anywhere in Hell but here." He tugged her left arm up, so that she

supported him with her right, and he pressed his lips to the soft
scales of her inner wrist. "And listen—don't freak out, but I'm
going to bind you to me as close as I possibly can."

"How—"

Shock stole her breath as his teeth—*his fangs*—sank into her
wrist. Like a vampire's.

But he didn't drink; his Gift tore through her, into her, as if her
veins were strings that he knotted together—and used to drag
her along behind him.

🔥

How very odd. Jake was shouting her name, others were screaming, and she was falling—

Oh, dear God.

Alice snapped her wings open, and it was the sharp slap of demon wings instead of her softer feathers. Jake's hand was
wrapped around her wrist, and he dangled beneath her . . . over a
river of bubbling lava.

The heat thickened the air, made it waver and dance, distort-
ing her vision as if she were peering through old glass. And when
she saw, she wanted to take it back, to forget.

The humans were being tortured—with contraptions, at the end
of demons' blades, with fire. All of them, screaming in anguish,
for forgiveness, for it to stop. There was rot here, the acrid stench
of burning blood, burning flesh—and a deep psychic stain, evil
and dark and agonizing, worse than anything her physical senses
took in. She couldn't block it out.

"Alice."

She tore her gaze from them, looked down at Jake. Not just the
air wavering—the moisture in her eyes, too. But even the tears
were heating, steaming from her cheeks.

"Try again," he said, and his voice was hoarse. "Think of anywhere in Hell *except* for the Pit."

Nodding, she closed her eyes. Not the Pit. That was where the
murderers went, the humans with black marks on their souls.
This was not where she would—

🔥

Her hands and knees burned with cold. No sound met her ears,
but inside her head they were screaming, screaming.

She was afraid to open her eyes. Her palms lifted to her ears but she stopped before covering them, fearing that she'd trap the screaming inside. The tears on her cheeks were ice now, and she felt one crack and fall, but though she was kneeling on the lumpy, frozen ground she didn't hear it shatter when it landed.

She knew the lumps were faces. She knew their eyes were open, that they could see her. She knew that in the Chaos realm, their bodies dangled from a ceiling of ice, and dragons devoured them.

She knew they were all humans and demons who hadn't fulfilled their bargains.

Then there was warmth against her cheek, a thumb that brushed away a trail of ice. She opened her eyes, but didn't look down. She looked into Jake's face instead, saw his eyes, the bleakness there.

He'd seen. And the tight mask of his face told her it was worse than she'd imagined.

His lips moved. She couldn't hear him, but she knew what he was saying. *Anywhere in Hell but here.*

Somewhere no one was being tortured, no one was screaming. Death was preferable to this.

❧

She felt Jake's teeth slide out of her wrist. They were falling, and somehow her wings were gone, so she formed them again. Feathers, this time, spreading wide.

Jake's weight was a painful strain on her arm, across her back—and it was an effort to carry him.

Alice sucked in a sharp breath. How could that be? A Guardian could lift his weight a hundred times over.

The ache in her shoulder flared bright as she pulled Jake up and wrapped both arms around his chest to hold him. She looked at the ground far below, the glistening red wet of it, thinking of the symbols carved into her skin, the sword used to make them, and she did not immediately comprehend what she was seeing.

But it was the death she had wanted.

Demons—and what must have been a battlefield. They lay thick on the sand, four and five deep, as if they'd been fighting on top the bodies of their brethren.

No, she realized. They'd fallen out of the sky. Now they all were piled together.

It wasn't silent, however. Enormous hellhounds, several times larger than Sir Pup, bounded across the bodies. Two fought over a demon corpse. Smaller creatures squirmed between broken limbs and peeked out from clean-picked skulls.

"How many?" she whispered.

Jake's voice was flat. "A couple hundred thousand. Half million, maybe."

Dear God. "I had no idea there were so many demons alive in Hell, let alone dead. And to think that one battle could kill this number . . ." She could hardly conceive of it. How many were left in the cities, in the armies? Millions, altogether? "I think we Guardians are very lucky that more did not escape to Earth through the Gates before they were closed."

"Yeah." He stared out over the carnage. "It looks like Lucifer lost this one."

Yes. Fewer of the dead wore Belial's armor. She let her gaze slide over them all. Shouldn't she have been heartened by this? They were demons. Heaven knew how many she and Jake had killed escaping the prison, how many the spiders had devoured. She didn't grieve for them, and didn't grieve for these. Yet all that she could think was—

"What a fucking waste," Jake muttered.

"Yes." It shuddered from her, and her chest was heaving. She bore down against it, feeling as if she was one of those horrid spiders, filled too full, bulging in all the wrong places—and with a shell that would burst open.

Jake turned his head, and she sensed his gaze on her face. He would feel the tremors wracking her, but she prayed he wouldn't comment on them. If they weren't mentioned, she could pretend that he didn't notice.

"Just one more, goddess. That way." He pointed to their left, where sand and rock rolled out to the red horizon. "Because all of the towers are in the other direction. Okay?"

She nodded, afraid that if she tried to speak, her teeth would chatter, or something vile and huge would pour from her open mouth.

Jake's fingers closed over hers. "Then we'll get on the ground. We're a target up here, too easy to spot from a distance. Belial will be looking for us—maybe Lucifer now, too. So picture us going that way as far as we can. We'll find someplace safe, and hang on until Michael figures out we're missing."

Was anywhere in Hell safe? But she couldn't allow herself to doubt. His mouth pressed to her wrist again. She stared out over the horizon, and let him take her.

❧

Alice's knees buckled as soon as they landed.

Jake caught her before she hit the ground, swept her up against his chest. Her wing tips trailed on the sand until she vanished them. She opened her mouth.

"Shut up," he said before she could protest, then wished it'd come out gently. Goddammit. Every jump had torn away her strength, stripped her emotional shields. Every fucking jump. But she'd done what was necessary—and so had he. He swallowed his guilt, softened his tone. "Just rest."

"How dictatorial you are." He sensed the effort it took her to smile before she laid her cheek against his shoulder. She folded her talons on her lap, and they clinked against her armored thigh. "But as sprawling on my face in Hell is one of my least favorite pastimes, I intended to say 'Thank you.'"

"Yeah? You're welcome. Now be quiet."

"Very well. We do seem to get along best when we don't speak." Her eyelids were slowly lowering, her voice was thick with exhaustion, and his heart was freezing in his chest.

Guardians could be knocked unconscious, they could drift—release all of the psychic buildup—by meditating, but they didn't sleep and didn't physically tire. And they could sweat, but not from exertion. Only severe emotional distress or sickness could have put that clammy perspiration on her upper lip, on the backs of her knees.

Alice tried to turn her head, and her horns bumped his neck. "Oh, dear," she said on a sigh. Her eyes didn't open. "I'm still a demon."

He felt her crimson scales shift into dark golden skin. Her body and her features became her own again. When he realized he was staring at her bare throat, he faced forward.

There'd be no looking down. The demon armor didn't hide as much as her dress—and he didn't doubt that if she hadn't been sick, she'd have already covered up. Taking a peek now seemed like a betrayal of her trust, an invasion of her privacy.

Maybe there was a chance that, one day, she'd invite him to look. For now, he kept his eyes up.

He began walking. The sand was soft beneath his boots. A tall pile of jagged stone loomed in the distance. He mentally marked it as north, set out in that direction. Unless something else inhabited the rocks, he and Alice could hide there, wait it out.

A small creature scurried ahead of him and disappeared beneath the sand. Scaly, with glowing crimson eyes and a long, skinny tail. A wyrmrat, he thought. Lilith had mentioned them before, had said they were mostly harmless. Once, when she'd been trying to frighten him into teleporting, she'd described a giant spider. He'd assumed she was lying.

Now he was trying to remember everything else he'd thought she'd lied about. There were hellhounds, wyrmrats, spiders—all hybrids that Lucifer had supposedly created from creatures in Chaos, because he couldn't control the purebreds. She'd mentioned some kind of snake. A basilisk, maybe. Bats.

He turned in a circle, paused to study a dark cloud in the northeastern sky. Hell didn't have weather any more than Caelum did. Something flying, then. No telling yet if it was demons.

Alice made a soft, agitated noise, and he slanted a glance at her face. Her eyes were still closed. Her heartbeat was quick, but regular. That mattered most. As long as her heart was beating, he wouldn't panic.

She still hadn't exchanged her armor for her dress by the time her psychic scent slid from wakefulness into sleep. She went limp against him. Her breath came in deep, ravaged shudders, like the aftermath of a crying jag.

His jaw clenched, and he trudged on.

❧

Walking through hostile territory—always expecting an attack but never knowing when it would happen—had a way of making a man start listing the things he had. Jake didn't know why that was, but he'd done the same before, when he'd been walking through jungles instead of over sand.

And after thirty-eight hours of walking, the list Jake compiled felt pretty damn comprehensive—if not all that impressive. It was one he liked better, though, than the list he'd made forty years ago.

Some things were the same. He had a packet of memories from his human years: Grandma and Granddad, cornfields and tractors, Billy Hopewell and Barbara. Those were mostly good. He'd added to them, almost four decades of doing nothing in

Caelum except training, studying, and bullshitting with Pim and the others. Those were mostly good, too.

But it also meant he had four decades of basically doing nothing. Getting smarter, but staying in one place. The past two years, though, had been a boot in his ass. He still had a stinging footprint from his failure up in Seattle.

Yeah, he had a nice little collection of fuckups. But he was reclassifying one thing that he'd always thought belonged there.

He had a daughter. Once, he'd had intentions that surrounded her, like getting out of Vietnam alive and going back to marry Barbara, staying in Kansas, being a good dad and husband, and making sure that his little girl wouldn't have to fight so hard to escape the same thing he had. Those intentions had become failures when he died, and later had become guilt when he avoided facing them. Now he had a different intention, one that didn't weigh so heavily.

He had wings, and they'd finally grown out to his ass.

Fucking pathetic, that.

He had a constant desire to kiss Alice awake. But even if it wasn't normal for Guardians, sleep was usually good. So he let her go on.

He had a toothpick in his mouth that he'd chewed down to pulp, so he vanished it into his hammerspace—where he had six pistols, two automatic rifles, eight swords, one dagger, three crossbows, twelve pounds of plastic explosives, and the four rocket launchers that Lilith wouldn't know he'd requisitioned until he turned in his next expense report.

He had an ass-chewing in his future. Maybe a literal one, if Sir Pup did it. But he had no regrets—he'd known he would end up in Hell, sooner or later.

He had a couple of hellhound puppies on his trail about a mile behind him, and he had an eye out for the mommy.

He had a hell of a lot of questions for Michael.

He had a Gift that he couldn't allow to go haywire anymore. And he had no idea how to control it.

He had a woman sleeping against him who was in danger of being trapped in a frozen, screaming wasteland, and he had a deep ache that settled in his chest whenever he thought of it. And whether she knew it or not, he had the burden of her bargain on his shoulders now, too. He had the dread and terror that came with it.

And he had every intention of freeing her, no matter what he had to do to accomplish it.

He had hope she'd change her mind about her bargain meaning that she couldn't let herself care about him or become involved with him—and that her talk of rubbing against him hadn't just been the sickness. Every hour, he had several hundred sexual scenarios run through his head, and only half involved her bloomers.

He had Alice in his arms, but he didn't *have* her—and she had over a hundred years' practice keeping anyone from getting too close.

And that, he thought, was the item that topped a list made in Hell.

CHAPTER 13

Alice didn't want to open her eyes. They were still in Hell; she could feel it on her skin, hot and arid, and against her mind, as if the dark psychic stain in the Pit permeated the entire realm. She could feel it in her parched lungs—though the stench wasn't as terrible. Either she'd become accustomed to it, or the odor had lessened as they'd traveled farther from Lucifer's territories.

But there was no point in hiding. She sensed the tension in Jake's arms, the subtle change in his gait. He'd realized that she'd woken.

Her hair fell away from her cheek as she lifted her head. What a mess she was. Jake stopped, but she didn't look at him—didn't want to see if *he* was looking—when he set her down.

The sand was hot beneath her bare feet. Her skin flushed, and she quickly called in her boots and stockings, her drawers and dress. Almost instantly, she replaced the armor with them, and turned her back while she fastened and arranged everything.

"I didn't peek," Jake said in a low voice.

She believed him—and felt doubly wretched. When scales had covered her demonic body, she hadn't given a thought to being exposed. It shouldn't have been different, yet it was. And though she had much to thank Jake for since they'd come to this realm, she'd have resented him if he *had* looked.

Now she was grateful that resentment would not be an issue.

"Thank you." Without glancing up, she began to braid her hair. Her fingers caught in the tangles. She tugged, pulled—then forced herself to stop and simply wind two sections back from her face and pin them.

"Of course, now that you're not unconscious, I'll probably try. I'm hoping for a nice gust of wind to blow your skirt up."

"How unfortunate for you that there is not even a breeze," she said, giving in to a smile. It faded when she caught sight of the two hellhound puppies in the distance. A scan of the horizon revealed nothing else but sand and rock—not even Lucifer's tower was visible.

They must have jumped much farther than she'd thought. "Where is the mother?" she asked.

"I dunno." Jake pointed to a distant, tall pile of jagged stones. His footprints led away from them. "A while back, I passed that rock—I'm calling that south, by the way—and heard the puppies. They started following me, but I haven't seen any sign of her. I'm not sure if they care for their young anyway." His gaze moved over her face. "How are you, goddess?"

Her shoulder was sore, but the weakness had gone. "Very well." She studied him, aware of a difference that she couldn't pin down. He looked older, perhaps—but she didn't think his features had changed. He hadn't become rugged or developed any lines. "Are you well?"

"Yep. I have an earworm, but other than—"

"A *what*?"

Jake rolled his toothpick from one corner of his mouth to the other. His expression told her that he was laughing, but trying to hold it back.

Her heartbeat slowed again. "You don't have a worm in your ear," she guessed.

"Nope. A song stuck in my head."

"Oh. Yes, that can be quite annoying." His scrutiny of her features continued even through his amusement. Unsettled, she struck out in the direction he'd been heading before she'd woken. When he came abreast of her, she asked, "What song?"

"Just one about a guy who walks five hundred miles. Then five hundred more. I have it on my 1980s playlist." He shook his head, looking pained. "There are days I wonder why I bother catching up on that decade."

"I'll be certain never to borrow that list from you, then." Five hundred miles? She frowned, and watched as he turned, began walking backward so they wouldn't have to keep glancing over their shoulders. "How long did I sleep?"

"Not quite sixty hours."

Astonishment dropped her mouth open, and she slowly closed it. She had nothing to say in response. And she was well now—there was no reason for her chest to be squeezing with fear and uncertainty.

She tilted her head back. The sky was a burning red that bordered on night, like a bruised, rotting pomegranate that had been split open. No moon, no sun.

"I wish there were stars," she said quietly.

"I wish there was a Gate to Caelum."

She laughed, and lowered her gaze to his. "Jake, there is no immediate threat. Do you think that you could anchor to this spot and teleport—"

"No. If Mommy Hellhound shows up, and you run—then we don't find you again."

"I could fly into the air."

He pointed into the eastern sky. "I think those are bats."

Alice saw the dark cloud, and clenched her teeth in frustration. "Damn Lucifer for not leaving well enough alone," she muttered. If not for the danger these creatures posed, she had no doubt that Jake would attempt to seek help.

"So says the woman who feeds vampire blood to her spiders."

With a narrowing of her eyes, Alice turned to stare at him, and found his hands held up in surrender and his mouth curved into a smile.

"Hey, I'm not complaining—by the time the first sentinel hit your web, I loved those spiders as much as you do. In any case," he continued, "I think the 'damning' part is pretty much a given. For Lucifer, that is."

"Yes." Hopefully not for her, though.

"And there weren't as many as I thought there'd be."

She was becoming accustomed to his jumps during a conversation. "In the Pit?"

"Yeah. Considering how long there have been people—and

how many people die a year—I thought there'd be more. A lot more."

"Yes. Perhaps they were somewhere else," she suggested, although that didn't seem right.

She had seen the edges of the Pit, the black cliffs that had risen all around it—but more than that, she had *felt* them. And she'd been disoriented, but thinking back, she couldn't recall seeing many more humans in the Pit than demons on the battlefield.

She related the same to Jake, and he nodded his agreement. "Did you see who was screaming outside the prison? Screaming *before* you freaked them all out with the spiders." When she shook her head, he said, "They were demons, not humans."

Alice considered that. If Belial was to be believed, he had just taken over Lucifer's territory. "Torturing the enemy for information?"

"Or for fun."

She glanced down at her hands. Despite the heated air, she could still feel the burning cold against them. "And the frozen field?"

"I couldn't count them all," Jake said. Then he added quickly, "But, Alice—most of them must be demons."

She looked up at him, curious. And, she acknowledged, eager to think of anything *but* humans in that field. "How do you suppose?"

"Well, they promised to serve Lucifer after the First Battle. So all of Belial's demons reneged on that bargain when they rebelled against Lucifer's rule—and as soon as they die, they're in that field."

The image of all those killed in the recent battle filled her mind. "What do they gain," she wondered, "that they would risk it?"

"You don't think it's a return to Grace?" Jake gave a wry grin when she snorted her response. "You don't think Heaven will take them back?"

"Surely I couldn't speculate what those Above—"

"Yeah, you can. I've never met anyone who doesn't want those Above to think exactly the same way they do. So, what would you do?"

"Keep Belial roasting here forever—preferably on a spit." When Jake's eyebrows lifted in mock surprise, she went on. "I think a human wearing wings offends him. I think that he blames

Lucifer for their fall, and can't admit to his own complicity in the rebellion—even as he covets the throne Lucifer gained. And I think that although he might want to return to Heaven, it is because he sees that return as an affirmation of his superiority."

"Is he better than Lucifer, though?"

"I don't know," Alice said. "It is like asking who is the better man—Hitler or Vlad the Impaler?"

"I'm pretty sure that if we hop over to the Pit, we could find out."

How awful was she for laughing as she imagined those two tortured there? But there were some things she could not feel sorry for. Jake was not, either, she saw. His laugh didn't contain even a hint of chagrin.

They spoke at the same time. "Did you know that Hugh—" She broke off, waited for him to finish. But his smile only broadened, so she said, "So Hugh told you about his encounter with Vlad, as well."

"Yeah. Considering how I died, I thought for sure Vlad must have been a nosferatu. Maybe a vampire."

But he'd just been a human who'd made a bargain with Lucifer. He likely wasn't in the Pit, but the frozen field.

Why couldn't she laugh at that?

Alice's amusement left her on a troubled sigh. She tore her gaze from Jake's and continued walking.

After several miles, she realized that Jake's attention wandered not just during conversations, but during silences. When she glanced at him, she found the unfocused expression on his features almost as often as she encountered his keen, watchful gaze.

And as the quiet between them was slowly annoying her, the tenth time it happened, she could not stop herself from asking where it was he went.

Then she had to ask again, when he didn't seem to hear her.

"Jake?" She lifted her hand, and the motion snapped him out of it. Exasperation shortened her temper. "What are you thinking about?"

His slow grin heightened her irritation. "Sex."

Blast. She lifted her chin, stared ahead—but she had no one but herself to blame for asking. "You do it rather often. I suppose the scenarios are quite varied."

"Yeah," he said easily, as if he hadn't registered the pique in her voice. "In this one, I had you on the sand. I stripped you naked, got handfuls of your hair, and when you interrupted me I was in the process of fucking you silly. So neither of us got to come."

Her mouth was open, her gaze locked on his. "Oh, dear," she said weakly. "I'm so very sorry."

Jake shrugged. "I had the same one about five hours ago. Since then it's been you on your chair in the Archives, after I went under your skirts and had my mouth between your legs until you begged to ride me. And there was one where you were sketching the frescoes in a temple, and you turned to me and said, 'How sexy you are, Jake! Ravish me!' So I did. Then I had you in Onan's Bathtub—"

"Onan's Bathtub?" she sputtered, uncertain whether the prickly heat that had taken up residence beneath her skin was from embarrassment or arousal.

Had he intended to shock her? He had managed, but not for the reason he probably assumed. These were situations that *she* could be in—not generic fantasies with interchangeable women.

"Yep." He slid his toothpick into the corner of his mouth, worked it with his tongue for a moment—and Alice wanted to close her eyes. She didn't. "Considering that it's the luckiest tub that ever existed, it deserves an official name."

"And you chose *Onan*?"

"Hey, I'm from the Bible Belt. You don't just go blind for stroking one out, you die. So Onan's a hero—a martyr for the fourteen-year-old-male cause." He continued over her laughter. "So you were straddling me in the water, and I was sucking on your nipples. Are they like blackberries? Because that's how I've been picturing them, and I'd hate to be wrong."

Alice pushed her gaze to the horizon again, controlled her breathing. Jake thought about her nipples more often than she did. But she was aware of them now, tight beneath the silk of her bodice.

She needed to turn this conversation, somehow. "How in heaven's name did you go from not thinking about sex with me at all, to this?"

Dear God. That had been as ill-considered as her original question. It was not a turn at all, but a leap in the same direction.

"It was your bargain," he said, which was just as frustrating as

the "I don't know" he'd given after kissing her in Caelum—
because she couldn't make sense of how her bargain was an attraction. "Anyway, you shouldn't bring that up. It was a stupid
thing to say; I admitted it, and apologized for it. You accepted the
apology, and should be telling me how sexy you think *I* am."

He was teasing, but she grabbed hold of her frustration, and
pulled it close. "No," she countered. "The apology I accepted was
over your assertion that I wasn't a real woman. I was not upset by
the other. Why would I have cared whether you found me attractive?"

A muscle in his jaw ticked, but his tone was still light. "Why
indeed? You don't care what anyone thinks."

Frowning, she came to a halt, crossed her arms over her breasts.
"That is not true. There are people I love whose opinions I care
about very much. But why should I care for the opinions of people
who don't matter to me? Do you?"

"No." His gaze had hardened, and she hoped that would end
it—but he didn't let it go. "So if the right guy comes along, and
you care about whether he wants you, you'd start parading around
in little skirts?"

She clenched her teeth, but the idea was so disgusting she
couldn't prevent herself from answering. "No. I have no desire to
let anyone look as they please." Only as *she* pleased.

"What, a little skirt isn't modest enough for your Victorian
sensibilities?"

She forced herself to move again. He was deliberately goad-
ing her, but her resentment overrode her discretion. "I do not allow liberties to all and sundry," she said coldly as she passed him.
"And I will never expose myself unless I believe he has as much
interest in my pleasure as his own."

It was a miracle that she did not stumble when his answer
came after her, as solemn as a vow.

"I would."

"I will keep that in mind," she managed stiffly. It would not be
difficult. Instead, it was an effort *not* to keep it in mind.

She blinked away the image of his hands in her hair, the hot
sand at her back.

"Drifter's one of them."

Alice spun around, her eyes wide with disbelief. "What a
ridiculous notion. Ethan and I have never—!"

"No." Jake was grinning again, and she realized her reaction had been exactly what he'd intended. "One of those whose opinions matter."

"Well, yes—of course. He is one of my dearest friends."

"Yeah. He's so close to you, but you haven't told him about your history? Right."

This time, she did not let herself be provoked. "You are mistaken. He knows my history."

"You were worried I'd told him about the bargain."

"I may have left out *portions* of my history."

His brow creased. "Why? Do you think he wouldn't help you? That he'd threaten you?" He was shaking his head, as if discarding the idea even as he spoke it.

"Oh, no," Alice said lightly. "I expect that of others."

"Irena?"

He didn't miss anything, she thought. And there was no point in denying it. "Only if I follow through on the bargain. And, no—I know Ethan wouldn't."

"Then why not tell him?"

Surely Jake knew—surely he'd realized the moment he'd learned what her bargain entailed. "I do not want him to know what a coward I am." She laughed without humor. "Too much of a coward, even, to tell him that I am one."

"A coward." Jake stared at her strangely. "I don't see it."

Her smile was faint. "You are too kind."

"Or missing a big chunk of the picture. Care to fill me in?" When she didn't reply, he gave her a wry look. "No? I didn't think you would. All right. So, you got pissed because of the 'real woman' thing?"

Now they would head back there? She sighed. "Yes."

"That was even a stupider thing to say than the not-sexy thing."

"On that, we are in agreement."

"Yeah, but if you didn't care for my opinion about one, then why get pissy over the other?"

"I believe anyone would find it offensive to be told that their value as a woman—as a person—resides in how attractive someone finds them. And I can't imagine that you cared for my opinion of *you*, but tell me: Did my response about learning to be a real man sting?"

He grimaced. "Point taken."

She was not done. "And I also find it offensive that I have only become a real woman to you because you now find me sexually appealing."

"Hey, just flippin' hold on a minute." He stopped walking, a frown darkening his face. "You're all backwards there. I started thinking about banging you *after* I noticed you weren't just a creepy, mechanical, spider-loving freak— Ah, fuck."

"I see." She concealed her smile as she passed him and collected the five dollars he held out. After several minutes, during which his psychic scent ran from the heat of self-directed fury to the bitterness of remorse, she said, "They *are* like blackberries."

She heard the breath he sucked in, the hitch in his stride. "Jesus. You're not just creepy. You're evil, too."

Her sound of agreement was met with a deep chuckle, and he caught up to her, resumed his backward-walking vigil.

She glanced at him sidelong. "Perhaps we ought to return to our safe zones. What manner of temple was I sketching?" At his puzzled expression, she added, "When you ravished me."

He groaned and linked his hands behind his neck, his elbows angled up toward the sky. She took a moment to blatantly admire the way his shirt stretched over his chest, how the raised hem revealed the tanned skin above his waistband, and the line of short dark hair that trailed down from his navel.

And she reveled in how the simple touch of her gaze stirred him to obvious arousal—and that he didn't attempt to hide it.

"You're killing me, Alice."

She cackled, and he burst into laughter.

Finally, he shook his head, gave her a narrowed look. "Okay, the temple. Jesus. In '74 or '75, I found a journal in the library. It had notes and sketches by one of the archaeologists at el-Amarna in the 1880s. I kept it for about a year, reading through it. So I based it on those."

"So *that* was where it had gone. I could strangle you," Alice said. "I had heart palpitations when it went missing from the Archives."

Jake made binoculars of his hands and peered at her through them. "Observe the Black Widow in her natural habitat—fierce, territorial."

The amusement in her psychic scent undercut her withering stare. "It was my father's," she told him. "Hugh found it and brought it to Caelum."

"No shit? Huh. And the sketches—were they yours?"

"Yes."

"Hot damn." He grinned as if she'd announced some significant accomplishment. "Don't take this the wrong way, but being a girl—being a girl back then—how'd you manage that?"

"I had more freedoms than most of the girls I knew." When she'd been with the British and American families, her Egyptian side had been blamed for her unconventional and graceless behavior. Egyptians had attributed it to her American upbringing. And her parents had simply spoiled her. "My mother was my father's second wife. Not at the same time," she hastened to clarify. "He was a widower before they married, and I was born late— my early years were spent on different sites. When I was thirteen, I convinced him that I had better eyes and a steadier hand than he did, and that I'd be invaluable as his assistant. Granted, he and my mother tried to prevent me at first, but . . . Well, it may come as a surprise to you, but I was rather obstinate when I was young. Quite insufferable, actually, until they allowed me to help."

"Nope," Jake said. "I'm not surprised at all."

She resisted the urge to poke her tongue out at him.

"What about your husband? Did you meet him in Egypt?"

Her gaze left his to skim the horizon. What should she say now? Should she admit that she'd seen Henry and had immediately loved him? That she'd dressed in sweet English gowns and curled her hair? That Henry never saw her dusty and perspiring, because he was like a golden prince from one of Scheherazade's tales, and she could never let him see her be anything less than well behaved and smiling?

Oh, how she'd wanted to be that for him. Wanted to be the ideal wife, and his intellectual partner.

"Yes," she finally said. "I met him at the site."

Why did she bother to flatten her tone, to try to dissuade further questions? Jake would ask anyway.

"So you worked with him after you married?"

"No. We traveled to England for the wedding. My parents returned to Egypt immediately afterward; Henry and I were to return later, but . . ." Henry had lost his passion for Egyptology. Had wanted to concentrate on making a perfect life with his delicate flower of a wife. Had been certain that by remaining in England, his family would grow to accept her and love her. "We did not."

"Because of Teqon?"

"Yes, in part." She increased her pace, her heart pounding. "I don't wish to speak of this."

Jake's disappointment was clear. This hadn't been idle curiosity or prying, she realized; he was genuinely interested in *her*.

What a coward she was. She'd been so foolish, all those years ago; now she was so afraid that Jake would know it.

Surely *that* was foolish.

"All right," Jake said. "Back to el-Amarna, then. Were you there when they found the—"

"Never compare me to a flower."

If he was taken aback, he didn't show it. His gaze was steady on her face. "Okay."

"I loved Henry. He was kind and generous. Intelligent and humorous. Always trying to please everyone, to think the best of them, to care for them."

His jaw clenched. "A paragon, I get it."

"Yes. Yes, he was." She took a deep breath. "And I was terribly unhappy."

Oh, dear God, how wonderful it felt to say that. Like Sisyphus, dropping his boulder and letting it roll. Despite knowing that it wouldn't change anything, for a brief moment the relief of its missing weight overwhelmed the compulsion to bear it.

"You want me to kill him?"

"He's dead."

Jake spread his hands. "Look where we are."

He could make her smile so easily. "I hope no one ends up here just for being weak."

"Weak? So you rode over him."

"No. As I said, he was very caring and intelligent. And he was quite certain that he knew exactly what was best for everyone— particularly me. He knew better than I what would make me happy." She sighed. "And it hurt him so when I was not."

Jake's voice seemed very flat and controlled. "So it was your own fault that you weren't happy. And your fault that he was hurt by it."

"Yes. Because I did not—could not—do as he thought best, do what he asked me."

Oh, and she had asked far too much of him. When she had expressed her disappointment in the marriage bed, he'd explained that he loved her far too much to degrade her in that way—and that he was shocked by the carelessness of her parents, that she'd even known of such things. And when she'd screamed her frustration at him, he'd beg her to stop—wondering why she couldn't see that he only wanted what was best for them, that he only lived to serve her and to make her happy.

And at the beginning, though they had regarded her with disdain, his family had not been so terrible. They kept their distance, and she hadn't minded. She was quite capable of keeping herself occupied.

But then they had begun to remark upon her strangeness, to advise Henry to curb her reading and studying, her correspondence. Such activities were too taxing, they argued—and Henry would follow their direction. How Alice had grown to hate that mix of subservience and condescension in him. Despised how he could never admit that they or he might be wrong.

Then she'd miscarried, and he'd been convinced it had proved him right. And they'd tried again.

Oh, so gently.

Jake's voice broke in on her simmering thoughts. "You know what a load of—"

"Yes. Yes, of course I do. Now." She shook her head. "No, that is a lie. I knew then, too. I tried to leave—to return to Egypt."

"You ran off by yourself?"

"Yes."

"Just unhappy, huh?"

She smiled a little to acknowledge the understatement. After her second miscarriage, she'd been desperate to return to her family. "I had little choice. Henry had begun vetting my letters, saying to any request for my parents to visit that it would be too dangerous. My father was so old, you see. And surely news of my melancholy—which could be cured if I would simply take Henry's advice—would only upset my father's health."

She stopped, surprised by the bitterness in her voice. Not that it was there, but that she was expressing it. "But don't we do the same? Determine what to say based on what we think is best for others?"

Jake, bless him, let her take that step back. "You mean Michael," he said. "And whether we're going to mention what Belial said in the prison about being Michael's father. Or if it's different than Drifter deciding last spring to keep what Belial said about teaching Michael from the others."

"Yes."

"What's your gut say?"

"To let it out there. If it is true, Michael can explain it—after all, it still wouldn't change what he is now. And if it is not true, he can put it to rest."

"Yeah," Jake said. "That's what mine's saying, too. But it isn't the same as what your husband did, not letting you talk to your family. Marriage isn't war."

"In theory."

His grin flashed over his lips, then faded as he said, "Michael *has* been hiding what he knows about Zakril and the temples. And maybe he has a reason for keeping silent, just like Drifter did. But whatever the reason, it's not staying buried."

"And if Michael is Belial's son?" But how could it be? To her knowledge, demons couldn't reproduce. Lucifer had created the nephilim, just as he had the hellhounds and spiders—but she did not know by what method. Halfling demons—like Lilith—had been humans once, transformed in a sacrifice. "If it is true, what then?"

"Maybe nothing," Jake said. "Or maybe we reevaluate what we know of demons."

"And feel guilty for slaying them?"

"What, and toss my cookies whenever I kill one?" He shook his head. "Have you ever met one that wasn't evil at its core? Can you think of any demon that the universe wouldn't be a better place without?"

She had to admit she couldn't.

"So, Michael's not a demon like the others—he's something else," Jake said. "That's not such a surprise."

No, it wasn't. He'd always been more powerful, had always been *more* than the rest of them. "How strange that I would rather be lied to by someone with good intentions or ill—to have them hide the truth—than be aware that good intentions were making my decisions for me."

"You mean, having a choice? Yeah, I prefer to fuck up on my own, too." He studied her face for a moment. "So, those good intentions. You didn't get away."

She took a long breath, wondering if she was ready to go back there. And she was.

CHAPTER 14

"Henry caught up to me in London." At the docks—and the smell there, she reflected, hadn't been much more pleasant than the odors in Hell. Of everything that day—the blinding sun, the cacophony of voices, horses, whistles, and engines—it was the stink that remained at the forefront of her memories. "I made such a scene—was such an embarrassment. When we returned to Manchester, he tucked me away. And I was restrained so that I couldn't run again. For my own good, of course."

"Jesus, Alice."

She knew he was remembering the attic, the bed there. "Henry brought in a physician, and I was diagnosed with female hysteria. And, despite my protests, was treated for it."

"Treated?" His brows drew together in a heavy frown. "You mean the doctor was . . . Onan's little helper?"

"Yes."

Alice took a small amount of pride in knowing that her voice didn't betray her humiliation. The physician had seen more of her than her husband ever had, and in his clinical manner had produced more of a response. Not attraction or arousal, but release. And Henry hadn't thought it degrading at all.

She continued in the same lighthearted vein. "But I had an outlet, after that—a way to settle my nerves that Henry could not prevent. It was, after all, his suggestion to let me be treated. And so I settled them quite often."

Jake didn't smile, didn't laugh. She dropped her gaze from his.

"And it was better, for a while. We traveled to Bath for an extended holiday, away from his family. It was supposed to be a restorative for me."

"But?"

"I believe Henry was trying to make amends. To give me a bit of home. And so he invited a man that we'd known in Egypt—an acquaintance through the exploration society—who would never have been welcomed in the same way by Henry's family."

"Teqon."

"Yes. And it began with simple tricks. He would shape-shift into Henry's form before my eyes, but look like himself again immediately thereafter. I would have conversations with Henry, who would later claim to have no memory of them. Eventually, Teqon flared his eyes, showed me his demonic face. And I tried to avoid him, certain I was mad—but it was impossible. Henry was determined to put us together, because it would make me happy."

"So you told him," Jake guessed. His gaze wasn't on her face, but searching behind them. "And he thought you were nuts."

Alice nodded. "I look back, and I see how easily Teqon manipulated me—and I want to call myself a fool. But I cannot. I do not blame myself for that. Only the bargain."

"What happened?"

"Henry had begun restraining me again—for my own good, of course. It should have been soothing; I had *such* a lovely view of the garden from my bed." Bitterness had crept into her voice. She smoothed it before continuing, "Teqon came to me in his demon form, and told me that he would not kill Henry as long as I brought Michael's heart to him. I had no idea who Michael was—and despite everything, I loved Henry. So I made the bargain."

"How does that make you a coward?"

Alice stopped walking, her brow furrowed. "Who trades the life of a stranger for another? I didn't fight Teqon—not physically, not with words. I begged him to go, to leave Henry alone, to leave me alone. But I didn't fight. Yet if I had, perhaps I'd have learned that he *couldn't* kill Henry—not without breaking the Rules and receiving Punishment from Lucifer. But I assumed he

had that power, and bowed down before it." Thinking of it made
her stomach churn with self-disgust.

Jake shook his head. "You're too hard on yourself."

"What if Michael had been a child? I didn't ask—didn't care
to know. Yet I agreed to kill him." She watched Jake's expression,
the struggle there. "You want to be kind to me. Don't be."

He scrubbed his hand over his hair, dropped it back to his
side. "Okay, yeah—maybe you could have been tougher. But it's
not worth spending eternity in Hell for. Did you know that was
part of it?"

"Yes. But I was determined to save Henry, to follow through. I
didn't consider the implications of it—that it would be murder."
She sighed. "And of course, once I was transformed, I realized
who Michael was."

Understanding spread over Jake's features. "Teqon gambled
that it would happen—that you'd have access to Michael and
Caelum. Did you die saving your husband?"

She nodded. "He and Teqon would spend hours talking together, and Henry's 'care' became even more caring." And always
accompanied by his crying, his pleading with her to be happy.
"One evening—after he'd spent the day with Teqon—he came
to bed, lay down next to me. He removed all but one of the restraints, asked me to hold him. He told me that everything would
be perfect."

"And then?" Jake prompted when she paused.

"Then I smelled the smoke."

"Jesus Christ. He set the house on fire?"

"Intending for us to die together," she confirmed. "So I coshed
him over the head, kicked him through the window to the garden
below."

"A delicate flower, huh?" An admiring smile curved his mouth.
"And you were transformed, so he must have lived. But you didn't
make it?"

"I knew I would not have much time, but with him there and
fighting me, both of us would have died. So I saved him by pushing him out, then tried to save myself." Alice wrapped her hand
around her wrist like a manacle. "But I couldn't get the last one
off. I couldn't go out the window, and I couldn't drag the bed
through the door."

"Jesus Christ in Heaven."

"It wasn't so terrible. Fortunately, I succumbed to the smoke, not the flames. I'm not certain if I was dead when Michael came, but most assuredly I was on the verge of it."

Jake was silent for almost ten yards. "I'm going to say two things."

"Oh, dear. Must you?"

His nod pulled a laugh from her. "One," he said, "that's badass. And you call it cowardly?"

"Perhaps not that part," she admitted.

"Damn straight. Two, your husband was a flippin' idiot."

"Yes, well. He could translate hieroglyphs and converse in ancient Greek, so it was a surprise to me, too." As was the discovery that she was capable of loving an idiot almost as much as she was sickened by his weakness and condescension. "But he was very handsome, and kind, and so I'm certain he found another wife to care for—one who wouldn't reduce him to tears on a daily basis. I hope, however, that he *did* cry every day." She fell silent, thinking. After a few minutes, she asked, "How do you suppose anyone could choose England over Egypt?"

Jake shrugged. "Beats me."

❦

Alice was describing the excitement that had surrounded the discovery of the Amarna Letters when Jake lost his focus again.

She pursed her lips, waved her hand. "How often do you do that?"

Despite her tone, she was not irritated—she was amazed. Surely his mental stamina was unmatched among mortals and immortals alike.

"Think about banging you? Once a minute or so," he said. "But this wasn't about that."

"Oh?"

"Nope. I was thinking about making a Gate."

She blinked, surprised by her disappointment that it *hadn't* been about her. And intrigued, as well. Hell's Gates had been formed through sacrifices and rituals, death and negative psychic energy—but there was no indication in the Scrolls as to how a Gate to Caelum was made.

"Go on," she said.

Jake crammed his hands into his pockets, his gaze intent on her face, his expression thoughtful. "Well, maybe we could just draw a circle in the sand, scribble a few symbols around it, and then have sex in the middle."

It took a heroic effort to maintain her composure. "What position would we have to take?"

His lips didn't even twitch. "I dunno. We could run the gamut. Eventually, we'd hit on the right one."

"Oh, yes. Excellent idea, Hawkins. And while we are both facing the same direction in an animal position, the hellhound puppies will surprise us from behind."

"Yeah, and my hot ass would go first. So that's out."

"It would have to be the Lotus position," she determined. "We could keep watch over each other's shoulders."

She met his eyes. They should have been laughing, she thought. Instead, she was only imagining herself sitting with him, her legs around his waist, her mouth against his. Rocking slowly, with Jake deep inside her.

Oh, dear. She wanted to stop walking. Wanted to lie very still, with her thighs pressed tightly together.

And she would *not* look away first.

Jake's sword appeared in his hand.

Alice swiftly glanced around them, saw nothing. "What is it?"

He dragged the tip of his sword through the sand, drawing a circle. When she laughed his name, he raised his brows at her. "No? Dammit," he said, straightening. "Okay, so you aren't gung ho for opening-a-portal sex. What about saving-the-world sex?"

"Would that require the missionary position?"

"However you like it."

She feared she might be agreeable to any he had in mind. "If it would save the world, I would likely say yes."

"Hot damn." He vanished his sword. "When we get back, I'm going to put the world in danger."

Her small, self-contained world was already in danger of cracking apart. He hadn't battered her defenses, but snuck through them. Just as now, he was walking backward directly in front of her, but slowing, slowing until her next step would bring her up against him.

Her gaze felt weighted; she couldn't lift it above his lips. Sense made her say, "This is not the wisest course to take now. Not with hellhounds behind us."

"Is there a Lotus kiss?"

"No. And you have a habit of jumping when we attempt one." She flattened her hand against his chest—touching him, holding herself back. His heart was pounding. Did she produce that intense reaction? "You did not even need a spider the last time."

"Hey," he said in a wry tone, but beneath it she felt the sharp point of his self-reproach. "That got us down here, didn't it? Started this fun little vacation?"

She looked up into his eyes. Oh, that had come out very badly. She shouldn't have said anything—should have just kissed him. "I didn't mean—"

"I freaked out over something." He lifted his hand to rub at the back of his neck. "Not over you. Well, not over kissing you."

"Oh." But somehow, she'd produced that intense *fear* in him? Uncertainty slipped into her, stiffened the muscles along her spine. She pulled her hand back. "When I returned to Earth after finishing my training, I thought my Gift would drive me mad. I was overwhelmed with senses that were not my own—and I had no idea where they originated." And when she did realize, she didn't use her Gift again for a year—until Irena had shamed her for her cowardice. "Then I learned to control it; yours will become easier, as well."

"Gee, thanks." Jake took a step back, then another.

With a sigh, Alice followed him. How patronizing she'd sounded—and dismissive. Whatever her troubles, her Gift had never landed someone in Hell.

Yet he hadn't teleported at the worst of moments, when his wings had been severed—and he had done very well teleporting them around within the realm.

Frowning, she lightly touched her opposite wrist. "Why did you bite me?"

"Because of Drifter and Charlie. She says his Gift feels different when she bites him. Like it's pure psychic energy through the blood. That's how they get through the shielding spell. So I thought it wouldn't hurt."

"Do you think it helped?"

"Dunno." His half smile softened the hard cast of his features. "Maybe it's just a mental thing. You know, giving me something more tangible than a psychic image. It didn't taste any different."

She contained her grimace. "Did you swallow it?"

"Well, yeah. Spitters are quitters," he said, and held out a five-dollar bill. When Alice realized what he meant, she snatched it.

His smile broadened into a grin, and her heart rolled over. "Nah, I'm kidding. I didn't drink it—I put it into my hammerspace. I can use blood as a strong anchor to you. That is, I could if those symbols weren't there. Do they still hurt?"

"They ache," she admitted.

"Want me to take a look?"

"What would be the point? Nothing can be done."

"I could kiss it better," he said, and she smiled.

"Another mental thing?" Like nerve-settling.

"Or practice for being a great-granddad."

"I—" Her gaze locked onto his face. He was looking to his left, his expression distracted again. Alice saw nothing but rocks and sand. "Forgive me, Jake. Did you say you were a grandfather?"

"*Great.*"

How incredible. Alice recalled him saying he'd written to his girl before he'd gone out to meet the nosferatu. It apparently hadn't been the girl she'd assumed. "And your . . . daughter? Have you spoken with her?"

"Not yet. I intend to when we get back." He met her eyes briefly, and she saw the hope and hesitation there. "I'm not sure how it'll go. But the four-year-old girl is a whippersnapper. Cute as hell. You saw her."

"The one who called me a witch?" At his nod, she said wonderingly, "And you will meet them? You are a lucky man, Jake. A very, very lucky man."

"Yeah. You wanted kids?" He'd been looking to his left again, but at that, his gaze snapped back to hers. "Ah, shit. What a stupid—"

"No, it's all right. And, yes, I did. But now I'd have to Fall before I could, and I'm in no hurry to be human again. I enjoy this life—and I would rather not add children to the list of things I'll never have if I don't escape my bargain."

"This is the place for lists," Jake said, then stopped walking. "Do you want to run or to fly?"

"What?"

"Both get us there faster than walking." He pointed to his left. "Take a look. The rock all the way out."

Alice studied it, trying to make out the distant shape. With no idea of how far it was, she couldn't determine its height. But it was solid, with a rounded—

She flattened her hand against her chest, felt her heart leaping. "It's the missing statue—from the temple in Tunisia?"

"Looks like."

"Oh, dear God." She formed her wings, ran to lift him up. "We'll fly."

❧

Alice's wings moved like a bellows, each beat puffing her full of excitement and trepidation. The statue sat amid a large collection of jagged, monolithic black marble stones, as if someone had tipped out sharp pebbles from a shoe, and not noticed the granite statue among them.

She could make out the statue's wings now, folded against its back, the long tips sweeping out behind it. Its head was bowed; the figure had gone down on one knee. His sword lay on the ground in front of him, his right hand gripping the handle, his left wrapped around the blade. There was submission in the pose, but it wasn't complete. Alice could see the tension carved in his arms, his hands—as if he was deciding whether to place the sword at her feet, or to stand up and use it on her.

"The puppies are chasing us."

Alice spared them a glance. "We can remain in the air for now."

It would be easier to study the figure anyway. Given its size, it was best taken in from a slight distance. Alice swooped toward the downturned face, her heart tight. She hovered just below the eyes, staring up at its features. Hair curled over the figure's forehead. His eyes were closed, and a slight frown pulled his brows together. His mouth was a firm line, yet it still gave the impression that it might tremble at any moment.

Indecision, pain—and love, impossibly expressed in a stone.

They stared at it in silence, until Jake said quietly, "I thought it'd be Michael."

Alice had, too. She tore her gaze from the statue's face, looked down. "Jake," she said. "His sword."

"Zakril's?"

"Or its mirror image." Movement on the ground near the knee drew her attention. The hellhound was in its demon form, scales showing through the spiked fur. Though a puppy, it was four feet tall at its shoulder. One of its heads fixed on them, the other two looking to its left. Alice glanced in that direction, and saw nothing. "Where's the other hellhound?"

"Dunno. My question is, why'd the other one leave *foot-prints*?" Jake strengthened his psychic blocks until his mind was impenetrable. She did the same. The trail of footprints ended a hundred yards from the statue. No one but Alice and Jake were in the air. "Pull up, Alice. Let's circle around."

Unease wound its way into her stomach as she rose higher. They'd both had their psychic shields down, just slightly, so that Michael could anchor to them. But there was no mistaking the shape of the prints—it hadn't been a second hellhound following them.

"Did you sense anyone pushing into your mind?"

"Nope." His crossbow was in his hands now. She called in her naginata, holding him with one arm around his chest. "But it wouldn't have taken much of a push, would it?"

"No." They'd both been expecting hellhounds. There hadn't been a reason to mentally probe those trailing behind them. And they might have mistaken any foreign touch for the psychic stain that pervaded Hell. "Only skill."

Alice turned them, made sure no one approached from behind. Jake made a sound of frustration.

"Put me up on the head, Alice."

Where he'd have a better vantage point, and his movements wouldn't be handicapped by their position—freeing her, as well. She set him down, performed another sweep around the statue. The hellhound lay like a Sphinx next to the left foot, heads lifted to watch her. Keeping a wary eye on it, she hovered ten yards over the sand, glanced beneath the stomach of the statue. No one.

What aren't we seeing? she signed, knowing that Jake covered her position with his weapon.

"Or hearing," he said quietly.

She'd been listening for a heartbeat. Her gaze ran over the sand, then to the trail of footprints, their abrupt end. Yet no one was in the air.

The memory of the symbols written over Zakril's skeleton struck her now, ripped a shiver over her skin. *She waits below.*

The sand was heavy, dense—dense enough to muffle a heartbeat, if someone was buried under it.

She felt a spear of realization from Jake the same moment she stretched her wings, prepared to shoot upward.

A geyser of red sand erupted beneath her.

Black feathers, obsidian eyes. Alice barely had a moment to

see them before she rolled. Her naginata sliced flesh. Blood spurted. Hands gripped her neck.

The thrust of an unfamiliar Gift ripped through her.

Jake slammed into them from above, tearing Alice from that powerful grasp. Powerful—but not painful. Alice hit the sand with Jake; they immediately rolled to their feet. The hellhound growled in front of them, jaws dripping foam, eyes flickering with hellfire.

Alice didn't let go of her weapon to sign. "She has a Gift."

She didn't need to say the rest—that only Guardians possessed one.

"I felt it."

Jake held his swords in both hands, his gaze on the hellhound. Her naginata at the ready, Alice narrowed her eyes up at the woman hovering over the hellhound's head. Multiple narrow braids failed to tame the riot of her ebony hair. Tiny vermillion symbols were tattooed from forehead to toe, forming an intricate pattern that tinted her bronze skin a deep orange red. A sleeveless black tunic fell to mid-thigh.

She was petite. And beautiful, in the classical sense—as refined as the Egyptian queen Nefertiti with her high, wide cheekbones, full lips, and tapered nose—but it wasn't the same face as the statue in the temple. Alice flicked a glance at the statue behind her. If that was Zakril, this was the feminine mold. The resemblance was unmistakable.

The woman returned Alice's stare, then looked beyond her, as if searching for someone. Confusion flitted over her features. "I am early," she said in English, and her voice was like Michael's, like Belial's—a harmony from a single throat. "Or Michael is late. I saw him with you, but you are here, and he is not." She tilted her head. The obsidian receded from her eyes, leaving irises of dark brown that focused on Jake. "You, then, are early—though it has taken you so very long to come."

"So long that you couldn't put on a nicer welcome? Yeah, right."

Ebony brows pushed together in a puzzled frown. Her Gift rolled out like a wave, crashing against them. Alice widened her stance and loosened her grip on her weapon; she could strike faster if her wrists were relaxed.

"Both of you are so weak," she said, as if surprised. "And that one—Alice—is corrupted by Belial's hand. But I see now that it was not of her choosing." She vanished her black wings, landed lightly beside the hellhound. Eagerness hardened the curve of her lips, sent a shiver down Alice's spine. "And I see that fire will cleanse it."

So she knew of the symbols carved into Alice's shoulder. Either she'd heard Jake and Alice speaking while following them, or she'd sensed it another way.

"And what, exactly, do you mean by that?" Jake asked as he vanished one of his swords. His hand caught Alice's. His fingers squeezed in a rapid code. *She considers Belial a corruption? Is that good or bad?*

The enemy of our enemy has never been our friend. Nosferatu, nephilim, demons.

Vampires go both ways. Humans, too. What about maybe-Guardians?

Alice had no answer—but she didn't think Jake expected one. Their exchange had taken less than a second, between one breath to the next, and the woman was only now responding, "I only mean what I said: fire will cleanse the symbols." Her gaze dropped to their linked hands. The force of her Gift gentled into a continuous ebb. "You will not leave here that way. Nor will Michael come for you."

Jake shifted his weight. *Was that a threat?*

Alice was also uncertain. The tone had been more informative than anticipatory, and had been delivered in the same manner as the strange, nonsensical greeting. Early, late—and she'd expected Michael to be here, but now she said he would not be?

No, Alice realized. She'd said she'd *seen* Michael with them.

Could her Gift be foresight, or an ability to predict? she suggested, and opened her mouth.

"Yes," the woman spoke, frowning again in confusion. "I am a seer. Did I not introduce myself? I was certain I did. Perhaps I only saw it."

"You didn't," Jake said—and simultaneously against Alice's fingers, *Nut job.*

She feared he might be correct. Not that Alice doubted her foresight—only her stability. *That does not make her any less dangerous,* she said.

No shit. He followed it with a soft squeeze, as if to assure her he hadn't taken her warning any way she hadn't intended. "So, care to fill us in?"

The lines of bewilderment between her brows deepened. " 'Fill us in'?" Her Gift washed over them in a heavy wave, and Alice felt it draw something back with it, psychic sand dragged by the tide. The woman's eyes closed, pain tightening her features. "I see that so much has changed. And that I should not rely upon only one of you for the language, when it, too, comes from the past. No, I do not tell you here. We are inside, for the nychiptera come."

I am completely lost, Alice admitted.

You're in good company, then. Jake paused. *But I think she just said you talk like an old lady.*

How he'd managed to interpret that, she couldn't say. Alice grabbed on to the one statement she had understood . . . partially. "What—"

The woman was already pointing into the southeastern sky. *"Those* are the nychiptera. Has Michael taught you nothing?" She lowered her hand, her expression taking on a faraway look. "Or did the threads pull them in after he left? I saw them come before he did, but I suppose they came after, for we only used the threads when we hid from him. Unless they were not drawn in by the threads, but brought here."

Alice didn't respond. She could see the bats that made up the dark cloud now, their fangs and sharp talons. The hellhound whimpered and growled, nudging the woman's hip with one of its heads.

She looked down at the hellhound, startled. "Oh, yes. Thank you, *meiraks.* We go inside. You will follow me."

Turning, she strode away from the statue, the hellhound at her side. Alice glanced up at Jake.

"Do not dawdle," the woman called. "I have already seen you discuss it. You decide to come with me. There is no reason to do it twice."

Jake's gaze held hers. *Waiting around for those bats isn't such a hot idea. But we don't have to go with her. We can jump.*

Alice looked back at the statue, then at the woman. With a sigh, she said, *You know I cannot leave now.*

His mouth tilted into a smile. *I can't, either. But I thought I'd give you a choice.* Still holding her hand, he began to walk after the strange duo—toward, Alice realized, one of the enormous stones scattered over the sand. *I think she learned English from you—by listening to your future. Then she picked up more from me, so that she could translate the slang.*

Her fingers went slack against his, transmitting her surprise and disbelief. Finally, she recovered enough to say, *I hope that means I have enough of a future to learn from.*

A future in which you say "dawdle."

Alice bit back her nervous laugh. The hellhound turned one of her heads to look back at them.

What is M-E-H-I-R-A-X? Jake approximated the spelling.

"Little girl." It's from the Attic Greek.

Damn. I guess I should have learned a few more ancient languages—because all of ten people speak them. He was grinning when she met his eyes, quickly, before looking away and pursing her lips to stop her own grin.

Was he trying to ease her anxiety, or his? Either way, she was grateful for it.

The woman paused in front of the stone, her figure an insignificant relief against the enormous wall of marble. Her fingers traced a vertical line over its surface. A tiny crack appeared; she pushed, and it widened before swinging open. She stepped into the darkness beyond.

"Ye-e-e-ah," Jake said slowly. *We're going in there?*

Alice glanced at the dark cloud scudding across the sky. *Yes.*

You know the story of Hansel and Gretel, right? If I see an oven, I'm grabbing you and jumping.

I thought we would push her in, instead. She could barely hear his quiet chuckle over the pounding of her heart. *At any rate, this entire realm is an oven. I'm not certain it is any better out here.*

That's true enough. And what's one crazy Guardian? But, Alice, listen— He stopped, and she looked at him; all trace of humor had fled his expression. *Stay close.*

She nodded, and they stepped over the threshold together.

CHAPTER 15

Whatever he'd been expecting, a dinner party wasn't it. Yet that was the only description Jake had for the four sculpted figures seated around a table in the center of the large chamber. Three males, one female. Jake recognized the faces of three—they matched the statue of Zakril in Hell, the female statue in Tunisia, and Michael. The woman dressed their nude bodies in tunics, speaking to each one in a soft, lilting language. They were as white as department-store mannequins.

Everything was white, with the appearance of stone. Not marble, though. Jake narrowed his focus on the table, then the statues, and his stomach lurched.

It was bone. Shaped and molded into faces, furniture, and overlaying the walls, ceiling, and flooring.

Threads of orange light, as thin as fiber-optic strands, were embedded in the walls. In the soft glow, he met Alice's eyes.

There are degrees of creepy, Jake said. *You're sexy creepy. Nephilim rituals are sick creepy. And this is* creepy creepy.

Yes. She averted her gaze. *How long has she been here, do you think?*

She must not have intended for him to respond; she let go of his hand and moved toward the wall. Apparently, something more than the bone bothered her, and he watched as she traced her fingers down the luminescent threads. She stood sideways to the wall, wary, but distracted, her naginata between her body and the woman fussing at the table. Jake angled himself between them.

Two more chambers led away from the room; the hellhound lay in the left doorway. From his position, Jake could see enough to guess that the interiors had also been surfaced with bone. All that white . . . was she trying to re-create the look of Caelum?

Pity rose up, and he squashed it. No Guardian he'd known would've appreciated it.

And he didn't know if this one deserved it.

"Spider threads," Alice murmured behind him. Jake felt the light touch of her Gift—and through it, her sudden confusion—before she shielded.

"Yes." The woman faced them, smiling brightly. "I have just seen your deaths, but now I see you alive. How lovely."

Yep, that would eventually make him crazy, too. "Are those deaths going to be anytime soon? Say, the next five minutes?"

If she said yes, he was taking Alice and jumping. Of course, he'd feel pretty stupid if he jumped them right into Lucifer's throne room—and died there, instead.

Her careless shrug didn't help. "Who can tell? The only ones I am certain of are those I intend to kill."

"I suppose it is very rare that someone shouts out the date in their death throes." Alice came to stand by his shoulder—close enough to defend him, far enough that her movements wouldn't be hampered. "How often do you turn to find someone alive in here with you?"

The furrowing of her brow underlined one of the few demonic symbols Jake knew: lock. It was intertwined with another, directly in the middle of her forehead, and surrounded by hundreds more that had been inscribed over her face. "How many years has it been since Lysander took Lampsakos?"

At the end of the Peloponnesian War. Jake hoped he didn't look as thunderstruck as he felt.

Alice's face was pale as she responded, "Two thousand, four hundred."

She slowly blinked, revealing more symbols on her eyelids. "Only that many? It felt much longer," she said, and Jake wondered if she'd accurately picked up the concept of "thousand" while rifling through Alice's future. "In that time, I have only turned my back on visitors once."

Them, Jake thought. "How many visitors have you *not* turned your back on?"

"One." She studied him with eyes that were rapidly becoming obsidian again. "You are accustomed to those who tell the truth, but not all of it."

"Occupational hazard. Was the other person Michael?" If the Doyen had deliberately left her in Hell—or brought her here— that'd be another reason to jump.

"No. He does not know I am here—yet." She turned, trailing her fingers over the shoulders of the male statue Jake didn't recognize. "When I saw him come, I did not think he would take so long. Or that you would."

Jake glanced at Alice, tried to gauge her response. The wariness had almost gone. With her eyebrows drawn, she stared at the woman, as if trying to work something out.

But they weren't going to get anywhere unless they asked.

"Ah," the woman said before Jake could speak. "I know this moment. This is when you wonder who I am, and I tell you that I am Khavi, of the grigori, sister to Zakril—and sister in spirit, if not flesh, to Michael and Anaria." She looked over her shoulder with a brittle smile. "Much less so to Anaria."

Whoa boy. Jake didn't even know where to start.

Khavi's eyes narrowed into ebony slivers. "You did not know." She pivoted, paced to the wall and back. Her fingers shoved into her tangled hair, yanked. "How can you not know? No, no—"

She came to a stop and pointed at Jake. "No. You spoke his name. I heard through the sand. You saw him, and you spoke his name."

"Zakril?" Alice walked to the table, her sketchbook in hand. "We only know of him from—"

"Why do you move like that?"

Jake's jaw clenched. Khavi's expression reminded him of a kid studying an insect through a magnifying glass. But he swallowed his angry response when Alice's lips thinned, her irritation plain.

Yeah, it was pretty much a given that anything not relating to Zakril, Michael, and whoever Khavi was, Alice would consider an annoying distraction.

"My Gift has left its mark." Alice moved between the statues of Michael and Zakril, opening her sketchbook. "Now, do you—"

"You can change your form, is that not still true?"

Alice breathed out sharply through her nose before she said, "Yes."

Jake wondered if he mistook the meanness in Khavi's smile, until she said, "Then why do you wear that face instead of a beautiful one?"

Fuck hellhounds, fuck nut jobs, fuck this whole fucking realm. Jake stepped forward, but Alice's calm reply stopped him.

"Because I already am." She met Khavi's eyes across the table. "And you *are* half-demon."

Khavi's dark gaze landed on Jake. "Yes."

He stared back, his poker face on. He should have known Alice wouldn't feel insulted by that. But Khavi hadn't known Alice wouldn't be hurt, so there was no doubt she'd *meant* to inflict pain.

So what was it about—was Khavi looking for their weaknesses? Probably. He'd been doing the same since he'd come in. Problem was, if Khavi's only emotional link was to the hellhound, there wasn't much Jake could threaten.

Luckily, Alice hadn't given anything away in her response. Not so luckily, he had.

But if Khavi thought that loving Alice was a weakness, Jake would be happy to show her how wrong she was.

With fury still flooding his veins, he began a wide circuit of the chamber, keeping watch on the table. His gaze swept over Alice's sharp features as she flipped through the book and turned it toward Khavi. Goddamn. Even a crazy demon should be able to see how flippin' gorgeous Alice was. Sure, not in the Hollywood sense, all sultry eyes and pouty lips—but for fuck's sake, all anyone had to do was look at her more than once or twice, and they'd realize it.

As if aware of his gaze, Alice glanced at him from under her lashes, a question in her pale blue eyes.

Jake shook his head. He'd sit out for now. Would just listen, and absorb. At least until cutting off Khavi's head didn't seem so tempting.

Not beautiful. Yeah. His hot ass.

"This is what we know," Alice said, smoothing her hand over a drawing of winged figures warring against the heavens. "There was the First Battle, waged between angels."

Khavi nodded, examining the sketch. "Lucifer's rebellion."

"We know that he and his followers were transformed to

demons, and those who abstained became nosferatu—and the angels came to Earth to guard humans."

"Yes."

No big surprises here, then. His lethal mood fading, Jake glanced into the right chamber. The terraced recesses in the floor were a smaller version of the baths in Tunisia. They were dry, with traces of red sand at the bottom.

He turned, found Khavi staring at him. "Both water and fire purify," she said softly. "But when we bathe, the water becomes muddied. Fire burns clean."

Was this a riddle—or something straightforward, in a flaky kind of way? "Fire leaves ash," he pointed out.

"The *flames* are clean. Regardless, there is no water in Hell." She studied the next drawing, of Lucifer riding at the head of the dragon, and Michael plunging his sword into its heart. "What do you call this?"

"The Second Battle."

Khavi sighed. Jake had seen the look she gave Michael's statue hundreds of times on Pim's face, on Charlie's face. It somehow combined familiarity, affection, and exasperation—and reminded a guy that females were the superior species, with more going on in their heads than between their legs.

"His strengths never included his imagination," she said. "What is the story of this battle?"

"Lucifer became envious of the angels, and brought a dragon with him to Earth. The angels faltered until mankind sided with them, and Michael—one of the men in the *human* army—slew the dragon. The angels gave Caelum to him, and the power to create the Guardian corps."

Khavi sat motionless, as if waiting for Alice to continue. Alice was just as still, waiting for a reaction.

Slowly, Khavi unrolled her fists. Jake hadn't seen her clench them. "Is that all?"

"In essence—yes."

She exploded into motion, backhanding the female statue. Its head shot toward Jake. He snatched it out of the air before the face smashed against the wall, his fingers stinging from the catch.

Alice straightened, her eyes guarded as Khavi stalked back and forth across the chamber.

Jake's gut twisted, a sick, heavy knot. "Is it a lie?"

Her fingers pushed into her tangles. She tilted her head back and screamed, the sound a hoarse rip from her harmonious voice. Frustration poured from a dark psychic scent that was as rich and powerful as Michael's—as the nephilim's.

Jake was beside Alice before the scream ended. But the anger left Khavi as quickly as it had come; she crouched in front of her hellhound, spoke in soothing tones.

I have often wanted to scream like that, Alice signed.

Tension no longer whitened her knuckles. *Maybe you should,* Jake signed, and held up the bone head. Unlike the statues outside and in Tunisia, no emotion or personality had been captured in the blank, staring eyes. *Clean break in the neck. She's beheaded it with a blade before. And there are dents and chips all over—this isn't the first time she's hit it.*

Alice's gaze skimmed the other statues. *And only that one.*

Jake began to reply, then realized that although Khavi was still facing the hellhound, she'd switched to English.

"The dragons are of Chaos," she said in that low tone. "They create, they destroy—there is no difference between each act. All Chaos knows is destruction and creation."

He frowned, glanced at Alice, and saw the same incomprehension on her face. The words made sense, but he had no clue what Khavi was getting at.

Before he could frame the question, she returned to the table. "It is not a lie."

But it wasn't all of the truth, either, Jake guessed—and his gut didn't untwist.

"Then Michael was human," Alice said.

"In every way that matters. He called himself a man, and he lived as one. He did not water his mother's fields with the sweat from his brow, but he *did* work them."

Alice breathed in and out. Wanting, Jake thought, to dance around the question.

He asked it. "Was Belial his father?"

"Yes. And no." The faint smile on Khavi's lips might have been mocking or sad—Jake couldn't tell. "Belial was not as he is now. He drank at the table of the dragon, was created and destroyed. When he was full, he became himself again."

Jake bared his teeth in a grin. "I don't suppose you could say that one more time, but without the woo-woo seer-speak?"

That Alice didn't hold out her hand for his money told him that she was just as frustrated.

Khavi's smile widened, sharpened. "Your novice friends will refer to me as Déjà Vu when I cannot hear. I will not appreciate it."

Was that why she was deliberately obscure, or was this just a crazy tangent? "I'll tell them not to, then."

"It is already done."

Great. Just . . . flippin' . . . great.

Alice's frown became thoughtful. "How is it you didn't know that you would have to tell us about Michael? Or that we don't know everything you do about the Second Battle?"

"I can only see what I know. I cannot see what you do."

For an instant, Jake considered shape-shifting and growing out his hair, just so he could rip it out. "So," he said, measuring each word, "Michael had a farm. He considered himself a man. Belial wasn't always such an asshole, and he was the father. Who was the mommy?"

"A human."

"*How* was she a mommy?"

Khavi tilted her head. "Surely you know how it is accomplished."

"With a demon? Not exactly."

"But I have already told you."

"Dragons," Alice murmured. "The hounds, the bats, the spiders." Her gaze lifted from her sketchbook. "Have they all drunk at the table of the dragon?"

"Yes." Ebony eyes gleamed. "And they ate through their mothers' wombs when they were born."

Khavi was going to have to work harder than that to freak them out. "Yum," Jake said, thinking it through. So, Belial had either eaten dragon meat or drunk its blood—as had the bats and spiders. Their offspring would have changed, generation by generation. The original destroyed, and something new created—except Belial, a demon, had returned to his original form when he'd stopped consuming it.

And considering the blinding brightness, maybe it truly was his *original* form—his angelic form.

"You said Michael worked his mother's fields," Alice said. "So he was not born so violently."

"No. He slid from his mother with wings of black, and his white-feathered sister not far behind." She sneered at the head Jake still held, and he remembered the name she'd coupled with

Michael's: *Anaria.* "And so we came, two by two, the dark and the light."

"And Zakril?" Alice asked quietly.

Khavi's expression softened. "Our mother was the demon, and Zakril was the white. There were many demons who dined on the dragon, but not all performed the mating of the human's free will. And of those who did, only five pairs were born."

It made a sick kind of sense. A human couldn't be transformed into a Guardian or a vampire without their consent. Apparently a demon couldn't conceive without it being willing, either.

"We were ten: the grigori, who watched the humans. Who saw their fear when they looked back at us. Their greed when they attempted to use us. Their anger and their hate and their envy."

"But?"

Her hand rested on the shoulder of the unnamed male statue. "But Lucifer had not foreseen friendship and family, that demons might care for their human partners and their children, or that the light would balance the dark."

Lucifer? Jake had been operating under the assumption that this had been one of Belial's grabs for power. "Hold on a second. Lucifer planned this?"

"Yes."

Something wasn't right about that. Frowning, Jake set Anaria's head on the table, gave himself a moment to think. Michael was stronger than any demon, except maybe Lucifer or Belial. Why create such powerful beings—such powerful potential opponents? Unlike demons and the nephilim, the grigori wouldn't have been bound to serve him. So it didn't make sense.

Unless Jake was going about this the wrong way. He shifted gears and tried to think as Lucifer would.

Because the angels couldn't completely hide their difference from humans, they'd been worshipped as gods—which had pissed Lucifer off. He'd planned to wipe them out using the dragon. And, like any power-hungry prick, he would've assumed victory.

But even with the angels gone, he couldn't do much to the people. Lucifer was still required to honor human free will and life.

So, what's a prick to do? Jake thought grimly. What else, but develop a race of powerful beings and raise them to despise mankind? The grigori wouldn't have had to follow the Rules.

Yep. That would have been one hell of a plan: ten hate-filled

Michaels, consumed by anger and loose on Earth with no angels left to fight them.

Just the thought of it coated his stomach with ice.

It took only a second to sign his conclusion to Alice. She nodded, her mouth prim, and crossed her arms beneath her breasts. Yeah, the idea unsettled her, too.

"Then you . . . and Michael" —Alice's lashes flickered as she added the name—"don't have to follow the Rules?"

"We do. It was a condition of our transformation—just as dying while saving another's life was. It still is?" Khavi waited for them to confirm it, then nodded. "We fought alongside Michael after he was changed. As you can imagine, it was not long before we were all killed defending others from demons or nosferatu, just as he was."

"*Michael* was killed?" Alice shook her head. "I cannot even imagine it."

"His death might free you, yet you never imagine it?" A hard smile touched Khavi's mouth when Alice stiffened, but she only continued, "I cannot imagine anyone emerging unscathed from a battle with a dragon—as Michael did not. And three of us—of the grigori—were killed simply defending themselves, and could not become one of the watchers."

"Guardians," Jake said.

"Yes. And for those of us who were changed, the difference was not so very great. We already possessed our wings, our strength and speed—and we could sense another's emotions. Afterward, we could alter our shape, move between realms, and we each had our individual abilities." She paused, and her Gift eddied around them. Pulling in the correct words, Jake realized. "Our Gifts. If we Fall, are no longer Guardians, we give those up—but we no longer have to follow the Rules, either."

Jake exchanged a doubtful look with Alice and said, "You can teleport." Yet she'd stayed here?

"I *could*—if not for the symbols. But I do not know where he placed the ones that prevent it." She gestured to the glyphs on her face, then behind her waist. "Somewhere I cannot see."

Alice's lips parted, and she touched her own shoulder. "Belial. He's the one who has been here, but that you haven't turned your back on."

"Never of my choice. Just as it is not my choice that he comes now to ask if I have seen you."

"He—" Jake's gaze snapped to the door, his heart kicking against his ribs. "*Now?*"

"Soon after the nychiptera disperse. No," Khavi said as Jake's hand sought Alice's. "You do not leave that way. Stay, a moment. I will see where the nychiptera are at present, and how much time you have before he arrives."

As she strode toward the entrance, metal guards formed over her arms, chest and legs. She shoved on a gleaming helmet with plates to protect her nose and cheeks, and a bow appeared in her hand. Skin hardened to scales; her fangs gleamed when she turned and smiled.

"It will be a wonderful surprise to find you alive when I return."

CHAPTER 16

The opening of the door brought in the scent of blood and sulfur, the roar from a maelstrom of wings, and chilling, high-pitched shrieks.

They were still ringing in Alice's ears as she walked through the bathing chamber, holding her sketchbook. She didn't call in a pencil. The silk soles of her boots muffled her heavy steps.

It was not so difficult to see into the future. She only had to look around. This was what awaited her if she chose to safeguard her soul by imprisoning herself. This . . . but without the company of a hellhound, or a door, or any event she could look forward to with hope.

She emerged from the chamber to the sound of a soft warning growl from the hellhound, who still lay across the entrance to the opposite room. Jake paused in his slow approach, and his frustrated sigh pulled a smile from her.

No, he could not stop himself from wondering about that chamber any more than she could. But neither of them was willing to challenge a hellhound to look.

"Damn." He turned toward her, his expression rueful. He pushed his hands deep in his pockets. "So . . . whaddaya think?"

Alice placed her sketchbook on the table. In truth, she did not know what to think. She was completely uncertain—about what was truth and lies, how they would escape Belial again, whether Khavi could be trusted, and if what they'd learned here had any significance at all.

She only had one certainty: how very glad she was that Jake had not been separated from her. That she could rely on his integrity—and that she could test her instincts against his, without having to maneuver through motives and half truths.

And she would do so now. Alice leafed through the sketches until she found Zakril's skeleton and the symbols written above. She'd debated showing it to Khavi, but refrained—uncertain, again, as to the other woman's reaction.

"'She waits below,'" Alice recited. "Michael said this referred to the woman who had betrayed them."

"Yeah." Jake joined her at the table. His leg brushed her skirts, and she wanted to lean against him. Not for support; just to feel his warmth and strength. "But that's not Khavi. Anaria's the one who betrayed them."

Alice looked at the statue's head, lying on its cheek, then up at Jake. "Why do you suppose?"

"Why she betrayed them or why I think it's Anaria?"

"The second."

"Good, because I have no clue about the first. As for the second, here—" He flipped to a drawing of the statue in Tunisia. "And outside. You have any brothers, sisters?"

"No."

"Me neither. Okay, let's use Drifter then. Say you saw a statue with him kneeling in front of this woman, looking like Zakril did outside. Obviously defeated, forced to submit, and hating it—even though he loved her. What would you do?"

Her chest tightened. Put that way, the woman's—Anaria's—serenity and benevolence were an insult. "Destroy it, or take it somewhere Anaria could never see, so she could never take pleasure in it. But I am not Khavi."

"No, neither am I." He flipped back to the skeleton, the symbols. "Michael said they were divided—that the others wanted to put a Guardian on the throne in Hell. And he said that Zakril wasn't one of them. So, two questions: If the betrayal was Khavi's, why would she stick his bones on a wall, and then bring his statue down here—removing evidence of his defeat?

Evidence that no one would have seen anyway, until you came along?"

"Guilt? Perhaps she was torn between ambition and loyalty. Or perhaps she brought it with her so that she could always look upon his humiliation."

"But it's Anaria's head she beats up? Yeah, right."

She smiled slightly. "And the second question?"

"Why would Zakril be bowing down to Anaria? Can you ever—*ever*—imagine Michael forcing anyone to bow to him? Even with Lucifer, he wouldn't bother with the whole debasing routine; he'd just chop off his head."

That was true. "Yet Khavi admitted that she had hidden from Michael."

"Yeah, and that's the part I can't work out yet. But she loves Anaria, too—she made it sound like they were quite the tight little group, didn't she?—so I'm guessing whatever her reason for hiding, *that* has more to do with guilt and conflicted loyalties."

"Yes," Alice murmured.

Jake's eyes narrowed on her face before he said, "You didn't think it was Khavi who betrayed them."

"No. But I feared I pitied her too much"—and saw too many parallels in their isolation—"to judge correctly. I wondered if my desire to think the best of her was clouding my vision."

"And here *I* was wondering if you wanted to think the best of Anaria because she's Michael's sister."

Alice smiled. "I want to think well of Michael, but I do not feel a blind loyalty that extends to everything—or everyone— related to him." How odd, though, that she had begun to assume— blindly, perhaps—that Jake would always attempt to do what was right. With regard to his actions, she was certain that she would always jump to the best conclusion.

If not always the expected one.

Jake's gaze held hers before dropping to her mouth. "Keep your eyes open, goddess. You watch the hellhound, I'll watch the door. And it'll help if you tilt your head. But if you don't, I'll compensate for it. You'll be able to see past me."

While kissing him. Alice's heart seemed to slide into her belly, and lifted again when she rose up on her toes. She would not waste this opportunity. "I—"

"Don't talk," he said softly. But his head stopped its descent, and he waited, listening.

"I only intended to say that I wish you'd thought of this earlier."

"Okay. Now, quiet." Would he still be smiling when he touched his mouth to hers? She held her breath, watching, until he reminded her, "The hellhound, Alice."

The puppy stared back at her with three pairs of eyes, and Alice was wishing that she'd had a door to watch instead, when she felt a light brush against the corner of her lips. Perhaps he'd missed while looking the other way. She adjusted the angle of her head, searching for his mouth, but he'd already found hers again, a warm press full against her lips.

What heaven this was. Dear God, but she felt *so* very much for him—she could not even name all of the emotions tumbling within her.

How was it, she wondered, that the pounding of her heart didn't shake her entire body? Or that this gentleness didn't leave her frustrated, but filled her with the sweetest content?

Content, though they stood in Hell. How could that possibly be?

His hand skimmed over her hair from her crown to her waist, a tender exploration that felt more intimate than the kiss. He lifted the strands, letting them fall slowly through his fingers, sweeping softly against her back.

Alice rested her palm against his chest, then sighed her disappointment as Jake drew away, his shoulder blocking her view.

It was, she realized, the same view she would have if ever she lay beneath him.

Desire whipped through her, lashing at her nerves with heated flicks, and she closed her eyes. Oh, dear. Perhaps there was frustration in this, after all.

"Hey." His breath traipsed lightly over her cheek. "You okay?"

Her nod, she knew, probably seemed very short, and her spine very rigid. "Yes. I am simply attempting to understand how that did not open a portal."

Dear heavens, how she'd come to love the deep sound of his laugh. Like the rumble of an engine, caught by fits and starts. And the way it took over his face, lit his eyes the most brilliant blue.

She would kiss him again, she decided. Perhaps even drag him into the bathing chamber, put up the shielding spell, and push him against the wall. If they went quickly, two Guardians at full speed, surely it would take no more time than the kiss had.

But she wasted precious seconds imagining it. His laughter

died; shrieks pierced the chamber. And as Alice called in her naginata and spun around, she consoled herself with the knowledge that her fantasies had improved of late, even if her timing had not.

The door opened and an arrow-riddled bat streaked inside. As tall as Jake, it scrambled awkwardly across the floor on knuckles and clawed feet. It turned red eyes on them.

The hellhound pounced. Bone crunched as she tore off the creature's head. The stink of the bat's blood made Alice's eyes water, her stomach churn.

The earsplitting sounds at the door were joined by scratching, the ring of metal. Khavi burst inside, her skin coated in the same putrid blood.

She looked at the hellhound, and spoke in the Attic Greek. "Create a mess, Lyta. The scent must mask theirs."

Alice signed the translation to Jake; Khavi turned to them and continued in English, "We have not much time. Belial is visible on the horizon." Her armor vanishing, she strode toward the second chamber. "I have erased your footprints and— What is that?"

Dread tightened in Alice's chest when she looked at the table, her open sketchbook. Khavi was already standing next to it, her eyes a deep black.

Jake's hand clasped hers. Ready, she knew, for any reaction. "A week ago, we found this beneath a burial chamber," Alice said quietly. "The nephilim opened it. This is Zakril."

Alice didn't protest when Khavi leaned forward, ripped out the page and vanished it. She didn't flinch when the other woman placed her hand over Anaria's face, and crushed the bone with a flex of her fingers.

Behind her, Lyta tore into the nychipteran, shaking the ravaged corpse and swinging ribbons of crimson over the white floor, the walls.

"Come," Khavi said. "And tell me how it is that the nephilim are on Earth. I knew they would be, but not how or when it would happen."

Knew they would be . . . Alice's steps slowed. Here, she realized, was the source of the prophecy. Dear heavens.

Dimly, she heard Jake explain that the Gates to Hell had been closed, but that hundreds of demons were still left on Earth.

Khavi nodded. "I see. Lucifer would not be able to go through the Gates. But the Rules must be enforced, and so he released the nephilim. Tell me, do they bring the demon back to Hell for Punishment, or do they slay him?"

Death or Punishment—the two consequences a demon faced after killing a human or preventing free will. A Guardian was given the choice of Falling or Ascending.

"They slay the demon," Jake said. "It's the nephilim's only option. They can't return to Hell."

An ironic smile twisted Khavi's mouth. "No. Lucifer would not dare risk it, would he? Better that they pose a risk to Guardians and demons than to his throne."

"Yep. But enforcing the Rules isn't all the nephilim are doing—" Jake crossed the threshold of the chamber and stopped. "Whoa damn. Alice?"

She briefly met his eyes before letting her gaze search the chamber. She knew the glowing strands in their odd formations had surprised him, but she only gave them a cursory glance. In one of the upper corners, she found the familiar mind she'd sensed earlier: a cave weaver from Tunisia, weak—dying. The others lay upside-down on the bone floor, their thin legs curled, their bodies dry.

"When I repair the concealment spell, the threads pull them in," Khavi said. "They cannot bring the higher forms of life, but they do animals and insects." She stopped in front of a waist-high black marble cylinder. Symbols had been carved into the surface; the luminescent silk strands were embedded in each symbol, so that they glowed with soft orange light. At the top of the cylinder, hundreds of rigid threads rose from a point to form an open, inverted cone. "The burial chamber must be this one. I knew it was one of these two," she said, nodding toward another cylinder, "for they are the last Zakril made. I did not help construct either of them, but this is the one I most recently mended—and it is during that time you must have entered it and found his remains."

More cylinders were placed irregularly around the room. Each one, Alice realized, hid a temple. "And which did you mend before that?"

Khavi pointed. "It is the one that held the statue of Zakril. These threads"—she gestured to the cone—"are the anchors. When we constructed the temples, we put the threads within the stone. Upon its completion, the ends of each thread were gathered together"—she made a fist, like a child holding balloons—"and teleported here. They stretch between the realms, and feed the spell from the cylinders to the temples."

"And the spell was supposed to hide you from Michael?" Jake sounded as if shock had a stranglehold on his throat, but Alice was amazed that he was even capable of speech. She wasn't.

"Yes, it does that—but it was humans who concerned Zakril and me. Except to Michael's eyes, the concealment spell does not function when someone is alive within the temple. Yet when they were eventually abandoned, they might have stood for anyone to discover. And so the spell mimics the appearance of the sites before the temples were built, and the temples themselves are pulled into the in-between."

"The what?" Jake's confusion echoed hers.

"Into the reflection. In Caelum, in Hell, there is nothing of those realms that reflects—yet we see it, walk on it. It is the in-between."

No reflection . . . and no pictures. Alice shook her head. She knew what Khavi was referring to, yet didn't understand it. But she imagined that even if they had more time for explanations, it would still not make sense. "If they are in-between, how is it that they appear on Earth?"

"The threads that power the symbols fade. I am sometimes very quick to repair them." She shrugged. "Other times, I am not."

Jake crouched next to a cylinder. "How'd you prevent just Michael from seeing it?"

"We used his blood." Khavi frowned. "I suppose I could remove that part of the spell now. The threads might not fade as quickly."

"That'd help. Especially if the nephilim plan to do their rituals again; maybe he could go in and kick some ass." Jake looked over his shoulder. "Why hide from Michael in the first place?"

Khavi moved toward the rear wall of the chamber. "We have not much time." A dagger appeared in her hand, and she sliced her opposite forefinger, began writing symbols on the bone surface.

The disappointment in Jake's eyes sharpened into calculation. "Alice has hot water."

How very clever. Khavi's hand stilled, and Alice sweetened his offer. "Enough to fill your upper *and* lower baths."

No blood dripped to the floor when Khavi turned; her finger had already healed. "You are bribing me."

"Yep."

"And so it seems that Michael has taught you something after all." Pleasure and anticipation danced in her brown eyes. She gestured to the ceiling. "We will make the exchange there—and quickly, so that Belial will not detect the moisture."

It was almost instantaneous; Alice dropped the water out of her cache into the air, and Khavi vanished it.

"Now, do not interrupt. There is much to tell you, for I cannot explain *why* we hid without explaining what it meant to know someone like Anaria." She cut her finger again, and spoke while drawing more symbols. "She was the light. Zakril was, too, and so were others—but none were quite like Anaria. She looked at the world without cynicism, and you wished you could see it as she did. She would speak, and you wanted to believe her. Unlike many humans we knew, she did not wear her goodness as a false face—that would have been impossible to hide from us. It went through to her heart; her thoughts were all kindness, even to those who did not deserve it. Her humor and her manner were as sweet as Michael's were wicked."

Alice opened her mouth at the same time Jake did. They caught each other's gaze. Instead of speaking, he grinned and signed, *Michael, wicked?*

She pursed her lips. No, she could not imagine it, either.

But she could also not imagine a woman like Khavi was describing.

Khavi pierced her finger again, watched the crimson drop form on her decorated skin. "Anaria balanced him. We all measured our kindness against hers, used her example as a guide when we felt called to walk the darker paths. Michael was always our head, and the strongest of us in spirit—but she was the heart. We loved her unreservedly. Zakril, more so than all of us, and Anaria him in return. Their bond formed when they were children; in the spring before Lucifer brought the dragon up from Chaos, they were married." Her gaze unfocused. "I have not thought of spring in years. What season is it now?"

The wistful query made Alice's throat thicken. "In the north, it is late autumn."

"I would go south, then." She licked the blood from her fingertip. "I do not know when Anaria began to visit Lucifer. A hundred years after we went to Caelum, or a thousand—it had become difficult for me to measure time. But the reason for her visits was clear, and when we eventually learned of them, I do not know why we were surprised."

"Let me take a wild guess," Jake said, his voice flat. "She

wanted kids and she thought Lucifer would know how to make some. What'd they get instead—the nephilim?"

"I . . ." Khavi blinked, her eyes hardening to obsidian. "Yes. But they were not *Lucifer's*."

"Zakril's?" Alice wasn't certain if it was sadness or horror weighing so heavily in her belly. "How?"

"Lucifer had—still has—the body of the dragon Michael had slain. I do not know the method or spells Anaria and he used, only that her body rejected their attempts. So the women in the Pit carried the children to term."

It was horror. Silently, Alice moved closer to Jake, until she could feel the warmth of his arm against hers. The skin over his jaw had paled.

"Let me guess. They ripped their way out."

Alice closed her eyes. Dear God. Only a man would voice that.

Or a half demon. "*Ate*," Khavi corrected. "But you must see that it was for the best."

"No, not exactly."

"The women were willing. I am certain that Anaria arranged the bargains. They traded the service for a fast burn rather than prolonged torment, and were released from Hell shortly after giving birth."

"They were released?" The questions lined up in Alice's throat like soldiers, eager to fire. "The punishment in the Pit isn't eternal?"

"Of course not. Only the frozen field is; the others are reborn after they've been cleansed—given another chance. As for the nephilim, the nature of their surrogate mothers prevented them from holding their forms outside of Hell. *That* is best, for it means the nephilim need to possess a weaker human body while on Earth." Khavi paused, studied their faces, and must have seen the confusion there. "The humans in the Pit aren't flesh," she explained, and touched her fingertips to her forehead. "They are this. Spirit, energy. It takes form in this realm. So the women in the Pit had bodies to carry the seed." Her mouth twisted. "Zakril and Anaria's seed."

"Their children," Jake pointed out, "but the nephilim serve Lucifer."

"They serve the *throne*." A smile ghosted over her lips before she faced the wall again, placing each hand over a crimson symbol. "I imagine that was Anaria's doing; once she realized how their experiment had failed, she made the best of it. And so Lucifer used the nephilim to enforce the Rules against his demons on Earth. A Guardian could find little fault in that. And if in Hell, Lucifer used them to keep other demons in line—slaying, for example, any who rose against him—a Guardian might not fault that, either. The grigori might, however, even though the demons slain were not as they once had been."

"Lucifer was killing each of your demon parents because they were rebelling against him," Alice realized.

"All but Belial," Khavi confirmed. "And only because Anaria intervened, and led the nephilim against Lucifer."

"Even though they served him?"

"If they had succeeded, Anaria would have been on the throne. As it was, disobedience only risked Punishment or death. When they were defeated, Lucifer destroyed half and imprisoned the others. I suppose he thought he would have use of them again." She cast a wry look over her shoulder. "I could have told him for certain."

One of the sarcophagi had been missing from the rephilim's prison. "Was Anaria locked in with them—then rescued?"

"Yes. Zakril, Michael, and I went for her. Lucifer was too arrogant to guard the prison well, and it still took half our blood, our combined voices, and all of our knowledge to release her." She smiled. "I believe he moved the prison after that, and shored up its defenses."

"He put it in the spider," Jake said with a faint grimace. "Good hiding place."

Khavi nodded. "Afterward, Anaria told us what she had done—all of it with the best intentions and kindness: to give Zakril children; to liberate Hell from Lucifer's tyranny. She'd intended to abolish the Pit, to let the humans be free in Hell, and never feel pain from the flames."

"Oh, man. Yeah, I can see why it'd be hard to give her a slap for that." Jake shook his head. "But I'm guessing the ones who are burning deserve it."

"Yes." Khavi pushed against the wall, grunting the words. "And without flames, never cleansed. Never released or reborn. Never given the chance to be human again."

Alice and Jake moved forward to help, but she stopped them with a sharp glance.

Oh, how she loathed feeling useless. Crossing her arms beneath her breasts, Alice asked, "What were your responses to her?"

"Michael and I were more forgiving than Zakril"—this time, it was the wall that groaned beneath the pressure; Khavi's feet dug into the floor, her back and arms shaking with strain—"who felt betrayed. For a time. Then he returned to us. I do not know how many years passed before Anaria decided to . . . make humans . . . *better*."

With a final shove, a seam split the center of the wall, ran along the ceiling and floor. Doors now—and they opened easily, revealing an empty black stone room.

A familiar hum filled the chamber, resonated deep within Alice's flesh.

A Gate.

Disbelieving, she turned to Jake—and laughed aloud as he snatched her up, swung her around.

He did not completely release her when Khavi made an impatient sound, but set her feet on the floor and remained at her back, his arms linked around her waist. How casually he did that. Yet it was with the greatest self-awareness that she lightly rested her hands on his forearms.

She felt very young when Khavi observed them with an air of indulgence that was both amused and annoyed. An expression, Alice feared, that resembled what *she* had bestowed upon her students whenever she'd found them with their lovers instead of training.

It was fitting, however—with Jake, she *did* feel younger than she had since she'd accepted Teqon's bargain. No less burdened—but so much more hopeful.

Khavi's gaze locked on hers, and she spoke solemnly in ancient Greek. "You will not fulfill your bargain, and so your companion will die."

Jake? Oh, God. Oh, dear God.

Desperately, Alice retranslated Khavi's words. The meaning didn't change. "No. I do not believe you."

Her denial meant nothing. Khavi shrugged. "I have seen it. In his attempt to free you, his heart will be cut in two by Teqon's sword. How could he survive?"

He couldn't. Oh dear God, he couldn't. No Guardian could.

And she could not conceive of this. She could barely speak over the panic tearing through her. "Show me what you saw."

A still image filled her head: Jake, his swords held out to his sides like a brash man inviting a blow. Determination had hardened his features; his blue eyes were filled with fear and hope. A black ribbon was tied around his left wrist.

And Teqon's sword was embedded in Jake's chest—through the Styx logo on his T-shirt.

Alice's heart suddenly seemed to be pounding against icy needles, each beat piercing, bleeding. This couldn't be a trick—Khavi couldn't have known about the logo; Jake hadn't worn that shirt since they'd been in Hell.

You going to fill me in anytime soon? Jake asked.

Alice tightened her fingers on his arm, unable to respond.

Without a shift in tone, Khavi moved into English. "Anaria slaughtered an army of humans. Those Guardians who assisted her were given a choice to Fall or Ascend. But Falling would not remove a grigori's strength, and her actions were no better than a nosferatu's—so Michael ordered her death."

Too numb to be surprised, Alice stared through the open doors, at the Gate she couldn't see. When she returned to Caelum, she would . . . she would . . .

What?

"It was as if Michael had removed his own heart by giving the sentence, and Zakril would not let him bear the burden alone. So Zakril claimed it was his right as husband to carry out the execution. But he did not."

"Michael thinks he did," Jake said.

Khavi smiled. "Unlike Anaria, Michael has no Gift to see Truth. Zakril lied. We hid her instead, hoping that with enough time, Michael's anger would lessen, and Anaria would be forgiven—enough to live, even if she was never transformed to Guardian again. And that she would also see the error she had made, and atone for it. Many others came with us, those who had believed in her, and who wanted her to try again for Lucifer's throne. Anaria shared with Zakril and me what she had learned from Lucifer. We built this place, the temples, and moved as often as necessary."

"Whenever Michael got close?"

"Yes, but he only knew that I was among those who had left Caelum, and I had nothing to fear from him. He would not kill us for believing what Anaria had believed. Usually, we moved because demons found us."

"So, except those times, you were all cozy together. What's with the statue of Anaria and Zakril, then?"

Behind them, Lyta whined softly. Khavi's face lost expression, but the quickness of her speech revealed her urgency. "I do not know. Zakril, Aaron, and I had been searching out a location for the next temple. When we returned, the statue was there, and most of the Guardians had been killed. Anaria told us she was tired of hiding, that she wanted to resume what she had begun." She turned away from them. "We subdued her. Zakril still had Lucifer's sarcophagus, and we sealed her within. We only intended to hold her until we could find a place Zakril could remain with her, and be completely isolated from others. We separated to look. He must have built two—probably a temporary one, and then a more permanent temple he built while he entrusted the remaining Guardians to guard the sarcophagus. And he must have done it quickly, because the concealment spells were already in place when Aaron and I came here to await Zakril."

"Who's Aaron?"

Khavi pointed at the table. "My husband. Like Zakril, he had a Gift for shaping stone. And he sacrificed himself to save me when Belial ambushed us."

Behind her, she felt Jake's wince. "Oh, damn. Sorry. I didn't realize."

Khavi frowned at him. "How could you not? There is a Gate. Obviously, a Guardian sacrificed himself for another here." Her gaze rested on Alice. "A Gate is not a companion."

No, it wasn't. Alice's throat ached unbearably. "Zakril never returned."

"I knew he would not. I no longer see him—have not seen him since I came here. Until Michael comes, there will have been only you, your companion, and Belial." She paused, and visibly shuddered. "Who has almost arrived. You must leave now, so I have time to close the Gate. Please, do not delay in telling Michael that I await him."

His arms still wrapped around her middle, Jake urged Alice forward. "We won't."

"A moment." Alice called in a unit of vampire blood. "Please feed this to the weaver. Perhaps she'll survive until we return with Michael."

Confusion crossed Khavi's face, but she accepted the bag. "I will try. Now—"

"Hold on," Jake said. "One more thing—Belial's been using you as his personal little oracle, hasn't he? You've been telling his future—"

He broke off as Khavi held out a rolled parchment. Alice took the scroll—and because it was not a *Scroll*, she vanished it.

"That is what you will request," Khavi said. "The prophecy I gave to Belial."

Jake laughed softly into Alice's hair, and paused in front of the Gate to ask, "Did you tell Belial the truth?"

"Yes." Her smile was thin and amused. "But not all of it."

CHAPTER 17

Shockingly cold water enveloped Alice the moment she stepped through the Gate. She contained her gasp, sealed her mouth. She'd breathed underwater once before, and did not want to repeat the experience—the burning pain as water entered her lungs, the indignity of heaving it out.

She swam forward, giving Jake room to clear the Gate. After a few arm strokes, she came up against a smooth white wall that completely encircled them, as if they were in the shaft of a giant well. Light shone from above; she could not see the bottom.

She couldn't guess where they were. Obviously not in the sea surrounding Caelum—not if the walls surrounded *them*.

The hum of the Gate disappeared. Khavi hadn't delayed closing it.

Her dark hair floated around Alice's shoulders as she faced Jake. He stared upward, and a grin slowly widened his mouth.

You won't believe what this is, he signed.

What? she asked, but he only took her hand, and dug the toes of his boots against the wall to propel them up faster than they could have swum.

They didn't have far to go—only one or two hundred meters.

Alice broke the surface first, blinking in astonishment through a sheet of falling water.

They were in a fountain at the center of an unfamiliar court-yard. But she recognized the buildings and towers around them; this was near the Archives and Michael's temple. From outside the courtyard, she heard several Guardians talking, and sensed more psyches than had been in Caelum at one time since the Ascension.

For the gathering Michael had called, she realized.

Behind her, Jake began laughing. First in relief, then harder. She turned just as he went under. He bobbed up an instant later, choking and sputtering, but still laughing.

Seeing that he was unable to share the joke, she swam nearer to him, and saw the words inscribed in Latin at the bottom of an obelisk.

"Deeper than you think," she translated in disbelief, and set Jake off again. He sank, came up, and coughed out another mouthful of water.

She couldn't hold back her own laugh after that. It shook through her, and she steadied herself against the obelisk, running her fingers over the inscription.

Someone had a very strange sense of humor.

Alice dried her clothes as they walked to the square facing Michael's temple, but the stench of Hell still clung to her dress, her hair, her skin. But there was no time to wash properly, and the smell would provide the answer of where she and Jake had been, without requiring a word to be spoken.

Beside her, Jake tensed. She listened, heard the mutterings, the raised voices. The ebb of conversation told her there were several groups, large and small; other Guardians had broken off into pairs.

"I think they've finished," Jake said quietly. "And I don't think everyone likes what they've heard."

"Did we?"

"I'm reserving judgment. I've still got questions." The set of his face was grim. "I'm hoping Michael has answers."

"Yes." She called in Khavi's scroll, opened it. "I hope that some of them are here— Oh, blast. I'd also hoped it would be in Greek."

Jake glanced over at the demonic symbols. "At least it's not a bunch of stick figures miming the prophecy."

Yes, there was that. "I hesitate to ask Michael for the translation. Will you—?"

"Yep."

Though he could have vanished the scroll from her hand, he closed his hand over the parchment, his fingers brushing her palm.

"Promise me," she said. It was difficult to breathe, as if she'd been tightly laced into a corset. "Even if you find something that will free me, you will wait. And that you won't face Teqon alone."

There was a question in the ultramarine glow of his eyes, but he only said, "And deny you the pleasure of kicking his balls in? Not in a million years."

She nodded and continued to the square, pausing at the edge to assess the mood. Almost everyone was shielding emotions, but there were aggressive stances, uncertain expressions. Several Guardians surrounded Michael; half spoke with hostility, the others trying to calm.

The novices huddled together, signing quietly. Alejandro stood alone, as still as the column he leaned against, his dark eyes focused on someone across the square.

She followed his gaze, saw Selah and Ethan sitting on the steps to Michael's temple and Irena standing in front of them, impatience and anger in the taut line of her shoulders. The giant doors of the temple were closed, the frieze of Michael and the dragon carved into the marble unbroken.

Ethan met her eyes. Slowly, he unwound his long body from the steps and formed his wings.

Half of the Guardians in the square quieted and turned to look at him, then around to see what had captured his attention. Several gaped.

Perhaps she should have braided her hair.

"Do you think," Alice murmured, "that Ethan is so tall on purpose?"

Before Jake could respond, Selah touched Ethan's hand and they appeared in front of her. Selah drew in a breath, gasped.

Ethan tipped his hat back, his mouth smiling. But there was something else—fear? relief?—in his voice as he drawled, "Well, sure it's on purpose. The air's a bit fresher up here." His gaze moved to Jake. "We figured you must have gotten lost. Once

Michael got done jawing, we were heading on out to find you. It would have been an awful shame if you missed your party."

"Yeah, I can't think of anything much worse than that. Listen, Alice needs Michael to heal her."

Selah vanished, reappearing next to Michael. Alice gave Jake her most withering stare, but he only gazed steadily back. Relenting, she looked away just as Irena pushed through the novices that had gathered around them.

She stopped, her nostrils flaring. "You were in *Hell*?"

The square fell silent.

Alice sighed. Her gaze locked with Michael's as he strode across the marble pavers. His healing Gift slipped over her, searching.

The ache in her shoulder flared. Alice gritted her teeth to keep from crying out against the unexpected pain.

In an instant, his eyes changed from amber to obsidian. "What was done?"

"Symbols," Jake said. "Carved into her skin with your sword. Belial said they prevented her from teleporting out of Hell."

"Then how did you return?"

Though his voice and touch were gentle, Alice hissed in a breath when his fingertips skimmed over the symbols. She saw Irena's eyes narrow into green daggers; they were, she thought uneasily, directed at Michael's back.

"We found a Gate. And Khavi."

His fingers stilled.

"Who?" Irena asked, her voice sharp.

"One of the grigori. I briefly spoke of her; she is Zakril's sister," Michael said, stepping back. His gaze didn't leave Alice's face. "I cannot heal this with my Gift. It has to be removed—and cleansed."

Jake sucked in a breath. "Tell me you'll do it with water."

"I cannot."

Alice felt the blood drain from her face. She grabbed for Jake's hand, gripped it tightly—for support or to prevent his response, she didn't know.

"Perhaps," she ventured, "we can wait until—"

"It is best done as soon as possible."

Her chin lifted. "Very well."

Michael's features softened. "Fortunately, you resisted—and so your body resisted it, as well. The sword pierced deeply into the muscle, but the corruption has not spread. Once it has been cleansed, it will heal naturally. A few hours at most."

She nodded, and Michael turned, signaled to Alejandro. Alice glanced at Ethan, willed him to look at her. His face had paled, and she realized that Jake had been signing, telling the others either what had happened to them—or how Michael intended to heal her.

It must have been the latter. Her green eyes glittering, Irena jerked her head toward Michael's temple. "Come with me, Alice. I will prepare you."

She finally caught Ethan's gaze. *Please,* she mouthed silently. *I don't want Jake to see me like that.*

Facedown, again—possibly held down. Cut into and burned, again. She knew he felt responsible for the first; he would this, too.

Surprise moved across Ethan's expression. When he gave a short nod, she slipped her hand from Jake's, faced him.

Knowing it would appear false, she did not attempt a smile at Jake. "I hope you and Lilith will have good news for me when this is finished."

His jaw clenched. "Yeah. I'll drop it off, then go back for it when she's done with the translation."

Ethan came up beside her, and as she'd hoped, he bluffed his way through. "I reckon it'll take us longer than that. I'm heading there to tell Castleford what Michael had to say. I figure you can fill them in on your trip at the same time."

"I will do the same here while I'm being healed," Alice said. If she could speak at all.

Jake looked from her face to Ethan's. Not fooled, she knew, for an instant.

"Please," she said softly. "The translation is important to me. And I would prefer if you were the one to explain to Ethan why it is necessary. I fear I haven't the courage."

"Yeah, right." Jake closed his eyes, and relief slid through her when he added, "All right, goddess. You need mice, too? More vampire blood?"

"Yes." Dear heavens, Nefertari must be so very hungry. "And if you could stop by my quarters—"

"Consider it done." He took a step back, then another. "If I can't jump when she does, you got any advice on how to get out alive?"

"Yes." Now her smile was genuine. She laced her fingers together, so that she would not hold her hand out to him. "Run faster than Ethan."

✿

Michael's temple was not partitioned into rooms, but was an open space separated into living—and practicing—areas. Irena had already set up a sterile metal table amid a collection of mismatched furniture, carelessly tossing sofas and armchairs aside to make room.

Given that there was a large, open floor next to Michael's weapons display, Alice assumed that Irena had been one of those displeased by everything he'd revealed to them.

"Alice."

She looked around to find Drusilla with her novice, Pim. For once, the Healer wasn't bobbing.

"We haven't seen an injury like this," she said quietly. "Do you mind if we observe?"

"Of course not." Alejandro, Michael, Irena. What were two more?

And how contrary she was, for now she wished that she had not sent Jake away. She'd convinced herself it was for the best, but after looking at the table, she thought that clinging to his hand might be best, too.

Just as he'd held hers when the demons had struck the wings from his back.

"Michael," she said, and wondered if her expression was as cold as her voice sounded. Wondered if they could see the rage that lingered inside her. "Belial cut off his wings."

She projected the image of Jake on his knees, and felt the dark touch of Michael's mind against hers.

The temperature did not drop, but Pim visibly shivered as ice speared from Michael's psychic scent.

"I will demand payment," he said softly.

She nodded. Beside the table, Irena held up a robe of blue silk.

"Remove your clothes. It is better to ruin this than your dress."

Alice pressed her lips together. Reluctantly, she began to unbutton the small fastenings at her throat.

Irena's gaze shifted to Michael and Alejandro, and she snapped, "Turn, the both of you. If you look at her, I will stab your eyes." Her tone barely softened as she added, "And you as well, Dru. Pim."

Alice's throat swelled with gratitude. Blast. She would *not* weep before a blade touched her flesh. She heard movement behind her, and when Irena appeared satisfied and closed her own eyes, Alice vanished her dress. After pulling on the robe, she climbed onto the table and lay on her stomach.

Irena called in a knife. "How much do you need to see, Michael?"

"A hand span around the symbols."

Alice quickly braided her hair, pushed it to the side. Irena cut a large circle in the silk robe, exposing her shoulder.

Irena's fingers brushed her nape. "If you like, I will snap your neck, so that you feel nothing until your spine heals. Michael and Olek—Alejandro—will have finished by then."

The thought of having no control over her body frightened Alice more than the coming pain. "No."

"Take this, then." A thick strip of leather appeared between Irena's fingers. "Unless you want to scream."

She did, but not here. Not for this. She placed the strip between her teeth and bit down. From the corner of her eye, she saw Pim slide her hand into Drusilla's.

"Now be quick, or I'll kill you both," Irena said over Alice's head. Irena kneeled in front of the table, met Alice's eyes. "And do not fear. If they *are* slow, I will give you his heart."

Alice smiled around the leather. *Whose?* she signed.

Irena shrugged and took Alice's hands in her own. "Either one."

❧

Alice might have given him the go-ahead to spill the truth about her bargain, but Jake had a feeling she'd only pulled that out so he wouldn't argue about leaving her. So if she was still uneasy about telling Drifter, then it was better all around if Drifter figured it out for himself.

Halfway to Odin's Courtyard, Drifter broke the silence between them. "Teqon's got her bound, I reckon."

"Yep."

"She supposed to kill Michael?"

"Pretty much."

"Meaning?"

"If she can find a way to give Michael's heart to Teqon without killing him, that'd get her out of it."

"Son of a bitch." Drifter shook his head. "She looking at the prophecy in hopes of finding something to exchange?"

"Yep."

"And that's what you've got for translating."

"I do."

"She bargained to save her husband?"

Husband? More like a fucking crybaby. "Yeah."

"So she figured herself yellow for not fighting."

"Yep."

Drifter swore again. After a few more steps, he looked over at Jake. "It sure is interesting that we ain't flying. Your wings broken?"

"Something like that. You in a hurry?" Jake wasn't. He had several hours to kill—through torture. His heart was back there with her, and the gaping hole in his chest widened with every step. His head was probably imagining something worse than reality. Just a little cut, a little burn.

Yeah, and if he told himself that enough, maybe at the end of several hours, he'd believe it.

"I don't reckon I am." Drifter pulled his hat lower over his eyes. "She sent me a look at her spider. It stood damn near past my knee. There any chance she was fooling me with that image?"

"Nope."

❧

With all of the Guardians up in Caelum and the vampires sleeping, Special Investigations was quiet.

Jake stuck his head into Lilith's empty office and frowned. "Is it a weekend?"

Drifter nodded, looking queasy. Not just from the jump—Nefertari *had* been hungry. Mostly, Jake thought she'd been kind of cute, but Hell had put things in perspective.

A second after they teleported to Hugh and Lilith's house, Jake projected an image of the giant mama spider and her babies. Drifter was still swaying when a barefoot Hugh opened the door.

Tomato and garlic scented the air. From the kitchen, Jake heard water boiling, a sauce bubbling.

He'd forgotten that Hugh and Lilith *needed* food. But then, it was hard to think of them as human.

Hugh sized up Drifter, and smiled a little. "Hungry?"

"I don't reckon I'll eat for another century. You ever seen a giant tarantula hunt down a few itty-bitty mice?"

"No. Perhaps Lilith has—although I doubt what she saw hunted mice." His gaze swept over Jake. Hugh's expression didn't change, but Jake sensed a new tension in him. "I don't need to ask if it was difficult."

Because it was Hell, or because Jake looked different to him? "It could have been worse."

Hugh nodded. "Alice was with you?"

"She's up in Caelum now."

"And you want to return soon." He stepped back, gestured for them to come in. "I'll get Lilith."

"Okay— No, wait. Hugh." He frowned, dragged through his memory. Khavi, standing in front of them. His arms wrapped around Alice. The painful dread that had flashed through her psychic scent. "Before I forget . . . what does this mean?"

Hoping he didn't screw it up, he parroted the first line Khavi had spoken to Alice, the one that had sent despair crashing through her.

Hugh's brow furrowed, and he echoed the words a few times, changing inflections until Jake nodded.

"Yeah. That sounds right. Is it Greek?"

"Yes, an old dialect. Someone said this to Alice?"

Jake nodded.

Hugh frowned. "Is she bound by a bargain?"

Ice slipped through him. Had Khavi told Alice something about the outcome of it? "Yeah. What was it?"

Hugh looked at Jake and sighed heavily. "They told her that because she does not fulfill her bargain, you will die."

"Huh." Jake called in a toothpick, began chewing. He worked the exchange through, considered alternate meanings. And every way he looked at it added up to the same thing. "That sucks ass."

But Alice's reaction to the news had been pretty sweet. He clung to that thought, and followed Hugh inside.

§

For decades, Jake had only seen Hugh wear a monk's robe, so the bare feet weren't so unexpected. But seeing Lilith in cargo pants and a Hell's Angels T-shirt, sitting cross-legged on an ottoman and twirling spaghetti onto her fork, was like stepping into the Twilight Zone.

And it didn't help that as Jake stood through his debriefing, Sir Pup was sniffing at his jeans and rubbing his huge heads up and down his legs. But at least the hellhound didn't go for his crotch, and the wicked amusement in Lilith's eyes whenever she glanced at the puppy was familiar enough that Jake didn't feel compelled to teleport around, searching for a way back to his own dimension.

There was a long silence after he finished. Drifter stood in front of a large painting of Caelum, his thumbs hooked into his suspenders. Hugh sat on the edge of his blue sofa, his elbows braced on his knees, his empty plate in his hands. Lilith swirled the red wine in her glass, her expression thoughtful.

Finally, she glanced over at Drifter. "I'm waiting to hear the rest."

"Well, there ain't much to add."

"Did Michael even tell you half of that?" Hugh looked doubtful.

"All of it," Drifter said. When Lilith's eyes widened, Drifter admitted, "I'm still working through my own surprise that he volunteered so much. And I'll tell you, not everyone was happy to hear that Michael is Belial's son."

"I imagine not," Hugh said dryly.

"And everything else Michael told us matches up to what Khavi told Jake. Michael didn't leave anything out."

"Did he tell you anything *more*?" Lilith asked.

"Not much. I figure the only bit Michael filled in was why Anaria thought she'd wipe out an army."

"Does it matter? She killed humans, and it wasn't in self-defense. We wouldn't give vampires any leniency if they did the same. We shouldn't the grigori."

Funny to hear a former demon saying exactly what Jake thought—but since she did, he didn't have to. He shifted his weight, trying to ignore the nuzzling behind his knee. If Sir Pup started breathing heavily, nothing was going to stop Jake from jumping.

Jake hadn't even detected any scent coming from Lyta, but the next time he came back from Hell smelling anything like a female hellhound, his flippin' clothes were heading straight into an incinerator.

Drifter shook his head. "No, Michael wasn't explaining his decision—her killing them was reason enough for her execution. This was what came up regarding the question of why it was such a bad idea to have her take Hell's throne."

Lilith's brows arched. "Because she's a psychopath?"

"That would hardly make a difference," Hugh said dryly. "Hell has a long tradition of being ruled by one."

Yeah. Being psycho was probably either a requirement for the position or an inevitability. "She wanted to make humans better," Jake said. "I'm guessing she thought stopping a war would do that. And I bet she didn't intend to stop just one."

"Was she a complete fucktard?" Lilith lifted a hand. "Don't answer that. Obviously, yes. But what did she think it would accomplish? Did she even choose a side, or just decide that killing off the enemies of one group would mean only friends were left, holding hands and singing?"

"According to Michael, that's exactly what she hoped would happen."

Her mouth fell open. "I was joking."

Jake fought the urge to jump when Sir Pup licked his hand. "That's because you're evil," he said, shoving his fists into his pockets. "What's a joke to you is serious to someone who's all good inside, with marshmallows and roses coming out her ass."

Lilith turned her dark gaze on him. "I forget sometimes why I like you, puppy. Then you remind me." She used her wineglass to point at Drifter. "So Anaria decided to wipe out a random army to stop a war—and likely had some plan to stop *all* wars in the same way: by getting rid of one side, so there weren't any enemies left. Disregarding, for now, the sheer impossibility of that—what would be the point?"

"Seems her idea had two parts to it. First was getting rid of fear, desperation—whatever drives people to do whatever puts 'em in Hell."

"Treating the symptom rather than the sickness." Hugh pinched the bridge of his nose. "People are the cause of that fear and desperation, not just the reaction to it. She could stop wars, but she couldn't root out what drives people to fight—on a large or small scale. Everything might look better on the surface for a while, but human nature isn't going to change."

"Well, that 'better for a while' is what allows her the second part. For a while, maybe you've got less hatred and cruelty—and fewer humans heading down to the Pit."

Lilith choked. "To weaken Lucifer?"

"That's what she figured."

Jake frowned. "How's that work?"

"Burning doesn't just cleanse them, puppy. It leaves the . . ." Lilith rubbed the tips of her fingers together, as if trying to mold a word, a description. "Stain. The dark energy."

She didn't look satisfied with that, but Jake nodded. "The ash. The evil shit that's left when the rest is released."

"Yes. And that energy, that power, belongs to Lucifer—or whoever rules Hell. It allows him to shape his cities, to fortify his magic, to strengthen his lieutenants. It feeds him. So, when Hell runs low on humans, Lucifer isn't as strong." She let out a short laugh. "Not as strong . . . but the difference wouldn't mean anything to most of us. But to a grigori, who he's taught to use magic, and who might be supported by the nephilim? There, maybe he's got something to worry about."

"And so would the rest of us," Drifter said. "Because the other half of that is, if she succeeds, that means there's someone on the throne who doesn't have to follow the Rules. And if *she* doesn't have to, then the nephilim don't. So she'd be getting rid of the Pit, freeing humans to live in Hell—and using the nephilim on Earth to keep more people from heading on down."

Jake shook his head in disbelief. "It's the same flippin' thing Lucifer was doing with the grigori, except he was hoping they'd become asshole tyrants. But Anaria would be doing it for the people's own good—and instead of ten, she'd have a hundred."

"More than that if she got around to creating new ones," Drifter pointed out. "And with them, maybe no more wars, poverty —"

"No free will," Lilith interrupted darkly.

"And that's the sticking point, isn't it?" Hugh said. "For Michael—and it is for me. How have those in Caelum responded?"

Drifter ran his fingers up and down his suspenders before just letting his hands sit at his waistband. Jake knew him well enough to see he was weighing his words—and was reluctant to say them.

"They're splitting along the same lines as they did when Michael told us Lilith would be in charge of SI," he finally said. "There's some who don't question him. There's others who are uneasy and looking to see why and how, but are willing to accept his decision if it all works out to the good. There's some who just don't see beyond the 'demon' part. And there's others I can't read at all and who aren't saying much. But the worrisome thing is: they're splitting."

Hugh smiled slightly. "It is to be expected. But it does not necessarily follow that the division will be permanent; dissent and self-examination can make the corps stronger."

"Eventually," Jake said. "Now's a bad time for it."

"I wonder if there is a good time." Lilith set her plate on the floor. Sir Pup hopped over, cleaned it with single swipe of his tongue, and headed back to Jake's pants. "But I agree that our balance has been more precarious of late. Tell me, puppy, what do you make of the nephilim in Turkey?"

"I think I have no clue."

"Well, shit. That's because my head's been filled with bargains and spiders since I saw you and Alice."

Drifter held up a folder, and Jake vanished it. Immediately, he pulled the file out of his hammerspace and flipped it open to a map. On either side of a strait of water—the Dardanelles—seven points had been circled in red.

"Those are seven small vampire communities," Drifter said.

A rock seemed to settle in his gut. "Wiped out?"

Drifter didn't need to answer that. "We got word three days ago. Michael's got a team patrolling, but those last two took place pretty much under their noses."

"Actually, behind their backs," Lilith said. "The nephilim broke pattern. They had been moving southwest along the strait. The next two were northeast, above the first community."

Doubling back might have thrown Michael's team off the scent for a short time. But if the nephilim were avoiding the Guardians, it would have made more sense to leave the region entirely.

Which meant they had a particular interest in the area.

He looked at the movements. They'd started over, but in another direction. Backtracking wasted time and energy. That wasn't what he'd have expected of beings who were so efficient they could kill—in a single night—every vampire in a large city.

"What are they searching for?"

Lilith's eyes narrowed. "More vampires to kill?"

"Nuh-uh. If they were just moving through the region, they wouldn't start in the middle." He'd bet anything that wasting the vampires was just something they did on the side. Out of frustration, for fun—or just because it was convenient. Like picking up a piece of litter not because you were cleaning, but because the trash can was right there.

Yeah. Searching, and although they didn't know exactly where to look they had a general idea of where to find it, because—

"Oh, fucking hell. The Scroll." The nephilim had taken it from the burial chamber—a message, left for them. "Telling them where to find her. Or her sarcophagus."

Hugh and Lilith exchanged a look.

"Anaria?" Hugh asked.

"Yeah."

"You reckon she's in that last temple Zakril built?"

"I dunno." Jake vanished the file again, linked his hands behind his head, and paced the room. Sir Pup followed him, sniffing. "Because that concealment spell doesn't work if someone's alive in it—and even locked in a coffin, she's still alive. And that's twenty-four hundred years of no one stumbling across the temple . . . or the ruins." He stopped. "Unless it's underground. Another hypogeum."

" 'She waits below'?" Lilith quoted.

"Yeah. Once Alice heals up, I'll jump over there with her, and we'll start looking."

"And what do you do if you find her?" Lilith mused. "Is more than two thousand years in a box enough of a punishment? Should you free her? Or should you just carry out the execution?"

Just the thought of working through those questions made him uneasy. "I dunno. Chances are, I wouldn't know how to open the sarcophagus. And Michael . . . shit, he doesn't even know yet that Zakril lied to him."

"I'd wager he does by now," Drifter said. "He wouldn't be leaving Alice alone, not until he was sure everything was healing like it should."

"Yeah." Jake would rather have been with her, too. But instead of jumping to Caelum, he called in Khavi's scroll. "I need a favor, Lilith."

"Are you certain you want to phrase it like that?"

Considering it was for Alice, he didn't mind being indebted. But Lilith had a point—and the anticipation gleaming in her dark eyes told him which way to go.

"I'll let you translate this prophecy . . . if you call your puppy off my leg."

"Done." She held out her hand for the scroll as Hugh laughed and gathered their dishes. Sir Pup flopped onto the floor with an unhappy whine. "And tell me about this bargain."

Jake only hesitated for a second. Alice hadn't asked him to tell anyone but Drifter—but if anyone knew their way around a

bargain, might find a loophole, it was Lilith. By the time he finished, Hugh had returned from the kitchen, a frown etched on his
forehead. Lilith met Hugh's eyes and sighed.

"Teqon's got her," she said, turning back to Jake. "The bargain
is so straightforward, there just isn't any room to move."

"So finding something to exchange is our best bet."

"Yes. Or a threat that forces him to release her—but unless he
has a compelling reason to release her without gaining anything
in return . . ." Lilith spread her hands. "It's difficult to find something a demon cares about more than himself. He doesn't have a
throne to lose—and you can't threaten his life, because slaying
him doesn't free Alice."

No, killing Teqon made it impossible for her to ever free herself. Jake scrubbed his hand over his hair, his mind racing. His
chest ached; his gut was a lump of hot lead.

"Do you think she could, I don't know . . . go to Teqon, and
bring Michael with her. She's technically brought his heart to
Teqon then. She just hasn't taken it out of his body."

He'd never seen sympathy on Lilith's face before. It made the
ache worse.

"No. There was an understanding between them when the bargain was made, of what it meant to bring Michael's heart. If
meaning could be changed so easily, she could ask Michael to cut
paper in the shape of a heart, and give *that* to Teqon."

"Well now, hold on a second." Drifter shook his head. "Charlie changed the meaning of Sammael's bargain. We both knew
when that bargain was struck, 'preventing any hurt from coming
to her' meant physical injury. She made it about emotional pain."

"Yes." Lilith nodded. "Another meaning can be layered over
the original—but the change has to be agreed upon by both parties. Sammael accepted her interpretation because it benefited
him. If he hadn't, how long would it have been before a Guardian
killed him?"

"About five days," Drifter said easily, but frustration heated
his psychic scent. "Four, if Irena had come visiting early. So there's
no other option for Alice?"

"She could wait until Michael falls in combat, then remove his
heart and deliver it to Teqon. But that might be thousands of
years—and runs the risk that Teqon or she might die before
Michael."

"Dammit," Jake said softly. His fists curled. But there was

nothing here to hit, to rage against. "Dammit. Then it depends on that prophecy. And finding something in there that he wants more than Michael's heart."

Lilith unrolled the parchment. Her gaze quickly skimmed over the symbols. "This will take a little while."

"I'll wait."

"Not here. Not unless you shower," she said without looking up. "The apartment over the garage isn't being used; Hugh can find you some soap. A box of soap. And change your clothes."

"And should I leave my flippin' pants on the floor for Sir Pup?"

The hellhound lifted his heads with a chorus of hopeful whines.

Lilith eyed the puppy. "*Not* one of the carpeted floors," she told him.

Jake opened his mouth, thought better of it, and just followed Hugh out of the room, with Sir Pup prancing along behind him.

CHAPTER 18

Alice sat beneath the tree in her courtyard, watching Remus and Romulus weave a new web between her portico columns, and willing the faint ache in her shoulder to subside. The pain was not so terrible now. And once the gaping wound had sealed over, she had erased the stench of burned flesh with a short bath and her first shampoo in years.

Perhaps it had been wasteful to lather the pink liquid over her skin as well as her hair, and absurd to sit in a cloud of strawberry-perfumed air, but the fragrance had been too heavenly to resist.

She wasn't certain why Michael hadn't left yet, but it wasn't due to that lovely smell. He sat quietly beside her without breathing—he never breathed unless he was talking. He'd already determined that she could be teleported without landing in Hell. Now she was all but healed, yet hoping that her torment would soon end.

In one hundred and twenty years, she had not passed this much time alone with the Doyen. If she had a choice, she never would again.

He was, she supposed, very pleasant to look upon. And his company was agreeable enough, but she'd have welcomed amusement—or even irritation—instead of being left almost wholly to her own thoughts.

Particularly when those thoughts so often drifted to her fate—and Jake's—if she didn't kill Michael.

How could one man be so very serious? And did anything discomfit Michael? Feeding her widows and rousing Nefertari from her mice-induced slumber had not. Boredom apparently wouldn't send him fleeing, either.

Very well, then. It was probably best not to lecture a man like Michael, so she would take another route. "Khavi told us that you were once very wicked."

"I was also once very young."

She opened her mouth, but could not voice the salacious question that sprang to her tongue. Not to Michael. In all probability, she would end up more uncomfortable than he.

Sighing, she tugged at her skirts, rearranging them over her lap. An ethnography describing urban vampiric cults—formed by humans who only knew of vampires through literature and films—waited in her cache; her time might be best spent reading.

Michael spoke before she could turn to the first page. "I find that I am uneasy with you."

How strange. Alice pursed her lips, searching for any pain in her emotional response, and discovering none. "I find that I am accustomed to producing unease."

"You must understand—" He hesitated briefly "It is because I have been in love with you the past one hundred and twenty years."

Oh, dear. Alice gazed at the sky through the lattice of thin marble leaves, wondering how one gently rejected the Doyen.

"And I would have opened my heart to you before," he continued softly, "but I live in fear that you will steal it."

Her book dropped to her lap. "Oh!" she exclaimed through her laughter. "You *are* wicked!"

His smile didn't sit as awkwardly on his mouth as she'd imagined it would. "Or I have observed that you are more at ease with people who have made you laugh. Particularly if they have made you laugh at yourself."

Was it so simple? "And what puts you at ease?"

"I have yet to find it. But one of us must be, or we will not be able to speak as we need to."

Alice sighed. "Of the bargain?"

"Yes. We have avoided it for too long."

Michael stood abruptly, and she realized that while he might never be completely at ease, he typically wasn't *uneasy*. Yet he was now; that part of his confession hadn't been in jest. She rose to her feet, crossed her arms beneath her breasts.

"If you need assistance," he said, "I will help you."

Had that been so difficult? "Yes. I know you would."

"But you do not feel comfortable asking for it. That, I feel, is unacceptable—and a situation that is of my creation. I know that you have struggled with your decision . . . as I have with mine. And that struggle is the reason for my avoidance, and for my . . ."

How very odd this conversation was. "Unease," she supplied.

"Yes. For although I would stand and fight with you, side by side, and die to save you—I find I cannot stand and allow you to kill me, so that you could save yourself."

Her knees went weak. "I would never expect you to."

"I know." His grave expression could have been sculpted from stone. "I expected it of myself. I cannot decide if it is a failing that I will not do it."

And so she reminded him of that struggle, made him feel that failure. Yes, she could see why he had avoided it—and her. "I do not think it is a failing," she said. "But I suppose that my opinion does not make your struggle easier. If you told me that I should not feel wretched when I imagine myself cutting out your heart, I would still feel it."

A twitch of his lips cracked the stone set of his face. "And do you imagine that often?"

"Oh, yes. Quite often. And so we will agree: you shall not feel a failure for wishing to live, and I'll not feel wretched when I imagine killing you. The only thing for which we will feel guilty is regularly breaking our agreement with each other."

"That is acceptable." He looked toward her quarters. "I believe you have been awaiting this."

Jake. She heard him opening the mice cage, the shuffling of tiny feet across wooden shavings. His shields were up. Did that mean he was hiding bad news, or hoping to surprise her with good?

Lacing her fingers together, she pressed them against her heart.

It leapt when Jake suddenly appeared in front of her. And it constricted painfully when she saw his face.

"Alice," he whispered.

He didn't need to say it. He'd found nothing in the prophecy.

Her body was rigid. She would not fall. There must still be *something*. "May I see?"

The sheet of paper appeared in her hand. It fluttered, and she had to force her fingers to cease their shaking. The words blurred in front of her. Dragons and blood. Caelum's voice. They meant nothing, there was nothing here—

"Oh, dear God."

Upon the destruction of Michael's heart, Belial will ascend to the Morningstar's throne.

She read the line again. Jake's hands circled her waist, steadying her. And she knew his tormented expression was not because the prophecy contained nothing to use as an exchange.

It was because Teqon would never accept *any* replacement.

"Jacob."

Jake pulled her against his chest as he turned to face Michael. Her arms trapped between them, Alice crushed the paper in her hand, vanished it. She would study the rest of the prophecy later. She could not read another word without screaming.

And she could not let herself give up.

But at this moment, she needed to push it away. She closed her eyes, and listened to the rumble of Jake's deep voice.

The nephilim were searching for Anaria. Earlier, Michael had not even blinked when she'd told him about Zakril's lie. His reaction to Jake's news, and the announcement that he and Alice would look for the temple, was just as flat.

"Very well. I will continue hunting the nephilim."

She felt Jake's nod. "And what about Khavi?"

"We must wait. If Belial is still with her and we appear, he will kill her rather than let her leave."

Sensing Michael's hesitation, Alice looked up. Reluctance cast a shadow over his features.

"The symbols *were* to keep you there, Alice. Belial cannot lie. He would have used Jacob to teleport, and formed a bargain to keep you both in service."

Alice frowned. Both in service? What could she do—direct spiders to devour Lucifer's armies?

The muscles against her forearms hardened. Jake's arms tightened around her, and fury heated his reply. "What—he hasn't had a Guardian to try it on? Would all of them get in on the action? What's the fucking deal with demons thinking they should have kids?"

Oh, dear heavens. Alice touched her stomach, felt sick.

Bitter humor twisted Michael's mouth. "It is an act of creation. They believe it will bring them closer to Glory."

But it was not all terrible. Not when it had been willing. It had created Michael. And yet Belial also looked forward to Michael's destruction, because he believed it would gain him a throne.

Jake shook his head, anger still sharpening his voice. "All I know is, if that's the path to Glory, I'm hopping off. And leaving a few land mines behind."

"If you give me notice, I will help you bury them." Michael smiled slightly, then gave a short nod. "Find me if you need anything."

A soft sound filled the air when he disappeared, like the pop of a champagne cork.

Jake's arms were still around her. She didn't want to pull out of that strong embrace. Didn't want to return yet to the prophecy, and her bargain.

" 'Jacob,' " she echoed, smoothing her fingers from his collar to his shoulders. Her eyes were level with his clenching jaw. How cowardly she was. "Is he the only one who calls you by that name?"

"Yeah. Unless my grandma is in the Guinness Book for 'oldest woman.' " The shadows on his face deepened when he tilted his head forward. "Listen, Alice—"

"Please!" Her fingertips covered his lips. "Don't say anything. Let's not either of us speak."

He dropped his brow to hers. His eyes were closed, and she shut hers, as well. "No talking at all?"

"None."

"For how long?"

"I will tell you."

His breath moved over her mouth in a silent laugh, and he nodded. Content, it seemed, to hold her and wait.

That would not do at all. In the silence, her mind was already leaping where she didn't want it to go.

But there was another leap she could make. And he would not ask questions she wasn't prepared to answer.

Such as why, when she knew it was best to shun intimacy, she wanted to lift her lips to his. And she would not have to look within herself to discover what had changed in the past week— would not have to find an answer to how "you must see that I can't" had become "please" and "now" and "quickly."

No gentleness. She didn't need it, didn't want it. Jake would never leave her frustrated. She only needed to have the courage to let herself go where he led.

Alice opened her eyes, and leapt.

❧

Hot. Damn.

Alice didn't want him to talk? He wouldn't talk. He'd do anything she asked as long as she didn't take her tongue out of his mouth.

Her hands ran down his chest. Christ, oh, Jesus Christ. Straight for the snap of his jeans. Straight for his dick.

He was hard so fast it *hurt*.

She ripped open his fly. Her slender fingers wrapped him in a tight grip. A groan tore from his throat—half need, half disbelief.

No way was this happening. Women didn't go from a couple of kisses over the course of a week to pumping a guy's cock in the middle of a courtyard. But damn if he'd ask why Alice had.

His palms slid to her ass. Not much there beneath the silk, but a handful was enough. He hauled her up against him.

God, she smelled good. Like strawberry pie in summer.

Her hands left his dick, but that was peachy, because her skirts slid across him and her legs were suddenly around his waist. She hitched up her dress, and—

Whoa boy. She was already naked underneath those skirts, and rubbing against him.

His brain should have exploded. Instead, the flippin' thing started working.

What the hell was she doing?

The thought stuttered to a halt as she reached between them, tucked the head of his cock against moist heat, and bore down. Jake staggered forward. Her back hit the wide trunk of the marble tree. Stone leaves shivered above them.

She squeezed her legs, drawing him in. Oh, fuck. This wasn't right. He was halfway inside her, she was hot and tight, but this wasn't feeling anywhere near as good as it should have. The flesh gripping him—*resisting* him—was moist, not wet.

She wasn't ready. She'd jumped him, but she wasn't even aroused.

Yet.

He grabbed her hips, held her still. A growly sound came from her throat—frustration, discomfort. Well, hell yeah there was discomfort. So he just needed a second to figure this out, to think, and he'd get them rocking.

Okay. He understood this. A trip to Hell + Belial + crazy Guardian woman + getting home safe + a healing more painful than the injury + crap news about the prophecy = a mindless fuck against a tree. Affirmation of life or some shit like that, and with the bonus of not thinking about her bargain while he screwed her silly.

And he was on board for that, but Jesus—he thought he'd get a chance to kiss her ear first, or get a look under her dress, maybe cop a couple of feels.

The pressure of her legs increased. Her kiss became more frantic.

Okay, then. So this time, a quick bang. And next time . . . He just had to make sure there was one. He couldn't fuck this up, and hope for a chance to fix it. He'd prove he cared for her pleasure as much as his own—more than his own—and next time, she'd let him take her dress off. So he'd get this right the first time.

He *had* to get this right.

Best-case scenario for that was: he withdrew and started over. That wasn't happening here. So he'd go for option two.

Slowing her down.

Her tongue was drilling past his lips. Her palm clapped over the back of his neck when he pulled away, but he got the space he needed. He closed his lips around her tongue, sucked lightly.

When she shivered, he licked his way back into her mouth. He hadn't forgotten the last time he'd done that, and her reaction was exactly what he'd been hoping for. She made a little sound of surprise and need, arching toward him. Meeting him lick for lick.

Her legs still wrapped him tight, but she forgot about pulling. He was sliding in anyway, her weight doing the job. But the going was easier, and by the time her hands were moving up the back of his head, her mouth sweetly devouring his, she was slick enough.

He pushed deep. Alice gasped; her lips and hands stilled.

Yeah, he wasn't going to move either. One little thrust and he'd probably come, and that wasn't on his list of priorities right now. And he wasn't going to think about how wet she was getting, or listen to that funny stuttered noise she began making, like a desperate keening that she repeatedly tried to swallow, or the way she began to buck, as if testing out the feel of him stuffed inside her.

The bucks became thrusts, the noises more demanding. Oh, Jesus. It'd be over in two seconds if he fucked her with the fast, hard strokes she apparently wanted.

All right. This called for diversionary tactics. He leaned in, pressing her heavily against the tree with the bulk of his weight. His hips ground in wide circles. It'd feel deep and rough, but there was more rolling than in-and-out. Good for him, because just thinking of baseball wasn't going to keep him sane, and he'd be rubbing up against her clit once he got her pelvis tilted at the right angle.

Her fingers caught on his collar. He vanished his shirt, and instantly regretted it when her teeth dug into his shoulder, biting him. Her tongue worked frantically against his skin. Oh, fuck fuck. Her mouth was as hot and wet as the rest of her, and now he was thinking of his cock inside her instead of trying to forget that he had one.

Angles, he reminded himself, desperate. She was pinned against the tree, so he let go of her hips and reached back. Her boots were still laced up to her shins, her silk stockings covered her knees and were held up by a ribbon tied around her lower thigh. His balls tightened as his fingers found the edges of her stockings, and beyond that, warm smooth skin—

Oh, Jesus. Mickey Mantle's career batting average was two ninety-eight. DiMaggio, three twenty-five. Willie Shoemaker's was . . . was . . .

Shit, oh shit. Shoemaker was a jockey. He rode—

No. No thinking about riding anything here. He needed to focus. Or *not* focus. Christ, he couldn't think.

He filled his hands with her bare ass. Lifted her higher, until her lower back curved and the base of his cock ground against her clitoris.

Alice cried out, panted. She bit and licked his neck. Baseball wasn't going to work anymore. Jake blanked his mind. That didn't do it. He tried to imagine what was happening to the jeans he'd left with Sir Pup.

That helped, a little.

So did Alice, when her legs began trembling and tightened. When the erratic push of her hips told him she was close. When she stiffened, reaching for orgasm. Her head fell back, and she strained and dug her nails into his arms, and he thanked God and began to fuck her as she'd wanted, as he'd wanted, long, deep strokes that made the leaves shiver and clink.

Until she made another sound, of disappointment and loss. He saw her frown in confusion, felt the tension leave her muscles.

Oh, no. No, no, no.

He tried to push it back, began to grind again, to bring her up with him again. He buried his face in her neck, felt the warmth of her skin through her thin silk collar. But it was like holding back the ocean; though he clenched his teeth and stopped moving, it boiled up through him, spilled over.

Shock and horror held him motionless, until Alice dropped her legs from around his waist, pushed at his shoulders. The hitch of her breath tore at him. He pulled back, and the sheen of tears in her eyes ripped out his heart.

He'd fix it. Jesus, please let him fix it.

He fell to his knees. Gathered the skirts bunched at her waist in his fists. She batted sharply at his hands, yanked the silk from his grip.

And walked away.

Jake stared at the twisting roots in front of him, the cracked pavers. Somehow, his blood wasn't all over them. There was a hole in his chest, but somehow, that marble was still white.

He turned. To beg, maybe. She'd reached her doors, but he caught the shattered look she sent after him. That wasn't disappointment.

That was failure.

That was the same damn thing he was feeling. But why the hell was she—

God. Because she hadn't come?

And he'd bet anything that was why she'd swatted him away; she was afraid it would happen again. That she'd get close and lose it a second time.

Stupid, both of them. Fucking stupid. She hadn't had sex in a century, and he'd been jerking off to pinups for more than a decade. What'd she think, that he just had to stick it in and she'd get off? Did *he* think he could stick it in and *not*? It was a miracle he hadn't blown his load the second she'd touched him.

That hadn't been a fuckup, and he was damn well going to get a next time.

Alice closed her doors.

Jake took two steps, and jumped.

❧

She walked right into him. Jake cupped her face in his hands and had his mouth over hers before she could say a word. His thumbs wiped the tears she'd allowed to fall. She sagged against him. She'd begun buckling, he realized, the moment she'd shut her doors.

When her lips opened beneath his, he jumped again.

❧

The air was humid and perfumed by strawberry, but the sweet psychic flavor once permeating this chamber had faded. She'd been absent too long, and although she'd bathed after they'd returned, she hadn't used her tub in the usual way.

He saw her look at it now in confusion. He brought her hand to her thighs and rubbed lightly, watching her face.

No talking, he thought, but he needed her to understand. His fingers pressed against hers. *Teach me.*

Her eyes widened, and his heart sank when she pulled away. But she didn't let go of his hand.

She led him through a library that was a mess of papers and books, thick rugs and low, cushioned furniture. With her every stride, her steps firmed and quickened, until she was gliding. The tip of her heavy braid barely swayed. He caught the ribbon, tugged, and vanished the looping black satin into his hammerspace.

They climbed stairs. The top floor was one large, empty room. No windows opened the walls; the roof peaked like an attic. Alice came to a halt.

A thick, pillowy mattress appeared in the center of the bare floor. Cushions and sheets of sapphire silk covered it a moment later.

Jake scrubbed the heel of his free hand over his chest, trying to rub out the ache that had been building since they'd left her bathing chamber. And to think he'd considered taking her back to his place and the cot he used when he drifted. Alice apparently drifted more comfortably than he did.

She pulled him forward. She didn't seem as tall now, and he caught a glimpse of her stockinged toes. He followed, vanishing his boots.

His heart was about to pound through his rib cage.

She let go of his hand and stepped onto the mattress. Her dress flared around her when she dropped to her knees in the middle. With abrupt movements, she arranged the cushions at the head of the bed.

She didn't meet his eyes as she turned and lay back on the cushions, her body as rigid as if she lay on a board. Her fingers seemed to walk along a moving plane of silk as she rucked her skirts at her waist. Her heartbeat raced as her hem drew up over her knees, her thighs.

Nervous as hell, he realized. Afraid, maybe. But fighting it so that she could do what he'd asked.

Jake slid onto the mattress beside her before she exposed any more. He didn't look down. He kissed her softly, slowly, until the stiffness left her.

The nervousness didn't. But his didn't either, so they were even.

He lifted his head, held her gaze. When she shifted her focus to the ceiling, his chest constricted. But she touched his cheek, and he realized she wasn't trying to shut him out.

She just couldn't watch him watch *her*. She could expose herself now, but only because she wouldn't see him looking at her.

Okay, then. He was all right with anything she had to do. He moved down the sapphire sheets, breathing again, inhaling that sweet berry scent. Her fingers rested at the small patch of dark curls that didn't quite hide her clitoris, though he couldn't see any more of her sex. She wasn't stiff now, but her thighs were locked together.

And they weren't wet. At some point, she'd vanished his semen.

Jesus. His cheeks heated. He should have done that for her.

She let out a shuddering breath. Her left hand fisted in her skirts, and her right moved through her curls. Her fore and middle fingers slid to either side of her hooded clitoris, and she began to rub with tiny strokes.

Jake didn't move. She must still be feeling nervous, shy. But as the seconds passed and she didn't change her rhythm, didn't delve deeper past her clit, open her legs or touch any other part of herself, he came to a different conclusion.

This wasn't the effect of shyness; this was efficiency.

And habit. Christ. When he'd been fifteen, he'd gotten so

good at whacking off he could be out of the bathroom within a minute or two. But that speedy orgasm—release, without any good buildup of tension—had eventually lost its appeal. Thing was, he'd had a hair trigger after that, and he'd pretty much had to relearn how to stroke one out.

Alice's lips parted. Her thighs tightened, trembled. Her back arched. Her clitoris pulsed gently between her fingers.

She lay back against the mattress and sighed. Smiling now.

Jesus, he thought. *Jesus.*

One hundred years. More than one hundred years.

He wanted to cry. Then go back to Hell and kill Henry Grey and her fucking doctor.

Alice lifted her hand, and he pushed her fingers back down.

She glanced at him, frowning. Irritation sparked in her pale eyes when he nodded for her to do it again. He grinned, and she looked up at the ceiling, her lips in a prim line.

Jake leaned over, let his mouth hover above her moving fingers. Let her feel his breath.

Yeah. Not so steady now, not so rhythmic. The hand fisted in her skirts flexed open. Her clit flushed a deep pink, peeked out from the protective hood.

Tension, arousal.

Moisture glistened. He licked it away, left his own. Alice dragged in a halting breath. His cock hardened to steel when he saw her use the pad of her finger to swipe across the flesh he'd just licked. Her speed increased.

Not so fast. Not this time.

He closed his lips around her, began to suck. Her hips jerked and she pushed at him reflexively, before making a low noise and running her fingers over his hair.

God, his dick ached from that rasping touch, like she was rubbing his cock instead of his head. His hand slid to her locked knees. He pressed lightly, and she let them separate.

Barely separate. But it was enough to work his hand up between her thighs, testing her responses as he went higher. All good. All good. She was slippery beneath his tongue now. Every time she twisted away, as if she couldn't bear it anymore, she came right back.

Her flavor was sweet, subtle. He wanted to search it out, drink in more. Wanted to push his tongue inside her instead of his fingers.

A groan rose through him when he found her drenched. She tensed, but it was anticipation. No fear. No discomfort. With two fingers, he fucked her slowly, drawing out each easy thrust of his hand, timing it against his tongue.

Within minutes, the familiar trembling began. This time, he didn't change speed or depth.

Her fingernails clawed the sheet, her silk-clad feet slid together frantically. Her knees snapped closed, her thighs clamping his wrist.

He rode with her as she arched and cried out, the sound too guttural to be a scream. Slick muscle clenched around his fingers. She came down, and he licked harder, pushed her up again.

Her breaths were little sobs when she finally lowered her hips. Jake rose up on his knees and lifted her, arranging her skirts as he sat back on his heels. Soft blue light brushed her closed eyelids, sparkled against her lashes. His eyes must be glowing. They flared brightly when he let go, and her weight carried her down over his rigid cock, her knees sinking into the mattress on either side of his legs.

Her nails dug into his shoulders. Though it almost killed him, he waited, studying the crease in her brow. Was he big enough? She felt so snug, but maybe she needed more. He shifted, just a little, until she was uncomfortably tight around him.

Her eyes opened, shining icy light that stole his breath. A shake of her head and her sound of distress had him quickly shifting back.

He went smaller, and her mouth flattened, her eyes narrowing to frozen slits. Her Gift suddenly crept over him, threatening, hinting at the consequences of remaining that size.

From somewhere downstairs, Nefertari purred.

He laughed silently and regained his shape.

Her lips curved. Her fingers explored his chest, pushed until he had to brace his hands on the mattress behind him. She lowered her head, flicked her tongue over his nipple.

Oh, Jesus. No fucking fair. He hadn't even gotten his mouth on her elbows, let alone her nipples. He bucked beneath her, but instead of glancing up at him so he could give her a warning look, she gasped and closed her eyes. Then rocked, driving him deeper.

Okay, he could live with that response.

He remained still as she rocked, then rolled her hips, then

lifted herself up and down. Testing each motion, as if deciding what she liked best.

Jake loved every damn one.

When she began to shake, he only moved to help her keep the same rhythm. Her legs hugged his tighter and tighter, and she rocked fast and hard.

And still lost it.

Her disappointment was not as severe as the first time, but the glow in her eyes faded. Jake levered himself up, held her against him, looking blankly over her shoulder. What was going on? He had no clue.

Except maybe even his hot ass couldn't immediately override one hundred years of conditioning.

He remained inside her as he maneuvered a pillow behind her hips and laid her on her back. She kissed him softly, and only frowned a little in confusion when he withdrew halfway, pushed her legs together.

And with his knees outside hers, he thrust back in.

Her eyes widened, and she choked out his name. Jake froze. Hot damn and holy hell, he hadn't been prepared for that. His body shook with the need to come. Tighter, not because he was stretching her too much but because she was squeezing his length, and so wet and hot that his blood was boiling.

Alice twisted beneath him, her fingers clenching on his ass. Urging him deeper.

He couldn't go as deep as he wanted. But her thighs were together, which was apparently what she needed to come. And they were slick and caressing the base of his shaft with every deliberate stroke; he was rubbing past her clit and still sinking most of the way inside her.

And oh Jesus, *Alice writhed*. Made strange, incoherent chittering noises in her throat that drove him insane. Pain streaked across his back as her nails raked him, breaking his control. He planted his hands next to her shoulders and plunged, fucking her off the pillow, fucking her across smooth blue silk.

He fisted his hands in her hair to anchor her in place, then used his tongue to fuck her mouth, deep strokes that matched the rapid thrust of his cock, that weren't deep enough until she tensed and trembled, screamed into his mouth, her body jerking and twisting.

It still wasn't enough. Jake slowed, and Alice wrapped her

arms and legs around him. He pushed in to the hilt, watched her eyes close in almost sleepy pleasure.

She moved with him, held him when he came. Kissed him until his shakes eased.

It had to be some kind of miracle that he was still alive when they did.

He didn't roll off her, but braced himself on his elbows. His hand wasn't steady when he pushed a tangled curl from her forehead. Her stockinged feet slid up and down his thighs.

He couldn't remember when he'd vanished his jeans.

He watched her face. Her soft smile didn't fade as his fingers found the tiny buttons that ran from her shoulder up the side of her neck. Her eyes remained closed, but he could detect a faint glow through her lids.

There were twenty-four, like tiny black pearls. His heart beat a thousand times for each one. He started at her jaw, and waited until he'd unfastened every button before peeling back the triangle of silk.

He pressed his lips to her shoulder. Her collarbone. Her throat. The upper swell of her breast, where the fold of black silk barred him from her nipple.

He didn't care. God, how he loved her. He could die now, and not have a single regret.

He lifted his head. Her eyes were open, watching him.

The feeling swelled, threatened to pop. He was going to kiss her, and probably never stop.

"Jacob," she said softly.

It exploded inside his chest.

And he jumped.

Alice blinked up at the ceiling for several minutes. After several more, she could finally begin to think.

Very possibly, his teleporting was for the best. Soon, he would have had to get up, and what would he have seen? She was in complete disarray. His fault, for stealing her hair ribbon and then tupping her within an inch of her life.

But perhaps her appearance wasn't so terrible. She vanished her dress and stood, dragging one of the sheets up with her. Her full-sized mirror was in her cache; she called it in at the end of the mattress.

Her mouth dropped open when she saw her reflection.

Oh, dear. She did not like using a mirror in Caelum, unless it was in a chamber full of her own things—it was too disconcerting to stand in a marble room and have nothing in the background but the blue sky.

But now, standing on the mattress, draped in sapphire silk, her hair in a wild tangle over her shoulders, she did not look as if she were floating into nothingness.

She looked like a goddess. Aphrodite, rising from the sea.

With a cackle, she vanished the mirror. How very silly she was—her smile was not serene enough for a goddess. Perhaps, though, it was just wickedly pleased enough for a witch.

And she would not have minded at all if Jake had seen her that way. No, her only worry was what he'd have heard if he had stayed.

As it was, she might have already said too much.

CHAPTER 19

His dick was freezing when Jake realized that he'd lied. If he'd died, he *would* have had one regret.

But it was too bad that when he met his daughter, she was taking out the trash, and he'd just landed naked and facedown in the snow. Snow was better than prickly grass, though—and night had fallen, so maybe she hadn't gotten an eyeful of ass.

She was still openmouthed with a trash can lid in one hand and a sack of garbage in the other when he formed jeans and a shirt. He didn't know if getting up would freak her out, so he moved his arms up and down, as if it were perfectly normal for a dead man to be making a snow angel in his daughter's backyard.

The bag dropped into the can, and the lid clattered over the top. She shoved her hands into the pockets of her puffy coat, took a step toward him.

God, she was beautiful.

She had her mother's hair. Thick and red, with only a few strands of gray at her temples, and she wore it in a loose ponytail at her nape. Her rounded face was his grandma's, and her eyes were his. Laugh lines had settled around the corners, but hadn't touched her mouth yet.

He frowned and stopped moving his arms when he saw her feet, her pink-painted toenails. She'd come out here in a coat, flannel pajama pants, and *flip-flops*. Jesus Christ.

But he held his tongue.

She didn't. "Are you nuts? Lindsey's going to see you and think she can come out here in her swimsuit."

Okay, that was fair. He stood, vanished the snow off his chest and legs. "Sorry. I didn't think about that."

"Well, maybe you should have—" She cut herself off, pressed her fingers to her eyelids. "Oh, Lord. *I'm* sorry. I go into Over-protective Mommy mode when I'm in shock."

She was? Maybe his own shock was preventing him from feeling it. He pushed his hands into his pockets. "It's fine. I'm actually surprised you aren't thinking that you've gone crazy."

"I might have if I hadn't sat on the fifty-thousand-dollar chair you left in Lindsey's bedroom. After that, I was ready to believe her when she said you scared away the monsters under her bed. And there are . . . other reasons." She pushed her coat closed, shivered. Her chin jerked toward the back door. "Do you want to come in? I could use a drink."

Snow crunched beneath his toes as he followed her to the stairs. He vanished the ice from the steps so she wouldn't slip, then felt like a dick when her surprise made her trip.

He caught her arm, then immediately let her go. "You know, it's probably not a good idea to invite strangers into your house."

Her snort of laughter was just like Barbara's. He grinned, but it faded with nervousness when she turned, her expression apologetic.

"Look, I should be up front about something. I'm not looking for another dad."

That hurt—but he was mostly just glad that she *had* a dad. "If we're being up front, I don't think I'd make a good one."

Not right now. If Khavi's prediction didn't come true, maybe someday—someday far in the future—he'd be ready.

She smiled and unlatched the screen door. "That's not what Mom said."

❧

Her name was Grace. She sat him down at the same table he and Billy Hopewell used to eat cookies and milk on—and when she gave him hot chocolate with marshmallows, he wondered if he should have appeared his age instead of looking like himself.

But she made the same for her own drink, left the room, and came back with a flat box. Several picture frames were piled on top. "Lindsey and Sarah—my daughter-in-law—are already in bed. This is Brandon." She passed him one of the frames, and Jake looked down at a replica of himself the year before he'd died. The uniform was different, though—Marine Corps. "He was deployed just after Lindsey was born."

There was a note in her voice that he couldn't ignore. "All right. I can jump over there now and then, see how he's doing." Probably would anyway, even if he didn't introduce himself. "But I can't . . ." He gritted his teeth, forced himself to say it. "But if it's something *people* are doing to each other, I can't interfere."

She bit her lip before nodding.

Fuck it. That was the Guardian line. But he had a personal line, too. "But if I was there and something *did* happen that I thought I could stop, I wouldn't just stand by." Even if it meant he had to Fall for it.

This time, there was a shimmer in her eyes when she nodded. "Thank you."

"Okay, but listen. The chances of being there at exactly the right time—"

"I know." Grace pressed her fingers over her eyelids again. "Drink your cocoa while I pretend I'm not crying."

Oh, man. "Is it good crying or bad crying?"

She looked up, waving her hands in front of her eyes as if to dry them. "Both. I just . . . He's my baby. He never met his dad, either. It was so stupid, a fling, the summer after I graduated, and I was feeling so old, ready for a little excitement before I hit college. And he was the type of guy . . . well, the type of older man who'd always speed up when he was changing lanes, even if no one was letting him in, instead of tapping the brakes and waiting until it was safe to merge. No surprise, he had an accident; I had Brandon. So it was just me and him for a long time, and I get weepy really fast when I realize he's not a baby anymore."

"Ah," Jake said. "Now I feel guilty for not being here. I think my granddad had a shotgun made especially for older men like that."

She snorted out another laugh, and pushed a new picture in front of him. "There's Mom and Dad, on their wedding day. And Dad probably would have taken his shotgun out if he'd known."

Barbara in white, a young Grace in pink, and—"Billy?"

"Yes. Bill, by then."

"Hot damn." Jake grimaced, looked up. "*Darn.*"

She shrugged, but he shook his head.

"No, I knew I'd be running into you sooner or later, so I've been trying to watch my language. I haven't been doing so well."

Her smile was soft and pretty. "Don't worry about me. Lindsey, though, is another story. She picks up everything."

"Okay." Still, he'd do better. And he hoped that meant he would be seeing Lindsey again. He looked down at the picture. "So, Billy Hopewell. He's good people. How old were you, though—ten? He waited long enough."

"That's your fault," Grace said, still smiling as she took a sip from her mug. "He'd been coming around Great-Grandma's since I was a baby, but Mom thought he only came out of obligation, because he'd been your friend—and Dad thought she was still hung up on you. So it took them a while to figure it out."

Jake could only shake his head and grin stupidly.

"You aren't hung up on her." There might have been relief in her voice.

"No." He met her gaze. "I did love her. But not the way a man does when he wants to spend his life with a woman."

Her eyes sparkled with sudden interest. "There is someone."

"Yes." And he'd happily spend a hundred lives with her. "Did Lindsey say anything about the Wicked Witch?"

"She did. Then she said you both disappeared."

"We did." Jake thought about giving a demonstration, decided it might be too much right now. "Why aren't you freaking out? That chain isn't really enough of a reason."

Grace opened the flat box, pulled out a yellowing envelope, and paused. "Do you want this stuff?"

A folded flag and a medal lay inside. Jake shook his head. "Those are meant for family, not for me."

She dug beneath the flag, pulled out a small flint arrowhead. "What about this? Great-Granddad said it meant something to you." She stopped. "He . . . I was about eight. Great-Grandma was the year after. Both went easy."

"Good." Jake fought the stinging at the backs of his eyes, reached for the arrowhead. Yeah, it meant something. He'd come across it in one of their fields when he was ten, and within two years had read every book on archaeology that the local library owned. Then reread them, because there hadn't been any other option.

He closed his hand around it. "Thank you."

"I'm glad I had it." She pushed the box aside. "So. When I was fifteen, this guy shows up here with a letter for me. Only, he didn't have my name—just Mom's maiden name—so it took a while for him to track us down. Because Mom had taken on your last name after you died. You know, to make it easier, even if it wasn't really legal."

"Yeah, I know," he said quietly. In a town like this, at a time like that—it was better to be seen as a widow than an unwed mother.

"And because she said when you told her you'd marry her, she considered that as good as a ring."

"As far as I'm concerned it was. I'm just sorry I couldn't give her a real one."

"She knew that. And it wasn't so bad. Hard, sometimes, but Dad was always there." She took a deep breath. "So, this man comes, and he has this letter you wrote me."

"Pinter?" Jake laughed to himself, shaking his head. The fucking new guy had made it out.

"Yes. And then he says he's got this story about how you ended up writing it."

"Oh, no." Nosferatu, a slaughtered village, and tortured soldiers. "He did *not* tell that to a fifteen-year-old girl."

"He did." Her face paled a little, and she licked her lips. "And, yes, Mom thought he was crazy. So many who came back were. You didn't hear much about it here, but in the cities . . . and that was where he'd come from. So she tried to get him to leave, but he stayed until he told it all. Until he told us about the white light, and the man with wings who took you with him."

Jake rubbed the bridge of his nose. So Pinter had seen his transformation. He remembered that light, how it had surrounded him, blazed through him.

"They never sent your body home. And it's always been in the back of my mind, so when Lindsey tells me that you've slain the monsters under her bed, and suddenly she knows who made her blue quilt, and an antique chair appears in her room that she says is from France, even though she has no idea what France is . . . I start thinking, 'Maybe.'" Her eyes were direct. "Now I'm wondering if our family should be afraid of those things Pinter talked about."

"Nosferatu? Probably not." He called in a card with SI's phone number, and then wrote his own cell and e-mail address on the back. "But you can always contact me if there's something you're unsure of, or if something threatens you. And demons . . . well, you probably won't know what they are. Mostly, you just don't let them tell you you're less than what you are, or that you aren't worth anything, or make you believe something that you feel in your gut isn't true."

He pushed the card across the table, then sat stock-still when she pressed her fingers to her eyes. They were calloused, he saw. A few tiny scars lined her fingers. She wasn't a stranger to working with her hands. "What'd I say?"

She did that waving thing in front of her eyes again, flapping the envelope like a fan. "Just . . . You told me exactly the same thing in this letter. About never letting anyone put me down. So I never have."

"Good." His throat was thick as hell. "Listen, do you need anything? I can't be your dad, but—"

"Yes." She was already nodding. "Yes. There is one thing."

There was no reason to delay her flight to the Archives. Jake could find her anywhere; it didn't matter if she was in her quarters. But Alice waited for several hours, finding tasks to occupy her, reading an erotic manual and picturing herself and Jake in every sketch, until she simply had to accept the obvious.

He wasn't returning.

And didn't that sound so very dire? She amended her conclusion as she strode into the Archives and toward the rear corner that she liked to think of as her own.

It wasn't that he wouldn't return. Something was keeping him away.

Or perhaps not. Alice drew to a halt, her lungs feeling very tight.

Jake was *here*. He sat at her worktable, sifting through photographs.

She couldn't return the smile he sent over his shoulder. She wondered why he attempted that welcoming expression at all; it was too false, strained.

And why had he not come to find her? "Have you been here long?"

"A little while."

"I see." She did not look at him as she picked up an unfamiliar aerial photograph. She couldn't focus, but she recalled that they intended to look for Anaria. "The Dardanelles?"

"Yep. I'm hoping these and the topographical data will give us a head start, a few possible locations. I'll have satellite images by tomorrow."

"Then shall we begin?" Dear God, let them begin. She needed desperately to leave this place, to fill her mind with something other than: he hadn't returned.

"Nope. The sun doesn't set for another six hours. We'll need to be flying around as we're looking."

And they couldn't risk humans glancing up to see them. Or, she supposed, teleporting in and out to specific sites. Stiffly, she moved around the table. "Very well."

"You'll have to carry me tonight. My wings won't be ready."

She gave a short nod, but he wasn't looking at her.

It was very odd, but he was still examining the same photograph he'd had when she'd come in. When had he become so slow?

And his breathing, she thought, was too steady. His face too still, his voice too even.

She had asked the wrong question. This was not about how long he had been here, but *why* he hadn't returned to her quarters.

It only now occurred to her that she wasn't the reason.

"Jake," she said softly. "Where did you go?"

"Kansas. Then SI. Then I took Pim to Malaysia to see her brother. Then back to SI. Then Baghdad. Then here."

So many jumps, but the first was the key. "Did you not find your family in good health?"

"They're fine." He swallowed with, she thought, some difficulty. But the wry humor in the glance he flashed at her was genuine. "All things considered, they've probably been better off without me."

"No." Alice sat, her back straight, her hands in her lap. Her gaze did not leave his face. "That is not the way to phrase it."

He stared at her for a long time. But not, she imagined, for as long as he'd been sitting here, trying to balance the relief of finding them well against the ache of witnessing how removed he was from their lives.

Men made life far too difficult when they insisted on neatly categorizing their emotions. When emotions became complicated, they brooded and struggled so mightily in an attempt to simplify them again—when, given time, everything would sort itself out and slide into its place.

As rational as Jake was, he'd have known his family would have moved on—but that knowledge was likely at emotional odds with the sense that he was unnecessary.

And he'd had forty years to prepare for it, but only hours to accept it. Surely he must know it would take more time than this.

Or perhaps he was only now realizing it.

Alice watched the tension ease from his body, and he finally said, "All things considered, everything worked out in the best possible way for them."

"And for you, too."

"Well, yeah. But considering I ended up a Guardian, and a couple of hours ago you had your legs around me, that goes without saying."

Alice smiled, vanished her boots, and curled back into the chair. "You met your daughter, then? Did you like her?"

His expression softened. "Yeah. And look—she gave me this."

Alice reached out to turn the heavy wooden book podium that appeared on the table. Apostles marched around the base in bas-relief, their features and robes exquisitely carved. "This is lovely. Did she create it?"

"Yep. She builds custom furniture by trade, but makes these on the side and sells them online. They're for displaying family Bibles. But I think we could use one of the illuminated manuscripts around here."

"In the Archives? You don't want it for yourself?"

"She said she was making me a personalized one. This was just something to take with me."

"So she plans to see you again." The painful threads wrapping around her chest loosened. Relief, for his sake.

"Yeah. I've got a standing invitation to Sunday dinner and under-the-bed monster slaying. And if you've got a few free hours one of these upcoming Sundays, I'll be taking Lindsey to see the pyramids at Giza. You want to come?"

"Oh, but surely I cannot—" She touched her fingers to her lips, halting the automatic response. She *could*.

What she could not do was recall the last time she'd made any plans that were more than a couple of hours in advance. She'd always feared that Teqon would reappear in her life, disrupting it entirely. And there were many reasons not to make plans now— Khavi's warning foremost in front of them.

But how many years now had she lived in fear, expecting her life to shatter around her at any moment? Far, far too many.

Even if that Sunday never came to pass, she would not let anything prevent her from looking forward to it.

"Yes, I would like to go," she said, and her heart tumbled over when Jake heaved a great sigh of gratitude and muttered about the energy of four-year-old girls. "How on Earth did this arrangement come about?"

"Grace asked me to make a point of telling Lindsey the places I've been, so that she'd grow up knowing there was a bigger world out there than a little town in Kansas."

How serendipitous. And utterly perfect. "So you told her you could do better than that," Alice murmured.

"Yep. And I'll see if I can talk Grace into a few jumps, too. Since we've come back from Hell, I haven't had a problem controlling them."

She had to laugh. "Except for—"

"Hey, now, that doesn't count. That was a higher power, kicking my ass to Kansas." His grin told her he didn't believe that any more than she would believe they'd opened a portal over her bed and he'd been yanked through it. "But—except for that—when I intend to jump, I've been going where I want to."

"Was it because of Hell?"

"I have no clue. But, yeah, maybe jumping there drove the point home. Or maybe it was just knowing that if I fu—*messed* it up again, you'd be hurt. And that I couldn't go back and fix it."

She looked away from him, waiting for the powerful emotions swirling within her to fall into place so that she could name them. They would not.

"So," he continued after a moment, "all things considered, everything is pretty darn swell."

He could not be serious. *All* things considered, "swell" was a gross understatement. She glanced at him from beneath her lashes. How unfortunate that he was not just attractive, but so incredibly appealing. There was nothing about him she did not like, so much that she admired, and everything drew her to him. He left no part of her untouched and unengaged; not her mind, not her emotions.

And not her body.

Oh, dear. Even now, as the result of a single glance, her breasts seemed fuller, her nipples tighter. Warmth spilled through her womb, and her mind was returning to the incredible pleasure she'd felt in his arms.

But surely it hadn't been *so* very good. Surely she hadn't been so completely lost and overwhelmed. Surely her surprise had blown her memory out of proportion to the reality.

Surely, in time, she would be able to go more than one or two minutes without remembering how agonizingly wonderful it had been, or thinking about taking him inside her again.

"Alice?"

The line of concern between his brows told her it hadn't been the first time he'd said her name. She snapped upright, placed her feet on the floor. "My apologies. I was not attending."

He sighed, shook his head. "Ah, goddess. I'm guessing you spent most of the time I was gone looking over the prophecy."

Oh, heavens. She had not given it a thought. "I— Yes. Quite absorbed by it."

"So what do you think?"

Alice called in the paper. It was still crumpled into a ball. She avoided his eyes as she smoothed it out. "The language is obscure. Do you think it is deliberate?"

There was amusement in his voice, blast him. "I'm sure it is. What's the fun in saying 'vampire blood weakens the nephilim' when you can write 'the blood that heals will release the dead unto judgment.' And even then, who knows if there isn't another meaning in there?"

It was difficult to find a clear-cut meaning anywhere. " 'She waits below. The dragon will rise before the lost two,' " she read. "The lost two what? Dragons?"

"That *could* be the grigori," Jake said. "Count 'em—she said there were ten. Three were killed and never became Guardians, then there's Anaria, Michael, Khavi, Zakril, Aaron—"

"Perhaps. She did not say Aaron was."

"Okay, yeah. But if he was, that adds up to eight. That's two left. And the dragon—is that the one Michael killed? Did it already rise or is it coming? When's 'before'?"

One line, and Alice's head was already spinning. " 'The blood of the dragon will create one door and destroy another.' " She looked up at Jake, who spread his hands. " 'Caelum's voice will sing it closed with ice and fire and blood, and be lost until she claims her new tongue and the dragon's blade. The blood that heals will release the dead unto judgment, and the judged unto Heaven. And upon the destruction of Michael's heart, Belial will ascend to the Morningstar's throne.' "

Finished, she carefully laid the paper flat on the table. Her blood pounded in her ears. "And this gibberish is why Teqon trapped me into this damnable bargain?"

"It's useless," Jake agreed. "Even if it's all true, it doesn't mean anything until you look at it after the fact."

Yes. There was nothing specific; it was almost all open to interpretation. The only clear reference was Michael's heart.

But perhaps someone more familiar with demons would recognize something they could not. "What did Lilith say?"

"That Khavi was a nutcase. And a bad poet. She said it rhymes in the Old Language."

She tried very hard to smile. And could not. Before she could tear up the paper, she pulled her hands back from the table, wrapped her arms tight around herself.

"Hey," Jake said. He vanished and appeared, kneeling beside her. His hand cupped her cheek, his thumb brushing her compressed lips. "So Khavi gave us nothing. But listen—"

"Blast it all, Jake. There *is* something she gave us. And it is specific. I ought to have told you."

"Yeah, that I was going to die because you don't fulfill your bargain?"

Shock rendered her speechless. How could he be so blasé when the very thought of his death tore her apart?

He smiled a little and shook his head. "Come on, Alice. Don't tell me you're going to believe it."

"Believe—? You think she lied?" Khavi had been truthful about everything else.

"Nah, not really. But, think about it. She'd give us answers to questions that she saw us ask, right?"

"Yes," she said, wondering how on Earth that would make her *less* inclined to believe Khavi's predictions.

"But we never asked the questions. She saw something that we would have asked, no doubt about it. Each time, the question was right there. But because she'd already seen it, we didn't have to say it. And hot damn, you're sexy when you're confused. How about you just tap my shoulder when you've figured it out."

With only that much warning, he braced his hands on the arms of her chair and lifted himself to her mouth. *Oh,* she thought, when his tongue slid past her lips. He tasted of chocolate and something light and sweet that she couldn't identify.

And he would have a very long wait if a functioning brain was her requisite for stopping him.

Especially now that his hands moved down to her waist, tugging until she half reclined in the chair. He pushed up her skirts, pushed himself between her legs, and then he was rubbing, rubbing.

His lips left hers and for an instant she decided to kill him. Until his mouth covered her breast, his teeth scraped over steel-strong silk, and his wet tongue circled her hardened nipple.

"Oh!" Dear heavens, how that lick made her ache. She pushed at his head, then pulled him back, loving the rasp of his hair against her palms. He suckled, and her body melted—except, it seemed, for the very tips of her breasts, which stood like buttons beneath her bodice.

He lightly pinched the nipple he wasn't licking, and her legs tightened around him, rubbing faster, faster.

His hands were traveling up her outer thighs when he froze.

Oh, no. He could not stop. "If you jump, I will feed you to Nefertari," Alice said, but her threat was ruined by her breathlessness.

"No. I just . . . Oh, God," he groaned as he withdrew from between her legs. "No way."

She could not see a problem. His penis rose thick and tall behind blue denim, her drawers were damp at the juncture of her thighs. Everything was as it should be, except that neither of them was yet bare, and there was empty space between them.

"Bloomers," he said in awe. "You have bloomers."

"Oh," she exclaimed, laughing, delighted. In truth, they were not precisely bloomers. Her simple black drawers were not gathered at the knee, but fell loose like a long pair of shorts. Only a small bit of lace decorated the hem.

However plain they were, Jake seemed quite taken with them. Her hips jerked when he dragged his finger up her wet center.

His voice was guttural. "Do you any with an opening? Like a slit here?"

Her lips formed an O before she cackled merrily. "I shall make a pair." They wouldn't be of spider silk, but she didn't need armor with him.

"Get them on." He leaned over, his mouth just above her left nipple. "And I'll get you naked *next* time."

§

How depraved they were.

Alice lay on her stomach beneath her worktable, the marble floor cool beneath her cheek. It was odd to be thankful for a slit in her drawers, but she supposed that if the opening had not been there, her bottom would now be exposed, and she simply did not have the strength to cover it.

Who could have anticipated that animal positions would be so draining? It was not as if she'd had to do much more than brace herself. Yet here she was.

"I have figured it out," she said with the little energy she had left. "What Khavi sees has a high probability of occurring, but is not inevitable."

Jake made a noise that sounded like assent. He, at least, had refastened his jeans after he'd rolled off her. His right hand rested on his taut abdomen, just above the bunched hem of his T-shirt, and his left forearm covered his eyes.

Depraved and satisfied, though they were both fully dressed.

She and Henry had always been clothed, as well, and some part of her had named that as the primary reason their lovemaking had been such a failure. But it had only been a symptom of the passion missing between them, not the cause.

And the cause was not that she had lacked passion—but that it hadn't been *between* them. Never shared, and so never flourishing.

What a rare and wonderful feeling it was when it did flourish. And so very frightening.

She only had to move her hand a few inches to touch him. It had never been difficult before—but before, there had always been a reason: to teleport, to comfort him, to steady herself, out of need and arousal.

Now, when it was simply because she wanted to, when it was only because it would please her, she hesitated.

In her marriage, she had touched Henry easily, without thought—coming up behind him to kiss his neck while he sat in his dressing room, linking arms when they went walking. That playful, innocent contact had been permissible between a man and his wife.

And she'd seen the ease with which Jake and the novices exchanged friendly kisses and embraces, his familiarity with Charlie and Selah. Why could she not do the same?

He would likely never know the courage it took to slide her hand across the marble and rest her palm in the crook of his elbow.

Or perhaps he would. He stilled, and raised his forearm from his face to look at her. She held his gaze, willing him not to say anything.

He moved her hand from his elbow to his palm, clasped her fingers, and turned onto his side. "Listen, Alice. There's something we haven't talked about, but we need to."

Oh, dear. "There is?"

"Yeah. About your bargain."

"Oh." She frowned, and came up on her elbow. "There is?"

His gaze was direct. "There's still a trade we could make: me. If Belial ordered Teqon to release you from your bargain—"

"No." She yanked her hand from his. "Do not even speak of it."

"I am speaking of it. We could put a time limit on my service to Belial, say fifty years of—"

"No!" Alice fisted her hands in her hair, closed her eyes as if she could shut him out.

He fell silent. But only for a moment. "Okay, then there's something else we could try. We'd intended to use Belial's demons to get information about the prophecy. We'd have to go a lot further with Teqon, but I'll do it."

Her lungs seized up. He meant that they could torture Teqon. And not anything like what they'd have done to Belial's other demons—those, she and Jake would have frightened, threatened, perhaps stabbed once or twice while subduing them. But they wouldn't have done more than that. If the demons had remained silent, they'd have been slain.

They'd have slain them anyway.

But Teqon . . . would take more than subduing. He had the advantage of knowing they would never go far enough to kill him, and that he would heal from anything they devised. It would have to be so terrible that he would beg for mercy, beg to release her. It would have to be like something from the Pit: slow, relentless, excruciating.

And inhumane.

"You cannot," she said quietly. No one with even a little compassion could stomach that sort of torture. And if Jake forced himself through it, he couldn't walk away undamaged by the experience. "Even to a demon."

"I will. You asked me once what I'd do if I had to make a choice. I can tell you now, my choice would be helping you."

"No." She drew a shaky breath. "If it has to be done, I should do it. And perhaps I could use my Gift to open myself to my widows so much that I would not feel any soft emotion."

His voice was oddly flat. "Could you come back from that?"

"I don't know."

"There'd be no point to freeing you if you just became a freak spider woman who wouldn't care if her soul was trapped in Hell anyway. And what if we have celebration sex afterwards and you bite off my head?"

"You said it was a good way to die."

"Well, yeah, I say a lot of stupid stuff." His gaze searched hers. "We don't have to decide this second. But we should keep it in mind. At this point, I don't see many other options."

Neither did Alice. She stared down at the marble, at her fingers trembling against the stone. And then cried out in surprise when Jake pushed her onto her back and came down over her.

His jaw was clenched, his expression tight, but warmth spilled from the blue glow of his eyes. "Scream," he ordered.

"What?"

"Scream."

"You cannot be—"

"Just for practice."

"It won't help."

"Oh yeah?" He caught her wrists, pushed them over her head. "Try it."

She didn't know whether to laugh or to hit him. "If I do, *you* will be the reason."

His cocky smile flashed. "Yeah, I bet. Do it."

"Why?"

"Because Teqon has your soul by the balls. Because your husband was a prick. Because I'm a dickhead. Because lately it's hard to tell if we're just grunts in a war where everything we believe we're fighting for is going to be blown out from under us by the guys higher up the chain."

So this was partially for him. Alice tilted her head back and shrieked. Short, piercing—and she could not hold it. She caught a breath, laughing.

He grinned down at her. "Come on. That felt good, didn't it?"

"Yes."

"Better than settling your nerves?"

Her laugh died. Familiar anxiety and anger tightened around her chest. This time, her scream ripped at her throat, went on until she had no air in her lungs.

When she finished, Jake was rigid above her. "Better?"

"Yes." Her voice was hoarse.

"Good. Could you ask Irena to remove her giant knife from between my legs?"

Oh, dear God in Heaven. Alice twisted beneath him.

Irena crouched beside the table, her eyes burning. The tattoos on her arms coiled like snakes preparing to strike. "This is of your choosing, Alice?"

Her mouth was too dry to answer. She nodded.

Irena stood. "When you have finished, you will come to my forge. Jake, too."

He rolled off her as soon as Irena's footsteps faded, and cupped himself through his jeans. "Oh, thank you, Onan. Everything's there." He glanced over at Alice, who was still trying to bring moisture up to her tongue. "Whoa boy. She scared *you*?"

"Yes." Alice swallowed, sat up, began straightening her skirts. "But not for myself. The next time I scream with you on top of me, we will put up the shielding spell first. I suppose that scene was not pleasant for her to come upon."

Jake frowned thoughtfully and turned his head, as if looking after Irena. "What happened to her? Was it that bad?"

"I am not certain." Alice stood. "But there are times I suspect it was worse than I imagine."

CHAPTER 20

Alice projected an image of Irena's smithy to Jake, and they were immediately surrounded by the scent of soot, smelted ore, and a dirt floor.

Even with the wobbling, it was much more convenient than traveling through the Baltic Gate and flying northeast for an hour. Irena had not yet arrived, but at eight times Alice's and Jake's combined ages, Irena was twice as fast; she would not be long.

"She should only be thirty minutes," Alice said, holding lightly on to his arm as she waited for the disorientation to pass.

Unaffected by the jump, Jake nodded, firelight casting uncertain shadows over his face.

There was, as always, a small fire burning in the hearth at the center of the lodge, and coals glowing in the furnaces squatting along the northern walls. Wind whistled across the ceiling hoods that released smoke into the air; sleet clinked against the metal roof as if the sky rained crushed glass.

"I thought she usually sculpted weird angry things," Jake said, looking behind Alice.

"She does." Now that her feet were solid beneath her, Alice felt confident enough to turn.

Her breath strangled in her throat.

"That's more minimalist. Or abstract." He approached the large steel cube, walked around the corner of it. He slid his palm up and down the smooth surface, then tapped it with his knuckles. A dull, hollow echo sounded through the thick metal. "Okay, and still weird."

He glanced back at her, and his amusement slowly faded. His hands pushed into his pockets. His gaze ran over the cube again, this time incisive, measuring.

Oh, blast Irena for forcing this. She'd known what Jake would see when they arrived.

"You know what this is?"

"Yes." Alice laced her fingers together over her midriff, strived for an even tone. "It is for me."

"Because of your bargain?"

She nodded sharply.

"What—to make sure you never fulfill it, she offered this as an alternative to killing you?" He teleported so close she had to tilt her head back to see his face. "Do I need to get you out of here?"

She felt his concern, as if he thought Irena was planning to push her into an oven. "No," she said, but knew it would not reassure him. "She likely only intends to show me that the box is ready."

Though he didn't move, he seemed to stagger. "This was *your* idea?"

"Yes."

He stared at her, his jaw clenching and unclenching. "This is your solution. The way you plan to make immortality last as long as eternity."

She could not look beyond him, could not avoid his gaze. "You don't approve?"

"Well, let's see."

He brought his hand to her cheek and they were plunged into a spinning darkness. His eyes glowed, red as a demon's, lighting smooth metal walls.

"Oh, nice. Comfy. Yeah, I could see you living here." He let her go to walk the breadth of the cube—four steps. "What is it, twelve by twelve? You have room to set up an armchair here, your tub over there. A spider or two in the corner, and books in your hammerspace. Everything you'll ever need, and a great view, too."

Alice closed her eyes. "That is enough, I think."

He took her hand and dropped it as soon as they were in Irena's forge again, the heated air filling her lungs. He crossed his forearms over his chest, his stance rigid.

"So, this is your 'I give up' box."

She pushed her response past her dizziness. "No."

"No? How is it any different than what you did with Teqon when you made your bargain? When you called yourself a coward? This box isn't fighting. This is deciding that 'what the hell, I can't beat him, I'm going to stick my head in the sand.' Why try if you're fucked anyway?"

She had nothing to say as he paced back and forth with his hands linked behind his head. She couldn't argue with him. It wasn't different than with Teqon; it *was* cowardly.

He spun back to face her. "Is that what *I* am?"

She stared at him, not following, but certain that she didn't want to jump where he had. Not if it had created that stab of pain in his psychic scent. "I don't under—"

"Your 'I give up' bang. A week ago, you said you couldn't touch me. I told you if you're screwed anyway, you might as well grab on and ride. Well, you did, didn't you? Right after you got that prophecy. So what am I—a couple of fucks before you lock yourself up? You lose all hope, and think, 'All right, I'll bang Jake'? Or would anyone have done?" He gave a hard laugh, spread his hands wide. "Oh, right. There's a bonus with me— when you're ready to go, you can just ask me to teleport you into the box. I'll do anything to help, right?"

The swirling emotions raged like a maelstrom inside her. She would scream if she opened her mouth, and so her denial was a faint shake of her head.

These were the same questions she'd been trying to avoid in her courtyard. And if she hadn't demanded silence, she would have had answers for him.

Jake let his arms slowly fall back to his sides. The acrid anger in his psychic scent drew in on itself, and she tasted the sour fear beneath it before he shielded. He turned away from her, slid his hand over his head.

"Jesus," he said softly. "The thought of you in there messes me up, but I shouldn't have—"

"Don't." She didn't want an apology.

She wanted—needed—everything to settle.

He nodded without looking back at her, his psychic scent heavy with regret. "Look, I just . . . I'm gonna take off. Tell Irena I'm sorry."

Alice smiled thinly. "Why should you be? I believe she is the one— Oh."

Sorry, not because he'd disappeared before Irena had come— but because he'd taken her box with him.

✦

"That was unkind," Alice said when Irena came through the door in a gust of wind and ice.

"But necessary, yes? And you are both young, so you will quickly recover." Irena threw back her white hood, stomped snow from her boots. "He has the cube, or you do?"

"He does."

"Good. I knew he would take it. You are a fool, Alice."

"Yes. But only because I am here and not flying to Caelum to find him."

"So we agree." Irena grinned as she moved to the hearth fire and stirred it, sending sparks dancing into the air. "And there will be no more talk of imprisoning yourself?"

"I was unaware that I spoke of it so often," Alice said dryly.

"You did not have to. It has always been here. In twenty years, I have not looked at you without seeing you inside it, and you have not looked at me without thinking of it." A jab with her poker sent up another shower of sparks. "Did you think I would like creating such a thing for you, knowing its purpose?"

"You create weapons knowing their purpose."

"Now you are impertinent. Someone has said they care for you, and so you revert to your novice days." Irena's eyes were hard. "Should I lecture you on the difference between forging swords to slay demons and forming a prison for a friend?"

"No." Alice sighed. "Twenty years ago, it seemed a sensible solution."

"Only an odd-brained ox would think it sensible."

"You agreed to it."

"You were petrified with fear, certain Teqon would have your soul in the frozen field the moment you left Caelum. You were like the novices who will not take their first dive without a mentor on the ground to catch them. A *sensible* novice knows that she will suffer the same injuries crashing into the ground as into her mentor, and that if she insists otherwise, two will be injured instead of one. But you were not sensible."

Alice stared into the flames until her vision blurred. What a strange picture of herself this presented. She'd always thought she'd formed a reasonable plan despite her fear, not as a result of it. But did reason ever come from fear?

She couldn't deny she *had* used the box as a safety net, as a way to exert some control over her fate. But it was a net that would hurt as much to land on as the ground—and hurt others as well. Irena would have had to build it, someone would have had to teleport her into it, and everyone would have known that she was isolated inside, slowly going mad.

In the end, it would be no different than the frozen field—except that she would have laid an additional burden on her friends by asking them to help her into it.

She blew out a soft breath. "I suppose a sensible mentor says she will catch the novice, but steps aside at the last minute rather than be smashed."

"She steps aside," Irena said, "because only a stupid novice would not be more sensible on the second dive. You are odd, not stupid."

"Yet I am a fool?" she asked, smiling.

"If Jake left, that means you did not tell him you no longer intended to use the box. That you had already decided against it, but were unsure if that decision came from reason rather than dread." When Alice didn't respond, Irena tilted her head, examined her face. "Why is he the one you test yourself against? I know very well that you think for yourself and that your mind is your own—yet when you were uncertain, you measured yourself against him."

"I do not know." When she had more time to consider the question, when everything she felt for him settled, she might discover the answer. "Or do you mean: Why him . . . and not you?"

Irena's eyes widened and she burst into laughter.

Alice had not expected more than a chuckle. Surprised, she asked, "Would that be impossible?"

"Yes." There was a feral edge to Irena's grin. "We do not have a common measure. Hate does not drive you; compassion does. A sense of fairness. You slay demons because you care for humans, because you know they are evil, because they take advantage of and twist everything good."

Alice's eyebrows furrowed. "We all hate them."

"You despise what they are, what they do." Green fire burned in her eyes. "I hate *them*. Every single demon, and every single drop of blood in their veins. You thrill at a fight, and relish a victory. I relish the break of their bones, the rending of their flesh—and above all, the kill." She drew back slightly, her gaze steady on Alice's face. "And so you would not be comfortable with my unit of measure."

"No, I would not," Alice agreed. She understood that hate—she felt it for Belial. But she could not conceive of it on such a wide scale—not against demons who had not personally harmed those she loved. Hate was too intimate.

And that much hate sounded far too exhausting.

She hesitated before asking, "And Michael?"

Irena's expression cooled. "If you decide to fulfill your bargain, and Guardians are queuing to take your head . . . I will no longer be standing in line."

CHAPTER 21

After three hours of flying and passing through several Gates trying to find Jake, she had never wished for the Gift of teleportation more.

It would not be much longer until he found *her*, she knew. In a little more than an hour, the sun would have set over Turkey, and they would begin searching for Anaria's temple.

And when the sun rose again, she would ask him to take her to Cairo—and harden her stomach to do what she must. She *would* have her Sunday in Giza.

She would have not just one, but as many as she liked.

Dawn had just come to San Francisco when she located Selah in the Special Investigations warehouse. A moment later, Alice was wobbling behind Jake, who sat on a flat cot with his wings folded at his naked back. A computer topped a small cart in front of him.

He didn't startle, but slowly stood in his jeans, vanishing his wings as he turned to face them.

Face *her*, Alice realized. Selah had already gone.

She linked her hands together. "I— Your wings looked well."

"Yeah," he said, his voice flat. "They aren't there yet, but they're close."

"How close? You should form them again, so they finish."

"I don't think so."

"Oh, but—" She stopped. No, she would not argue. She would irritate *herself* if she argued. As it was, she feared she'd begun to flit. She moved to the nearest wall in order to cover it. "You have a great many books here." The usual variety of literature, the expected archaeology texts—but also a large number of titles regarding military history and tactics. "You do not keep them in your cache?"

"No. They aren't mine."

"Oh. Scavenged?" Left behind in other quarters after the Ascension—and likely why he didn't carry them in his cache. If anything happened to him, they would be lost.

"Most of them. Some from the Archives. Are you here about my books?"

"No. I—" She turned, and encountered a pair of large breasts in a tight white shirt, partially unbuttoned to reveal an extraordinary cleavage. Alice took in the arched back, short red pants, curled red hair, and pouting lips. "Oh."

Across the room, a brunette slinked in a nightdress and stockings. A voluptuous blonde in black heels straddled a motorcycle seat. And taped on the ceiling above his cot, a laughing blonde tried to hold down the white skirt billowing up around her legs.

She'd begun to walk over, craning her neck to get a better look at the woman's dress, when they all vanished.

"Alice. They aren't—" Jake closed his eyes, pushed out a breath between his teeth. A dull flush stained his cheeks. "They're just *here*. I don't even notice them anymore."

"I see." She frowned, studying him. "When we were in Seattle, you took the shape of an actor. Why do you not do that more often?"

"I didn't know you wanted me to," he said stiffly.

"Oh, no. *I* do not. But during your free hours, it would have been very easy for you to meet women who looked like these women. And they would be willing."

He frowned. "Yeah, and that'd make me the biggest asshole on the planet. Speaking of, I'm not giving you back your box."

"Very well. I do not believe I have a use for it." She sat on the cot, her back straight. "I have not for some time."

"Gee, that's good to know *now*."

"Yes, I thought it would be. You should also know, however,

that you were wrong. It was not my 'I give up' box. It is my 'I am scared senseless' box."

Warmth melted into his voice, and dulled the edge of his sarcasm. "Then maybe you should make it your 'I need to scream somewhere I won't risk Jake's balls' box."

She glanced at him from the side of her lashes, then quickly tore her gaze from his bare chest. For at least five more minutes, she should not let herself be distracted by lustful thoughts. "With her Gift, Irena could still come through the metal."

"The *shielded* 'I need to scream' box."

Alice smiled, and to avoid his nude torso, she looked at his computer. Another map filled the screen, but in this one, she recognized several of the pinpointed locations. "What is this?"

Jake hesitated.

She glanced back at him. "What?"

"I, uh— Okay. I was thinking about the temples, and those cylinders with the spells, and how that one cylinder hooked to the last temple that Zakril built—the one we're looking for now. But there were all those other cylinders around them, and we know which temples at least three of them coordinated with. And I was thinking about how, despite everything else being symmetrical in Khavi's place, those cylinders were randomly positioned. But they weren't random."

Alice frowned at the computer display. Each pinpoint, she saw, was overlaid by another. She shook her head. "Are you saying that the locations of the cylinders in the room correspond with the temple locations?"

"Yep. It didn't work at first. The three reference points were a little off, and the farther away from the reference points, the bigger the difference. But then I realized I wasn't accounting for the Earth's curvature. So I adjusted, and they lined right up."

Her heart pounded. There were several points that had no temple marked. The Indonesian islands, Siberia, South America. She either hadn't felt the disturbance, or the spell hadn't needed to be repaired—and so she'd never found them.

And one pinpoint lay directly over the Dardanelles.

Over the *water*, she realized, and her excitement faded. They hadn't had time to sketch or measure Khavi's chamber, so the placement couldn't have been exact. "This is still an estimate—the approximate location of Anaria's temple."

Which they'd already had, thanks to the nephilim.

"Ye-e-e-ah," Jake said, and rubbed awkwardly at the back of his neck. "About that."

Alice's blood froze. "You went to Hell without me?"

"What, you wanted to go again?" He held his hands up when she rose to her feet in a swift movement. "Look, it was just popping in and out of the chamber. A few minutes to measure. Khavi wasn't even there."

"You went *alone*?" She shrieked the word.

"No." His brows snapped together. "Hell, no. You think I'm stupid? Maybe there'll be times I have to go alone. But if I've got a choice, you bet your ass I'm bringing backup. So I took Drifter."

"Took— Oh." She stared at him, her body still vibrating with anger, fear.

He crossed his arms over his chest. A toothpick appeared in his mouth, and slowly, a smirk formed around it. "So. I guess I don't feel like such a dick for going off on you earlier."

Shocked by her response, Alice averted her face, smoothed her hair. "Perhaps. But you are to blame for my screaming."

"It's music to me, goddess."

"I don't know why you make me want to—" She stopped, met his eyes. "That was a lovely thing to say. And I . . . Do you know, I have something for you. Two things, actually."

"I am trying *so* hard not to ruin my one-hit lovely streak by letting something out of my filter."

Her laugh felt full instead of thin and nervous, and when she pulled his swords from her cache, her hands did not shake. "Irena had these ready for you."

He made a sound of pure male pleasure when his hands closed over the grips. "Oh, damn. Feel that. A guy doesn't even need a dick if he's got these." The air whistled around the blades as he gave them a spin. "Want to practice before we head to Turkey?"

"We will soon." She called in her gift, closed her fingers over it. "I also have this, but I must first explain it. And you must realize how very brave I was to get them for you. Irena had just frightened me a little, yet I remained, and asked her to make them."

His brow creased, as if he could see that she wasn't completely joking. "What did she—?"

"Nothing. It is nothing; I am just delaying."

He vanished his swords, glanced down at her closed hand. "Then go on."

Oh, dear. *Now* she was not quite steady. "I find," she said, "that I have been very foolish. It has been some time now that I have been looking at many things upside-down. The box, for one. And when I thought of the novices who Ascended, I blamed myself for not inspiring them—for not being able to make them understand why Guardians are so very important. I have thought that perhaps they sensed my cowardice and my fear, and that with me as a model and mentor, they could find nothing honorable in being a Guardian."

Jake touched her cheek. "Alice. That is such bullshit."

"Yes." She smiled weakly. "But you have done the same. You wonder if we are nothing but pawns, unimportant and replaceable, manipulated by the demons, the grigori—perhaps even the angels. You wonder if their only purpose is to grab power or to rule, that we have been lied to about our reasons for fighting, that it taints our purpose. And you feel it here." She rested the back of her hand against his stomach. "I know you do."

"Yes," he said softly.

"But we don't fight for *them*. We fight for your daughter, and her family. We fight for young wives tormented by demons and young men hunted by nosferatu. That is what I told my novices, and if they could not grasp the importance of that, it is not *my* failing."

"Damn right it's not."

"But you *do* know what is important, and you still doubt. Yet no matter what the purpose of those stronger than us is, so long as your reasons for fighting and your actions reflect what you believe, there is nothing that could taint you. We could discover that Michael's only purpose is to enslave every human on Earth, and it would not make our fight less worthy—it would only mean that we would begin to wage our war against him, as well. And that is why I made you these."

She opened her fingers, and lifted a pair of platinum tags by the chain.

"Dog tags?" His breath seemed shallow as he cupped them in his palm, used his other hand to turn them over.

She hadn't known what to inscribe, so she'd only had Irena write his name, with "Guardian" below it. "Yes. I have heard it is customary for soldiers to have these. I thought you should have a pair now that you're fighting a war you can believe in."

Jake turned them over again in his palm.

She twisted her fingers together. "If you want something else written—"

"No." His voice was thick. "No. It's just right."

Relief shuddered through her, and she held up her hands. "May I?"

He nodded. His gaze never left her face as she placed the chain over his head. She sighed when the tags jingled.

"They make noise. They'll give your location away."

"Let them find me. They aren't coming off."

She touched the tags, then let her forefingers separate and follow the curving line of his pectorals. "Perhaps I can wrap them in a transparent web to muffle the sound."

"Alice. Jesus, Alice. You can do whatever you want. I'm such a dick. I don't have anything to give you. Except this." Jake caught her right hand, pressed it flat over his heart. "But the truth is, it's already yours."

Oh, God. Oh, dear God. Her chest tightened unbearably. She pressed her lips to the hand over hers, his throat, his mouth.

He cupped her cheek and lingered over the kiss, slowing it before lifting his head. "You're afraid."

And in front of that keen gaze, so exposed. Without moving her hand from over his pounding heart, she slid around his arm, held him with her cheek against the back of his shoulder.

It had been so simple before. One look at Henry, and love had fallen neatly into its place—and had eventually been battered and squeezed and bruised by every other emotion crowding around it.

But with Jake . . .

She raised her head, opened her eyes. With Jake, it would not settle, no matter how long she waited. No, her love for him was not a small piece to be put in its place. It shifted and changed, was both made up of her emotions and more than the combination: a complicated web whose pattern and texture altered as threads were weaved in or cut—but always remaining a web.

And even the razor threads were silk.

Turning her head, she kissed his shoulder. His heart beat steadily beneath her hand; Jake stood motionless, but his posture wasn't rigid as he waited for her to speak.

Comfortable with his feelings. Secure in himself. And likely with more confidence in *her* than she had.

She traced the fingers of her right hand down the hollow of his spine, and watched his muscles flex in the wake of her touch. The whole of her body seemed to react in the same way, as if the warmth of his skin seeped into her through her fingertips. "Oh, dear."

Jake turned his head to look over his shoulder, his brows lifted.

"Since the moment you teleported to Kansas, I have not been able to go more than a few minutes without having a salacious thought. Even when I *ought* to be attending to other thoughts."

He grinned and faced forward again, and she marveled at how his neck looked just as strong and masculine with the chain against it. Strange, but she supposed that although it was a necklace, it was not jewelry.

"Are you having one now?"

"Not salacious. Admiring." She skimmed her fingers over his shoulder blade. "I wonder that you do not wear your wings. I would find it very difficult not to wear them even while on Earth."

"They're a little too stubby for that, goddess."

Stubby? He could not be serious. "You lost them so that I would not be hurt. Because you knelt when you could have easily jumped—when you had to fight *not* to jump. It was the bravest act I have ever witnessed, and while they heal, your wings are a visible badge of your courage. I would wear them, and wave them, and parade myself through the streets of Caelum."

Jake made a strangled noise, and his shoulders began shaking.

Alice sighed. "The tags even jingle when you laugh. But you should not laugh at this. You hide your wings, as if you should be ashamed of their appearance. I see them much differently. No," she said, when she felt his weight shift. "Do not yet turn, or kiss me. There is more I have to say before my next salacious thought."

He lifted her hand from his chest and kissed her fingertips. "I've already had several."

"I wonder how you function; I find them quite distracting. Always before, I'd determine when they would come. I would choose erotica to read or allow myself a fantasy. But these are completely unbidden." She glanced down at her fingertips, which were rubbing themselves along the ridge of muscle above his hip. She would have to delve into his jeans to explore it farther. "Not unwelcome, however."

"I just had about ten more, Alice."

She laughed and rested her brow on the hard curve of his

shoulder. "Very well." With an effort, she made herself stop rubbing. Anxiety fluttered high in her throat, and she swallowed it down. "Earlier, you said that there was a bonus attached to you."

"Yeah, and I was being a dickhead."

"Perhaps. But you were correct—except that it is not teleporting." She met his eyes when he looked over his shoulder. "You make me uncertain," she admitted.

"And that's a bonus?"

"Yes. Not very long ago, I was utterly certain."

Understanding smoothed the crease from his brow. "About Teqon."

"Yes. Because of the bargain, I would either be in the frozen field, in a box, or standing with Michael's heart in my hand. I had hope—very small hope—that I might find a way out. But I didn't believe I would." She searched his eyes. "That is something you have given me. Something I know didn't come out of me by itself. You irritated it out. Now I am uncertain of what the future holds. I believe, truly believe, we can find a real solution—believe it even over predictions and probability."

He looked down at her hand on his chest. His throat worked before he said, "I'm all for that kind of thinking. But you know, believing in something despite the odds might be just craziness, not optimism."

"Very well." She linked her arms around his shoulders. "If I am crazy, then at least I shall live up to the novices' expectations."

"Yeah, well—I'm going to be talking to them about some of the stuff we've been saying."

"Oh. Must you?"

"Don't tell me you enjoy it."

She cackled against his neck.

"Witch. You creeped us out on purpose?"

"Not on purpose. I am how I am. But I am not unaware of how people see me."

"So you made sure you were extra creepy when we were around."

"Perhaps."

He reached back, caught her hips. "Why? *Aside* from the entertainment, because it wouldn't be efficient for you to go out of your way to creep us out just so you could get a good laugh. Was it to get rid of us?"

Of course it was. She glanced over his shoulder, but could only see the hard angle of his jaw. "Is that surprising to you?"

"No. No. But you know, they're not that bad. The novices."

"I never thought they were." She pulled back to look at the taut line of his shoulders, wondering at his tension.

"You never— Okay. Forget it."

Oh, how very obtuse she was. These were his friends. "I would not try to make them uncomfortable now. Not deliberately."

His hands flexed on her hips, and he bumped lightly back against her. "Unless it'd be entertaining. Then go for it."

"Well, yes. Sometimes they are unsettled so easily I cannot help myself."

"Hey, that's good for them. My creeped-out threshold is pretty high now."

She bit his shoulder.

"Yeah, see? But don't do that to them. Will you bite me if I turn around?"

"Yes." She laughed and held on when he did anyway, lifting her feet so that she was still at his back when he stopped. "I would have said no if I'd realized you wanted it."

"You haven't had even one dirty thought yet?"

"Yes." But mostly wonderful thoughts of pleasing him, of concentrating wholly on him, of returning even a small amount of what he'd given her. Her hands fell to his abdomen, and she slid her fingers over ripples of muscle, circled his navel, and traced a narrow path of coarse hair toward his waistband. "And that is why you cannot turn around."

"Hot damn. But listen, goddess—if you've shape-shifted, be gentle."

She smothered her cackle against his shoulder, attempted to pinch the taut skin below his navel. She couldn't be sorry that her fingers didn't find any extra flesh to squeeze. She settled for tugging hair, then traveled lower when he pretended a wince.

"You *are* a little evil."

"Mmm," she agreed, in the moment before her fingers encountered the bulb of hot flesh that protruded above his waistband. "Oh!" she exclaimed. "Oh."

"Yeah," Jake said, his voice strained. "I'm about to do that, too."

Heat roared through her as she swept her thumb over the broad head of his penis. So unexpected. She'd anticipated unfastening a button, lowering a zipper, teasing, then finally touching.

Now she ripped open his jeans to fill her hands with him. Oh, dear heavens. How incredible. The few times she'd practiced shape-shifting into a male form, the genitals had always produced the most acute discomfort, as if an alien appendage grew from her form—a discomfort that had intensified if the flesh hadn't remained flaccid. She'd certainly felt nothing like this fascination now, as she explored Jake's rampant erection.

Jake groaned through each tentative stroke, locking his fingers together behind his head as if forcing himself to let her touch him as she willed, without direction or interruption.

And once her initial curiosity had passed, there was so much more to learn. A firm grip made his knuckles whiten, and if she went fast, his head fell forward and he gritted his teeth.

Oh, why hadn't she done this before? Why hadn't she known she would love this—that simply by touching him, her center would be wet and her nipples aching, as if he'd taken his tongue to both.

She pictured that, tried to imagine his reaction, and her need wound tighter, until she could think of nothing but tasting *him*.

Slowly, she drew her left hand up the length of his rod and collected the moisture at the head against her forefinger. Her right hand continued stroking him as she brought her finger to her mouth.

"Alice, Alice, Alice," he chanted, shaking. "What are you doing?"

Her lips closed over her finger, and she knew he would hear the slide of her tongue as she licked the salty drop. Odd, but not unpleasant, and her excitement heightened when he stiffened.

"Oh, God." He bent forward a little, as if in pain. "Don't do that again."

She took him firmly in both her hands again. "Shall I do this?"

"Yes. No—not like that. Hard's only for emergencies."

Her touch lightened. "Such as?"

"Such as: my head will explode if I don't come in three seconds."

"I see. And if I cannot bring your wetness to my mouth again, shall I come around and taste it directly?"

His ragged groan might have been a denial or a plea.

"May I? My tongue here"—her fingers danced over his crown—"and here, and suckling you, and when you finish, I will drink—"

His hands clamped over hers, stroked hard once, twice. A rough sound vibrated through his chest; his shaft pulsed beneath her hands. He shuddered. The next stroke was slick, and the slide of her palm easier.

Yes, she decided. Next time, she would use her mouth.

Jake weaved on his feet. She licked the nape of his neck, then caught the chain in her teeth, drawing it back, letting it fall in a loop between his shoulder blades.

When he took her face-to-face, those tags would jingle between her breasts.

Her skin flushed with heat. Her gaze fell to the gap between his backside and his jeans, and her lips parted. She tugged at his belt loops and exposed just enough to see the Vietnamese characters tattooed on his right buttock.

She read the black lines, frowning. *No fear but fear.*

"Oh, no." Jake groaned, then added in a rush, "Okay, so I was in Saigon, and walked into this place, asked the guy there to do it. I was trying to inspire myself, right? I was thinking that if I actually made it a part of me, I'd be able to accept everything."

Oh, she realized. *Nothing to fear but fear itself.* The translation was imprecise, and she could easily imagine him in a small parlor, trying to communicate exactly what he'd wanted the tattoo to say. Attempting to make sense of where he'd ended up and why he was there, and how he would get through it.

She smoothed her fingers over it. No, a tattoo would not magically change him—but over the years, this *had* become a part of him.

"Anyway." He shrugged, still vaguely embarrassed. "It made sense when I did it."

"You were drinking?"

"Yep." He glanced over his shoulder. "I forget about it most of the time; I can't see it."

"Oh," Alice said, and firmed her lips. "Then you haven't made certain the translation is correct?"

"No. Why?"

"It says, 'Only simpletons ask for tattoos they can't read.'"

"*What?*" His psychic scent shot arrows of disbelief, and Jake turned around and around, looking over his shoulder, as if he turned far enough about he would see it.

Then he froze, straightened, and pointed at her. "You."

She lifted her brows.

"I love you."

"Oh," she said, her hands flying to her chest to keep her heart within it.

"That's right. And we've got about ten minutes before the sun sets in Turkey. We'll be fast."

"No," she said as he strode toward her, and he stopped. "Let me . . . do this."

Her fingers found the buttons at her neck.

"Alice," he breathed, and then surprised her by pressing a kiss to her throat.

Why had she been certain he would only stand and watch? Had she assumed he would look at her like he had his pinup girls?

She should have known better. With every inch she exposed, he was there, worshipping it with his mouth. He replaced every button with his lips, followed silk with his hands.

And by the time he pinned her to the wall and told her she was the most beautiful woman he'd ever seen, she believed him.

CHAPTER 22

Even a dress of spider silk did not make for easy swimming. When her legs tangled in her skirts for the third time, Alice exchanged it for a short black chemise, but kept her drawers and stockings.

Jake glanced over, the glow from his eyes illuminating the sediment clouding the water. *This should clear out when we hit the lower current,* he signed. Then, *How would you have managed if you were here with Drifter?*

Though she would have worn her swimming trousers, Alice sent him an image of a swimsuit she'd once seen on a Brazilian beach.

Then he's never coming treasure hunting with us. Okay, see anything?

She shook her head, and held out her hand.

He teleported them deeper. The visibility was better; she could see the bedrock now, stones worn smooth. Ship debris gathered in front of uneven shelves and the odd protruding boulder, and was held in place by the current.

The strait was narrow, and relatively shallow—and had been heavily traveled for thousands of years, strategically important for both military and commercial interests. Any temple of size and distinction wouldn't have gone unnoticed. Perhaps before the technological advances of the past century—but not after submarines and side-scan sonar had been developed. And because of the history of the strait, maritime archaeologists and salvagers had combed the seafloor extensively, searching for wreckage and jetsam.

Alice turned to Jake. *How near are we to the estimated location? Right on top of it. Should we jump around this area, take a look from a few different angles?*

Her nod started them on a dizzying trek though the water, but after fifteen jumps that had taken them from one bank of the strait to the other, still nothing had appeared to her as out of the ordinary. They began a searching pattern, moving with the current—then against it—all without success.

The night had half-gone when Jake teleported back to their starting point. He floated on his stomach, staring at the seafloor with his brows drawn.

He turned his head to look at her. *Do you know what?* he signed. *I'm an idiot.*

His Gift pulsed once, twice. He didn't vanish, and Alice had just begun to frown when he pulsed it rapidly again, twelve, thirteen times—

And disappeared.

A second later, she almost sucked in a lungful of water when he reappeared in front of her, grinning. He smashed his lips to hers, and then she was wobbling, dripping water onto a damp white floor, dragging in a breath of freezing stale air. The temple spun around her as Jake swept her up, his deep laugh echoing off the decorated marble walls.

This time, she kissed him back.

But they didn't linger over it; he was just as eager to explore as she.

It was remarkably like the enormous chamber in Tunisia, but of white marble instead of black granite. A dais and the black sarcophagus stood where the statue had been, but the colonnade around the room was similar, as were the friezes lining the walls. For a long moment, Alice simply turned in a circle, taking it all in.

She looked over at Jake, who'd tilted his head back to frown at the domed ceiling. "How did you find it? Why were we idiots?"

"Because I was thinking like me instead of like Zakril. He

could teleport, and his Gift was working with stone. And he didn't want Anaria to escape once he'd let her out of the sarcophagus. She'd Fallen, so she didn't have an ability to teleport . . . so, I realized, why wouldn't he just make a hole beneath the seafloor? And I can't jump into anything solid; if I try, I just don't go. So I kept trying until I hit the pocket of air."

Incredible. He was simply incredible. "How deep was it?"

"Not deep enough. Look." He pointed up, and Alice saw the water seeping through tiny cracks in the dome. "Maybe two thousand years ago it was, but the current has worn the seafloor above it down to about six feet of basalt. I'm guessing the dome butts right up against the bedrock, and that's not going to be enough to support the water above it. Not for much longer. One little earthquake, and it's probably coming down—if this chamber doesn't fill up with seepage first."

Yes. She could hear it now, when she listened closely. A drip here and there. Could see it in the faint paths trickling down the walls.

She looked toward the dais. "Will you think me heartless if we do not immediately return to tell Michael we have found his sister, and—"

"Record the site first?" Jake grinned, and his camera appeared in his hand. "Honestly, goddess—I'd call you heartless if we didn't."

§

Once she'd taken a closer look at the friezes, Alice wished she'd been heartless. She held her sketchbook, but couldn't bring herself to draw them.

These were not scenes of Guardian history, but Anaria's and Zakril's history. As children, happily laughing as they shared a bowl of dates. Two young lovers in a field of exquisitely carved wildflowers. A wedding, and a bed. Zakril, holding Anaria as she wept over Michael's broken body, the dragon limp behind them. Anaria, smiling up at Zakril in front of Michael's temple in Caelum. And there were more—dozens more, of them fighting side-by-side, making love, or simply looking at each other, sharing a private joke, a moment of pain, a moment of comfort.

Jake came up beside her. No longer with his camera, she saw.

Her throat felt raw when she said, "He must have loved her very much. And how very hard he must have prayed that being here would remind her of what they had."

"Yes. What now, goddess?"

She closed her eyes, saw Zakril's skeleton pinned behind her lids. "I want to leave her here to let this place fall down on top of her. But that cannot be my decision to make."

"Yeah, it can. No one knows we're here."

She smiled faintly, shook her head. "No."

"All right, then. How about this—we leave it for now, and while we're still both pumped full of this righteous anger on Zakril's behalf, go and beat the shit out of Teqon."

"Yes," Alice murmured. "Why not?"

🦢

Alice had always loved predawn in the Egyptian desert. The cool air, the quiet.

With her Guardian hearing, it was not as silent as it had once been—but the sight of the full moon setting behind the pyramids affected her exactly as it had more than a century ago, and her heart still skipped into her throat as the moon seemed to slide down Khafre's steep side before falling into bed at Khufu's base.

She sighed with pleasure and turned to Jake.

"This expression you're seeing on my face," he said without looking at her, "is called 'Whoa, damn.'"

"Yes." She tucked her hand in the crook of his elbow. "We should have chosen another location to prepare for our attack on Teqon. It is difficult to maintain righteous anger here."

"Yeah. I suppose it is a good place to soften me up, though. Where you might say something like, 'Just in case Khavi was right, and your heart is going to be chopped in two, why don't you let me face Teqon alone?'"

Alice flattened her lips, tugged her hand back. "Blast you."

"Oh, come on. You don't even sound angry."

No, she could not be. But she could be irritated that it was so. "What a stubborn donkey you are."

"Because I won't let you do what you think is best for me?"

"It is best for *me* that you live." She crossed her arms, frowning at the pyramids across the stretch of desert. "With Lucy and all of her children in his home, I will know exactly where Teqon is, where he moves. I can shoot through his walls, and slow him before I draw close enough for him to retaliate. I will weave webs at his doors to catch him should he try to escape. I will have him at my mercy within moments."

"And then you torture him."

"If I must."

"I'll do it, Alice."

She smiled. "And now who is trying to do what he thinks is best for the other?"

He fell into frustrated silence. In the distance, a call to prayer sounded, signaling the approaching dawn.

"I wonder, however," Alice said when it faded, "if I have not been looking at Teqon upside-down, as well. Because he has had so much power over me, I haven't thought of him as a pawn."

"Belial's pawn?" Jake sounded thoughtful. "Yeah. How much is Teqon really willing to endure if whatever he gains isn't personally for him? You wonder if a demon is willing to take one for the team."

"Yes. And I think that because I've been afraid of him, I never considered the possibility that *he* might be a coward. Perhaps we don't need to torture him now. Perhaps we just need to give him something to look forward to."

"You mean, scare the shit out of him."

"And if we fail, perhaps we can torture him next week."

"Right on. Now we just need—" He broke off, gave her a considering look. "You don't still have that dress you wore in Hell, do you?"

"Yes." Alice grimaced. "But I have not had an opportunity to wash the smell out."

"Good—especially if some of that smell is from a female hellhound." He shoved his hands into his pockets and looked out over the pyramids, grinning. "You never know what kind of bribe might come in handy."

❧

Though her plan of attack played out very much as she'd told Jake it would, Alice had not expected that she would be literally looking at Teqon upside-down.

But the most sensible thing to do with the demon after she'd wrapped his body in enough silk to form a cocoon was to hang him from the date tree in his private courtyard. He'd struggled against the web, at first. And when he stopped, she feared it was not because he'd given up, but because he'd realized they did not intend to kill him.

And demons, unfortunately, did not appear to have an irrational fear of spiders.

Hellhounds were another matter entirely.

Sir Pup in his demon form stood taller than Alice. The sun gleamed over his scales and the barbed spikes that ran the length of his enormous body. He did not growl, but stood salivating as Alice asked whether he preferred to eat demons from the feet to the head, or the top down.

"I suppose you would have to start at the feet," she mused. "And stop below the heart, or else it would kill him. Once it all grew back, however, you could begin again."

The hellhound stretched his left head forward and took the whole of the demon's head between his jaws, as if measuring the bite. He drew back, swiped his tongue over Teqon's too-handsome face, and snapped his teeth closed a centimeter from the demon's nose.

The demon's pulse raced. But, Alice realized with growing dismay, this fear was not the whimpering terror that she'd hoped to see. Teqon was afraid because any sensible creature would be—but with an enduring strength and resolution behind it.

Even if Sir Pup *did* eat him slowly, he would still not release her.

Very well, then. She reached out with her Gift, holding it steady as she called the widows to her. "I could have them come and devour your eyes," Alice said softly, "but I do not see the point in it, and I do so hate to be wasteful."

"It is good that you do not leave them." Teqon's eyes flared. "I would rip off their legs, one by one."

"Would you? Sir Pup, his left leg. Just the bone."

They'd agreed upon a signal that would let the hellhound know if any command she issued was designed to merely frighten the demon and not be carried out.

She did not give it.

Sir Pup lifted his heads, closed his jaws over silk, and bit down. There was a snap—two, three. Teqon hissed.

Alice crouched until she was even with his face. "I don't know if you can feel empathy. I imagine that, despite knowing that what you feel now is similar to what the spiders would, you'd still enjoy inflicting that pain."

"Perhaps," Teqon said through his clenched teeth, "I would not enjoy it so much now."

"Perhaps," Alice agreed. "Do you know, when I was in Hell I witnessed the oddest thing: there were demons who were concerned—horrified—when they saw that a young winged child had been injured. I'd have thought they would rip his wings off, as if he were no more than a fly."

"No." The demon's heart pounded. "You *saw* a winged child?"

"I held him in my arms," she said in the most wistful tone she could muster, and rose to her feet again. Her stunned gaze met Jake's. He'd been standing silently behind her.

Oh, dear God. Dear God. There *was* something Teqon wanted. But how could she possibly use this?

She didn't know. But if she did not try, she would gain nothing. "That is why you follow Belial, is it not? In hope that when he ascends to the throne, he will give you children."

Teqon remained silent. Alice held Jake's gaze, seeking inspiration. He gave a tiny shake of his head, and the tags beneath his shirt clinked softly.

And it came to her easily, as if it had always been lurking there.

Jake had given her his heart in return for that gift. And Michael had already cut out his own—metaphorically—when he'd given the order for Anaria's execution.

"And yet," Alice said, turning to face Teqon, "if you destroy Michael's heart, you destroy your best chance for having those children."

"I think not, Mrs. Grey."

"You will, when I tell you of a woman in Hell, who was the one to give the prophecy to Belial. The woman who told us that Michael's heart was his sister—once Lucifer's pupil, and the mother of the nephilim. It is she who already has the knowledge to allow demons their children." She leaned in close. "I know where Anaria is, demon. I know where she waits."

It was, she thought, the name that did it. Teqon hesitated, but only long enough to say, "I do not agree yet, Guardian. You must release me, and then I will see if this alteration can be made to our agreement."

Though she wanted to take a wary step back, Alice held her ground. "You cannot decide now, demon?"

"Or maybe," Jake said, "he can't make the decision on his own."

"So we let him down. And that was when he talked to a demon buddy on his cell phone."

From the lowest step of Michael's temple, Jake watched that sink in on the faces of the Guardians in front of him. Some of them, anyway. Michael's expression hadn't changed since Alice had announced they'd found Anaria. Irena had grinned through the description of how they'd caught Teqon in the web and his fear of Sir Pup, but her face had slowly darkened through the rest. Pim looked concerned, Drifter thoughtful.

"You got any inkling of who it was he called?" he asked.

"Nope. And he was speaking demon so fast I didn't pick up anything. But I'm guessing he was told what offer to come back to us with—and that was the change to Alice's bargain."

"Which is?" Selah's gaze was concerned when she looked to Alice.

Jake had noted who hadn't appeared so understanding when Alice had explained what her bargain entailed. And they could all go take a fucking leap into Caelum's sea, and keep on swimming.

"Michael's heart, or Anaria." She stood straight, her hands clasped behind her back as if she were at ease. But Jake could see how her fingers were clenched. "And both in the same condition."

"Bloody?" Irena's smile was feral.

Alice didn't return the smile as she shook her head. "They must be outside of the container they come in. Michael's heart from his chest, or Anaria freed from the sarcophagus."

"Now why does that matter? You figure demons ain't going to be able to open it'?"

"Yes," Michael said. "Only the grigori, the nephilim, and Lucifer would be capable." He met Alice's eyes. "If it is what you wish, I will open it for you."

Alice's fingers twisted tighter. "Yes, well—that is why we are here. It is not my decision to make alone. We cannot know the consequences of releasing her."

"I can imagine one." Drifter had his thumbs in his suspenders, his gaze intent on Alice's face. "And that is, Teqon isn't able to hold her, she takes up with the nephilim, and the vampires they've been slaughtering suddenly have a whole lot more trouble to deal with."

Selah paled. Becca shifted her weight from side to side, looking uneasy.

"And it means you're turning over a living person to a *demon*," Pim said.

"*Demon-spawn* to a demon." Irena arched her brows in response to the chorus of indrawn breaths. "If you give a dead body to him, will it still fulfill your bargain?"

"No," Alice said.

Irena shrugged. "So you will release her to him, and we will hunt her down."

"She was once trapped with her back against a stone wall, and facing twenty of Lucifer's sentinels. She fought rather than tele-port," Michael said softly. "She will not be so easy to hunt. Or to slay."

"Will she be coming after us if we don't fall in line?" Drifter asked.

"I cannot say. But if we oppose her—and if she decides to lead the nephilim, we *must* oppose her—she will strike back."

Even Irena appeared troubled by that.

Alice drew in a short breath, as if her throat was hurting. "It may be that Teqon will only take her to kill her. I do not know."

"Since when do we let demons carry out Guardian execu-tions? Or trade the life of one Guardian for the soul of another?"

Since that had come from one of the pricks Jake wished was swimming, he didn't even let Alice take time to acknowledge it. "There's something else. Khavi said that if Alice doesn't fulfill her bargain, I'll be killed."

Michael closed his eyes. Jake wished he could do the same, and shut out the second round of exclamations and comments, questions and guesses. But no goddamn answers.

And Alice must have been on the verge of screaming. His chest was tightening along with her fingers, and he thought, pretty soon, something was going to snap.

But it came quietly. In a sudden lull, Alice asked softly, "Michael . . . what choice would you make in my place? What is best?"

He shook his head. "There is no 'best.' This cannot be decided to everyone's satisfaction, yet someone must decide. And as it is your soul at risk, Alice—that decision must be yours."

CHAPTER 23

Alice was cutting the webs from the frames in the *Nephila* room when she heard Jake return. After the gathering, she had come back to her quarters, but he'd been responsible for taking a third of the Guardians back to their assignments.

One look at him told her how that had gone. She hadn't missed the hostility or the sympathy, and she imagined that there had been many vocal in both as he'd teleported them wherever they needed to go.

Michael had made it her decision, but whatever her decision, it would not please many. She cared for some of their opinions— and though there were some she did not, she *did* care if her decision endangered their lives.

But she would think no more of a disapproving glance than Remus and Romulus did her smile or her frown.

It was Jake, she thought, who would bear their anger—and, because of his association with her, be a target for it. He would be judged for her actions, blamed for her decision.

She took in his clenched jaw, the flat stare he directed at nothing. Anaria was still in her box, and already, she thought, some of the blame had begun.

Carefully, she cut the tether lines of the next web, then vanished it into her cache. When she glanced back, Jake was watching her hand.

"How long does it take them to make a new one?"

Was this curiosity—or a safe zone? Her throat tightened. "Only a few hours. I harvest them every couple of days. I could more often, I suppose, but it seems rather cruel to force them to always be spinning."

"Would they care?"

Alice shook her head.

He tilted his head back, as if looking through the ceiling. "And the widow babies you brought back from Teqon's? They're, uh . . . settling in?"

"Some of them. Some will be killed by the other widows."

"Nature taking its course?"

"Yes. I once tried to stop them with my Gift. It was painful."

He was quiet, then said, "Listen, Alice. Michael said this decision could only be yours, so I'm pretty useless around here right now. And you won't need me to help you out anymore, since Michael can teleport you—and if you decide to make the trade, he can open the sarcophagus. So maybe I ought to start working with Drifter again."

"I see," she said evenly. "Yes, I suppose that is for the best. Ethan is such an agreeable companion."

"Yeah, everyone likes him. And you and me—well, we can remain friends." Nodding, as if in agreement with himself, he repeated, "Friends. Yep. Just like Irena and Alejandro."

The wretch. "Very well. Do have a nice life. I hope that you think well of me."

"Could you say that again?"

She faced him, frowning. "What?"

"The 'I hope you think well of me' part." His hands slid into his pockets, his shoulders hunched in that very tall way. He was, she thought, laughing to himself. "I'm thinking that's pretty close to you saying you love me."

"I suppose it is." She sighed, and threw her knife to the floor.

His brows rose. "Your hammerspace is full?"

"There are times when it is just so much more satisfying to throw."

"I bet. Especially when you think you're going to do what's best for me, *again*, and—"

"I love you," she said crossly.

Jake drew in a breath and appeared in front of her, cupping her face in his hands. "Yeah?"

Her tone softened. "Yes."

"I know."

"How irritating you are."

He grinned. "And now I'm looking forward to when you say it without screwing your face up like you've been sucking—"

"Do *not* say lemons."

"I wasn't going to." His grin faded. "So, some Guardians aren't going to like what you decide. I'll deal with it. No sweat."

Alice closed her eyes, nodding. "I don't doubt you can deal with it. But I did not want to be the reason for it."

"I get that." With his thumbs, he smoothed her hair back from her temples. "So what's the plan?"

"For you to hold me while I try to think."

He pressed his lips to her brow. "I can do that."

❧

Jake held her until she rose to her feet, began pacing through her rooms. The movements of her legs and arms were jerkier than usual, her eyes unfocused. Completely lost in thought, he realized.

He sat up and she shrieked, hopping back with her hand covering her mouth. He tensed, but her expression faded into a laugh. Just startled, then.

"I guess that you aren't *trying* to think anymore."

She nodded, resumed her pacing. "Yes, but I have not completely determined how it will be done."

"How?" There wasn't much to it, was there? She only had to decide whether to release Anaria or not. "Are you going to release her?"

"Yes," she said, and his gut twisted into a knot.

He dreaded what might happen with Anaria out—but more than that, how much Alice would blame herself if anyone died because she'd been released.

But there was no real choice; given her options, she'd chosen the best one.

And maybe after two thousand years in a sarcophagus, Anaria wouldn't be a psychopath.

Yeah. He could keep telling himself that.

"Will you need anything?"

She paused. "Do you still have the box?"

"I dumped it into the sea. Off the Boreas edge."

Amusement rolled through her psychic scent. "I will need it."

And so he was going swimming.

❧

It took five jumps before Jake saw it, and only a second to pull the giant cube back into his hammerspace.

So she was freeing someone from one box and taking along another. He floated in the water, considering that, and the sick knot in his stomach slowly unwound.

It wasn't just a decision she was making, then—it was also a plan of attack. Hot damn.

And releasing Anaria meant that she'd need Michael in the temple—which also meant Jake had a trip to Hell coming up.

❧

Jake found Drifter walking with Irena not far from Odin's Courtyard. Maybe they'd both go; Alice couldn't scream at him for two backups.

On the other hand, he liked her screams—and judging by the vicious anticipation glittering in Irena's eyes, he thought either she or Khavi wouldn't be coming out of the encounter alive.

"Jake." Drifter nodded, his jaw tight. "We were just coming looking for you."

Yeah. This was not good, whatever it was. He'd fought alongside Drifter enough to know when the man was out for blood. The question was, whose?

"Funny," Jake said. "I was just looking for you. You need a ride somewhere?"

"Egypt."

His blood cooled. He knew what was coming up. God damn, he should have *seen* it coming. "Oh, yeah?"

"I'm thinking we need to have ourselves a little talk with Teqon."

"And would that talk involve knives, swords, thumbscrews?"

Irena tilted her head, studying him. "You want to join us?"

"Maybe I would if I could see the point."

Drifter frowned. "The point is, it ain't Anaria that's our problem. She's doing just fine where she is. But Teqon's given Alice no choice but to let her go."

"And Alice does not have the stomach for what must be done."

No question that Irena did. Jake looked to Drifter. "And you do?"

"I've got Charlie, and I've got Alice. I'd kill for either one, and this'll be providing help to both. I figure that measured against Charlie's safety and Alice's soul, I can stand bringing a lot of hurt onto a demon." There wasn't any eagerness in his voice, just resolution. "In any case, I'll mostly just be there to make sure Irena doesn't kill him too early."

"It won't work," Jake said. "He won't break. All you might do is destroy any chance Alice has of getting out of her bargain."

"We will see. Will you take us, or will we find Selah?"

Fuck. Fuck fuck fuck. But he didn't see a way out of it.

"Yeah," he said. "I'll take you."

❧

Jake took them about ten feet deeper than where he'd found the box, and got the hell out of there.

❧

Still sopping wet, he jumped into the air above Khavi's bathing chamber. Tattooed breasts floated in the steaming water below—

Oh, shit.

He didn't see her move. His back slammed into the ceiling. Ribs cracked against her hands. Her roar echoed through the chamber. Her black wings whipped furious gusts around them, swirling steam.

Her hand caught his chin, and his head whacked stone. Pain burst behind his eyes like flashbulbs. For an instant, another face shimmered beneath hers—reptilian, patterned with iridescent scales. Then the stars faded and she was just Khavi again.

"Stu . . . pid," he wheezed. "Knock . . . next time."

The pressure against his chest eased. Khavi blinked up at him, and her wings slowed to a steady beat. "This is strange. I did not see this."

"Yeah. Great. Lucky me."

"Your heart will still be pierced by Teqon's sword. And Alice will ask you to change your shirt."

Fuck this. "Did you remove the spell that prevents Michael from entering the temples?"

"Yes."

"Are you sure? You didn't just see yourself do it?"

Her withering stare was pure female. No dragon.

"Okay. Hold on. I'll be back."

With his heart in one goddamn piece.

❧

Alice almost could not comprehend what she saw. Jake's lip was bleeding, his clothes were soaked and carrying the faint odor of Hell. "Oh, dear God. What in heaven's name . . . ?"

"We've gotta go quick, all right? God knows who else is thinking the same thing and heading out for Selah."

"What?" She pulled in a handkerchief, dabbed at his lip. The cut had already healed. "Why?"

"I need to know before we go—are you done thinking?"

"Yes, yes. Now—"

"Tell me what it is."

"We release Anaria, and give her to Teqon. My bargain will be fulfilled. Anaria Fell, so she can't jump anymore; she and Teqon will have to be teleported out of the temple. And so you will take them into the box instead, leave them inside, and we will use your rocket launcher on the dome."

"Jesus Christ, I love you." His mouth covered hers, fierce and hot. It only lasted an instant. "I just did the same damn thing to Irena and Drifter. Only, I left them in the sea."

The laugh that burst from her was half-disbelief. "Why?"

"They were going after Teqon. We need to get to him first."

"Yes," Alice agreed, her heart pounding. "Yes, yes. What of Michael?"

"I can't jump to him. He must be blocked or behind the shield-ing spell. But we'll get Teqon down there and wait as long as we have to. And I'll keep trying. You have everything you need?"

She took his hand. "Yes."

"Okay. Shit, I'm soaked. Hold on just a sec while I—" He vanished his clothes, instantly replacing them with a dry shirt and jeans.

Then he stilled, as if struck by a thought, and looked at her.

Alice could not tear her gaze from his chest and the Styx logo. "Not that one," she whispered. "Change it."

"Alice—"

"I saw it. *Khavi* saw it—showed it to me when she said that you would . . ." She had to swallow past the ache in her throat. "Change it."

He did, into something blue. She couldn't read his expression when he kissed her softly, but she couldn't miss the resignation that filtered through his psychic scent.

"Don't think it," she told him. She placed her palm over his heart. "It won't happen. Not today. Not *ever*. We'll beat the odds."

Jake nodded. And then kissed her again before they jumped.

❧

Passing time with a demon was much worse than with the Doyen. She and Jake did not speak much, either; she had learned more than a hundred years ago that it was best not to reveal your heart to a demon, and so they maintained a physical and emotional distance that was almost painful. So much of their future depended on the minutes after the sarcophagus was opened, and yet she could not spend the minutes leading up to them with Jake.

Perhaps it was a small price, however, compared to the prize of success.

She busied herself with sketching some of the less intimate friezes: a group of Guardians in Caelum, battle scenes, a celebration. Either Michael had worn a smile more often then, or Zakril had preferred to carve him that way. And yes, she thought as she filled in a shadow at the curve of his mouth—there was something a little wicked about it.

The sarcophagus was not any different than those in the nephilim prison, and the same frustration rose up in her as she looked at it. How very maddening those symbols were. Given their potential power, she understood why Michael had never taught Guardians to read them—but it seemed such a waste. How much time had they lost, how many missteps could have been avoided if they'd only had the ability to read them?

At the very least, to *speak* the demon language. It was the height of foolishness to have two demons talking in front of a Guardian, and the Guardian ignorant of what was said.

And she would tell Michael so at the next opportunity.

Or, perhaps, slightly after. She glanced back at Jake when he sent out another pulse of his Gift. He would disappear when Michael's psyche was no longer shielded, and lead the Doyen back. She wiped a drop of water from her cheek and turned back to the sarcophagus. Hopefully, it would not be too long—

Another drop. Then a fine mist. Oh, dear God.

She looked up as the burst of power slammed through the chamber. Alice staggered, caught herself before she fell.

A crack split the dome. Chunks of marble rained down on a thin sheet of water.

Teqon was in the air, his wings holding him aloft. "Earthquake?"

Alice met Jake's eyes. No. No, they'd felt this before. The nephilim's ritual opening—not a burial chamber this time—but the temple.

The psychic thrust of Jake's Gift hit her, harder and harder, as if desperately trying to find Michael. Then chunks of marble became slabs, the noise of the water and breaking stone deafening.

Jake appeared in front of her; they jumped to Teqon, and then again.

Cold water surrounded her; a current pushed at her back. Below them, a female nephil lay dead inside a ring of four. Her body suddenly rolled over, buoyed by a bubble of air escaping the cracking bedrock beneath.

Horror clutched at Alice's throat. The bubbles were a steady stream now. Her fingers tightened on Jake's. That wouldn't have to matter. They didn't have to breathe. The chamber could fill with water, and they could still return for Anaria.

The crack became a fissure.

It was my Gift, Jake said against her hand. His profile was hard as stone as he stared at the ground. *They found us because I was pulsing my goddamn Gift.*

The bedrock tilted at a drunken angle. The nephil's body rolled into the fissure. Air belched from the crevice, and the ground collapsed.

Through the cloud of debris and churning water, Alice could make out the edges of a sinkhole as large as the temple beneath.

Numbness settled into her limbs, her chest, her mind. Her horror was gone. There was nothing but cold despair.

The nephilim swam into the murky depths.

Teqon's eyes glowed crimson as he turned to them. *If the sarcophagus survived, it is buried under tons of rubble. There is only Michael's heart now, Guardian.*

She looked up at Jake, her fingers squeezing his. *Do you see any way? I will do it. I will cut Teqon to pieces and leave only his heart. I must try.*

No, goddess, he said, and touched his lips to hers. *Not that way. I'll fix this.*

How?

Jake turned to Teqon, and signed, *I will bring Michael to you. You will soon have a heart, demon.*

Alice yanked on his arm. *Jake!*

He touched Teqon and, a moment later, left her alone with him in the demon's courtyard.

❧

The problem with Guardians was that they'd stop. Each one of them cared about Alice too much to *really* threaten Teqon—and Teqon knew it. They killed him, and she was fucked.

And the only way to win this was to make sure Teqon knew he was fucked twice as hard.

Jake strode through Caelum, his Gift ripping through the realm so hard that Guardians were flying over him to see what was happening.

Nothing was fucking happening. They needed to put a fucking bell on Michael so that he couldn't—

Jake jumped to the Boreas shore. Michael stood between Drifter and Irena, as wet as they were.

Irena's mouth drew back in a snarl, but dropped open when Jake said, "Alice is with Teqon. And you're coming with me, Michael."

Michael's eyes turned black. "Very well."

Jake pulled Alice's black hair ribbon out of his hammerspace, tied it around his wrist. His arrowhead went into his pocket. Of all the stuff he had collected over the years, those were the only two things he cared about keeping. He gripped his swords and dumped the rest of his shit in a huge pile on the ground.

"No," Drifter said, his voice hollow. It filled out as it rose in volume. "Hell, no. You son of a bitch. What the ever-fucking hell do you think—"

"I think I'm taking Michael with me this time instead of waiting for him. I think that Alice had a damn good plan, a way to get out of her bargain and to keep Anaria imprisoned. I think that if you and Irena had asked her about that plan instead of trying to do what you thought best, we could have taken this slowly, so there wouldn't have been any fuckups. I think maybe the nephilim wouldn't have found us."

He sent them images of the temple, of the cracking dome, of the sunken bedrock.

"And now I think Alice doesn't have any choices left. But I do. And I think that if I go at him fast, Teqon won't notice the difference in me until it's too late for him. His sword will be though my heart, and then *he* won't have a choice—except letting Alice go. But that'll be up to Michael, because Alice won't be in a place to bargain with him."

"Yes," Michael agreed.

Jake was shaking, with relief and a whole load of other emotions he wasn't taking the time to name. "And if I make it through, Alice is going to kick my ass after. Anything she does to me, it's of my free will. She won't be breaking the Rules."

"Christ Jesus, Jake," Drifter said.

"Well, yeah. We do whatever it takes, right? And if I do live through this, you have to kiss my hot ass."

"I'll kill you, more like." Drifter strode forward.

Jake hadn't known hugging could be manly, but he felt more like a man after. Then even more so when he survived Irena's crushing embrace.

She drew back, said fiercely, "Do not let her make your sacrifice worth nothing."

"I won't." He gathered his breath, looked at Michael. "Okay, then. Let's get this rocking."

❧

Though she'd only taken her widows out of the courtyard that morning, three new spiders had already moved in. Alice sat on the bench near the date tree, sliding her Gift around them and doing her best to ignore the demon who stood on the other side of the fountain. Jasmine scented the air, the sun was warm, the fountain pleasant. If she could disregard everything else, this was actually a lovely day.

Until Jake and Michael teleported in—so close to Teqon—and everything became a nightmare.

Jake strode forward, his gait looking oddly heavy, and he held his swords out to his sides like a cocky, stupid novice. A black ribbon—

Alice shrieked a denial and leapt forward, calling in her naginata. Michael appeared in front of her, and she crashed into him. She fell, screaming, and he held her down.

"You want a heart, demon?" she heard Jake challenge. "Come and fucking get it."

Teqon's sword appeared in his hand as he thrust it forward.

"No!" *Too late, too late, too late—*

The point of the blade speared through Jake's back. Made a short slice upward.

No, no, no. She tried to scrabble forward, her nails ripping on the flagstones. Her shrieks weren't even words anymore. She heard Jake's strange "Gotcha." Saw Teqon's eyes widen, and she was going to kill him, blast her soul and her bargain and the frozen field.

Jake staggered backward off the sword; Michael let her go and she caught him. Oh, sweet heavens. He was . . .

Jake was *human*.

Michael spoke, but she barely heard him.

Only the thin breath that bubbled in Jake's lungs. Saw only his face. Felt only the weight of his shoulders on her lap, and his hand weakly clasping hers.

"You have Fallen? Why have you done this? You foolish, stubb—" Her voice cracked like an old woman's.

Hold on, goddess, he said, and it was so slow. *You won't have to fulfill your bargain.*

"I don't care. Do you know what you have done to me?" she whispered, and kissed his cheek, his brow, leaving streaks of tears. She could feel herself slipping away with him—back to that place without hope. A future without him was a slow descent to Hell. "I love you. Please. Please, you cannot do this to me now."

Listen, Alice. Listen to Michael.

She did not care what Michael was doing, what Teqon was doing. Her breath coming in sobs, she gathered Jake close—but she did as he asked.

And listened.

"When Jacob dies, the nephilim will come for you, Teqon. And they will show you no mercy." Michael's words raced—a human couldn't have understood anything spoken at that speed. "You have not much time to decide."

Time . . . to decide what?

"Heal him," Teqon said, and she heard the panic beneath his

voice. "He is human. You can heal his injuries. You can prevent his death."

Oh, sweet heavens. Hope surged through her. Teqon was right. Jake *could* be healed.

"I can," Michael said. "But you must release Alice first—"

"No," Alice interrupted, her voice hoarse, her words quick. "Now. Heal him *now*."

She would Fall, and live with him. And she would cherish every moment she had before death, before she went into that frozen field.

Michael's reply was cold, hard. "Will you make his pain worth nothing, Alice?"

Teqon didn't give her time to respond. "If the nephilim kill me, Mrs. Grey will never fulfill her bargain. She will be damned."

"She will also be damned if you do not release her. There will be no difference in her fate if the nephilim come; the only difference is that you will be dead." Michael paused, and she felt the searching touch of his healing Gift. "He has but seconds to live, Teqon. Release her, or die by a nephil's hand."

"You won't let *him* die."

Michael's tone chilled Alice to her bones. "You forget who I am, demon. And what I am capable of."

Alice held her breath, tucked her face against Jake's cheek. *Please, God. Please—*

"A new bargain, then," Teqon suddenly babbled. "If I release her, you will heal him. You will not let him die. And you will not kill me, you will never lift a hand against me."

Michael's silence and the pounding of Alice's heart filled an endless second.

"Accept it, grigori! Accept!"

"It is done," Michael agreed.

Teqon's psychic scent swelled with palpable relief. "Then I release Alice Grey from her bargain. Now heal him!"

She lifted her head, kissed Jake's mouth. "Thank you, you wretch." She turned to Michael. "Heal him. Heal him now."

"Not yet, Alice," Michael said, crouching and placing his hands on Jake's shoulders. "You sacrificed your life for the soul of another, Jacob Hawkins. Do you willingly accept the transformation?"

Alice gasped her shock; Jake's eyes opened wide. His breath was gone, but his lips moved in an unmistakable "Yep."

She laughed, bent to kiss him again, but Michael signed against Jake's chest, *Alice. There is a demon who almost killed a human, but I cannot slay him. You know what you must do.*

Yes. She reached out with her Gift, and didn't have to look away from Jake as she called in her whip, lashed it behind her. Teqon's body and head thumped to the ground at the same moment she was blinded by the whitest, most incredible light.

She kissed him and kissed him and kissed him again. He grinned, blast him.

A shadow fell over his face when Michael stood, and Alice looked up.

An odd expression crossed Michael's features as he vanished Teqon's body and head. "I am fortunate, I think, that you did not want to kill me, Alice." His gaze fell to Jake. "This is your second transformation, and so there will be changes. You will be stronger and faster. You will develop another Gift."

Jake sat up and disappeared. He was back beside her a moment later.

"*Another* Gift," Michael said. "Not a different one."

His jaw slackened. "Hot damn." Then he frowned, twisted, and rose to his feet. Alice put her hand in his, and he pulled her up. "How many Gifts do you have?"

Michael smiled, and it was slightly wicked, Alice thought. "Several."

Alice slid her fingers against Jake's. "You have Fallen?"

"And sacrificed my life again, and been transformed. Several times. In all my life, do you think I have never broken the Rules or taken time for myself?"

Apparently, he had. Her brows drew together. "Who transformed you back? Who was the Doyen, if you were not?"

"You have met her." Michael formed his black wings, exchanged his tunic and pants for a toga. "And I believe it is time to bring her home."

❧

How very odd.

Khavi and Michael faced each other for the longest time, simply staring without speaking. Then Khavi laughed and spoke in the demon language. Michael sighed and bent his head, and let Khavi rub her hands over his shorn hair.

"It's the Twilight Zone," Jake said.

Friends, do you think? Alice signed with an arch look.

I can't tell. Holy hot hell. Is the hellhound coming to Caelum?

Alice felt a little faint at the thought—but she supposed everyone else felt the same at the thought of Nefertari. *I wonder if Khavi will teach—*

"Yes," Khavi said. "You will learn from me. The symbols, the magic. The demon language." She frowned, and looked to Michael. "I can already see that she will be a challenge."

"Oh, dear. How lovely my future seems."

"Yes." Khavi's gaze didn't move from Michael's. "But not yours. The nephilim will find Anaria. I believe they already have."

Michael nodded, touched her forehead, then a glyph on her cheek. "We will not falter." He turned to Jake. "Will you please ask Alejandro to come?"

"He does," Khavi said. "Very quickly."

🔥

Alice gave Khavi the same strip of leather that Irena had given her; long before Michael called a halt to the cleansing, Khavi had bitten through it.

And they had not removed even a significant percentage of the symbols from her skin—only those that prevented her from teleporting and altering her human appearance. Now Khavi could shift and conceal the symbols remaining on her skin until she was ready to cleanse them.

So it was enough, Alice thought later as she sat with Jake on the steps to Michael's temple, watching Lyta sniff uncertainly at a marble column—watching the other Guardians uncertainly watching Lyta.

Then Selah arrived, and it was not much longer before the delayed celebration for Jake was in full swing. Alice hadn't attended the last few celebrations before the Ascension, but she suspected this one was quite different from any that had been thrown before.

With a slice of pizza in his hand, Ethan dropped down beside her, stretched out his long legs. He pulled a second slice out of his cache for Jake, and passed it to him over Alice's lap. She lifted a piece of pepperoni as it went by, but waved away the offer of a whole slice.

"I'll eat yours, then," Ethan said. "You figure anyone's ever played . . . What do you call this, Jake?"

"Nine Inch Nails," he supplied, and Alice laughed as his T-shirt changed.

"Nine Inch Nails in Caelum before?"

"No." Alice glanced over at the large battery-powered stereo one of the novices had brought. There were many things in the past one hundred and twenty years that she needed to catch up on. Music, she decided, would be at the forefront.

"I've played it here," Jake said. "Just not at this volume."

Alice's gaze landed on Khavi and Michael, who were speaking with Alejandro across the courtyard. "Perhaps the volume is a blessing—she might not hear everything that is being said of her."

Jake shook his head, his jaw tight. "What they should be saying is, 'Thank flippin' God that we've got two grigori on our side now that Anaria's loose and with the nephilim.'"

"Well, according to the prophecy, the nephilim will be defeated—one way or another." Ethan met Alice's eyes. "Is it right that everything she told you would happen, *did* happen?"

"Yes. I didn't fulfill my bargain; Teqon put a sword through Jake's heart." Her voice was steady, but she slid her hand over Jake's, and reassured herself with a touch.

"Except my shirt," Jake said, squeezing her fingers. "Alice changed that."

"But Khavi didn't tell you the rest—that Jake had Fallen first, and that he'd live through it, be transformed again. Or that you wouldn't need to be fulfilling your bargain after you were released from it. Didn't she know?"

Alice couldn't claim to be surprised when Khavi appeared in front of them. Michael joined her a second later.

"Of course I knew," Khavi said, frowning. "But they might have acted differently if I had told them the outcome. This way, he Fell on his own, rather than at my suggestion."

"Yet you still influenced their actions when you told Alice what you saw," Michael pointed out. "Nothing is inevitable—but you cannot deny that everything you decide to reveal, you choose because you believe it will improve the probability of the outcome you desire."

Khavi narrowed her eyes at him, then turned to Jake. "He has never approved of my Gift. And there are times when I am too confused by what I see to enjoy it, as well. Such as now. I am told that this celebration is due to you having recently been made a full-fledged Guardian—which means that you were recently a novice?"

"Yep." Jake nodded. "That's the way it seems to work."

"But how can that be? I have seen many battles in which your strategic command— Oh." She shook her head. "No, I will not reveal this. I suppose every general was once a soldier."

Alice smiled, and Jake's dog tags jingled softly when he laughed and slid his hand over his head. "Yeah, well—most generals have that rank by the time they're sixty years old."

"Yes," Michael said, "but most do not spend thirty of those years in an orgy."

Alice barely held back her laughter. "I suppose a man must have his priorities," she said.

"Well now, that reminds me," Ethan said. A rolled sheaf of paper appeared in his hand, and Ethan didn't make a sound when Alice poked her elbow into his ribs. He passed the sheaf over to Jake. "I have this for you; I suppose you might call it a gift from your mentor in honor of your promotion. It's the one thing I ain't willing to teach you." Ethan waited until Jake glanced at the first page before adding, "Alice was the one who transcribed it, and she sketched all them pictures."

"Yeah?" He grinned and looked up at her with glowing eyes. "Hot damn."

Alice fought the urge to drag him off to the Archives building. "It needs to be improved," she said with pursed lips and her primmest tone. "Everything within is based upon human physiology. Guardians have many capabilities that aren't used to their full potential, and that aren't addressed in the manual."

Khavi sighed. "I have nothing for you, Jake."

"Maybe you can tell me what my new Gift will be."

"No."

"Ah, damn," he said easily. "Well, I had to try. But, I don't really need you to tell me anyway. I can guess what my future is: Alice and I are going to spend a couple of thousand years fighting demons, then we'll Fall and make a ton of babies, then grow old together and reminisce about the good old days, when kids didn't talk back to their parents."

That, Alice thought, would be absolutely perfect.

Khavi's mouth curved. "I do not know how many years it will be, but that is not too far off. And I suppose I can tell you that together, the two of you will be feared by demonkind. You will be known as 'the Weapon and his Witch.'"

"The Witch and *her* Weapon," Alice said.

Khavi's Gift rolled out in a soft wave. "Yes," she said. "Now it will be the Witch and her Weapon." She glanced over at Michael. "You see how easily they catch on?"

Michael rubbed the bridge of his nose before dropping his hand to his side. His eyes were obsidian now, Alice noted with sudden unease. "I have something for you, Jacob—but I do not know that I would call it a gift."

The amusement faded from Jake's expression. He rose to his feet, and Alice stood with him.

"When you could not locate me earlier," Michael said, "I was retrieving these. They cannot balance what was taken from you, but I demanded them as recompense."

The music in the courtyard was still loud, but Alice heard the silence that fell over the Guardians when the two white-feathered wings appeared on the steps at Jake's feet.

Not Jake's wings. These glowed subtly, as if they'd once shone brilliantly and the light within hadn't completely faded.

"Belial's wings?" Alice whispered.

"Two of them," Michael said. He lifted his gaze to Jake's. "And now they are yours."

Jake shook his head. "One goes to Alice, for what he did to her."

Khavi nodded. "Yes." She met Alice's eyes. "They have power within them . . . witch."

How strange. How utterly and wonderfully strange it was to vanish a glowing wing into her cache. And she felt it against her psyche, like a gentle, soothing hum.

She looked to Jake, saw by his expression that he'd experienced the same sensation when he'd vanished his. Then quietly, she sat again. He joined her, and they waited until Michael and Khavi had moved off, until Ethan had left to speak with Selah.

Jake took her hand, held her gaze as he brought her fingers to his lips. "So," he said, "it looks like I'm going to be as badass as you are when I grow up. Wanna take a victory dance?"

In the courtyard, a few Guardians were moving to the heavy beat of the music. "I will dance," she agreed. "But only if you will wear your wings."

"You drive a hard bargain, goddess." But he stood and formed his wings.

His full-sized wings.

"Oh!" Alice's laugh pealed out. "You wretch! You didn't say they'd finished healing."

"They didn't. I didn't have time." Jake turned his head, his brows furrowing as he studied them over his shoulder. "How much you want to bet it's because I Fell and was transformed again?"

"Yes," Alice said. And in their natural size, they were much larger than her own. She would have to remember to amend that, and shift hers. When he wasn't looking, of course, so that it wouldn't be too obvious.

Jake glanced at the courtyard, then at the sky. "Dancing—or fly?"

She stood. "Let's fly."

❧

This, Alice thought, was cleansing.

The glass-smooth sea that surrounded Caelum lay below. She and Jake skimmed above their reflections, so quickly that her dress whipped her legs and her hair came free of its braid.

For the first time in over a century, *all* of her was free of its bindings. What an exhilarating feeling it was.

Jake rolled in beneath her, flying on his back, grinning as he stole a kiss. She gave him the next one.

"So," he called over the wind, "next Sunday?"

"Yes." And the next and next and next. "What shall we do until then?" She would make plans for the next hundred years. Starting with the next hour—she planned to fly and feel the wind on her face and think of nothing but the present.

Until her gaze slid down Jake's taut form, and—unbidden— an abundance of salacious thoughts rose.

His grin widened. "Wanna ride?"

And how lovely it was, that she could alter her plans whenever she wished.